CANOPY OF SILENCE

Margaret Graham

C000065897

ARROW

Published in the United Kingdom in 2001 by
Arrow Books

1 3 5 7 9 10 8 6 4 2

Copyright © Margaret Graham 1992

The right of Margaret Graham to be identified as the author
of this work has been asserted by her in accordance
with the Copyright, Designs and Patents Act, 1988

First published in the United Kingdom in 1992 by
William Heinemann Ltd

Arrow Books Limited
Random House UK Ltd
20 Vauxhall Bridge Road, London, SW1V 2SA

Random House Australia (Pty) Limited
20 Alfred Street, Milsons Point,
Sydney, New South Wales 2061, Australia

Random House New Zealand Limited
18 Poland Road, Glenfield
Auckland 10, New Zealand

Random House South Africa (Pty) Limited
Endulini, 5a Jubilee Road, Parktown 2193, South Africa

Random House UK Limited Reg. No. 954009

A CIP catalogue record for this book is available from the British
Library

The Random House Group Limited supports The Forest Stewardship
Council® (FSC®), the leading international forest-certification organisation.
Our books carrying the FSC label are printed on FSC®-certified paper.
FSC is the only forest-certification scheme supported by the leading
environmental organisations, including Greenpeace. Our
paper procurement policy can be found at
www.randomhouse.co.uk/environment

ISBN 0 09 927952 5

Printed and bound in Great Britain by Clays Ltd, St Ives PLC

For Dinkie and Norm

Acknowledgements

Stephen Shaw of Margaret River Tours not only took me to the forests and caves of South-West Australia but talked to me in great depth about its life and times. My thanks to him, and to Peter and Vicki of Australian Pacific Tours, who were an endless source of information and fun as my coach journeyed from Sydney to Melbourne.

I must also thank Amanda Male and her family of Hanerika Farmstay, Yerong Creek, NSW, who took me yabbying, burning-off – you name it, we did it. Thanks, too, to my sister Jude in Sydney who sent me material over the months leading up to my trip and then put up with me on this leg of the journey. And of course, as always, Sue Bramble and her staff of Martock Library.

Finally, thanks to my family, who managed far too easily without me whilst I disappeared on my travels – and then had to look at all my photographs.

The Road to *Canopy of Silence*

As I settled down to think about my fifth novel I knew that I wanted to write about Australia, setting fictional characters in amongst an actual 'happening', preferably a little known one – but what?

I live in a small Somerset village and was chewing the problem over with my local pharmacist, Patricia Trawford, when she lent me a self-published book, *Over The Bridge*, sent over to her mother from Western Australia. It described the Group Settlement Scheme begun in that area in the 1920s.

This was a scheme introduced by the Premier of Western Australia, Sir James Mitchell, who dreamt of making his state self-sufficient in dairy produce. British and Australian ex-servicemen and their families were enticed to the South West, and it was only through their efforts, and after facing a life of hardship and struggle that the dream became a reality. I had never heard of it before and it was fascinating, heartbreaking, inspiring – I was on my way!

Indeed I really was, because there was very little literature on that particular episode of Australian/British history available over here. I realised I'd have to fly to Australia to hunt down the facts for myself, but more than that – I'd have to *experience* the forests, the terrain, the environment that these settlers faced, because it seemed so far removed from our British lives. But where should I actually go, and who could I speak to about those days?

Extraordinarily the manager of Bath Travel in Yeovil, our nearby town, is Australian and was flying to Western Australia to visit his sister at this particular time. Whilst there, he stumbled on a re-constructed Group Settlement Farm in Margaret River.

I knew now where to go. I told my village postmaster, David

Farrow, of my plans. 'But I still have no-one to talk to,' I wailed, knowing that a great deal of time could be lost locating the right people. But – wait for it – David had an aunt, Dinkie, in Margaret River. I wrote to Dinkie and Norm Sutton. Dinkie, it transpired, was the daughter of a Group Settler!

Leaving my older children to look after the younger ones, and my husband to look after them all – and tear his hair out – I set off on my great adventure. I'd never travelled abroad on my own before and was scared stiff but everyone was so friendly and helpful I found it an absolute pleasure. I also found an absolute gem in Dinkie.

She and Norm took me to her old home. I couldn't have done what she and her family did. The sheer size of the forests, the huge trees which had to be cleared before any production could begin. The torrential rain, the searing heat, the bush fires, the isolation, the lack of medical facilities.

She took me to a neighbour, Joyce Payne, whose grass Norm cut each week. It was Joyce who had written *Over the Bridge*! I drank tea in her kitchen and told her how I had read her book in my Somerset village.

Dinkie took me to the Margaret Cecil Nursing Home in Margaret River and told me how Lady Alicia Cecil and her daughter Lady Margaret had heard in England of the atrocious conditions the Group Settlers were experiencing and had travelled to see for themselves. Shocked, they'd returned to England and asked all the Margarets in Britain to contribute a shilling for a nursing home for the women of Margaret River. Many did and the Nursing Home was built.

As I left for the sheep station in the East where I was to stay and work, providing material for the first half of *Canopy of Silence*, Dinkie said: 'You're a Margaret too. You've seen what it was like, please tell them back home for us.'

I hope I've done so Dinkie, for you and every other group settler.

Margaret Graham
Somerset, 1992

Book One

CHAPTER 1

The white roses were still tightly budded but by tomorrow morning they would be open. Deborah held the finished bouquet to her face. It was cool and fragrant, the myrtle leaves glossy, a rich dark green against the white. Their scent was strong.

'For worthiness and for constancy,' her aunt murmured behind her.

Deborah nodded, feeling the hand on her shoulder. 'Yes. Susie will be happy, I'm sure of it. The trenches changed Will very little. He's steady isn't he, Aunt Nell? Worthy of love and they are both very constant.' Did she sound stilted, as though the words hurt? Because they did, so much.

She balanced the bouquet on two canes over the bowl which was half filled with water. The cool scullery and the added damp would keep the roses fresh until tomorrow. She must think of this and she must remember the lace and the starch.

'I'll put the lace around tomorrow. It's starched, isn't it? But I'll do the buttonholes now.'

Deborah picked up a single rose and a thorn tore her skin. The pain of a thorn prick far outweighed the actual wound, she thought as she watched the blood well up on her thumb. She must think of that, not of how very lucky Susie and Will were to have all this when she had nothing.

She took another bunch of myrtle from her mother's old friend. Nell would miss Susie, even though her daughter would only move from the Somerset farmhouse to the small

3

cottage by Lower Road. Mother would have missed her too in the same circumstances. But no, she must not think of her parents, because then she would certainly weep, then it would be just too much.

How strange it was that history could enter into lives and change them so easily, so dreadfully easily. It was 1922 and she was twenty-four, nearly an old maid. Her mother was dead, her lover, her father too.

Deborah took the scissors from her aunt's hand. 'How many buttonholes shall I make?' Her voice was unsteady. 'It's these thorns, they hurt.' She sucked, the blood was warm and so were her tears.

'It's not just the thorns, my love.' Aunt Nell's arm was warm round her shoulders and the smell of the cakes she had baked all afternoon clung to her skin and hair. It was the smell of happy summers, of crackling fires, of refuge. Deborah leant her head against the plump shoulder.

'I am happy for them, really I am, but I shall miss Susie.'

'Life goes on, Deb. It will for you too.'

But where will it go on to and with whom? Deborah wanted to shout. But so many were asking that question and nobody knew the answer.

She cut the thorns from the roses then, measuring up the myrtle. This is what she would go on to now, this minute; cutting roses, measuring myrtle. This was her best friend's wedding and this kind woman standing behind her had loved her, nurtured her for the last two years when there had been no one else to do so, allowed her to stay in the cottage she and her mother had lived in since her father died. So now she would smile and bind the myrtle to the rose, just so. And another. And another.

'Will your Australian relative be coming?' she called as her aunt carried the ham through to the bluestone in the pantry. Her voice was quite steady. Yes, absolutely steady.

'Patrick? Who knows. He wrote back saying yes but not her, not that stuck up old witch of a mother. Mrs Prover it

4

is, you know, never Eileen. She's never liked our side of the family.'

Nell cut a small slice off the ham and walked over to push it into Deb's mouth.

'Not too salty, is it?'

Deb pushed a tail in with the back of her hand. 'It never is, you know that. Mmm, no it's good. I've done fifteen. Shall I do another for him?' Her voice was steady again, it would be all right, for a while.

Nell shrugged as she closed the pantry door. 'Might as well but I'd have thought he'd be here if he was really coming. Said in the letter he'd come for the wedding and then go on to see where Great Uncle Robert lived, out on the Levels somewhere you know. Got to get these jellies done, Deb.' Nell walked into the kitchen to fetch the kettle from the trivet clipped to the bars of the grate. 'Maybe he's changed his mind. It's a long way. Didn't expect him to come at all. It was only politeness that made us ask.'

'What's he like?' Deborah finished the last of the button-holes, her fingers sore from the wire, the thorns, the water.

'I don't really know, but he was in France like your poor Geoff, only he came through. He was in some hot place, Gallipoli or something like that before then. His mum's a snob, I know that much. She made it quite clear she didn't want anything to do with our side when she married into the family. Can't think why, lots of them Australians went out as criminals. The boy doesn't seem to be like her though. He wrote a nice letter.'

Deborah propped the buttonholes between three rows of canes slotted across an enamel bowl with two inches of water in the bottom, then she carried two steaming bowls of jelly out into the late March afternoon. It was warm and snowdrops were growing in clumps along the side of the yard. She tied thick string around the curved edges of the bowl, and lowered them into the well. Her voice echoed back to her as she called.

'What did Great Uncle Robert do anyway?'

5

'Stole some slate off a church roof, or so the story goes. Here, move over.'

Deborah brushed her hair from her eyes as Nell put another two jellies down the well. Deborah watched them merge into the darkness, then touched her aunt's arm. 'Well don't tell the vicar for goodness sake, he'll refuse to marry them tomorrow and give us a sermon about the sins of the father being visited on the son, and his son and his son, or daughter . . .'

They were laughing as they returned to the scullery and when Deborah left after tea her aunt called, 'If he comes, make sure you take him under your wing. These foreigners need looking after. And don't forget the knives.'

Deborah waved. 'I'll be back in the morning to help set out the food. Give my love to Susie when she gets back from Will's.'

She did not say that any man who had been through Gallipoli and France would probably not need any looking after – either that or much too much.

The shadows were long down the main street of the village. Valerian grew out of lichen-crusted walls and the hamstone was golden in the evening sun. She passed children standing with their ears to the telephone pole outside the Post Office, waiting to hear the words they were convinced came down the line into the phone. She smiled.

She passed the orchard with the swing tied to a bough. Geoff had said he would swing her on that, the day they were married. It had been his last leave, but they didn't know that then.

She nodded to Mrs Briggs who stood at the door of number ten. She'd grown the white roses used in the bouquet and buttonholes. 'Susie is going to be so pleased with her bouquet, Mrs Briggs. That conservatory of yours is a godsend. I'll see you tomorrow.'

'That you will, m'dear. I've bought a new hat.'

Deborah continued to smile as she walked up the path to the back of her own cottage which was at the end of the terrace right beside the brook. A steam engine had woken her this morning as it pulled in for water. The ash was still there where the fireman had left it. There was a pile of stones ready for the stone breaker who would come and sit at his work with sacking across his shoulders against the cold.

During the war, convoys of soldiers with horse-drawn wagons had halted here too. But never Geoff, though sometimes she had half believed she had seen him, leaning into a horse, rubbing its neck. There was no smile now on her face as she opened the door and entered, only the image of the face she had last seen five years ago.

The cold struck at her. The fire was out. She had feared it would be and without that heat the flagstones sweated a chill into the air. Deborah drew her shawl around her shoulders.

As she bent down for the poker her shawl slipped and, catching it, she saw Geoff's hands. He had so often drawn her shawl around her, knowing how she hated the cold. He had been cold himself that day in Windsor Park when she and her parents and his mother had travelled to watch Kitchener reviewing his New Army, reviewing her Geoff.

She held the shawl to her face now because she didn't want to think, she didn't want to remember. She wanted to be back with Nell, cutting myrtle, cutting roses, but instead in front of her was the image of soldiers who had not been allowed to wear overcoats on that bitter review day in Windsor Park. How they had fallen as they stood whilst one hour, two, three, then four passed before Kitchener came. Not one had complained but several had died.

'Why didn't any of you damn well complain?' she said aloud, and though she was glad to hear the sound of a voice, she would have been even gladder to have heard the sound of a reply. She and her mother and Geoff's mother had taken one man to hospital in the car they had hired for the day. The wind and rain had gusted in through the cracked celluloid windows on to the young soldier who lay rigid on their laps. Her mother had wrapped her shawl around him. It hadn't been Geoff. He hadn't collapsed. 'The stuff soldiers are made of,' her father had said. No, he hadn't collapsed or died then. He had waited until Ypres.

She hadn't believed until then that hearts could really break, that they could tear and shred as though they were tissue paper, but now she knew that this was a truth.

They should all have complained, then, that day. They should have stopped it all happening somehow, but they hadn't; she hadn't. Had they colluded then, was that the answer? Colluded with a fact of history. One that had changed her life, torn her apart, made her want to die. People don't die when they want to though, do they? Only when they are like Geoff and want to live. Only when they are like her father.

She laid newspaper, kindling and coal and lit the fire. Her father had saved several young soldiers' lives that day, but then he was a doctor and that was his job. And he was very very good at saving people's lives, wasn't he, except his own. Oh God, Father, why did you do it? Why did you leave us?

Deborah straightened and felt at last some heat on her face as the fire caught and burned steadily. There were things to do. The hens needed feeding and then perhaps she would clean the knives, find her hat, wash her hair, anything to fill the empty evening, anything not to think.

Her mother had said when they moved here from Yeovil that idle hands, idle minds were the enemy of peace. 'We must never complain,' she had said. 'We must accept.'

Had Deborah accepted? She didn't know, all she knew was that she must climb the path which Tom had cut into steps and feed the hens. Yes, that's what she must do. She stopped to collect corn from the outhouse, then there was silence as she threw it to the hens, watching them jerk and peck and there was comfort in the relentless actions of these birds. Even in the rage of the cockerel when it came at her as it always did.

'What would Kitchener have done with you, my fine friend?' she whispered. 'Probably steered you towards the Germans and given you a great big medal but I, on the other hand, will eat you.'

She laughed gently, her anguish fading as tiredness overcame her. She knew that the cockerel would still be here next year and the year after that and that Tom would still be telling her she was a bloody fool.

Later, as the oil lamp flickered, she worked the knives up to a fine shine with the emery board before climbing the stairs, the candle she carried dripping wax on to the saucer. There were three windows in the bedroom, one of which had been filled in and shelved. On it was her hat. Her dress hung on the back of the door; warm blue velvet with a Honiton lace collar.

Her mother would have told her to take it down into the kitchen to air it. Deborah ran her hands down the material she had travelled to Bristol to buy. It was smooth, gentle, like her mother had been to her father, and would have been to her, if only she had lived longer. You would have been, Mother wouldn't you?' she whispered aloud.

She carried the dress down the stairs and hung it on the airer. She had aired her mother's laying-out gown two years ago too because she had looked so small, so white, so cold, as though it mattered – and it had, to the daughter who loved her. 'And now you're all gone,' she said aloud, retracing her steps, hearing the stairs creak beneath her slow steps. 'You're all gone.'

She leant against the wall, then sank on to the landing. Tomorrow there would be a wedding, but it wouldn't be hers. 'I'm alone,' she whispered, 'and I'm frightened that I will stay alone for the rest of my life.'

Tears were in her mouth, words in the air, but there was no reply. Of course there was no reply. 'There's no one here, you fool,' she shouted, forcing herself to her feet, moving into her room, searching for Geoff's letter, wanting words of love, however silent.

There it was, in the drawer. She must be gentle with it because it had been read so often it had worn thin at the folds. She could hear the sound of her breathing and wished that it was the sound of his words that she heard, for the sight of them was not enough.

> Dearest Deb,
>
> I want you here so that I can hold you, feel you against me. I shouldn't write like this, I suppose. It's hardly decent, but then, what is any more? Nothing here, certainly. I just want you to know that I love you. I want to live most of all to hold you again, to come home to you.
>
> If I don't, though, I can't bear you to be alone, though it's hard to think of you with another man, Deb. But you need someone to share your life, to love you, someone who needs you. You must marry someone else, if there's anyone left after this mess. I must go now, the barrage has begun again. Think of me.
>
> Geoff.

He hadn't lived. He had died in France, in the mud.

'Brave boy that one,' her father had said. 'He'll be glad he did his duty.'

'How can he be,' she wanted to shout. 'He's dead!' He was dead, her Geoff, the one she had scrumped apples with from their neighbour's garden in that middle-class street in Yeovil, the one who had planned to be a teacher, who had planned that they should have two children who would never be away from them, who wouldn't just be brought down for half an hour as she had been, and she cried and raged all night for the loneliness which loomed today, tomorrow and for ever, and for the two children, the family, she would now not have.

The sun was warm the next day and the kitchen and front room of the farmhouse were bright with daffodils. The kitchen smelt of bacon from a breakfast which Deborah had been too late to share.

'But only because I was eating Penny's double yoker and my own very fine bacon, thank you, Nell.' She grinned, and was glad that the darkness of last night was past, that her eyes were no longer red. She carried through yet more white plates on to the long table. She had already put the lace around the bouquet and wired it but wouldn't show it yet to Susie, who was slicing the ham in the kitchen.

'So did he come, your Australian?' Deborah asked as she put two small vases of crocus on the draped mantelshelf above the fire and put out clean antimacassars on the chairs.

'He did, you know. Nice boy, well, man really, Deb.' Susie nudged her as she passed. 'Very nice indeed. Different somehow. Not English if you know what I mean. Quiet. Talks a bit clipped I suppose you'd call it.'

Maidenhair ferns blotted out the light from the east window and Deborah moved one on to the mantelshelf. Nell nodded. 'Good idea. This isn't a wake, it's a wedding. We need a bit of light.' She gave Deborah a hug and they laughed, really laughed, and the sun seemed to fill the room. Yes, this was a wedding and she would be happy, even though it wasn't hers.

'Now don't you forget, you've to look after this stranger, Deb.'

'Well where is he?'

'Gone to the station with the milk. Wanted to go. Got up early to go. Strange people, these Australians.' Again they laughed and Deb went with Susie to help her into the white, lace-trimmed dress before putting on her own velvet. They would stay up here until it was time to leave for the church. The sun shone deep into the room, lighting up the quilt, the rag doll Deborah had given Susie fifteen years ago, the photograph of Will in his corporal's uniform in 1917.

Deborah picked it up and looked closely at that young face. Geoff would always remain this young to her but would he know this woman who was no longer a girl and had the rough hands of a farm help, a woman who made her own dresses.

She replaced the photograph and looked out across the

11

fields with a profound sense of loss because she could no longer remember the tint of his skin, the shine of his hair, or feel his skin as he grew from eighteen, to nineteen, to twenty. He had never known what it was to be twenty-one. She would never know how he would have looked at twenty-five.

'You look so beautiful, Susie.' Her voice was quite steady and she was surprised.

'You will marry too, one day, Deb.'

'Yes, perhaps I shall. It's time we went down to pick up your quite extraordinarily beautiful bouquet and get you to the church.' Her voice was light but still quite steady and she was still surprised.

Tom helped Susie into the cart that was to take them to the church. It was decorated with ivy and just a few roses, and the villagers and relatives milled around talking and laughing, and said how beautiful the bouquet was, how well Deborah had made her dress and Susie's too, then Deborah saw Tom waving his whip above the crowd and soon the procession was walking along behind.

'Thank heavens there was a spot of rain in the night.' Mrs Briggs said to Deborah.

'Yes, it's settled the dust a bit but don't get too close behind the cart or we'll end up looking like part of the road.' Deb tucked her arm in Mrs Briggs'. 'She's such a beautiful girl with those green eyes.'

'Brown ones have their advantages my dear, and so does rich dark hair, you just take my word for it.'

Yes, to you maybe, Deborah thought, but who else is there to notice it? Nell was walking ahead of her, waving towards her, beckoning her over. Her face was red and her hat tilted too much to one side. Deborah patted Mrs Briggs' hand. 'I'll be back.'

Nell was pulling at her arm. 'It's no good, my feet are killing me. I shall have to go up in the cart with them.' Nell called to Tom. 'Stop that cart a minute. I need a ride. Now, you look after young Patrick here. He's a stranger, I've already told you all about him. Come on, give me a bump up, young man.' They were alongside the cart now and Deborah watched as a tall dark man put both hands on Nell's waist and lifted her with ease into the cart before dropping back to stand beside Deborah.

'Give him this,' Nell called. 'I forgot.'

It was the buttonhole and Deborah took the pin from Nell and fixed it to Patrick's lapel, smiling into a face which stiffened at her touch and eyes which became blank. She paused, unsure, and then he spoke and as he did so his face relaxed.

'G'Day, I'm Patrick Prover, I'm a relative of Tom's.'

His handshake was firm but his skin wasn't hard. His eyes were dark and half closed against the sun and his skin was tanned. Susie was right, he was different somehow.

She said, 'I'm Deborah Morgan. I'm not a relative, just a friend.'

The cart was moving now and they walked on in its wake. More villagers joined them and Deborah pointed out the Post Office which had had its phone installed in 1917, and the baker's which had had its roof blown off in a freak storm, and each time Patrick nodded but said little.

The church door was studded with hand-forged hinges and Patrick walked down the aisle with Deborah who had to pull him back as he moved into the second pew.

'No,' she whispered. 'That belongs to the squire, he pays rent on the first two.'

He turned and looked first at her, then at Will who stood waiting for his bride, and then at the pew.

'So, all this is still alive and kicking back here too?' He tensed as he had done before and then looked at her and smiled. 'Well, Deborah Morgan, lead me to a seat I can sit in. I'm in your hands.'

The church was festooned with ivy as a symbol of fidelity and the organ wheezed and groaned as it was pumped too much or not enough. The choirboys looked perfect in their white surplices but young Joe Tanner hadn't cleaned his boots. Deborah raised her eyebrows at him and then grinned,

13

because he had winked at her and she loved this particular child. His father had died with Geoff at Ypres.

Patrick didn't sing Abide With Me and neither did Deborah. Her throat was full because this had been her mother's favourite hymn.

They threw confetti and presented horseshoes in the porch and followed the bride and groom down to the lychgate, through the gravestones and there were primroses everywhere and violets too. The hills rose behind the church and the new wheat was just glistening through the dark rich soil of Barton's Field which butted up to the church. Trees and new grass climbed to the summit. Her parents were not buried here, they were in Yeovil where they had lived when her father died and today she was glad of that, glad that she could look across to the peak of the hill and to the sky and just think of how beautiful it was, free from the echoes of pain.

'Tom farms all this land, does he?' Patrick asked as they walked back to the farmhouse, jostled and nudged by the others. 'It's so green, so fertile. I thought that when I landed in Plymouth. I had forgotten.'

'Forgotten?'

'Oh yes, I convalesced here for a while. No problems. I'm fine now.'

'We had some Australians where I nursed. Well, helped the nurses. Some were very new Australians, they sounded just like any British lad. Not like you.'

'It seems a long time ago, in one way, and yesterday in another.' He was smoking a cigarette, and squinting up into the sun and there seemed nothing else to say. He dropped back and Deborah moved up to be with Mrs Briggs but then he was beside her again.

'So does Tom farm all this? Do you help?' He was pointing to the fields leading up the hill and across by the brook.

'Yes, Tom does farm this, and I do a bit now that I live in the village. He owns it. It's sort of come down through the family, but then your grandfather must have told you that.'

'I think he probably did, but you don't listen when you're

young. It's only when they're dead and you are older that these things seem important. He loved this area best and I can see why, though he lived on some place called the Levels. That was the place he talked about most. He fell in love with a girl here when he was over this way seeing a cousin; maybe Tom's grandfather. Families are complicated, aren't they?' He looked down at her.

'Yes, I think perhaps you could say that,' said Deborah as they moved in through the open door of the farmhouse into the front room.

Cider was served in the kitchen, cowslip wine too and Deborah felt her cheeks warming as she moved through the room with plates of sandwiches, cakes and bowls of trifle, laughing, talking and nodding at the old men, the young women, the children.

Patrick stopped her as she moved through the kitchen to the scullery and took a sandwich from her, pointing to the shotgun on the rack.

'What do they use that for?'

'You're a farmer, you should know,' she laughed up at him. 'Rabbits sometimes, when Tom gets really angry. But mainly they're netted. Sometimes they're crated and sent to Smithfield. Tom lost a fifth of his crop last year. Do you have them on your farm?'

'I think you could say that. We have a few problems, a few million problems. They've pretty much ruined Australia. On the sheep station it's a permanent state of war where they're concerned. Some crazy Englishman brought them over to hunt with his horses and his fine coat. It got out of hand, shall we say.' He drank more cider. 'You don't hunt them here then?'

'No, we don't hunt them here, not like that. We hunt foxes. My father hunted foxes, and my mother too. I didn't.'

She walked away then, into the scullery and listened to Tom introducing Patrick to the vicar, whose wife would not have to cook lunch or supper today judging by the amount he was tucking away.

At five o'clock Susie changed into a pale grey dress and walked down the lane with Will to their cottage, taking her bouquet with her. After two days she would plant a sprig of myrtle which would grow into a bush as Nell's had done and one day she would make a bouquet from it for her own daughter. Deborah waved and laughed and felt loneliness crowd in again.

'Have some more wine,' Nell said.

The glass was cool. She held it to her cheek. She and Nell had made this last year.

She told Patrick that.

'Where's your cottage?'

'It's not mine. Nell and Tom have allowed me to live there.' She wanted to add that she owned nothing. I thought I did you see but I was wrong. Mother and I were both wrong, but how could we ever be angry with him about anything, when we both loved him so? Instead she said as the wine slipped down her throat, 'You live with your mother. You're lucky.'

Patrick leant back against the triple-fronted sideboard. The brass handles were bright in the lantern light. 'Am I? I don't know. You called Lenora a farm but it's a sheep station. My mother is a grazier's wife. To call her a farmer's wife is an insult. I guess you grow out of all that.' He looked down at his glass. 'Not many young men at the church today were there?'

He turned and walked from her, into the front room, over to where Tom and the older men were talking, knocking foul-smelling pipes out on the fireplace.

'No, there were not,' she whispered. 'But I need no reminding of that.' He didn't ask her again where her cottage was.

It wasn't until eight o'clock that Nell called them all together and made Tom stop playing the harmonium and Mrs Briggs from doing the jig with Mr Evans.

'Come on, it's off down the lane now. Time to do the bride's bedding. You keep an eye on young Patrick there, our Deborah, he could get lost in the dark you know.'

16

There was laughter and Deborah felt Mrs Briggs squeeze her arm. 'It's been a lovely wedding hasn't it, m'dear. A simply lovely do, but I'm going home now. Mr Evans will take me.' She kissed Deborah. 'You look very lovely, my dear. Just like your mother.'

Deborah smiled and hugged the old lady.

'Here are the buckets then. You get one too, Pat.'

Deborah watched as he held the bucket and the stick, turning them over in his hands, watching to see what the others did. She moved towards him, saying gently, 'Don't worry, you only have to bang it under their windows, the poor things.'

Patrick looked at her for a moment and then laughed. His whole face changed and she leant forward and kissed his cheek because for an instant he looked vulnerable, unsure, and the age that he was, a mere twenty-seven.

She took his arm and Tom's too and they walked along the lane, brushing the catkins as they passed, hearing the screech of foxes, the hooting of owls in the distance, seeing clearly by the light of the moon.

'Is your country as loud as this at night? Do you have owls, do you have birds in the daytime? It must be hot, so beautifully hot. I hate the cold. I love the spring, seeing the plants come up, putting the vegetables in, feeling the sun on my face.'

It was the wine making her talk. It was the feel of his arm through hers. It was his youth, his difference. It was the fact that she was walking to the bride's bedding with a young man. It had been so long since she'd held a man's arm, and Patrick was so nice.

He would be gone tomorrow but she mustn't think of that. She would tell herself that it didn't matter when dawn came up and another day loomed and she was alone again.

They passed the orchard where the cider apples grew.

'That's where your cider came from this evening. Our wine came from all these fields. Nell and I picked the cowslips here.'

Patrick didn't answer but looked across at Tom who nodded. 'When she's not tested her own wine as freely as she's done tonight, she's a sensible girl. Makes a rare cheese, does this one.' He laughed, and Deb laughed, then Patrick did too.

There was the sound of banging buckets, and the barking of dogs, there was laughter and singing.

'Well, is your land like this?'

Patrick turned, his stick beating on the bottom of the bucket. 'Where is your cottage, Deborah?' He was beating the stick more loudly now.

'Come on, lad,' Tom called, grabbing Patrick's arm, pulling him across into a circle where the villagers were dancing. 'The cottage by the brook,' she called, 'number twelve.'

She thought she saw him nod.

CHAPTER 2

In the morning as the sun threw shadows across the windowsill Deborah brushed her hair, coiling it into its usual bun. Would he still be there at the farm, the morning after the wedding, this quiet Australian?

He was, but already in his coat, standing by the doorway, moving back as she entered. His face was drawn, his eyes distant. His hat was in his hand. His kitbag was humped on the flagstones of the farm kitchen.

'Thought you'd never get here,' said Nell, handing her a package. 'Now, I want this to go to Mrs McGregor at Sudden's shop over near Muchelney. Tom hasn't time. While you're at it, you can show young Pat the Levels. He's heading off there today so you can give him a good start.' She was turning Deborah towards the door, pushing her out, handing her a thick shawl that hung behind the door. 'Hurry now, you'll miss that bus. And here, give this to Patrick.' She handed Deborah the buttonhole and whispered, 'He's quiet today, strange. Thought it best he have someone with him.'

They talked little as the bus jerked and roared from village to village and the hills gave way to flat misted plain. Deborah felt his thigh against hers. His kitbag blocked the aisle and he lifted it over on to the seat behind, apologising to the old ladies all around, nodding to them.

'I hear it was a good wedding,' said Mrs Ringwold from Martock.

'Yes, a fine one. Susie looked beautiful.' Deborah leant forward. 'And how's your Bet, has she had the baby yet?'

19

It was easy to talk to these people. Patrick was stiff and quiet and she remembered the kiss she had given him and wondered if that was why he was so cool. She looked at him again. His eyes were still distant, his hands were turning the buttonhole, again and again. Its scent rose between them.

They stepped from the bus well before the village when Patrick said, 'This is Grandfather's land. Can we walk from here?' He had risen, leaving the buttonhole on the seat.

They stood at the edge of the road, and Deborah felt the cold wind through the shawl, heard the driver move up through the gears and groan off into the distance but Patrick wasn't listening, he was looking at the miles of level mead.

'You forgot the buttonhole. Here, I've got it for you,' Deborah said and watched him take it, hold it, drop it. Then she watched again as he stooped and ran his fingers through the wet grass over and over.

'It's myrtle. I can't stand it any more.' His voice was sharp, taut, quiet and Deborah said nothing, just looked as he pushed it from him with his foot.

'Grandpa told me about these pastures.' Pat stood with his hands in his pockets, taking deep breaths, looking past her out over the meadows.

'The dykes are called rhines,' Deborah said, holding the package in one hand, tucking a strand of hair back with the other. There was nothing else to say. He knew who had made the buttonholes.

'Oh yes, I know. I know all about it. It's as though I've lived here, been here.' His voice was unsure. 'I'm sorry, Deborah, about the buttonhole. I'm just sorry.'

She watched him draw out his cigarettes, lighting one with trembling hands, drawing the smoke deep into his lungs but his eyes were distant again. Deborah knew that he wasn't seeing the Levels, he was elsewhere, deep inside himself and she remembered the glossiness of the myrtle, and the look on this man's face when she had put it in his lapel yesterday. She hadn't recognised it then but now she did. She had seen

20

it before on Geoff's face once the war began. It was a blanking off, a retreat.

She looked out across the rhines, the meadows. Some were sheeted in silver water, half merged into the mist from which pollard willows reared in fisted stumps.

'The withies have all been cut,' she said quietly, because she knew that Geoff had liked to hear her voice when darker thoughts had claimed him, even if he didn't hear the words. She knew now that she had brought this look to Patrick's face.

'I knew they would be. I know about the floods too. They're good for the basket willow as well as bringing the water weed. They follow a pattern don't they, Deborah, but what happens when the pattern blows apart? Tell me that.'

He threw his cigarette on to the wet ground. Soon it was sodden, dead and she allowed him to stand lost in thought, though the wind was like a knife and her feet were wet and numb.

He looked at her then. 'You're a patient woman, Deborah. We'll walk, you must be cold. Which way is it?'

Deborah nodded to the north and waited as he swung up his kitbag. She wanted to lean forward and kiss the thin strained cheek, and take his arm as she had done last night, but then she had been drunk on cowslip wine and today there was just the cold, cold wind.

They walked along the straight road, through the thinning mist, and soon the early sun broke through. It was red, a large red orb, staining the mist, staining the water.

Patrick had stopped again.

He looked out across the fields and his lips hardly moved as he said, 'They dropped us at the wrong bastard shore, you see. We pushed through that surf. It clung to our legs, the shingle slipped beneath our boots, everyone's boots. We drowned. So many drowned.'

Deborah said nothing. She knew that he wasn't speaking to her, not really.

'Gallipoli. Nice name, nice place at any other time.'

21

She nodded again and put her hand on his arm. 'It was a terrible time. No one complained. We should have done. My fiancé died.' Her voice was quiet and she no longer saw the silver-sheeted meadows, the red-stained sky and earth but that cold parade ground, Geoff's letter.

'We should have complained. We were careless with life, with dreams. Your dreams, your lives, and our own.' Her voice was a whisper and she knew he hadn't heard because he was rushing on, as though the words were a stream which couldn't stop.

'Dave died. My mate died. Not then, he had a bit more time. We went on through the bullets coming down from Ari Burnu. Gaba Tepe was way over to the right, that's where we should have come in. They're not going to get us, Dave said. We'll get back to Lenora.'

Deborah watched as the mist cleared completely and the sun shone. Her hand was still on his arm, her gloves were sodden from the dampness in the air, droplets clung to Patrick's coat.

He walked on then stopped again. 'God, it's wet. So wet. Gallipoli was dry but so is Australia. That drought when I was eight. How did we survive? My grandfather was some tough old man, Deborah. He'd not put too many sheep on the runs you see. We just made it. He held his nerve.'

Deborah heard the sound of horses' hooves behind them and stepped well back on to the verge, pulling Patrick too.

'You needing a lift?' An old man drew up. His hat was pulled down to touch the scarf he wore around his neck.

Deborah looked at Patrick who nodded. 'You don't mind?' she asked the old man.

'Wouldn't have stopped if I did.' There was a dewdrop on the end of his nose and his hands were large jointed with knotted veins. 'Next village?'

'Yes, next village,' Deborah nodded. They climbed up and sat tightly together, the package and kitbag in the back with the torn sacks of wood the man was carrying.

'Bit of water about today,' Patrick said, nodding to the

fields, the distance gone from his eyes. He was stiff, embarrassed, but Deborah said nothing, just nodded. The distance would return. It was at the edge of his voice still.

'Dare say but won't harm 'em. Good dry summer backalong and the cutting was done in time.'

They passed cattle grazing on the higher pastures while ducks swam beneath them and Pat laughed aloud at the sight of a field gate which showed only its top bar above the water.

'Dave would never have believed a sight like that.'

'You from London way are you then?' the old man asked, tapping the pony as its stride shortened.

'Bit further than that. From Australia. Back here to see where my grandfather came from.'

'Spect you find it a bit cold here then. Bit hot and dry out there, or so I heard from a lad that was back here in the war. Got hurt, he did. But then a lot did.' The old man was silent. 'I was too old but they said you could hear the guns some days. Bit deaf I am. Good thing too I reckon.'

Deborah nodded. Yes, maybe it was a good thing. You hear too much that stops a heart from healing. They were trotting between grey stone cottages now. Smoke rose from the chimneys and was the same colour as the clouds that were banking up from the north. It was cold.

'It's them damn northerlies. They set my bones off real bad,' the old man said, hunching himself further down into his coat.

'It's the northerly back home that gives us problems too, but that's because it brings winds like the breath of a red hot oven, in the summer anyway. But that's when your winter is here, if you know what I mean.'

Deborah smiled and the old man said, 'Can't say I rightly do but the thing is, where do you want to be put down? That's the thing really.' He pulled up the pony and looked across at the pub. 'If you be wanting to stay, then Mrs Gibbons next to the pub is a fair woman. You should try there.'

'Can I give you anything for the ride?' Patrick asked as he

heaved himself down, holding up his hand for Deborah. He was strong, taking her weight without effort, then bringing his kitbag with him, and passing her her package.

'Buy me a drink one night if we meet up in there, that'll be the thing.' The old man nodded and clicked at the horse, not looking at them as he left.

Patrick watched the cart and Deborah watched him, the stiff shoulders, the tense jaw. He turned.

'I'm sorry if I embarrassed you, Deborah. I shouldn't have spoken like that. It just comes sometimes. It was the myrtle you see.'

She didn't see why it was the myrtle but just shook her head. 'You didn't embarrass me. I understand. I've heard it so many times before.' Deborah smiled into his eyes. 'Really, everyone needs to talk sometimes.'

'Even you, Deborah Morgan?' His voice was soft.

'Even me, Patrick Prover.'

Mrs Gibbons was old and lived in a cottage with old beams, old chimney seats and a bread oven.

'Everything's so old here, so old, so small, so green. England's so very green, especially where you live.' Patrick sat opposite Deborah at the table before the fire. They drank thick tea with the bitter sweet smell of the red hot peat all around. She bent forward and felt its heat on her face. At last she was warm, her toes throbbing with the heat. She would get chilblains. Would this man talk to her again? He needed to, it was in his face. It was in his movements as he prodded the fire with the poker. He had good hands, strong hands. She wanted to reach out and touch them.

'I expect you burn peat in your country, don't you?' Mrs Gibbons said.

'No, but I know all about it. My grandfather was from round here. His name was Robert Prover. Do you know of him?'

Mrs Gibbons shook her head and took their cups from them. 'Can't say I do. Which village did he live in?'

'Never told us. Said that part of it wasn't important. My

cousin Tom Steadman from Stoke says they're all long gone to other parts – he thought they were from around Langport. But you know, all this is just as Grandfather said.'

They walked all afternoon after delivering the package, out along the road, in the apple orchards just beginning to bud, listening to the birds, which Deborah told him were peewits.

They walked along the droves, trodden strips of pasture crossing the moors, and Deborah told him of the flat carts laden with cut withies, gold, green or violet skinned, but he already knew of them.

He stood and looked at a cottage with peeled withies leaning against the orchard hedge to dry. The wind was sharp and rustled and moved them, rustled and moved his hair.

'Did Grandfather live in a house like this?'

But Deborah knew he wasn't asking her. These were his thoughts.

'But not the cold, not the damp, not the smell of the peat burning. I didn't know those things,' he murmured and she nodded because he was talking to her now, looking at her with eyes that were intent. Then he turned away.

'These must have been the things that made him stop and roll himself another cigarette, and remember. I wonder if my voice would become unsteady if I ever left Lenora for ever.' Deborah said nothing, just looked at him, at his face which was far distant again, and it was such a handsome face.

They walked through orchards, past stripping sheds and barns stacked with tied bolts of withies ready for transport. Yes, he recognised all this, he told her.

He would recognise, too, any man who fished with a bucket fixed to a pole, full of squirming silver elvers caught by the sieve. If he put his hands in they would slide and slip as Grandfather had told him, and Deborah nodded and said nothing, just let him talk.

They didn't catch elvers at Lenora, he told her. They caught yabbies; crayfish that sank into the mud at the bottom of the dams which had been built to catch any rain that ran off the sloping land.

But then he stopped and looked at her, at the orchards, at the sky.

'But I'm wrong, Deborah. I don't catch yabbies now. Because Dave's dead and it was the two of us who yabbied. Besides, I'm not a child any more. That's the problem, isn't it, Deborah? We grow older, those of us who can, and I've known other things, other challenges that pale beside sheep and cattle.'

Yes, she thought. Yes, those of us who survive know other things but she didn't speak because there wasn't room for her own bitterness here, only for his.

He squatted down beside the river. The water was swirling as the wind blew stronger. It streaked the flooded fields to his right with white lines.

'No, I don't go yabbying any more. I just try to make sense of the life I've still got, whilst Dave's has gone.' He was whispering into the wind, over the wind-whipped water. Had he forgotten that she was there? It didn't matter. She would wait. She stood quite still and then he turned.

'There was no water lying on the land at Gallipoli. We found a gully after the remains of the force had forced their way ashore, over the bodies of our friends. The company tried to stay together, it helps damp down the fear, being with people you know. But the gully split and the gap grew wide between the two halves. Then it split again and there were cross-cuts. But we stuck together, Dave and I.'

He took out his cigarettes, put one in his mouth, lit it and let it hang on his lip, the smoke drifting up past his right eye. He left the cigarette in his mouth as he talked.

'Dave's father was a boundary rider turned shearer. Not a suitable friendship, my mother thought. We were mates, though – always have been, always will be, Dave said.' Patrick turned to her. 'I can't help talking like this, Deborah. I've never spoken of it before but yesterday there was myrtle in my buttonhole.' His voice was unsteady.

Deborah nodded and again said nothing. She merely waited,

staring at the trees in the orchard, knowing that Patrick was seeing something else.

He pitched a stone flat across the water. In spite of the wind it skipped once, twice, three times. Ducks and drakes, she thought. Did he call it that? She knew better than to ask.

'The fire went on and on, Deborah, from the trenches above, and on the flank from field guns and mortars. That pattern never altered from the day we arrived until the day I left.'

He threw another stone, his fingers were muddy. He rubbed at them, then took the cigarette from his mouth and threw it away, watched it arc and die.

'It was dust there, not mud. We had no water to drink by the third day. Carriers scrambled up the slopes with containers. The water was warm and there was too little of it. As the day wore on the heat became heavier. By evening there was a soaking drizzle. I opened my mouth just to get some moisture. We laughed you know, Deborah. It was all so damn useless. We smoked, talked.'

'Dave said, "See the world, the buggers told us. See the sand and rocks and the bloody Turks with the sea at our backs and no place to run."'

'But he didn't die until May when the Turks stormed us, forty thousand of them, or so they said later to make us feel better.'

I don't want to hear this, Deborah thought. I don't want to hear this and be reminded of my own lost love, the lives that burst into nothingness. Dear God, I don't want to know anything about it. But she had listened to Geoff, she had listened to the men she had nursed and so she would listen to this.

'You didn't know that, though did you, mate? You didn't know anything bloody much,' Patrick murmured as he watched the rain bear down hard on the water and on the droves and rhines. He shut his eyes. Was he seeing the face of his dead friend? Could he still see the tint of his skin?

'He was going to come with me if I ever came back here. We told Grandfather before he died. I didn't miss him as much as I thought I would because I always had Dave. Fifteen we were when he died and we'd just sheared our first hundred bloody sheep and he bought the beer. Mother nearly killed him – and us. The Turks killed Dave instead.'

Deborah saw that the rainwater was falling in his mouth now. Had he noticed? It was so much harder than the drizzle had been. It was soaking through her coat and she was shaking with the cold, with the sadness of it all.

She stood, waiting and then he looked at her.

'You're so cold, so patient,' he said.

She felt him take her arm, and they walked without speaking back towards the village, towards the cottage. She made him stand in front of the fire, because he was shaking too. She hung both their coats on Mrs Gibbons' airer while the landlady put ham and potatoes on the table.

'Do you feel as cold as I do, Deborah Morgan?' he asked.

'I'm used to it. I stand at the cheese stall in the winter, and work in the dairy. I feel it, but I'm used to it.'

'You'll be lucky if you don't get your death, you being a foreigner and all,' said Mrs Gibbons to Patrick, patting Deborah on the shoulder as she passed. 'You'd be doing yourself some good, young man, if you went in next door for a drink and some dominoes when you've dried out. But not before you have, mind.'

She turned to Deborah. 'And you, child, should be getting on home the minute that coat's dry. There's a bus in half an hour.'

Child, that was nice, Deborah thought as she ate the moist, sweet ham, but not the potatoes. They were too dry. Her mouth was dry, her throat was tight. It wasn't the cold or the wet. It was the pain in Patrick's eyes, it was the myrtle she had made him wear. It was the memory of Geoff, and it was the loneliness which clung to her as she rode back to Stoke in the bus alone.

Patrick smelt the burning peat, which had sunk deep into the wool of his coat, as he stepped out into the darkness and then into the gas-lit bar, nodding to the men who were already there. He sat on an oak settle and looked at the stuffed moles in the glass case on the windowsill opposite.

The cider was flat and strong, like the cider at the wedding, but this time there was no myrtle, and no Deborah Morgan either and he missed her. Had she gone away thinking he was mad? She had said that she understood. That everyone had their memories, their pain. She had said that her fiancé was dead, and her parents. Poor Deborah Morgan. Poor Geoff. Poor Dave.

At least I've got my life, even if I don't know what to do with it. You see, Deborah, stepping into a grazier's shoes is nothing, not now, not after learning to survive, learning to graft, learning to live. It was nothing when your friend's life had gone, when there was a gaping loneliness, a desperate restlessness.

'You been out then, today?' The old man who had given them the pony ride was standing by him. He pulled over a rush-bottomed chair, and sat down, as Patrick rose to buy him a drink.

'You had a good look round, did you?'

'Too right, but there's more to see. I want to find the peat diggers and then head off to Exmoor before going to Ilchester, Dorchester. He was a convict you know, walked to the hulks from the gaol there. Then I suppose I'll go back.'

'Lots were. Took a sheep I suppose.'

'No, lead off the church roof.'

The old man laughed and jerked his head at the others who were nodding. 'Best not let Mrs Gibbons know that, she's well in with the Rector, passes on all she hears.'

Patrick watched as the old man carefully spilt some cider on to the floor.

'Got to keep them gods happy, you know. Keeps them quiet, lets the willow grow, lets the apples set well.'

The landlady called across. 'Best not let the Rector catch you doing that either, Ned. He'll keep them of us who goes on Sunday in for another half hour.'

She wiped a glass and put it on the bar, calling across to Patrick, 'You should be here for the wassailing. These old fools get themselves round the oldest tree and fire their darn great guns in the air to scare the evil spirits away. Too much spirit in them already, I'd say.'

Ned sipped his cider. 'Works though, doesn't it. Nice cider for you to sell at rack and ruin price, young Prue.' He winked at Patrick. 'Don't suppose you have apples over there. Just sheep isn't it? Sheep and fires, so we hear. You got a farm have you?'

'No, not a farm, a sheep station. We run sheep, shear them, breed others up for eating. Grow a bit of wheat.' The moles in the case were clutching a moss-covered plaster hill. They were like him, clutching at something, but he didn't know what. Would Somerset tell him?

'Sheep are stupid creatures. Don't care for 'em myself. Farming though, that's different. You put things in, watch 'em grow. Close to it all, you are, if you know what I mean. Have a few cows, get into a rhythm. It's a good clean life, is farming.'

Deborah Morgan had said much the same thing. She had kissed his cheek too, last night. Her lips had been soft, her hair had brushed his cheek. She had crushed the myrtle and its scent had risen strongly in the night air. You gave me the buttonhole, Deborah, and today you listened to me. Today you were kind and calm but I still haven't seen off the memories. He looked around the room. Maybe I need you all to wassail me?

'I be going to the Exmoor tomorrow, if you want a ride.' Ned was pushing at the elm log with his foot and Patrick nodded, drinking up his cider and calling for another.

'Yes, that'd be good.' It would be good to be with someone too.

Patrick's head ached in the morning.

'Too much of that Prue's cider,' Mrs Gibbons sniffed as she placed thick fatty bacon before him. 'Eat this, you'll feel better and it'll keep the wind out if you're going off with that Ned.'

It was cold on the cart and Ned smelt of the cider he had drunk the night before. They passed men weeding the withy beds.

'Silly buggers. They should have brought their sheep in, they'd have kept it clear. Eat back the willow shoots they do too. Better harvest later on. But your grandfather would have told you that. Miss it all did he, out there in Australia? Spect I would have.'

'He didn't miss the damp,' said Pat.

But he had missed the girl he loved as he was taken from Dorchester Gaol in chains to walk to Portsmouth and this was the route that he, Pat, would follow before he left England. He knew it by heart.

'The prisoners had to march from Dorchester to the ship. They walked fourteen miles the first day and then, at the red signpost they were turned right down a lane towards Boxworth. They had to paint it red, you know, because the guards couldn't read.'

'Can't say I hold with reading much. Don't need it here somehow.' Ned pointed towards the mist. 'It's rising now, it'll warm up soon. You got marsh marigolds have you in that land of yours?'

Patrick looked at the yellow flowers, the glossy leaves and shook his head.

'Your grandfather must have missed them, the flowers and the trees,' Ned said.

'He missed his freedom most of all. He said it was the chains that brought it home to him, that and the faces of the people they passed as they walked. If he'd gone from Ilchester he'd have travelled by cart but he took the lead from a church outside the parish. Said it felt less bad somehow.'

'Why'd he do it anyway?' Ned asked.

Patrick shook his head. 'He didn't really know why himself.'

` . He remembered his grandfather sitting on the verandah of

Lenora, swatting away flies, squinting across to the horizon, across the miles of land that he owned. I needed to get out, he had said. Ten of us in a cottage, no food, no clothes, aching joints from the damp. I needed to start again. If I wasn't caught I knew I'd have enough to start a farm near Stoke. If I was, I'd be deported. Either way, I'd have a start. Others did it but it made me feel bad. I shouldn't have done it, I should have taken a sheep we could eat.

Patrick laughed quietly as he felt the cart lurch beneath him. More than enough sheep now out there, old fellow, he thought, thinking of the four thousand they ran, and then he shuddered because he hated the thought of them.

They were passing orchards heavy with mistletoe and great brown stacks of willow bark strippings.

'Bring me marrows along beautiful,' Ned said, coughing as the cold wind caught him. 'Bit of that on the garden works a treat.'

Three sheep had strayed through a broken fence up on to the bank where the primroses and violets were thick, and Patrick thought of his own fences on Lenora. Would they be right? But then he relaxed. He knew they would be. Taylor had been brought in as manager when he left for Gallipoli, Taylor was still manager. He would remain manager. He deserved it, he was good. So what was Patrick? His mother's son.

He shifted on the seat, glad of the wind which cooled his anger.

'You grow oaks over there, do you?' Ned pointed to the gnarled tree they were passing.

'Some people grow them near Melbourne but no, we have gums. They don't shed their leaves, they shed their bark. It changes colour too.'

Ned nodded and flicked at the pony with his whip. 'Strange kind of a world, isn't it? Why don't you have a bit of cheese?'

Patrick took a hunk of bread and cheese from the tin Ned pointed to. Yes it was a strange kind of a world. Grandfather had gone straight from the ship to building houses, roads, a church. That was what had wiped out the crime in his mind, that and the flogging he had received for an offence he hadn't committed.

'Bought his own place did he, your grandfather, out there in Australia?'

'Married into it, you could say.'

Ned took some cheese and chewed. ''Tis a good thing to have a woman. Need it in life. Two's better than one.'

Patrick looked back at the oak which was quite small now. He looked across at the rhines, at the small orchard in the distance, at the mistletoe and he thought of Deborah Morgan's kiss. Then the smell of crushed myrtle reached him again and he no longer saw the Levels of Somerset but the gullies and dust of Gallipoli as the Turks charged.

There was a field of standing corn splashed with poppies, there were guns, screams. There was chaos, there was Dave to his right. And then, as the Turks withdrew there were thousands of bodies ahead of the Anzac posts. Throughout the day the heat grew, as did the hum of the flies which almost drowned the groans of those who lay out there, unhelped.

He and Dave and the other Anzacs had waited and listened and been driven nearly mad by the stench, the cries, the flies, until at last an armistice was declared. They had gone out, brushed crawling flies from the mouths of exhausted men and held water bottles to their lips – their own men, and the Turks, and they found that the Turks were not the fiends they had been told. They found them in dips and in gullies where their bodies had crushed the scrub-oak and the myrtle. They found layer upon layer of them because there had been many more of them than the Anzacs.

Dave was shot the next day, when it was quiet. They had been talking of the annual Lenora horse race that Patrick or he would win one day. Of the new lives they would make for themselves, the challenges they would find. Patrick had heard the shot only after Dave had crumpled and fallen. He had clutched at Dave's shirt, and it had torn. He had turned his friend's head and seen the wound and he saw that there was no life in Dave's eyes. But there had to be – they were mates, they always had been. They always would be. When he hugged him there was the smell of myrtle on both their clothes and a scream in his chest which wouldn't come out, which had never come out, which just twisted, turned, ached. He was alone, for Christ's sake. He was alone.

He had been alone for the rest of the war. He went home alone, to Lenora where his mother held him to her and said that he would be safe now, safe with her, safe at Lenora. And he had felt the air being sucked from his lungs and despair digging even deeper.

A week later, at the inn where he stayed, he wrote to Deborah Morgan.

Deb walked up the path in the middle of April. The stones were still in the parking space by the brook, there were ducks nuzzling the bank. She was tired. They had been making cheese again and her hair and hands smelt of it.

She pulled out some groundsel as she walked round the cottage and through the bottom garden, calling to the hens that she knew would be there.

'Keep your comb on, you noisy creature,' she called to the cock, throwing the weeds on to the compost. 'Just keep yourself and your women in order for a moment, can't you?'

The fire was still in, the smell of elm rich in the kitchen. 'It beats the smell of damp every time,' she said, and wondered what people would think if they knew that she talked to her hens, and to herself.

She walked through to the stairs, to pull off her clothes, and so tear from her the smell of the cheese, to rub cream into her hands and take away the redness. It was then that she saw the letter but didn't know that it was from Patrick. She had not allowed herself to think of him since she had returned to Stoke.

She thought of him now, as she read about Exmoor. He was grateful to her, he said, for taking care of him through the wedding, through the bedding, grateful for the kiss. But most of all he was grateful to her for listening. She felt the heat of her blush, saw her hands shake as she read his last words. 'Perhaps I can see you if I come back to Stoke. I hope so. Yours, Patrick Prover.'

CHAPTER 3

It was May and the nightingales were singing. Their song poured from the hill into Deborah's bedroom, pure and beautiful. There was a stillness in the air. She stood at the window and watched and listened until there was silence. Patrick Prover had not come back to Stoke, not yet, though each night she thought of him, his thin face, the tremble in his fingers as he had delved deep into loss.

She took out Geoff's letter again, held it to her lips. Yes, I do need someone, she thought. I need to get away from here. I need a future. But would there ever be one? Perhaps Patrick would never return. It was she, after all, who had given him the myrtle.

Next morning, in the dairy, she stood by the large wooden tub of milk, watching as Nell added rennet. Deb stirred the mixture until it coagulated and then left it for the curd to form. It was cold standing on the concrete floor and her back ached, but it was a job. It's not quite what we imagined, Geoff, is it? It's not what I thought my life would be. I was someone who need never work, I would just have At Homes like mother.

'Can you make a start on the butter now, Deb? I want to make sure that Tom's loading the cart with the right cheeses and then we'll be off.'

Deb poured the cream into the churn which looked like a barrel with a handle on it. 'You should at least produce some music,' she panted as she turned. 'Not just slurp, slurp. How about "Knees Up Mother Brown".'

Here she was again, talking to herself. Was she quite mad?

'Leave that now, Deb, Susie'll take over. We've got to get off, you know,' Nell called from the yard.

It was market day and Deb heaved herself on to the cart. At least now it was warmer. At least now they needn't clasp cups of tea between their hands and move their feet to stop the cold hurting, then numbing. At least she wouldn't feel the beginnings of chilblains until next year. Deb shut her eyes. No, don't think of next year, and the year after. By then the baby Susie was expecting would be a child, and she would still be alone, for there was no one else here in the village of an age. They were younger, or older, or married. Her old friends were in Yeovil, embarrassed, awkward to see her as she now was. Some married, taking all the available men. One had sent her an invitation to an At Home. She hadn't gone.

Many had not married but were teaching or doing good works. They were living in the houses they had grown up in, moving in the social circles they were used to, she was used to. They wouldn't know how to make butter, or cheese. They had no need to know, their fathers were still alive, their fathers were still providers.

Deb turned to Nell. 'I do love you, Nell, so much.' She squeezed the plump hand. 'You've been so very kind to us, to me.'

'Your father was kind to the villagers. He treated them whether they paid him or not, you know. I know he made his mistakes but it's because of him that the villagers have taken to you so well, you being an outsider and all.'

Deb nodded. 'Yes, he was a good man.' And felt the familiar headache begin.

The market was noisy and in the adjoining field there was a fair. The sound of the music mingled with, rose above, then fell beneath the bleat of black-faced lambs, the lowing of the cattle. Cockerels were crowing, the stall holders were shouting their wares. I should have brought the churn, she told herself. It could have learned how to make music as well as butter.

She jumped down and unloaded the cheeses on the stall

that Tom was putting up. She wanted to keep her hands busy and her head full of nonsense because always these first few moments made her throat tighten as she remembered her father and mother bringing her here for the first time when she was eleven to buy her a pony.

It had been white, almost completely white and she had stroked it, feeling the heat beneath its coat and had looked up at her father, who held her mother's hand in his, as he always did. She had heard him tell the seller that they would walk around and think just once more.

They had walked across frost-frozen grass, and she had felt the blades crush beneath her feet. Her parents had walked before her as they always did, and she had tried to walk in their footprints because it made her feel part of them. She had held her ungloved hand to her face to smell the pony. It was warm, alive, it had nuzzled her hand. It would take her riding with her parents for the first time. At last she would go with them. She had taken bigger strides so that she could draw closer to these two people whom she loved so much. She had watched her father touch her mother's face.

'But you are the only one I want to ride with my darling love,' he had whispered and her mother had laughed. They had left then. Her mother and father arm in arm, still walking in front of her, their heads inclined towards one another. Deborah had fallen back, no longer keeping in their footprints, looking over her shoulder to where the pony had been, then back at her parents and those words had never left her.

But they *had* loved her. They must have done because she had loved them so much. They would both have become soft and gentle if only they had had time. They would both have loved her as her mother had done by the time she died. She had told her. 'I love you, Deborah,' she had said. But she didn't want to think of it now, none of it, because her headache was coming again.

She lifted the cheeses from the cart, built them up carefully, so carefully into a pyramid, then lifted the butter on to the table. It was heavy.

'I'd like to buy some chicks today, Nell. Could I have a break before they all go?' Yes, she would think of today, that was all, just today, and look, the headache was going already.

Nell was looking over towards the sheep pens, waving to Will and Archie who had driven the sheep across as dawn was breaking.

'Yes, I'll go for some tea, then you slip off when I get back. Don't be too long, mind, it'll be busy today with the fair. Thank God we've a good supply.' Nell slipped off and Deb watched her weave between the crowds. Yes, Nell was kind, really very kind, but she was the boss, there was no doubt of that. It was still a strange feeling.

Deb sold eight cheeses and three pats of butter in the next half hour and it was good to talk to the regular customers, good to laugh at their jokes and listen to Mrs Jones's most recent wedge of gossip about 'er as lived in next village.

'Must keep you busy, all this neighbour watching,' Deb said patting the butter, watching the water ooze to the surface, wrapping it, passing it across.

'That it does,' Mrs Jones agreed as she took the butter. 'Loneliness get to you. You'll find that maybe one day.'

Deb just nodded and took off her apron as Nell returned, folding it quickly because she must be back in half an hour herself.

The crowds were thicker now. A group of children were by one of the vegetable stalls. The stallholder scooped out new potatoes, tipping them into an old woman's basket, keeping up a constant stream of chat, never for an instant taking his eyes off the children. Deb knew that they'd still manage to pinch a few of what they fancied, they always did.

There were a dozen yellow chicks in each box heaped up on the egg stall. She bought a box though she knew some would be dead by the time they reached Stoke, and some more wouldn't survive being popped under Penny, but maybe five or six would live.

She carried it past a stall with dead pigeons tied in bunches by their rich pink feet, another with pots of clotted cream. She and Nell hadn't brought any this time. She frowned as she saw someone buy two pots. They must next week.

She moved on past an accordion player who had set up his pitch too close to the fiddler. The music merged, jarred, irritated. The auctioneer's voice was drowned by the cockerels he was selling. Deb looked closely at the hens, the Golden Wyandottes, the Light Sussex. No, the chicks would do, but one day she would like some geese. They were solitary, beautiful and would give that darned cock of hers a run for its money.

She laughed as she moved across to where Tom would be with the sheep. She only had five minutes left.

It was then that she saw Patrick Prover and he saw her and for a moment the breath went from her body so that she heard none of the noise of the market, or the fair, but the bleakness of the Levels, the feel of her hand on his arm.

'G'day again, Deborah Morgan.' His hand was still tanned, she saw as he lifted his hat. People had to move out around them. She felt a basket clip her arm, knock her chicks. She heard them scrabbling, cheeping.

'You haven't left then?' was all she could say but what she thought was, you haven't left, but you haven't been to see me either, though I spent that day with you.

'No, I haven't left but I've almost finished the things I have to do. Almost, not quite.'

Deb only had two minutes left. She nodded and looked beyond him to Tom, who had turned and was beckoning her over to the sheep pens.

'Tom's over there. Why don't you just go on over and say g'day to him too.' She turned away, moving back through the crowd, back past the fiddler and the accordion player. Back to the stall. The chicks were still scrabbling and cheeping. The cheeses were still there, the butter too. She washed her hands in water she poured from the jug. She cut and patted butter, nodded at customers, spoke when spoken to, but all the time her mind was saying that he hadn't come to see her, even though he had been so close and she was angry, with him for not coming, and with herself for turning from him, because she knew now that she had wanted to see him again so much.

'You're quiet,' Nell said, passing her some bread and cheese at lunchtime. 'Bad day or something?'

'Or something,' Deb replied, chewing the moist sharp cheese that she had made. She was looking at the people who passed, paused, bought or went on. Patrick Prover was never amongst them. Patrick Prover, who had been in England and whom she had kissed, whose words she had listened to, and whose letter she had held, hadn't come though he had been near, so near. She told Nell and then she added, 'I told him to go and say g'day to Tom and walked away.' She watched as Nell laughed, and coughed, and laughed again, and soon she was laughing too.

'Get back out there, you stupid girl. Get back out there and don't think you're coming back on that cart with me until you find him. Good grief, you know what these country men are like, gormless as the day they were born. You have to organise them. Now go on.'

Nell was untying the apron from around Deb's waist. 'Go on, at least give yourself the chance of a ride on the swingboats with a young man. Been too many years without, it has.'

She was pushing Deb now, turning her back towards the sheep-pens, but there was no need for Patrick was coming, walking towards her with his loping stride, his eyes squinting against the sun. He walked up to Deborah and took her arm in that same tanned hand.

'I've said g'day to Tom, now come back with me and we'll continue with our conversation.' He turned to Nell, tipped his hat, and walked at Deborah's side, guiding her back towards the sheep-pen, and she could think of nothing to say, she could only feel the touch of his hand. Then he spoke again and people turned at the sound of his accent, and it was a sound that she liked.

41

'I knew you'd be here, Deborah. Tom said at the wedding that you always came with the cheeses.'

'Yes, put me in a bit of gauze like them and you'd never know the difference.' Why was she saying this, why wasn't she walking with him, talking with him as any sensible woman would? But there was nothing in her head other than the thought that he had known she would be here and he had come and found her. At last someone had come looking for her.

Patrick looked at her from under his hat. 'I rather think I would.'

Deborah flushed.

They were at the sheep-pens now. The blunt-nosed South Downs, the Suffolks with their sharp-pointed black faces and the horned Scotch Blackface, bred for bleak moorland heights, bleated at them. Deborah leant on the wooden rail. It was warm, the grain smooth from years of other arms leaning on it in just this way.

'Have any of yours got black skins like that?' She pointed to the Scotch Blackface. This was miles from talk of gauze, miles from the flush which had risen on both their cheeks.

Patrick was smoking, lifting his head to exhale above her head. 'Not the sheep, only the abos. And they're so black you can't believe it.'

'Do you have them on your farm, I mean sheep station?'

He nodded. 'We used to have them as stockmen but not so much now. They're mainly half-caste, lighter you know. The tribes are broken up. Good workers except when they go walkabout.'

'Like you're doing over here in England? Are you all right, Patrick?' She didn't look at him.

'Yes, I'm all right, Deborah. Thank you for asking. Thank you for listening. Thank you for making me remember. It made me think about my life when I return.'

'So you are going back then?' Deborah reached over the bar, touching the Blackface's long mantles which looked more like hair than wool. She didn't want to look at him

42

when he answered. She didn't want to think of him going away because she realised now how much she wanted him here.

'Yes, I'm going back, Deb.' Patrick ground out the cigarette beneath his boot.

She nodded, feeling a heaviness in her body at those words but at least there was still some time to talk, to laugh, to feel warm with someone. She would tell herself that and it wouldn't matter so much. But it did.

They walked over to the fair then and though his hand no longer guided her she felt more aware of him than when it had.

'I look into all the markets that I pass. Gets to be a habit when you've lived with sheep. I always think that just maybe I'll find one here that would improve Lenora's stock but I haven't. Grandfather did it all.'

'They're good for whooping cough you know. The child should breathe in the air around the sheep, or so they say.' Deborah walked past the entrance to the clairvoyant. No, she wouldn't be going in there. Today must be enough for her. She must tell herself that.

'Must be the lanolin in the wool,' Patrick guessed. 'Glad they're good for something.'

They had reached the swings and Deborah stopped. 'Don't you like sheep?' She nodded to the boy and gave him sixpence, climbing the ladder into the swingboat, taking the rope, watching Patrick come up and settle himself on the seat before the boy released the anchor tether.

Deborah tugged on her rope, and felt her muscles tighten as Patrick pulled effortlessly. He smiled at her and his face was twenty-seven again. 'Don't you ever feel lonely, Deborah? You lost Geoff.'

Deborah looked up in surprise.

'Yes, I can listen too, you know.'

Deborah thought again of the Levels, of the man opposite whom she thought had heard nothing of her pain.

'Do you ever feel like a change, Deborah? Do you ever feel

that life has more to offer? Sheep make me itch.' He laughed but the laughter didn't reach his eyes.

'Yes,' she said. 'You could say that there are times when I feel life has more to offer.'

The month of May passed and Patrick didn't come again. He had left as the sun was gaining strength. He hadn't said whether he would return and she couldn't ask, somehow she couldn't ask, because that was what she had said to Geoff when he had returned to the front for the last time.

The hay was cut by the end of the month and stacked and still he didn't come. That one day at the fair would have to be enough. But it wasn't. Damn it, it wasn't, for she had allowed herself to dream that the loneliness was about to pass, that perhaps she would live her life with a man she could grow to love, a man whose arm felt good in hers, a man whose hand was strong when he steadied her.

In June the pea pickers arrived, travelling along Somerset's lanes, some in yellow caravans with bedding, cooking pots and children in lilt-carts, most in small, fast pony-carts. It was these who pitched their tents in Tom's Lower Field, then the women walked through the village with babies on their hips knocking on doors, selling pegs.

Each household bought because there was always the fear of a curse. Deb bought too, watching as the men, wearing long coats with sleeves which hung to their fingertips, walked into the village inn. They would graze their ponies without permission in Tom's fields until the peas were in. Nothing changed. Oh no, nothing changed, though I would dearly like it to, she thought.

She was washing for Nell this morning, swirling the clothes round in the copper, then scrubbing them on the drubbing board, putting them through the huge mangle, hearing the water pouring, then dripping, into the bucket at her feet.

She paused to rake out the fire beneath the copper, then added coal and swirled the clothes again. In Yeovil they had never washed their own clothes. Did Patrick do this on his sheep station? She knew that he did not. She knew that his life was as full of ease as hers had once been and she envied him. Dear God, how she envied him, and he had a mother too.

She stopped turning the mangle, put her red swollen wash-day hands to her face and wept for the mother and father who had died too soon, who would have loved her.

She washed her own clothes and folded them in the wicker basket to hang in her garden because she was to go home at lunchtime today having been up early to milk with Tom at five a.m. The cuckoos were calling, the bees were busy in the foxgloves which grew behind the cottage garden walls. She waved to Mrs Briggs.

'The climber's doing well,' she said as she walked up the path and round to the back of the cottage, the wicker basket digging into her hip, heavy with the weight of the damp clothes.

Patrick was there sitting on the hamstone wall, leaning forward, his elbows on his knees, his hands hanging loose at his sides.

'G'day.' He rose and took the basket from her and she nodded. She had known he would come because she hadn't tempted fate – she hadn't gone into the clairvoyant's tent, he hadn't said he would see her again, she hadn't asked. She had known, but the relief made her turn from him, taking pegs from the tin on the ground, shaking out the damp sheet, then the pillow cases, then her tablecloth.

'Worse than the gypsies aren't you, for coming and going?' she said, her words indistinct from the peg she held in her mouth. Then she saw that her petticoats were next and she took the basket from him in confusion, and the peg from her mouth.

'I'll do these later,' she said, taking the basket inside. She returned with lemonade, passing him a mug, sipping from her own.

'So, you're still here then.'

'Yes, still here, but not for long.'

'So you said before. Sit down again. I'll bring some cheese. It's good, I promise you. Made by these fair hands.' She laughed as he sat again, but stopped as he reached up and took her hands. They weren't fair. They were red, swollen, rough, and she shrugged from him. 'I'll get the cheese,' she said, all laughter gone.

It crumbled as they ate and they tore the bread into pieces and dabbed up the cheese from their plates.

'Make your own bread, do you?' Patrick asked, tipping the last crumbs of cheese into his hand, licking it. His tongue was pink, his lips soft and Deborah felt a shaft within her. It was so long since a man had held his lips to hers, so long since his tongue had brushed around her mouth. So long since Geoff had been home.

She looked down at her hands. 'No, not often.'

She was sitting on the wall opposite. She pulled at the weeds, stroked a budded rose free of greenfly, then stood and checked her lettuces, stamping on two snails. Her own peas were ready. She picked some, handing some pods to Patrick.

'Eat these, they're sweet just now.' She sat next to him, leant across, showed him how to open the pod, and run his thumb along the peas. He was too fast and they fell to the paving stones. He picked them up and ate them.

'You can't do that.'

'I can, I did.' He looked at her and his eyes were so brown, his lips were pink. 'You like all this, don't you, Deb.' He pointed to the garden.

'Yes, this is fine.' Yes, she wanted to say, but I preferred what I had. I preferred Geoff, I preferred Father, Mother. Oh, I very much preferred what I had. But she said nothing more, just watched as he ate more peas.

'Come and show me your world, Deborah.' Patrick stood up, brushing the breadcrumbs from his clothes, looking at the pods in his hand. Deb threw them on the compost heap.

They walked out past the parking space. There were three

bags of coal left for the steam engine which had stopped here the day before. It would come back laden with logs and drop its long pipe into the brook and refill its tank with water.

Their heels sank into the moist ground, and the Devon Reds that she had milked this morning swished their tails at the flies as they passed. Deborah crouched by the brook, leant forward, pulled up some dripping watercress. Its leaves were dark.

'Try some, it'll be strong. It's watercress.' She laughed at his face. 'It won't bite, just burn a bit.'

They ate it as they walked along listening to the lapwings and the constant call of the peewit. He told her of his travels on the Levels, of the peewits he had heard then.

In Dickons Field the pond was green with pondweed and full of tadpoles.

'When I used to come and stay with Susie we would put them into an old boiler and when they became baby frogs I would come back and we would put them on pieces of wood or cork and wait until they jumped off. We were helping them leave home, we said.'

She looked down at the water. It seemed so long ago.

Patrick stood still, his head down, and then he removed his hat, wiping his forehead. 'Lucky bloody frogs,' he murmured. 'Maybe I should tell that story to my mother. Sometimes mothers love too much.'

'Parents can never love too much, Patrick,' she whispered. 'Just not enough.' But that wasn't true. Hers had loved her, she knew they had, all parents loved their children. She watched a newt as it swam beneath some weed. Another was motionless at the side. 'Look, see them.' She pointed but Patrick wasn't looking. She shook his arm. 'Look.' Because she mustn't think of her father, her mother, she must think of today, as she had done all her life. Just today.

He grasped her hand. 'So, you help frogs to leave home. You are a very wise lady, Deborah Morgan.'

His face was close to hers, his lips, those soft full lips touched her cheek. 'I wish my mother could meet you.'

She said nothing, nothing at all, just stood and felt those lips on her cheek and wanted his arms around her too. She wanted words which would change her life, which would hold her close. But now he turned and walked on.

'You're lucky to have a mother,' she called softly, but he didn't hear and as they walked towards the squire's estate yard beyond the big hill she thought of how little time she had had with her parents before they died. She thought of the years of ease before, the parlourmaids, the housemaids, kitchenmaids, the man who cleaned the knives. The loneliness, but they hadn't meant it. Of course they hadn't meant it.

They had let her help old Ben in the stables when they went hunting, hadn't they? She'd stirred the linseed gruel on the stove, and the cat had licked the stick clean at the end. She'd watched them ride out, watched them return. Watched them pull off one another's boots, the mud so thick always. She could still smell the hot whisky, see the lump of sugar they added, still hear her father saying, 'Soon you can come, Deborah. Soon.' But I was almost a woman then, Father. When could I have come? But no. The headache was coming again and it was only through love that he had protected her from the dangers of riding, wasn't it? Wasn't it?

Or perhaps it was worry that made him exclude her so much from their lives. The worry of living a lie because he owned nothing. He mortgaged everything and spent it. When we lost you we lost everything. But not quite, Father. Mother told me she loved me, just before she died. I know she did.

She called to Patrick, drowning out the peewits, the lapwings, the anger which so often stirred and which she didn't understand. 'You're so lucky to have a mother.'

He stopped and turned. 'One day perhaps you'll meet.' And then he walked on, to the estate yard, looking at the carpenters', painters' and masons' shops. Wood was being planed by hand and the carpenters stood knee-high in shavings. The smell of newly planed deal was rich.

'Do you have anything like this in Australia?' Deborah asked though she wanted to say, Ask me, ask me to come with you. Tell me you need me. I want to be needed then love will come. I want a mother again.

'Lenora's like this. My mother is queen of the castle and I'm the prince.' His voice was distant.

'Lenora's as grand as this? But I thought all Australia was hard, and arid and poor.'

'Not the graziers, Deborah. The graziers are like the squires. Australia is like England used to be. Feudal in a way. That's why some of your gentry's younger sons came over to our hot large land.'

The sun was failing now, clouds were blowing over and they returned through the lower fields and Deborah couldn't stop thinking of a place like Lenora and the family that existed there.

Patrick stayed for the village dance. The floor had been scrubbed. It was impossible to glide and they all lifted their feet as though they were trampling straw. The men kept leaving to drink cider in the inn, while the women dished up food, and talked, and Deborah told Nell of Lenora, of Mrs Prover and her love for her son. Nell nudged Susie and they smiled and Deborah smiled too because Patrick had said that perhaps one day she would meet his mother.

She danced with Will and with Tom and Susie took Patrick out on to the floor and then he asked Deborah. His arms were strong, his skin smelled of the sun and she wondered if she would be able to taste watercress on his lips. He said nothing, just danced and then Archie tapped him on the shoulder. 'Excuse me,' he said and Deborah grinned and danced away with Archie.

Patrick came up behind and tapped, but said nothing.

'You must say excuse me,' Nell shouted across.

'Excuse me,' Patrick said and took Deborah in his arms again, and they were close this time, so close. 'We just tap

49

in Australia,' he said. 'We don't use many words. We're not used to women.'

Deborah nodded, it was so long since she had danced with a man who was not an old friend of Tom's. It was so long since she had danced with a young man, one who had been in Geoff's war, her war.

They ate cake, sandwiches. Then he danced with her again, only with her, and then he took her outside and held her hand, kissed it. 'Do you like change, Deborah?'

Deborah looked at the moon which was so bright that the street was clearly lit. 'Yes, I like change, Patrick.'

'Come to Australia. Marry me there.'

His face was close to hers, and when he kissed her he tasted of cider, not watercress, and she hadn't known him for long enough to love him, or he her. It was too soon. Much too soon but they were the words she had wanted to hear all day.

'I need you, Deborah. I need you so much.'

He left the next morning, without an answer, but she had looked at his face in the moonlight and then at the village behind. She had barely slept that night, talked little the next day. She read Geoff's letter again and again until it tore at the folds, until it was in four pieces.

She opened her mother's trunk, took out the foxfur, the lace handkerchiefs and then shut it again. She thought of the mother's love she had only known for two short years. She thought of Geoff who would never come home again. She thought of her father.

She leant against the window and listened to the silence of the house. It was an end to loneliness that Patrick Prover was offering, it was companionship and it could be love in time. She knew that it could. She would make it be love.

CHAPTER 4

Deborah told Susie the next week that Pat was to leave for Australia at the start of July, and that she was to follow, had absolutely promised to follow in August. He was buying her ticket, one way, to leave from Tilbury on 31 August. Susie kissed her, and wept because it was so soon, and so far away.

'But I know it's the right thing, Deb. What else is there for you?'

Deborah nodded. She knew that Susie would understand, for she had known the depth of Deborah's loneliness.

Deborah took Patrick down the Somerset lanes when he returned from Ilchester, and again when he returned from Dorchester. They held hands, he kissed her farewell at the back of her cottage, where the scent of thyme, sage and lemon balm were heavy on the warm air and there was a stirring of heat in her body. There was a longing for his arms around her and a calmness deep within her when he said, 'I need you Deborah. I'm relying on you.'

'Make sure that she comes,' he said to Nell and to Tom as Archie brought round the cart. 'Just make sure that she comes.'

They took him to the station and he waved from the train, and then sat and watched Somerset, then Devon, then Cornwall pass. He drank tea from the thermos, ate ham from the pig which Mrs Briggs, the baker and Deborah had jointly owned. He remembered the bacon joint hanging up in her kitchen and then this ham, pink and moist as she had taken it from the bluestone with those strong, capable hands. The first time had been for sandwiches which he had carried with him to Ilchester.

'Might as well have something to eat as you poke around Somerset on this walkabout of yours.'

Well, the walkabout is almost over now Deb, almost over. Can you hear me Grandfather, can you, Dave? The walkabout is over and the rest of my life is about to begin. I knew what I didn't want to do and now I know what I do want. At last I know what I do want.

The ship was anchored in Devonport Roads and he threw his coat over his shoulder as he eased down the narrow gangplank into the tender. Some returning Diggers who had been on duties in England threw their bedrolls, suitcases and packages from the dock above. He squeezed past trunks and crates.

Outside the mole it was choppy until they came up under the lee of the ship but then he was on board and soon they were under way. He nodded as he watched Mount Edgecombe lose definition and fade. Yes, you came this way too, Grandfather. You came, you made Lenora yours, you made it what it is. There is nothing more I can do, there. It's my turn now. Are you listening, Mother?

Deborah drifted through July, picking foxgloves from the high grass, and pinks from her borders and placing them in large jugs with lemon balm. She washed and packed the Wedgwood tea service which was all that had been left after they had settled her father's debts. She packed the ornate gold-coloured clock which stood on the mantelpiece and had been given to her by Geoff's mother. She packed into the trunk what clothes she would not need on the voyage, what vases and photographs stood on her shelves. She emptied buttons, buckles and shopping lists from the two pewter beer mugs and packed these also. The trunks would be sent ahead.

She packed no cooking utensils.

'We are to live with his mother on the sheep station, Nell. There's no need.'

Nell sat on the trunk while Deborah buckled up the leather strap.

'Did Patrick tell you that then?' There was doubt in her voice.

'Oh yes, he said we would marry before Christmas near Lenora, that I would like the life and I know I shall, Nell.' Deborah stood up, shaking the dust from her skirt. 'I just know I shall love it.'

Her aunt stood too and held her, stroking her chestnut hair. 'I just want you to be happy and he's a good boy, but it's so far away. It'll be so different and I'm worried about his mother. She should have written to you. But then, I expect she's busy.'

Deb nodded, breathing in the warmth of this woman, then lifting her head and looking around the kitchen which the sun never warmed, even in the height of summer. Patrick hadn't written either, but he had said that he might not be able to. That he had things to do. That was enough for her, wasn't it?

'I want to be settled. That's what I want more than anything. To have a home, to be loved, to love. I must take my chance now. It might not come again.'

'But I just wonder if you might still find somebody here.' Nell stood back from her, concern on her face, in her voice. 'That Mrs Prover is difficult. She's a snob, she holds on too tight to her family.'

'But that's what I want, a family to hold on tight to me and it's not too far. It's only the other side of the world.' She stopped then and looked at Nell. 'It's only the other side of the world,' she repeated quietly and a silence fell between them.

In August she passed the hay stacked to the roof in Tom's Dutch barn and knew that she wouldn't see the bullocks ripping at the fodder in February. She saw the poppy-splashed fields of ripe oats, barley and wheat and knew that she wouldn't hear the rooks cawing over the ploughed, seeded spring fields, or hold Susie's baby, and she turned from the hills, so rich, so green and went to Yeovil to Geoff's mother and then to the house where she and her parents had once lived to say goodbye.

She remembered the At Homes, the morning dress, the afternoon dress, the carriages, the maids. She looked at the steps leading up to the front door, the drive sweeping round to the tradesmen's entrance. Perhaps Lenora was like this, father. Perhaps I shall have a family again and a man who needs me, who will give me a child to whom I can whisper 'I love you' every day. But yes, it was the other side of the world and she would never hold Susie's baby and she felt the ache deepen inside.

At the end of August the harvest was almost in, the summer had been kind to them and now Deborah watched the horse-drawn self-binders with their flip flop fans which guided the falling corn on to the revolving platform and then flicked the tied-up sheaves into rows. The men had hung their jackets on a broken branch of the oak tree as they always did, and broke for lunch to eat their pasties and their cheese, drinking cider from the jug.

Nell looked across at her. 'Don't forget us.'

'Oh no, how could I ever do that?' She remembered the picnic that Geoff had taken her on. The potted meats his mother had made, the visit afterwards to Nell, the swing in the village that he had said he would push her on on her wedding day. She wanted to feel safe like that again, cared for again. She wanted to feel that there was someone who would swing her in the orchard. She wanted to go but she wanted to stay too.

'Have you enough dresses now, for the voyage?' Nell asked for the second time that day because it was tomorrow that Deborah would leave.

'Bristol must be out of all its muslin,' Deborah laughed. 'And that old sewing machine of yours will be red hot for the next two weeks after all we've put it through.'

'Then it will remind us of you and we shall touch it as we pass and think how we miss you,' Susie said, easing her back, stretching a little. Her belly was swelling almost daily.

There were flying ants, silver in the dusty air. There were grasshoppers rasping, tortoiseshells fluttering in amongst the thistles, the cardoons of which drifted in the air. Think of this, Deborah told herself, not of tomorrow, not of leaving the people you love.

She rubbed an ear of corn between the palms of her hands and ate the grains. Her hands were tanned and rough. Soon they would be smooth. Think of that, but there were tears down her cheeks now and Susie's too, and Nell's. The men looked away, at the children who sat on the sheaves and waited for the rabbits to emerge. But Tom cried too, as she left in the train for Tilbury the next morning.

At Tilbury she saw the small launch which would take her out to the Orient ship and then looked at the people all around who were waving to friends or relations, then clutching handkerchiefs to their mouths, their eyes. She looked back too, though there was no one here craning forward for a last glimpse of Deborah Morgan and she waved, to England. She waved again to the receding shoreline as the ship's band played 'Auld Lang Syne' and nodded as the young man beside her said, 'I didn't think I'd feel sad, but I do.'

She nodded because she couldn't speak, because her heart was breaking as she left the only world she had known, the world which held Nell and Tom and Susie. The world which held her parents' grave, both of them in the one. The world which held echoes of Geoff. And it wasn't enough now, as she turned to face the wind, to think of Patrick, to think that he needed her, to think of the end of her loneliness. Because now she was frightened. Now she was more lonely than she had ever been in her life and she wondered why she was leaving her own land to marry Patrick Prover.

Why? she called into the wind. Why am I doing this?

*

She dressed for dinner, feeling the lurch of the ship beneath her wondering if she could bear the sight of food, wondering if her misery would stop, remembering the sewing machine as she smoothed down her dress. Would they touch it as they passed? She knew they would. She knew too, that if her parents had been alive they would have wept at her going. Yes, of course they would.

The Captain was waiting at the entrance to the dining room. She shook hands but couldn't smile, and was shown to her table. There were flowers in the centre, carnations. Would her pinks be dead? Cutlery gleamed on the circular table, the napkins were stiff and white. An elderly couple opposite talked and laughed, to one another and then to their companions.

The steward placed a terrine before them; it gleamed. The ship shuddered and rolled, and when Deborah clenched her hands, her nails were sharp in her palms where the grains of wheat had been. There was sweat on her forehead. The ship rolled back. She rose, moved as it rolled again, and then there was a hand on her arm, the voice from the rail again.

'I'll help you to your cabin.'

The young man who had been sitting on her right had risen with her. She felt the ship shudder and roll again and didn't know how she moved across the room so quickly. Her cabin key was in her hand but she couldn't use it. She didn't watch as it was fitted and turned. She didn't turn to thank him, or to speak, she just fell on her bunk as the wind and waves brought chaos to the ship.

The stewardess came, soothed, comforted and told her that many other passengers felt the same. In about four days she would have gained her sealegs. How could Deborah tell her that it was misery too? That she was turning her face to the pillow because of the people she had loved and left and perhaps would never see again, because of her parents and Geoff whom she was also leaving behind. Because there was no letter from Patrick that she could hold when she was alone.

Flowers arrived on the second day, beautiful flowers, but couldn't the young man see that she didn't care? On the fourth night she slept without tears, without sickness, and when she woke she was hungry. The sun was shining, the sea was calm and so was she. It was too late to turn back. She was committed. She was going. She had wanted a change, a family, a lover, and that was what she was going to have. Patrick would meet her at the dock, marry her.

She had not brought the myrtle Nell had given her because it would remind Patrick of the bodies which had crushed the shrubs, he had told her of the smell of it on Dave. She would learn to be a good grazier's wife, she would hold her own baby. She was twenty-four and a woman, not a child. Soon this loneliness which she had felt for so long would be over but beneath it all was still the pain.

She left her cabin and breathed in the fresh air, and then walked along the deck towards the dining room.

The young man rose as she approached the table. 'Good morning,' he said. 'Are you well?'

Deborah nodded. 'It was very kind of you, and the flowers too. I feel so foolish.' The steward brought her coffee and a warm soft roll. The butter was good, the marmalade too. The elderly couple were not opposite. She looked at the man – Edward Lucas, his card had said.

'Are they unwell too?'

He smiled. His hair was fair, like wheat. 'Most people have been, you've recovered more quickly than some. I have the constitution of an ox. It's been rather lonely really. No one to chat to.'

Deborah looked round. Yes, there were gaps. She had not been alone in her absence. She smiled at Edward Lucas. 'I'm Deborah Morgan. I'm travelling to Melbourne to be married. I suppose everyone else is to dock there too?'

'Oh, no my dear.' A woman with steel grey hair spoke, her accent like Patrick's. She had just sat down at their table, thanking the steward with a nod of the head. 'Perth is my home. I shall be disembarking at Fremantle, then you'll 'continue on to Melbourne, and if I remember correctly you will too, Mr Lucas, will you not?'

Edward nodded and began to speak but Mrs Warbuck went on with barely a pause to draw breath. 'A teacher if I remember correctly. Such a worthwhile profession. And you, dear, are you a professional person too? Brave to be travelling alone. I know you are alone. They've put all the singles on this table and on the one beneath the chandelier.'

Deborah remembered the elderly couple and looked at their places. Mrs Warbuck was still speaking, buttering a piece of roll, dabbing it with marmalade, then squeezing a fresh lime into her water. Surely she must stop to breathe? Deborah watched, waited until the roll was in her mouth, then turned to Edward. There was laughter in his voice as he said, 'Yes, I thought they were together too, but the Captain matches up his guests very well, with a few exceptions.' He was really laughing now and Deborah grinned as Mrs Warbuck began to speak again.

Deborah sat for the morning in a deckchair, feeling the sun on her arms, a book in her hands, but she wasn't reading, she was just letting her body rest, and her mind too. There had not been time to stop and sit since her father's death, since she had had to work at the farm and care for her mother. At first the tiredness washed over her in great waves, then eased and finally left her as the days passed and she felt almost young again.

In the second week Mrs Warbuck discovered that the quiet woman on her right had a relative in Yorkshire, which was where her own grandfather had come from.

'Was he a convict?' Deborah asked.

For the first time since Mrs Warbuck had sat at that table there was a silence so profound that the elderly couple, Mr Lucas and the woman with whom he had been talking also fell silent.

Deborah watched as Mrs Warbuck turned and looked, her cheeks flushed, her mouth tight. At length she said,

'My grandfather was most certainly not a convict. He was a free South Australian settler. My lineage is impeccable.'

Deborah looked down at her plate in the face of the woman's anger. She heard the continuing silence at the table, the murmuring on the periphery, the clatter of knife and fork on plate and wished she were back in Nell's kitchen, wished she were back in her parents' home, wished nothing had ever changed, that there had never been a war, that Geoff hadn't died, that her father hadn't lived a lie. That he hadn't died.

She wound the napkin around her fingers and realised that her calmness was only skin deep, that panic and despair could still break through, that loneliness was waiting.

'It's difficult for those coming out from England to understand the fascinating origins of Australia as it now is, Mrs Warbuck. Forgive us, I was talking to Deborah only this morning about the convicts and how most people were descended from them. As a teacher I should have known better. Perhaps you would join me for afternoon tea to tell me more about it?' Mr Lucas was leaning past Deborah, smiling at Mrs Warbuck. His hand clasped Deborah's for a brief moment.

That evening after dinner Deborah stopped behind Edward Lucas as he leaned on the rail, watching the phosphorus wake. The wind was ruffling his hair.

'That was beyond the call of duty, Mr Lucas. You deserve a medal, instead you have my undying gratitude. Are you quite well after two hours of undiluted Mrs Warbuck?' She sounded so in control, so mature. She allowed her hands to relax out of their fists.

He laughed. 'I'll be quite well if you dance with me tonight.'

Deborah looked out across the sea. The wind tugged at her dress. The stars were bright and the music was playing and somehow they were outside their real lives here.

'I'm only asking you to dance with me. Your Patrick, love

59

of your life, won't object I'm quite sure. Everyone dances on board ship. Let's be friends, Debbie.'

Yes, the stars were bright. Geoff had liked the stars, he had written to her of them. She didn't know if Patrick did. She wished he had written, that she had words she could read as she lay in bed.

Yes, the music was playing and it was so long since she had danced on a dance floor, rather than in a village hall but then, at least it was with her grazier, the man she was to marry, and yes, she did feel almost young.

'Everyone is dancing,' he said again. 'Evenings like this shouldn't be wasted. We are travelling companions, that's all, Deborah. We are two British friends in a bevy of Australians. Let us cling together.' He was smiling, and he was right. They were two people from the same land, two friends. He had been good and kind, he had cared for her.

So she danced with Edward Lucas. Not just one dance, but all evening until well beyond midnight and they glided together in time and in tune as they hummed to the music. Over cool lime drinks he promised that he would tell her of Australia, of its beginnings, its growth, of the graziers, of the class into which she would be marrying and he leaned back and looked into her eyes.

'You see, we are fellow travellers. You and I are alone, leaving England, not yet arriving at our destinations. You and I need one another, Debbie.'

He walked her to her cabin door at two in the morning, then kissed her hand, and she slept that night, her body tired, her mind full of music, of laughter, of youth.

The ship arrived at Tenerife the next week and it was warm and balmy as Deborah shaded her eyes and gazed out towards the large volcanoes that reached towards the sky, looming over the town of Santa Cruz.

'Mrs Warbuck says that the island's in fiesta. I shall go. Will you come, Debbie? The Joneses are coming too. I was talking to them over breakfast. Slipped on to the next table

60

since you weren't there. Where were you?' Edward stood, leaning sideways to her, his elbow on the rail, his eyelashes throwing shadows on his cheeks. Did Patrick's do that? She hadn't noticed. Geoff's had.

'I was tired. I haven't danced night after night for years. I'd forgotten what fun was I suppose. And it is fun, Edward.' She looked at the tenders drawing out from the shore as they dropped anchor. Smaller craft were also approaching and now passengers crowded the decks, pointing and looking as the boats arrived and shouted up their wares. Money was thrown and men dived into the crystal clear water to retrieve it.

'Here, dear, let me through.' Mrs Warbuck had a bucket tied to a piece of rope, lengths of which the steward was passing round. 'I want to buy some fruit, then I'll come along and talk to you.' Mrs Warbuck lowered the bucket towards one small craft and Deborah left quietly with Edward. Mrs Warbuck for the afternoon was more than flesh and blood could stand, she told herself as she crowded into the tender.

The beaches were black, the sea clear and clean and warm, or so it looked.

'Makes you want to swim.' Edward stooped and ran his hand in the water.

No, it didn't make her want to swim. She didn't like the water, not now, not after it had taken her father. She looked up at the road winding its way through the buildings. To the right a cliff reared high up out of the bay. She wouldn't think of anything but Tenerife. England didn't exist, not at this moment. They were between two worlds, they were nowhere. They were where memories didn't belong.

Mr Jones pointed to the tiny square building she could just see surrounded by palm trees.

'That's the hospital. We're building one in our township in New South Wales.'

Father would have been interested, she thought. He and

Mother would have taken donkeys up that path. She would not have been allowed to go unless she went with nanny later, but in time it would have been different. In time she would have gone too.

She turned to walk through the narrow shaded streets with their decorated stalls and balconied houses, easing past the milling townsfolk, the passengers from their ship. They ate spiced food and fresh fruit, then congregated for a bullfight where it was much too hot.

Deborah pulled her wide-brimmed hat further down and her lace gloves further up, over her wrists. Her muslin dress was cool. Edward was laughing with Mr Jones, Mrs Jones had returned to the ship.

'The noise, dear,' she had said. 'These things always get far too hot and noisy.'

Yes, it was too noisy, but was even worse when the bull came and the crowd stood and roared at the matadors making their feints as the bull pawed at the ground. Was it terror or anger in its face? There would be blood and pain. Deborah stood, touching Edward.

'I'm going. It's too hot, too noisy.' But that wasn't what made her leave, she thought, as she turned and pushed away through gaps in the crowd, brushing too close to bodies that smelt of sweat and garlic until she was free and out on to the road. It was too hot for memories here where the heat shimmered and rose from the streets and buildings.

She took the tender back to the ship and it was quiet as they rode the calm seas. The fans were stirring the air on the ship and lifted her hair as she removed her hat. She felt it cool the sweat beneath her hair line. In her cabin she bathed her face and lay down. It was good to be back in a place which was, for now, her home.

That night she walked with Edward on deck and stopped beneath the lifeboat.

'I'm sorry it was so noisy but you'll need to get used to the heat, Debbie. Australia will be hot. Living on a sheep station will be hot.' He was stroking her arm with his forefinger. She moved away.

'It wasn't the heat. It was the war. There's been too much terror and anger, too much blood and pain. Didn't you feel it?' She was looking out now, towards the island, towards the flickering lights. She could see Geoff's pain, Patrick's too. 'Didn't it remind you?'

'I never reached the front. I just flitted about doing clerical jobs, then took up my teaching again. I was lucky.'

'Yes you were very lucky.' Deborah turned and looked at him, seeing Geoff and Patrick where he stood. They had not been so lucky. She felt a gulf between her and this man who was doing the job that Geoff had longed for. 'And why are you leaving England and coming to Australia?'

'Why are you, Debbie?'

'I'm coming to get married, to live a different kind of life to the one I've been living.'

'And this Patrick Prover, he'll give this to you? I wonder, Debbie. The graziers don't like interlopers. They like their own kind. I wonder how his family will like you?'

Deborah moved out from the lee of the lifeboat. Edward's face was angry as he said, 'I can't help the fact that I wasn't properly in the war. I can't go on paying for the rest of my life, Debbie.' He stopped. 'I'm sorry, I shouldn't have said that. Forget it. Just forget it.'

He was smiling now, anxious, his hand outstretched. 'Forgive me please. Let me tell you why I'm coming.'

Deborah relaxed, sank back against the rail. The moon was bright enough for her to see his face. 'Tell me then, about your future, Edward Lucas.'

He told her about the small school he was going to start off in, how he wanted to move into one of the Public Schools.

'They're like our Eton and Harrow. They like their Englishness, these graziers. They have got money and class. It's what I want more than anything. There's prestige, status. It will be a good life.'

Deborah turned and looked out over the sea, her breath

was light in her throat, it was gloriously cool. So cool. Perhaps Geoff and I could have come out here if he had found a clerical job, she thought and she felt the bitterness twist inside her.

'So, you went into town today did you, my dears.' Mrs Warbuck had found them and Deborah had no more peace until she reached her cabin. She read Geoff's letter that night and longed for one from Patrick. She dreamt of Geoff, teaching, touching her, laughing, and then he became Edward, with his English voice, his English ways, his blond hair close before her.

In the morning she felt anger rising with the heat. Why should this blond young man have life when others hadn't?

The next day she remained on board while Edward went ashore. She didn't want to see him. She didn't want to spend a day with him, becoming familiar and relaxed.

She played quoits, threw down money to the small boats whose owners were calling their wares again. She took the fruit that she had bought and put it in the cupboard next to her bunk. It made the cabin smell of Christmas at Nell's, the stockings they still all had with nuts and apples and an orange. She was homesick. She was between two worlds. It was too hot, too different, too unreal.

She stayed in her cabin and ate just fruit that night and took her meals alone as they sailed on into the tropics. She watched the flying fish, like arched silver flashes, like flying ants; she watched the dolphins at play in the wake, chasing the ship, always chasing, and she felt as though she were the same. Chasing thoughts in her mind, always chasing.

The heat was closer, heavier, and on the Monday of the next week Edward sat next to her deckchair at the side of the pool and they talked of the heat, and of his plans, and of Mrs Warbuck, and she knew that though her anger remained, she had missed him too. Missed his Englishness, his charm. What was it Patrick had said about being with Dave in Gallipoli? It damped down the fear. Yes, it did. Being with someone damped down the fear of the unknown.

He swam, she didn't. His body gleamed. She had never

seen Patrick's, she had never seen Geoff's. She walked away along the wooden deck, and looked down on to the lower level where a canvas pool had been erected and children splashed. The sound of their laughter came to her. One day, she would have children too.

One man looked up and grinned. 'Good view from the dress circle is there, Missus?'

'Very good, thank you.' She laughed, returning his salute and moving on.

She took dinner in the dining room and asked Edward where the steerage passengers were headed for.

'They're assisted emigrants, heading out to the "lucky country." They'll try their luck in the cities or on some of these new schemes being set up to carve out farms. I believe there are some being set up in Western Australia. They come with nothing. Whether they make it or not is luck. They all work hard, but I wouldn't choose it. It's such a raw new country, Debbie. It's tougher than we can ever imagine.'

Deborah looked at the menu written in French, at the flowers on the table, at the cutlery gleaming. She was lucky, and Patrick was so kind and if he wanted her, surely the others would too, wouldn't they, in spite of what Edward had said? She felt angry again, with this blond man and his easy tongue.

She heard him now as he told her and Colonel Evans of the plans he had to make it to the top out here, and then return to England, to Eton or Harrow, or even to retire.

'Most graziers look to England. They send their children to public school "back home" or to the equivalent in Melbourne and Sydney. They like British teachers, they import headmasters. I know I can do well.'

'Patrick didn't go away to school, he stayed on the sheep station with Dave and the other children on the station. He had a governess too, he said, just so that his mother felt he still had the edge over the others, that there was still that division. He laughed but he wasn't amused. Is there really that division? Are they really that unfriendly,

Mrs Warbuck?' She looked at her hands. They were no longer red and rough.

Mrs Warbuck wasn't listening but Edward was. He pulled at his lip. 'It's unusual to keep a boy at home but it's quite usual to keep the division.' He laughed, then said quietly, 'But you, Debbie, will be loved by them all. Forgive me for what I said before. How can you fail to enchant? How can you fail to *be* enchanted? So much land. so much affluence.'

Was there an edge to his voice? But no, he was smiling, his face was gentle. Deborah nodded. He had said that she would be loved and she felt the stiffness ease from her shoulders and her neck. 'Yes, they've got thousands of acres though they're not like ours. Not lush and rich. He's got an air about him, you know. He's quiet but strong.'

She looked at her hands. Yes, they were no longer red and she did know how to behave with servants. She hadn't forgotten.

Edward was talking now, but not to her, to Colonel Evans.

'It was a chance to live out a dream, you see, for the early colonists. Not the convicts of course, but even some of those grew into graziers. Here was this empty country where they could establish the rural traditions again after they had been destroyed by the industrial revolution. Their workers had to be totally loyal because there was really no other employment to turn to. It's changing now though, there's more than sheep to Australia, more than cattle.'

Deborah rose and excused herself. She wanted to feel the breeze in her hair and have peace to think of Patrick. She felt the warm night air as she walked the deck, nodding at the other passengers who were doing the same. There was no haste, no pressure. There was just the sea and the sky and hours to relax in.

The next night they danced, as everyone did, and they sang and laughed, but the next day the tropical heat closed in on them, beat them down and Deborah walked the deck at two a.m. as others were doing, seeking air, seeking relief. She stood by the lifeboat and looked up at the sky. There was a low large moon which was soon hidden behind the smokestack. The breeze was full enough to whisper amongst the guy wires, the lifeboat davits flickered in and out of shadow as the boat shifted and rose, then fell lightly and smoothly.

'So, Patrick Prover, I'm coming. I'm really coming. Can you see this sky too? Are you looking up at it now?'

Edward was there beside her. She hadn't heard him. 'I doubt it, little Debbie, he'll be running that sheep station of his, flapping at the flies, talking to his men. It's a tough world out there you know.'

She looked up at the sky. 'It seems so close, so bright.'

'That's Orion, up there with his club, and there his belt, and his sword. Can you see?' He was pointing and she leant back, her head tilted, up and up again and then his face was too close to hers. He was bending over her and his breath was on her face as he spoke.

She pushed at him, but he was speaking into her mouth and his hands were strong, holding her, pulling her round, pressing hard against her and the shock of it numbed her, but only for a moment.

'We're friends,' she said, pulling from him, forcing his hands away from her hair. She heard her hairpins drop to the deck, heard the swish of the water alongside the ship as its bow clawed forwards, felt her hair drop around her face and neck. 'We're friends, that's all. I thought you knew that.'

She heard again those low words of desire, the heat of his breath.

'We're friends, Edward, that's all. I need a friend. I already have a lover.'

He tried to take her hands again and she pulled away from him, running along the deck, her hair streaming out behind her, down into her cabin.

Didn't he understand that she needed a companion to remove the fear, not this? Didn't he understand that a man had asked her to spend the rest of her life with him? Didn't he understand that no man had tried to kiss her like that since

Geoff? Didn't he understand that it must be Patrick? It wa
Patrick who had offered her a new life. He needed her, h
would love her. She would love him. Surely Edward coul
understand that?

Deborah threw her evening bag on to her bed and lear
against the porthole. She was so far from England, so fa
from Patrick that everything was unclear. She took out Geoff'
letter, stuck together now. She read each word and wished sh
had Patrick's to clutch to her breasts.

They arrived in Cape Town one week later. She had no
spoken of that night to Edward again. They had played quoit
separately, eaten dinner together politely. She had stayed i
her room when the others were dancing. She had felt the hea
of his breath on her lips, his hands in her hair. She wantec
Patrick to be here. She wanted it to be his hands that tool
pins from her hair but, dear God, she couldn't remember
what he looked like. She couldn't remember the feel of his
lips, or Geoff's.

At Cape Town she stood at the rail and watched as they tied
up at the wharf and coaling began. The railway wagons were
loaded with coal and shunted alongside the ship. Planks were
placed between the ship and the wagon. She watched closely
and tried not to look for the young man who had become her
friend before he had tried to kiss her. She mustn't look for him,
because Patrick was waiting and it was him she wanted, not
Edward.

The blacks were dividing into gangs, grasping spades,
shovelling coal into the large wicker baskets, running with
them on their shoulders up the planks, tipping the coal into
the hold, returning by another plank, again and again. The
coal-dust was in her mouth, on her skin. She ran her finger
along the rail, it was on the wood too. It was in her mouth.
She looked up at Table Mountain. She would like to go,
but Edward wasn't here and she didn't know if she had
the courage to go alone.

She had. She went around Cape Town, took the cable car
to the top of the mountain and there picked silver leaves from

a tree, for good luck. She looked out across the land to the sea. It was so big. She felt a stranger, alone and lost. She went to the Botanical Gardens and walked among the plants smelling their lushness, their strangeness.

Each day when she returned the coaling was still continuing. Hour after hour, day after day. The loading and unloading of goods. Each day she was alone. She sat at dinner but he was not there. She should have been relieved but she was not. No one spoke of him, no one seemed to notice. She stood by the rail and looked out across the town at night. 'Nell, I want to come home. I'm tired of being alone. All my life I've been alone.' But then she pushed the thought away because it couldn't be true. Because deep down she had been a daughter who had been loved.

They set sail again and soon, please God, they would be in Australia. That night Edward was at dinner, and he talked to her, laughed with her, told her of his stay with friends and she wanted to grip his sleeve and tell him that they must forget what had happened. They must be friends because they were going to a strange land and perhaps they would need their friendship. Instead she smiled and nodded and talked of her trip up Table Mountain, her walk around the Botanical Gardens.

'I suppose South Africa's like Australia; vast, different,' she said.

'Yes, there's a similarity but Australia has a dead heart, and there is nothing but farmland between the desert and the coastal area where I shall live. You will be close to the dead heart.' His voice was level and very quiet, his eyes locked on to hers.

'The men who live there are hard. They have to be. That's why they make good soldiers, Debbie, and bad husbands.'

She kept her voice level, her eyes met his and didn't show the hurt. 'At least they fight in wars,' she said quietly. She turned to Mrs Warbuck.

'Is the north-east of Victoria the dead heart of Australia, Mrs Warbuck?'

'Good gracious me no, dear. Quite fertile, quite goo
Lots of money up there.'

Deborah felt Edward push back his chair and lea
felt no sense of victory.

The fancy dress dance was in the sixth week of thei
Deborah dressed as a milkmaid and wore a mask that sl
made herself. The lights were low in the ballroom, the
played and her mask was hot. The fans whirred, m
the warm air around. There were devils, there were
Indians, jockeys, even a teacher in a mortar board l
was not Edward.

She danced and as she danced she thought of Pa
because soon she would see him. She would go to Le
to his family. Thank God, she would soon be at Lenora,
they could fall in love and go on with their lives. She sat w
cool lime drink and watched the dancing, no longer humn
along, just sitting because there were many long days
Australia.

Edward came then, dressed as a farmer, his mask gleam
He didn't smile, he just put out his hands to her and she t
them. She remembered the scent of the flowers he had s
as he took her in his arms. She remembered the heat of
breath, and his cold cold words. She couldn't smile.

They danced and then moved out towards the rail, towa
the lifeboat, and she told him that one day she would lo
Patrick, one day he would love her. That she and Edwa
were two young English people who were just travelli
companions from the same land, amongst strangers, needi
one another.

He nodded, he agreed, he kissed her lightly. 'Just travelli
companions,' he said. 'And friends.' They looked deep in
one another's eyes and Deborah saw her fear for the futur
mirrored in his. Then they clung together for comfort, and
was as though passion had never existed between them, jus
friendship.

They were together every day after that. They were together

at dawn on a summer day when the blur on the horizon became a blur of land, then a distinct coastline, then Fremantle. They were together when they breathed in the smell of land, and he told her that his capital for the trip had come from a trust fund which had been set up by his grandfather to care for his uncle.

'He was born dumb, silent. He was put in a mental home until they discovered he could hear. They had thought he was stupid. He was looked after by a housekeeper then, taught sign language. He became an ornithologist. He died last year. The money paid for my passage.'

They looked down at Mrs Warbuck and waved, then smiled. 'The opposite ends of the pole,' Edward said.

That night they danced, then conga-ed with the others as they left for Melbourne, breaking off as others did to look up at the Milky Way with its great band of luminous cloud studded with countless points of light.

'It won't be long, Debbie. It won't be long before we're there and it will all be spread out before us. Are you as frightened as I am? No, you can't be. At least you're going to your grazier. At least you'll be with someone.'

Yes, but who? I can't even remember his face. Will he remember mine? He said he needed me. He said he was relying on me, but it was all so quick. Nell, what have I done?

CHAPTER 5

They stood at the rail by the dock, all of them, waving, looking. The steerage passengers too. This was Melbourne, this was Australia, this was the future. She and Edward should be smiling and laughing, as Mr and Mrs Jones were doing.

Deborah felt the pressure of Edward's hand on her elbow, she knew she would see the same uncertainty on his face that was on hers. Yes, this was the future, this blue sky, this harsh sun. This was Patrick's country. She shaded her eyes, and looked at the docksheds and wharfs, the cranes casting deep dark shadows.

They moved from the ship, down the gangway, stopping and starting as a handbag caught, or a foot slipped and the line halted. Deborah felt the heat of the rail beneath her hand and the sun above it. Edward was here, behind her. Thank God he was with her.

'Are you all right Debbie?' Edward's voice was soft, his hand touched her back.

She had said that to Patrick as they swung on the boats at the fair. She could remember her voice but she couldn't remember his. She could remember the rope between her hands, the boy who took the sixpence, but she couldn't remember Patrick's face.

'Yes, I'm all right,' she replied. Was her voice steady?

She felt the heat and longed for the cool of October in England. Oh God, Patrick, what are we doing, you and I? Why haven't you written? Perhaps you're not coming. That was it. He wasn't coming. She could go back. She stopped, half turned. She must leave again, go back to England where it was cool and green and she knew Nell's face, her voice.

'Go down,' said Edward and smiled gently.

They were on the quay now, and there were people all around the customs shed. It was strange, so strange. The voices of the officials were like those on the ship had been. Like Patrick's?

She stopped again and looked around at these people, listened to the accent. She turned to Edward. She wanted to cling to him as she had done before and there was the same fear in his eyes, and sweat on his forehead.

'You'll be all right,' she said. 'We'll write. We'll stay friends. The other teachers will be pleased to see you. Some of them will be English too.'

But Patrick wasn't English. His mother wasn't either.

'They don't have dead hearts do they, Edward?' she whispered.

He held her arms, his blond hair falling over his face. There were deep lines from his nose to his mouth which had not been there two days before. 'No one could have a dead heart near you, Debbie. I was wrong. I was cruel. I was hitting out because I wasn't sure what the hell I was doing on a ship alone, going to a strange country.' He laughed but it was a tight sound. 'I wonder that same thing, right this minute.'

There were people pushing past them in the airless shed. Sweat ran down her back.

'Come along there please.' An official was beckoning to Deborah, to Edward. 'Keep moving please.'

Edward dropped his hands. Deborah's sleeves were wet where he had gripped them, wet from the sweat which clung to them both, to them all.

'Then let's go and see if your man is here, Debbie. Let's get ready to say goodbye.'

He stood aside and let her walk before him. She couldn't see him but she could hear his footsteps.

The light was blinding, the sun harsh, but at least outside she could breathe. There was nothing familiar here, no smells, no sights, no faces. Then she heard the seagull. Yes, that was familiar, but that was all. She looked around, stood on her toes. No, there was no one here for her. No one.

She brushed her face with her hand, but her muslin glove was damp. She wrenched it off, dropped it, tore at the other one, dropped that too. She looked again. There were voices all around, tears, people embracing. She recognised some of the passengers. Taxis in the background, the sound of horns, of ship's hooters, of voices calling. She looked. Again and again she looked but Patrick wasn't here. Oh God, she'd come all this way and he wasn't here.

She turned back to Edward, her hand outstretched. It was tanned brown. 'Oh God,' she said and then she heard that clipped Australian voice that she had thought she would not recognise. She turned and Patrick was pushing his way past Mr and Mrs Jones who were hugging their grandchildren. He lifted his hand in a salute towards her, then tipped his hat at Mrs Jones, apologising, stopping to pick up the case he had knocked over.

Deborah felt Edward's lips on her fingers, the pressure of his hand on hers. She looked away from Patrick, back at Edward, at the lines on his face, the blue of his eyes and he nodded, and his fingers still touched hers, just for a moment.

'Goodbye Debbie, my friend. Remember me. I'll write.' He touched the brim of his hat, moved past her, past Patrick who had straightened and was nodding to Mr Jones.

'Goodbye,' she whispered as she watched him go.

Then Patrick blocked her view as he walked towards her and took her hand. He bent and kissed it, then her cheek. Deborah looked at him. He was browner, leaner, but he was the same. She would have recognised him. She looked beyond him towards the place where Edward had been but he had gone and her vision was blurred and she could only nod when Patrick said, 'I'm so glad to see you, Deborah Morgan.'

'I wish you had written, Patrick. I do so wish you had written.'

They took a cab through Melbourne. 'I thought you'd like to see the city before we head for Lenora. It's pretty British I think. I thought it would make it seem less strange for you.' He touched her arm. 'It must be so hot for you. I'm sorry, Deborah, I should have written but I had places to go, things to sort out.'

Yes, it was hot. It was so hot she thought she'd die. It was so strange she thought she'd die. What were she and this man doing together when they weren't even friends.

They were just two strangers, sharing a cab, looking at buildings that cast sharp shadows across the street. They could stop the cab, say goodbye and there would not even be a ripple in their hearts. He had merely kissed her hand, her cheek after all this distance, all these weeks. He had not held her, drawn her to him, made her feel as though she might one day belong with him.

She said, 'I'll be all right, Patrick. It just takes time I suppose.'

She looked out through the window, her nails digging into her palms. Patrick was pointing out the yellow sandstone, the bluestone, the Portland stone buildings. They were like St Pancras Station, the Albert Memorial. I want to go back. Had she said it? She should have brought Edward with them. She should have brought her friend to see all that he had told her about. He had held her when panic surged through her. They had held each other as Patrick had not done, as her father had never done.

Yes, Edward, this is like England but bigger. Yes, Edward everything is bigger, hotter. Everything is strange. This man is strange.

'It was built up around the railway really,' Patrick said. 'Grew much bigger after the Gold Rush of course. See the trams?' They were in the centre of Melbourne now. He pointed to the cable trams and she nodded as he continued. 'Wide streets too. Wider than London.'

'Ninety-nine feet wide, just as Robert Hoddle planned it.' I'm seeing it, Edward. Are you? I wish you were here. I wish

I was seeing this with someone I know. She wanted to run back to the ship, up the companion ladder, into her cabin, then home. But where was home? She didn't have a home.

She looked along the street. So big, so spacious, so important. Oh God, she wanted the village, she wanted Nell, the softness of her shoulders, the smell of her. She wanted the narrowness of the street, the greenness of the fields, the scent of autumn in the air, the smell of apples in the loft.

Patrick leant back in the leather seat and laughed.

'Ninety-nine feet wide, eh? You know more about it than me.'

Deborah smiled. Her back was rigid, her nails were still digging into her palms. 'Not really, someone told me on the ship. I made a friend. He's a teacher.'

She could remember Edward's voice, his English voice. She could hear Nell's too, Susie's, Mrs Briggs'. Her roses would be over now.

'The Treasury,' Patrick said pointing to the side.

They jolted and slowed down near the towering buildings. She looked but could see nothing through the blur of tears which she would not allow to fall.

'The Houses of Parliament.' She could feel his arm brush hers as he pointed past her but she could not see his gesture.

Would the stone breaker be crushing the stones by the brook with his sacking on his shoulder? Would her cockerel be in the pot? Tom had promised that he wouldn't. The voyage was over. She was no longer between two worlds. She had arrived and she felt a stranger in a strange land.

'I'd rather get to Lenora, to my new home.' Had she spoken aloud?

She had, because she felt him touch her arm. 'We'll go now then, Deborah.'

They travelled by train, and Patrick sat opposite and told her that one day he would bring her back to Melbourne when it was less hot. They would go to the beaches, and to Luna Park.

'It's a bigger fair than the one at the market,' he smiled, then touched her arm again. 'It will be all right. I promise you. I will make it all right for you.'

She leant back on the seat, letting her body relax into the drumming lurching motion and looked at this land unfolding in front of her like no other she had seen. She looked at the man next to her. He had remembered the fair. She remembered his hands on the rope, she remembered how he had come for her. She remembered the Levels and his voice as he told her about Dave.

'Do you remember the old carter on the Levels?'

He nodded and smiled.

'So cold. You were so cold that afternoon, Deborah, but you stood and let me talk. Such a patient, wise woman, Deb.' His hand stroked her arm.

Hold me, Patrick, just hold me. But he didn't.

He turned from her towards the window and she looked at his strong back and the arms that had helped Nell up into the wedding cart. She looked at the hands which had thrown the pebble across the water of the mist-covered Levels. She must cling to those images. She must make a bridge between them.

They sat back on cushions as they rattled over a low bridge which drowned all speech and the air which came in through the windows became more dust-filled and hot as the miles passed. So hot, even hotter it seemed than the air in the carriage. Even hotter than the tropics. They rattled over low-trestled bridges, through rock-cuts, stopping at gravel platforms with booking offices that looked like sheds. There were weatherboard houses in the distance, and some orchards at first, then cattle grazing, then pale sparse grass and gum trees, a few sheep. A church.

'I want us to get married before Christmas, after the shearing.' Pat stroked his trousers, looking at them, not at her.

She looked at him, then back out of the window. She had thought he would propose properly. She had hoped he would take her out under the moon as Geoff had done, beg her to marry him so that he could hold her for the rest of his life, run his hands over her body, love her, know the feel of himself inside her.

Her father had agreed, his face filled with pleasure. Geoff's mother had said it was because he was looking forward to her leaving here, but she was wrong. Surely she was wrong. Her mother had bought a hat, written out invitations. She and Geoff had smelt the honeysuckle as they sat on the stone bench beneath the stars and he had kissed her mouth and neck and groaned with longing for her. He had been recalled early. He had died.

'Yes, I see, the shearing.' She looked out of the window again. The horizon shimmered in the heat, sweat ran between her breasts. Her gloves were still lying in the dust of the port at Melbourne. She lifted her fingers to her mouth, she could still feel the pressure of Edward's touch. She needed a friend now. She needed arms around her. The Levels were fading, the market too. There were tears on her cheeks now, tears that ran down on to her chin and neck. She brushed them away but more came.

Then Patrick came to sit next to her, put his arm around her, held her and stroked her face, her hair. He took it from her eyes, lifting it back from her face. His hands were gentle. 'We must wait for the shearing, Deborah. That's what this land is like. Then we can be together. Then neither of us shall ever be alone again.'

He sat with her for the next hour, holding her, stroking her arm, her shoulder, and she slept. For the first time for two days she slept and dreamed of England and sheep, and gum trees whose bark twisted and turned into shredded strips like her life had done for the last four years. She dreamed of Patrick Prover who had lifted the hair from her eyes as Geoff had done and who had held her in his arms at last, giving comfort, not passion, but perhaps that would come.

When she woke she drank barley water that Patrick had asked the hotel to provide, then ate some fruit and chicken and stared out at the parched land, the groups of gum trees, the distant hills. She listened as Patrick told her of the time his grandfather when still a convict had worked as a shepherd on Lenora, how he would allow the sheep to feed at their leisure, making sure that they were spread over the ground while feeding. How he would travel four or five miles then bring them to rest under the shade of some trees. How he would return to his hut by a different route so that they could have fresh pasture on his way back.

'The loneliness could drive you mad. Grandfather said that with two of you anything was possible, alone it would be impossible.'

She looked not at him, but out of the window. She felt again the arm which he had put around her, the hands which had brushed the hair from her eyes, his shoulder under her head when she had woken. Edward had said graziers would not accept her. This man had. He had asked her out here. He had held her. He had arranged the wedding. He would love her one day.

'Who did your grandfather marry?' She wanted to keep the air between them full of words, she wanted to listen to Patrick, she wanted to hear him speak, to get to know him as his friends did. She wanted to hear of his past, his present, his future. Their future.

'The owner's daughter. A beauty Grandfather said, small like the bud of a willow.' Patrick was peeling an orange, the pith was thick on the flesh. She watched as his fingers, brown against the white, eased it clear. He halved it, handed segments to her, one by one. She watched this and tried not to see the budding willow along the rhines, along the lanes of Somerset. She must stay here in her mind.

The juice was fresh in her mouth. Yes, feel it, taste it, talk to him.

'But he was a convict.' The train lurched and rattled and Patrick steadied himself against the seat.

'No, an emancipist by then. He'd served his time, paid his dues. He was a freeman, a shearer by that stage. He'd taken off from Lenora, earned some money then came back as overseer. Stayed when others went off after gold. Kept other hands there too. He loved her, you see.'

'But I thought owners didn't like convicts. Your mother doesn't. Or is it just that she doesn't like most people?'

Her nails were sharp now in her skin but her voice had been level.

She watched as he laughed but the laugh didn't reach his eyes. It never seemed to, when there was talk of his mother. He passed her another segment, then licked his fingers before wiping them on his handkerchief.

'None left I'm afraid. Would you like another?'

She shook her head. 'No, no thank you.' Her hands were sticky, she unclenched them, eased her fingers. Patrick tipped water on to her handkerchief. It was warm on her skin. Why hadn't he answered?

'Your mother doesn't like convicts?' Deborah repeated.

'My mother is a grazier's wife. She forgets that the man who built up the wealth was my grandfather, not the original owner. She forgets that the man she has to thank for the life she leads was a shellback, marked by the whip. Someone who fought for what he wanted. She forgets that sometimes people need to do that.'

Patrick's anger was in his voice and he was putting the remains of the picnic back in the hamper. The train was slowing.

'Graziers are good people. They work hard, they are paternalistic. In other words, they look after their people, they like them but they do not eat with them, they do not dance with them. Some go further, like my mother.' The train was stopping. 'This is Hurstland, Deborah. We're nearly at Lenora.'

She looked out at the dusty red road, the grey weatherboard houses, the feed and grain merchant's sign. As she stepped out on to the platform Pat told her it was eucalyptus and stringy bark that she could smell. There was dust in her mouth and nose, on her skin, in her hair. It was like the coal dust on the ship.

She looked at Patrick then, and there was a distance in his eyes as he looked out across the town to the horizon and she put her hand on his arm.

'Grandpa knew this when it was a muddle of slab-built bark-roofed humpies. Those must have been the good times, the challenging times.'

To her, it looked little more than that now, with its peeling weatherboard, its heat-blistered signs, its whirling dust and shimmering heat, wagons and drays.

'Come along,' she said. 'Take me to Lenora.'

They put their bags into a two-wheeled sulky which Patrick had arranged should be there, and she sat with him as he took the plaited leather whip from the brass holder and touched the horse gently.

'Come on then, Densie,' he called.

She looked up as the train rattled on out of the station. What are you doing now, Edward? Have you found your lodgings? Have you met your colleagues? Do you feel as strange and lost as I do?

The thin rubber-tyred wheels made furrows in the red dust road. There was dust on her dress, her skin, in her eyes. They passed paddocks at the edge of the town dotted with bluegum, sheoak, cootamundra. 'They're rented to a local dairyman,' Pat said. It was full of cowpats, full of flies.

They travelled for two hours, walking up the hills to allow Densie a breather. There was a single telephone wire strung from occasional high trees. A kookaburra laughed once. There were no peewits, no housemartins, no swallows. There was nothing that was full and green, nothing that was cool. There was just space, so much space, and an unending silence.

They opened gates that interrupted mile upon mile of fencing, passed through and closed them.

'To keep the sheep in, that and the fencing,' Patrick said.

They passed a small square wooden house with a galvanised iron corrugated roof, dazzling in the sun. There were two round water tanks.

'Dave's house. We'll come tomorrow,' Patrick said.

They passed cattle grazing in the distance on grey-green grass.

'More intelligent than sheep,' Patrick said.

They passed sheep with eyes that stared out from between thick wool tufts. 'They'll be cooler soon when the shears get on them,' Patrick said.

Would she? Her dress was sweat-soaked, her hands were burning. She tucked them beneath her thighs. Her hair was wet beneath her hat.

They passed a dam.

'We built that. Grandfather, Dave and I. We caught yabbies in there.'

And now he no longer caught them, she thought. She remembered the cold mists of the submerged meadows, the pain in his face, in his voice. It was there again. She put her hand on his arm and he turned and looked and nodded.

They followed the track which wound on and on. Kangaroos bounced across in front of them, kicking up dust. An emu too. Patrick said nothing and neither did she. The muscles in his cheeks were tense now.

'Is the grass always so pale?'

'There's been a drought, again. It's sparse. The sheep have pulled up the pasture here. Taylor let them graze on it too long.' His voice was clipped. 'Mother should have listened to me.'

There was a stream.

'A creek. We'll dam it and swim there.'

No, she'd never swim. She tried to push her own thoughts away but was too tired, too hot, too alone. She could never swim, not after her father had died in a river. Not after he had dived in, fully clothed, fully booted to save the Master of Hounds. Why did he do it? Why, before he had told her that he loved her? Why, before he had taught her to ride and taken her out hunting with them, made room in his life for her?

She had pressed her cheek to his cold lips when they brought him back and her mother had pulled her from him. 'He's mine,' she had screamed and covered his face with kisses. But you would have kissed my cheek one day, Father. You would have. Mother did, when you were gone. I asked her when she was dying and she said, 'I love you, Deborah.' It was faint but I'm sure that's what she said, not Denis, not you.

Densie was walking up a curving rise.

'No, I won't be swimming, Patrick,' she said and felt the headache begin, felt the pain of the memories, but he was leaping from the sulky, opening the ornate wrought-iron gate. There were pine trees ahead and there was a house, a big blue-stone house.

'Lenora,' Patrick said.

'Home,' Deborah whispered, pushing back her father, her mother, her loss, pushing it far down and leaning into the pain of her headache which always made the memories fade beneath its ferocity.

His mother wasn't there. She had been driven in the landau to Mrs Wentworth's for her usual bridge, Edna the maid told them, showing Deborah her room. The curtains were tightly drawn. The bed was high. It was dark, hot and there were flies.

There were flies too, in the sitting room where the curtains were drawn.

'Fly screens help, but not altogether,' Patrick said, showing her the covered verandah running along three sides with its red gum floor.

'We'll dance on this at Christmas.'

He showed her the bathrooms, telling her that the maids would bring water to her room each evening before dinner. That they would help her dress for dinner if she wished. He was stiff, he was listening and so was she, for his mother's return. It wasn't supposed to be like this. There was supposed to be arms like Nell's, there was supposed to be a family here to love her.

He took her through the house, out through the back into the blazing light, the blazing heat which made her headache sharper, if that were possible. Then Mrs Prover came, walking around the back of the house, standing still as Patrick and Deborah now stood still.

'You should not bring your guests out through the back of the house, Patrick. This, for those who aren't used to it, is for the use of station hands to bring in such things as wood. Neither of you appear to be carrying wood. The front door is for the use of guests.'

Deborah waited. The heat on her face had nothing to do with the sun.

Patrick put his hand against her arm, pressed gently then moved forward.

His voice was tense, tired. 'Mother, perhaps you have forgotten. This is not a guest, this is Deborah Morgan who is to be my wife. She is going to be part of the family. She used the back door because I did.'

Deborah watched the woman move forward, her black dress soaking up the heat, her hat shading her face. Yes, Nell, she does look like a witch, Deborah thought, because she had to keep the panic at bay and stop the headache from banging as it did.

'I'm so very pleased to meet you, Mrs Prover. I understand that it must be a shock for you to hear that your son is to marry so suddenly, and an English woman.'

Deborah drew breath. Yes, she thought, a woman. I am not a girl any longer and this man is to be my husband. This man is to be my partner so that neither of us are alone again.

Mrs Prover hadn't moved. The horses were scuffing the ground in the paddock beyond, there were flies on Deborah's face. She flapped at them as she remembered Edward saying Patrick would be doing. No, she was not alone out here. She had her fiancé. She had Edward too. She put her hand by her side.

'My father would have liked to meet you, Mrs Prover,' she continued. 'He enjoyed hunting so much. He would have admired your horses.'

Mrs Prover moved closer still.

'Your father was a doctor I believe? Not related to the farmers of Stoke?'

Deborah shook her head. 'No, we are no relation to the Steadmans. We are town people. My father preferred it, but I don't. I love all this. It's so beautiful, no one would ever want to leave it. My parents are dead you see. I've wanted to belong to another family ever since their death.'

There was a faint smile now on Mrs Prover's face and her hand was out and Deborah shook it carefully; it was so thin, with rings that dug into her skin.

'Patrick told me of you, Miss Morgan. I'm glad that you like Lenora, and that you like family life. It can work successfully, if nothing is disturbed. We shall eat at seven tonight.'

In the bathroom Deborah cupped her hands and sluiced water down her back, her front, her face, her hair, washing away the sweat and the dust and at last the headache. The sun was gone, but the moon lit the sky, the land. The generator throbbed and the electric lights fluctuated. She dressed in the bedroom without the aid of maids. There was a fireplace, two long windows. Out of the window was the endless pale green plain, the dark windbreaks, the faint line of wire fences, the sheep huddled in corners of paddocks too big to comprehend.

Below her in the forecourt was the sound of Densie champing in the stable, the banging of a screen door. The sounds of an alien world.

In the dining room she sat halfway down the twelve-foot jarrah table. She ate though she wasn't hungry. She talked of Melbourne, all that she had seen. But Mrs Prover said that Patrick should have taken her to the Botanical Gardens.

She talked of Cape Town, but Mrs Prover had been through the Suez Canal. She talked of Somerset but Mrs Prover had not been there. She talked of her parents, and how she missed them. She talked of the beauty of Lenora, though she had barely seen it. And all the time the clock ticked in the corner and the maids brought in and removed food.

Patrick answered her, Patrick talked to his mother. Patrick smiled at her and pulled out her chair when his mother said, 'Go for some night air now. It is fortunate that we are close enough to Hurstland to be able to entertain for just an evening. I shall arrange a dinner party. Now go and let Patrick show you over my property.'

Mrs Prover remained sitting. She nodded as Deborah came to her.

'Goodnight, Mrs Prover.'

'Goodnight, Miss Morgan.'

Patrick stooped and kissed his mother's cheek, then took Deborah's arm, walking with her through the house, showing her the piano that he had been made to play as a child.

'I never play it now.'

He steered her out through the front door, along the verandah, out to cross the square to the fence which surrounded the horses.

Deborah could hear their snorts, see the shake of their heads. There was a mare with a foal in the near corner.

'She'll let us close, but keep the other horses at a distance. She's protective, you see. Like Mother.'

'Yes, I do see.'

'You did well with Mother. She likes to feel that she can suck you in too. She likes to feel that you are looking for a mother. You are a wise woman, Deborah Morgan,' He bent and kissed her forehead and then her hand. Then he pointed out the gum trees which were filling the air with the scent of eucalyptus and told her it was the mopoke which was calling, when everything else was quiet. And she forgot to tell him that she had only spoken the truth.

CHAPTER 6

The night had not been easy. There had been a great silence
as the hours wore on. She had looked from her room out
over the land as she had done in England, as she had done
on the ship. No screen doors banged, no horses champed in
the stables. It was as though it was all waiting or all dead.

As dawn came the horizon appeared grey then blue, then
shimmered into nothingness. She heard the whine of the
cream separator, the cracking of a stockwhip, the barking
of the kelpies. Shouts, a wagon. She waited to be called,
but no one came. She ate breakfast alone in the great dark
dining room with its curtains still drawn. To make Mother
think it's a provincial town, Patrick had told her last night.
She's a solicitor's daughter.

Deborah shook her head at the offer of steak and eggs.

'Just tea, please, Edna.'

The tea was strong and the stillness of the room was
broken only by the flies and by the clock. Where are you,
Patrick? Where is your mother? She poured another cup but
ate nothing. On the ship there had been stewards, laughter,
light. Edward. What was Edward doing? Was he sitting
at a strange breakfast table too? Was he feeling the heat,
remembering the ship, remembering the silver flash of flying
fish, remembering her? She would write, she would reach out
to someone she knew. She would do it now, she would seem
to be busy. She would hide.

She stood and picked up her cup, walked from the room,
down the long wooden corridor along which Edna had come.

There were scatter rugs and oak chests, carved Indian ivory elephants and a ruler on an inlaid table.

Patrick called her then, from the front door, shutting it behind him, cutting off the brief shaft of light. 'Leave that in the dining room, Deb. Edna will come for it.'

She stopped, uncertain, embarrassed. Yes, she should have known that.

He was dusty, his boots were red, there was a smudge across his cheek. His hat was in his hand and he held out one for her.

'Come on, put the cup back – or no, I'll come with you. You should see the kitchen. You should know your way around for when I'm working. You'll be alone with Mother then.'

Deborah clenched the saucer tightly in her hands. But I've only just arrived, she wanted to say. How can you start work before I've come to know you? I shall be marrying a stranger. But instead she said slowly, 'I didn't know when to come down for breakfast. Am I very late? Where have you been?'

'Just sorting out. No, you're not late. We didn't ring the gong. Mother said to leave you. She's gone into Hurstland to buy specials for the dinner party.'

He was walking ahead of her, slapping his hat against his trousers, brushing against the oil paintings on the wall, pushing open the door into a hot light room. It must have been twenty yards long. Deborah watched the cook walk the full length of the kitchen from the scullery carrying a jug.

'G'day, Sarah,' Patrick called and the cook nodded, smiled, then grinned, coming towards them.

'So this is Miss Morgan. You'll be glad of the company, young Patrick. He's been out of sorts you know, Miss. Only been back a week or so and all sort of restless.' The cook was pouring water from the jug into a pan on a wood stove. 'Mark you, he's been restless since he came back from that war.' She was wiping her hands on her apron. 'But there's many that's like that.'

Patrick's boots made a hollow ring on the flagged floor as he walked towards the back door.

'Come on, Deb. I'll show you the rest.' His voice was terse, his eyes narrowed.

Deborah stopped as he opened the back door, the blast of light shutting her eyes. It was the back door. She looked round.

'She's out,' Sarah said quietly and nodded.

Patrick was standing at the bottom on the steps, holding out a leather hat for her.

'Wear it, it'll keep the sun off.'

'Why did your journey take so long? You left in July,' she said as he walked towards the long low weatherboard buildings on the western side.

'Business, Deb. Just business. This is the carpenter's work-shop. Over there's the store room. That's the coach house and stables. Grandfather built that himself. 1860 it was. Over here's the barn. Used to be a mill. Horse used to turn the main shaft.' He was standing still, just pointing to each building, his eyes narrowed against the sun. There were men working, moving, speaking.

'Wheat? Do you grow it?'

He nodded, then moved down a slope towards the home paddock fence they had leant against last night. The mare was still there, arching and preening as Patrick whistled to her softly. He turned and pointed to a weatherboard building at the bottom of the track which ran along the fence.

'Shearers' quarters. They'll be full in three weeks' time. And the station hands' quarters too. Those houses near the creek are the workers with families. The kids use the school.' He nodded across to a long low building. He was leaning back against the fence now and the mare was nuzzling his shoulder, tipping his hat. The foal scrambled up from where it had been lying and ambled over.

Deborah felt the sun on her back. It was harsh, burning through the cotton of her blouse. 'So that's where you were taught. You and Dave.'

She watched his face as he looked at the ground. 'Yes, that's

89

where we were taught. This is where we grew up. Behind it's the creek. Over there is the woolshed, where we sheared our first hundred sheep. Grandfather built it. The shearers reckon it's a top shed.'

Deborah looked at the buildings, at the sky, at the horizon and the land which disappeared into it. It was too big. Just too big and too hot to be believed. Was it hot for Edward in Melbourne? She would write and ask. She would write to Nell and tell her. She would wait for their replies. Each day, she would wait.

She walked towards the carpenter's shed, reached out, touched the wall, feeling its roughness, feeling the heat in the wood, smelling the shavings inside.

There had been shavings in the squire's shed when they had walked across the estate. There had been peewits, lapwings sweeping above meadows of green moist grass, there had been lights at night when you looked out of the bedroom window. There had been flowers in the meadows, watercress in the stream. She stooped, picked up a handful of dry curled shavings, then let them drop through her fingers.

Patrick's shadow fell on her, taking the heat away from her body for a moment, standing behind her. Would he touch her? Would he kiss her and make her feel that she was not quite so alone, not quite so far away? Would his arms come round her, hold her? She stood still, waiting.

He said, 'Does it remind you of your squire's shed? Does it remind you of the paddocks there? We must remember the frogs, Deb. Whatever happens, we must remember the frogs.'

And then the sun was harsh again as he moved away, back towards the paddock.

'Why just the frogs, Patrick?' she called. 'I remember it all.'

But he wasn't listening, he was bending, feeling the sparse pale grass.

'Too damn dry for October,' he said as she joined him,

standing at his side as he looked towards the horizon, towards the creek and then back at the horses.

'There's not much grass for them,' Deborah said. She could smell him, his sweat, his dust.

'You're right. Had them brought up last night, the brumbies anyway. They'll be down at the creek again by noon.' He shifted, flapping at the flies about his face. They were around hers too. Edward had said they would be. He had also said that it was a land of hard men but she mustn't think of that and the fact that Patrick had not waited for her to rise this morning. It was enough that he had held her in the train. One day he would hold her again.

'It's strange being so far away from everyone. It's lonely, Patrick. You must tell me what to do, when to get up in the morning. What to do in the day, if you're working.' She kept her voice level, calm.

'Don't worry, Mother will explain the rules, she always does and don't worry about the daytime.' He paused. 'Tom explained something to me at the market, Deborah. He told me that you should have been given a pony. Susie told me that you were never taken hunting.'

He spoke slowly and put his elbows on the fence. The brumbies were cropping the sparse grass. There had been mud at the market, not dust, not horses pawing the ground or sidling up to the mare who snorted, ears back, until they skirted away.

'He would have bought me one, if he had lived,' she said as the mare nudged her foal. 'Mother said he would before she died.'

There was silence between them, silence only broken by the snickering of the brumbies. She didn't want to think of it. She would think of the sun which was too harsh, the light which was too strong. Her head was aching again.

Patrick took his hat from his head, ran his fingers through his hair. There was a red sweat mark around his forehead. Was there one on hers? Her father had always had one when he returned from riding.

Patrick whistled at the mare. She came, he stroked her muzzle, as Deborah gripped the wood of the fence beneath her hands.

'They're brumbies bred from an Arab strain. I mustered them with Grandfather. They'll turn on a plate and they'll race.' Patrick was nodding towards a grey. 'That's Dave's. The chestnut's mine. He's coming on well. Pick one, Deborah. Choose your own. I've been out this morning sorting them. Try the bay, or the black. They're both gentle.'

He put his hand to her cheek, then kissed her gently on the mouth. 'You kept your promise, Deborah Morgan.' Pleasure was coursing through her, it was loosening the tightness of her head, her shoulders, the grip of her hands on the fence. It was making her smile, then laugh as she flung her arms around him, kissing his cheek, his mouth, his eyes and for a moment he held her, then the mare pushed him from behind and they laughed again. He patted the mare and drew back, but the heat of him remained, and the feel of his arms around her. Patrick Prover was a good man, she wanted to shout.

They walked then to the tennis court where tea had been served at the nets before the war and there was a distance between them now, and embarrassment, and neither looked at the other, but each knew the other was there and it was a good feeling.

'We have an invitation to a tennis weekend at Shellrick, a property to the west of Hurstland, but not until December. You'll enjoy it. The Bensons are fun.'

He took her into the library, the study, the second sitting room where his mother had arranged buffet dances during their own weekend parties.

He told her how Sarah had mixed fruit salad in barrels, how she had lined up meringues in tiers and how he had picked at one, how glazed mutton and ham had covered the dark jarrah sideboard in the dining room. How his father had played the pianola.

He sat at it now, flipping the shutters aside. She saw the long metal pierced bar, the zinc-lined cabinet.

'Choose a tune, Deb.' Patrick opened the cabinet at the side.

It was dark in here, removed from the world. She felt happy. He was beautiful. His eyes were deep and his lashes had indeed cast shadows on his cheeks. She took a roll, he inserted it into the sockets, pulled it down over the metal bar, hitched it to the bottom roller and started pedalling the treadles. It was the William Tell Overture and she danced to it, up and down and alongside the table, round and round, and didn't stop even when her breath was heaving in her chest because Patrick was singing and laughing with her.

Then Mrs Prover walked into the room and the pianola died and there was silence as their laughter died also. But then Deborah heard the clock still ticking, the flies droning.

'My husband used to play that. It's a good sound. I'm glad to hear you laughing, Patrick, I'm glad to see you happy at Lenora again. Old familiar things do this to people.'

She nodded at Deborah, at Patrick and then left the room. The smell of eau de cologne remained.

Patrick drove her to Dave's in the sulky that afternoon.

There were wild oats growing along the little-used ruts. There was a dam off to the side which Patrick told her his grandfather had created from a depression, digging drains out from it like the spokes of a wheel to collect what rain fell, building up the sides, planting pine trees to give shelter from the winds which evaporated the water far quicker than it fell.

They passed sheep digging in their feet as they walked. They and the rabbits had eaten out the roots of the grass.

'Can't they do anything about the rabbits?'

Patrick looked at her, smiling. 'Yes, they make hats out of them.' He pointed at hers. She laughed with him, wanting to reach out and touch him because his mother had seemed pleased today and he had given her the horse she had never had.

'You must be careful, Deborah, when you ride out here.

It's riddled with rabbit holes. Your horse can take a fall, you can lie out here for too long. You can die. You can get lost. Always take water. Always tell me where you're going. I'll teach you to ride, but you must obey the rules.'

'When will you teach me?' She was looking at the shadow of his lashes, then at the endless land where people still became lost, still died. He wanted her to be careful. She wanted to shout it to the empty sky.

'Tomorrow, that all right by you?'

She nodded. She wanted to be taught by this man with the strong hands. She wanted to glean those minutes with him. She wanted to be part of his day, of his life and she wouldn't think of the space out there and the unheard sound which so many people must have made before they fell silent.

'Who taught you, Patrick?'

'Grandfather. He taught me everything, or almost everything but never taught me to deal with Mother. He didn't teach Father that either. He was frightened of her I think. He died when I was ten. Killed just before the February race. Dave and I said we'd win it if we got back.'

He flicked the whip in the air, Densie picked up speed, the dust gathered behind them, then around them and there was a distance in his eyes again and she said nothing more.

Dave's mother met them. She stood in the shade of the weatherboard house. Pipes which led from the galvanised iron roof into the water tanks were dry. Washing drooped on the line, the skinned stringy bark prop was motionless. The air was motionless. It hung heavy, hot. It cloaked Deborah. It sucked the air from her lungs. The woman smiled. She was thin, worn, sad.

She poured them warm milk, she gave them scones. They ate them on the verandah beside the Coolgardie safe. The strips of towelling were wet. Would it cool anything without a wind? Deborah thought not. Tomatoes were growing near the house. A kerosene tin, the top peeled back, was by the shade of the step. Red geraniums grew in it, the leaves were yellowing from the heat.

94

The butter had been in an earthenware dish beneath a double walled beehive. It was soft, but not liquid. How could it not run in this heat?

'I'm so sorry about your son,' Deborah said.

The woman looked out across the stark bare land. 'He had a lot of life to live.' That was all.

Geoff had had a lot of life to live too and she understood why this woman left her blinds open as she did and allowed the sun to sear and fade her carpets because nothing had mattered to Deborah either when Geoff had died, when her parents had died.

They walked to the vegetables, to the henhouse as the sun gave way, and darkness fell. She listened to the White Leghorns, the Black Orpingtons scrabbling in the dirt. She watched Dave's mother milking the house cow and was glad that this job would never be hers again.

She listened as Patrick talked of the times that he and this grief-stricken woman's son had known and she looked away as their voices shook, because hers would have shaken too.

She heard Dave's mother say that her husband was in Queensland shearing, that in three weeks he would be at Lenora. She put her hand out to the woman as she faltered because Dave would not be there.

They drove away from the house along the oat-strewn track in the light of the kerosene lamp, rabbits scattering before them like a sea and Deborah heard Dave's mother call. 'Do as you said. You've a partner now.' And she didn't understand, but when Patrick put his hand on hers and raised it to his lips it didn't seem to matter.

'I shall miss Dave when the sheep come in,' is all he said but the distance had not left his eyes.

They were late, the guests had arrived. Mrs Prover was on the front porch. There was no light from the shuttered and curtained room. You have your son, Mrs Prover, Deborah thought, you have no need to open your curtains in your despair. She stood on the gravel, looking up at the woman dressed in black for a husband long dead. You have a future. You are so very lucky, I am so very lucky and when the darkness lifts from Patrick he will know that he is too.

She looked around at the home that Patrick's grandfather had built up into this dream. Yes, we're all so very lucky and she didn't mind when Mrs Prover said, 'In my house there are rules. We are never late. In my house we have responsibilities. In my house we have courtesy.' Her father had said the same and his words had disguised his love for her.

Deborah dressed in her room. Her pale blue taffeta was washed, ironed and draped on the bed. There was water in the jug on the dressing table but she bathed first, quickly. The dress clung to her still damp skin, her hair she wove into curls. She put on false pearls.

The guests were in the sitting room. The decanter glowed as she stood in the doorway. Patrick was there by the unlit fire. The curtains were drawn, deep pink, shadows flickering from the candles. There were no electric lights tonight.

She stopped, her hand against the doorframe. She had stood in Yeovil like this. She had gazed at guests, at candles, at her mother so fine, so fragrant. She had gazed at her father, dark-jacketed, hair gleaming.

'Not now, Deborah,' he had always said. 'One day when you are older you may eat with us and be trusted to carry out your duties as a hostess. One day when you are old enough for these responsibilities.'

But you died, she thought as she slid her gloved hand up and down the wood. You died before I could walk in as I am doing now. You died before you could take my hand as Patrick is doing now, bringing me in, including me.

She looked up and smiled at the man she would marry. The man who had given her the horse, the man who had kissed her with warm light lips and then she looked at his mother and in her eyes was the same expression that had been in her mother's when she had screamed, 'He is mine.'

But then that look was gone and it must have been a trick of the light because Mrs Prover came to her, took her from

96

Patrick. Handed her from guest to guest, poured her sherry, talked of England, the misty sun, the green of Hyde Park. Mrs Prover smiled at her, at Patrick, at the guests, and she was as a mother would have been. As her own would have been in time.

They talked, when seated, of coaling at Cape Town and Deborah spoke of Edward, her friend, the teacher. Mrs Prover talked of Suez at Easter, of travel overland, of the pyramids and donkeys, of camels and rejoining the ship at Port Said.

Dr Mitchell asked Patrick if he had seen the pyramids when he sailed for the war.

Patrick sipped his wine, then drank it to the dregs. He poured himself more and with that distance still in his eyes told them of Egypt. Of the training camp alongside the pyramid, of the lines of tents, so neat, so straight. Of the drill in the sand, the trench digging, the camel rides, the flies, the heat.

'But did you see inside the pyramids?' Dr Mitchell persisted, leaning back, his iced soup finished, droplets of it on his moustache.

Patrick looked at the doctor through his glass, holding it in front of his face, focusing on him, seeing him, Deborah knew, quite clearly because Geoff had done this with her too. She held her napkin tightly as she waited.

'Yes, Dr Mitchell, I saw inside the pyramids. I went along the galleries to the stone coffins. They were empty. We stood, all of us. We were going to France, to see the world, we'd been told, and there were all these empty coffins, there in front of us.'

He drank more wine. His hand was shaking.

Dr Mitchell spoke then of sheep as Edna brought in steak, potatoes, tomatoes.

'Sheep just feed and then are shorn, Deborah. The shearer rams him staggering down a slide into the counting pen beneath the woolshed. Or they might be killed for meat if they're not being bred for wool.'

'Or they'll be sent to make tallow,' Patrick said, cutting

97

across the doctor. 'Does it remind you of something? Does it remind you of your Geoff?'

'Patrick, please make sure our guests have wine.' There was ice in Mrs Prover's voice. There were flickering shadows on the deep red curtains. There was heat, the smell of candle wax, the smell of steak. There was distance in Patrick's eyes and Deborah put her hand on his arm though she knew he couldn't feel it. And yes, it did remind her of Geoff but she didn't want his death discussed here, amongst strangers. She began to speak but Patrick was talking again, too loudly, too slowly, a smile on his lips.

'I was at Dave's today, Mother. Have you been there since the news came? Did you know that in Somerset the curtains are drawn for grief? Dave's parents have opened theirs. They allow the sun to fade the carpets because there's no one coming home any more. There will be no grandchildren to play on the colours. Have you visited? It would be a courtesy.'

Deborah watched the candles flicker, the shifting glances around the table, heard the heavy silence that descended and cloaked them. Mrs Prover's hands gripped her knife and fork so hard that her knuckles whitened.

'The trip seemed so long to Australia,' Deborah said, squeezing his arm, watching the sweat roll down his face and neck, soaking into his starched collar. The lace of Susie's bouquet had been starched. The myrtle had been dark against it.

Her words were too loud, too fast but it didn't matter. 'So long. It's all so different here. At home it will be autumn, the leaves will be falling. Your leaves don't, do they? Tell me, Dr Mitchell, how long have you been here?'

There was the sound of knife and fork on plates again, there was a slow mutter of conversation from people who had been released from embarrassment.

The doctor was a fat man with a kind face, his neck bulged above his collar. His wife was talking to the Revd Wentworth who had told Deborah earlier that he came every second Sunday and took services in the sitting room.

'How long, Dr Mitchell?'

She kept her hand on Patrick's arm and he drank again, and then again, though he said nothing. For now he said nothing but she saw that his eyes never left the doctor's face.

Dr Mitchell answered now, slowly, his eyes not meeting Patrick's. 'Not long, a mere thirty years. I was twenty. It was all a big adventure. It worked well but I miss the hunting, the snow, the crispness of the wind as you take a hedge.'

'Dave was twenty-one when he left for his big adventure,' Patrick said, his food barely touched.

Deborah felt his arm tense and said, too quickly again, 'My father hunted. He boned his boots until he could see his face. They were covered in mud within two minutes. Why do people bother? One day I thought I would hunt. I haven't but I shall ride. What can you hunt out here?' Answer me quickly, Dr Mitchell, because the words are in his throat, are building and are going to come and I don't know what he'll say, but it will be blood and tears and pain and this is not the place. The place had been the privacy of the mist-covered Levels.

Her eyes were tight on the doctor's and he nodded. He understood. 'We have rabbits, too many rabbits, Miss Morgan – or may I call you Deborah? I have a niece called –'

Patrick was speaking now, loudly, slowly. 'Deborah Morgan, we have ferrets too.' Patrick turned to her now. 'We send ferrets down after our rabbits. They scream.'

His mother moved then, ringing the bell, instructing Edna to remove the plates, bring in the fruit, remove the wine. There was still the murmur of conversation but the doctor was quiet and he shook his head at Deborah, and then at Mrs Prover and sat back and they all waited. Patrick kept his hand on his bottle and Edna left the room.

'Turks scream too.'

'Please Patrick.' Deborah said. 'Please, not now.'

He looked at her, and then at the bottle but he wasn't seeing her she knew, he was seeing the past.

'They scream when you go in after them through the cracks

99

in the covered trenches. Lone Pine they called it. Jesus, it wasn't lonely. It's quiet when you're lonely. There were guns firing from loopholes, there were rifles, bayonets. Every corner could bring death. Do ferrets feel fear? Do they feel anger? Do they come back unchanged? Answer me that, Dr Mitchell. Do they come back unchanged?'

Patrick sat back, lifted the bottle, poured more wine for himself, for Deborah, his mother, the doctor. Then he relaxed his hand and smiled.

'I'm sorry, Mother. This is Deborah's welcome.' He bowed to her, to the Mitchells, to the Wentworths. He picked up Deborah's hand and kissed it but his lips were cold and his eyes did not see her.

The doctor then spoke quietly of the grief of war, the legacy it leaves. Mrs Prover spoke too of the photos in the newspaper, the medals that were won, the comfort they brought. They had had to choose between jam and butter on scones for the war effort. They had had to knit in the heat and had put on tableaux to raise funds. The rector spoke of his brother's son who had survived but returned a morphine addict after hospitalisation.

'You know him, Patrick. Perhaps you'd visit. It would perk him up. Make him shrug himself out of it.'

'I already have, Rector, but I doubt if he'll get out of it at all.' His voice was tired now, the tension gone from his arm and though he ate nothing more he talked with the rest of the party. He talked of the February race, as they did, and said that this year he would win. They nodded and smiled and hoped that he would.

They moved to the verandah for coffee and there were lights from the quarters, from the workers' houses. The stars seemed so near. Where was Orion? She could see the Milky Way. Edward, what are you doing now?

Patrick was standing on the step, looking out across the paddock where her new horse had been, his cigarette bright red as he drew in on it.

'Is my bay by the creek now, Patrick?'

He turned, nodding, listening as Dr Mitchell talked about the post-war boom in wool prices, the increase in stock, but not too much. Never too much on Lenora. 'Careful husbandry, my dear Miss Morgan. That's what's got this place where it is. Lots of hard work and now all Lenora needs is a steady hand to keep her going along steadily. With Mr Taylor around it's going to give you two young things the time you need to relax, to unwind, to give yourselves a good life. There's nothing left for you to worry about.'

Patrick wet his fingers, squeezed his cigarette between them, stood on the stub, picked it up and looked at it.

'Nothing left. Grandfather did it all,' he said quietly.

When the guests left, lighting their way by hurricane lamps to Dr Mitchell's car, he took her hand and traced the line of her fingers with his.

'I behaved badly. It was unforgivable. Sometimes I just want to beat at the bars, Deborah.' He looked at her, but didn't see her. 'I miss Dave, I miss Grandfather.'

Deborah nodded. His face was tense in the light from the house. The petrol engine was throbbing. The candles had been doused as they left the rooms, the curtains and windows thrown open. Mrs Prover was on the gravel drive. 'So sorry,' she was saying. 'Stressed, the war you know. Tired. Unfortunate about the sheep, and then the rabbits. Do hope you understand. Bridge as usual next week, Mavis?'

Patrick looked up at his mother, at her friends, watching as they drove away.

'So very sad, Deborah. So very sad to send ferrets in after rabbits.' The smell of cigarette smoke mingled with the heat of the night, the scent of eucalyptus.

Yes, she thought, looking around at this land which was still so strange. Yes, so very unfortunate, Geoff, Dave. All those broken bodies she had nursed.

'Jam or butter eh? We are from the generation that knows more than that, Deborah Morgan. We alone tonight know more than that.'

He bent down to her then, kissed her on the mouth. She

could taste his cigarette and remembered tasting the cider on his lips before.

'I'm glad you came, Deborah Morgan. I'm so very glad you came. Together we shall be all right.' He turned from her then, walking out into the darkness and Deborah climbed the stairs to her room. She stood at her window and watched as he leant on the paddock fence.

Yes, we know more than that, Patrick. You and I know more than that, and she peeled her clothes from her, lying naked on the bed, legs outstretched in the heat, feeling his mouth on hers, hearing his words. 'Together we shall be all right.' Tonight she had been included. For the first time ever she had been included.

CHAPTER 7

That week, in the home paddock Patrick began to teach her to ride, showing her how to strap on the sheepskin saddle as his grandfather had done for his father, and then for him. His mother had never ridden, she preferred the sulky or the car.

'But you, Deborah, you will need to ride.' His face was firm as he looked at her.

She had divided and sewn her linen skirt into leggings the previous evening because there was no way she would learn to ride side saddle, Patrick had said, not here in Australia, although his mother had frowned and said that the sulky was sufficient.

Deborah had to catch her bay with a whistle and sugar, holding her hand so flat that it almost bent backwards because Ned had told her of a groom who only had three fingers after a horse bit too hard and too well.

Patrick laughed as she told him this, losing his set look, his face turned towards her, and she laughed too, and wanted to kiss the smile which lingered on his face. Instead she said, 'I know it's not true, but it's best to be safe. I need a finger for my ring.'

She didn't look at him as she said this, but eased the bit into the horse's mouth, smelling her father's hunter, feeling the soft warm muzzle, hearing the clink of metal against teeth. She had said the same to Geoff and he had swung her round, held her against him, told her that he loved her more than life itself, that he would put the ring through her nose if they ate all her fingers off.

Patrick said nothing but he touched her arm with his hand, gently, and it was enough for her.

She stood with her foot raised behind her and felt his hands on her ankle lifting her up into the saddle. As she fitted her feet into the stirrups he led the horse by the bridle and she ran her hand down the mare's arching neck. 'We're beautiful, you and I, Penny,' she whispered.

Patrick led her endlessly round the paddock and the horse fluttered and wheezed under the hot sheepskin. The next day she was stiff and sore but she rode again. Each day she rode again, trotting, and then cantering along the driveway and track. The ground here was not treacherous with rabbit holes but it was hard when she fell from the horse and thudded to the ground.

There was no time to groan though, no time to catch the breath which flew from her body. There was only time to hear Patrick's voice shouting to her to catch Penny, catch her and mount again.

'Damn you,' she called, between gasps. 'Damn you.'

Patrick laughed, loud and long, running down the drive to her, dusting her off, hugging her, tight, so tight.

'You'll make it, Deborah Morgan.'

He let her go and she wanted to cling, but he pointed to Penny.

'Get her, mount her.'

'Damn you,' she said again, and walked towards Penny, her hand held out, her fingers relaxed. There was nothing to give the mare. She whistled and watched as Penny came, her bridle dangling, sweat dark on her flanks, just as it had been dark on the shoulder blades of the Revd Wentworth's black alpaca coat in the schoolroom service last Sunday.

She talked to Penny all the time, telling her she was more beautiful than the rector, more hair, you see, much more hair you lovely girl. She heaved herself back into the saddle, groaning when Patrick took her stirrups away.

'As a punishment for being rude about the Rector,' he

murmured, looking up, smiling, checking the reins in her hands. The leather was soft with her sweat.

He made her walk, trot and canter, that day and the next, and the next, all without stirrups.

'But why?' she said that night after a dinner taken decorously, distantly, with his mother.

'Because you must be able to cope. You must be able to ride better than you would ever have to in England. That's a vast land out there. You need to stay on that horse, on any horse, wherever you are.' He pointed across to the land that she knew was out there, though the heavy drapes tricked her into thinking sometimes that it wasn't.

Each day too, she looked for letters from Nell, from Edward because October was becoming November and it was so long since she had seen either of them. It was so long since a woman had held her, and loved her, so long since she had heard an English voice. But the only letters were from shearers booking a stand because November was to be the start of the shearing.

'There will be bonfires at home,' she told Penny in the paddock. 'Crispness in the air, a scent of winter approaching, of fallen leaves, of apples in haylofts. There will be potatoes, charred and burnt in the fire, but delicious.'

At night she lay awake, feeling the sweat running from her breasts on to the sheet beneath, unable to believe that there was anywhere cool in this bleak and stark country. It was a land which grew hotter every day. A land where the grass was fading to an ever paler green. Where the gum tree leaves hung limp and dustier each day. A land where everyone scanned the horizon for the shadow of smoke, for fire. Could it get hotter? Patrick said this was nothing.

She ate lunch the next week with Mrs Prover, Mr Taylor and Patrick when ram buyers came. She sat quietly as Mr Taylor discussed prices, as Patrick crumbled his bread into small round tight balls, as Mrs Prover nodded and smiled and kept her hand on her son's arm, pursing her mouth when he began to speak.

There was nothing that Deborah could contribute to the conversation. She could do nothing but listen, and watch the tension build in the man she was to marry after the shearing.

Patrick spoke once to query a price but his mother patted his arm as Mr Taylor paused, looking at Patrick, then at Mrs Prover.

'Good point, Patrick,' Mr Taylor said, 'don't you agree, Mrs Prover? Patrick was quite right about the sheep overgrazing that pasture. Let's consider it.'

They considered it, and then compromised, splitting the difference and Deborah wanted to say that it was Patrick who should be leading the negotiations. It was Patrick, the son of the owner, the love of his grandfather's life who should be sitting where Mr Taylor was sitting with nobody's hand on his arm. He had earned it after all those dreadful years.

But she said nothing then because Patrick didn't but that night as he stood on the verandah, his brandy colourless in the moonlight, it was her hand that was on his arm, it was her voice that said, 'You must consider all this. You must speak to her. This situation is making you so unhappy, so tense. You deserve more.'

'Don't worry, Deborah, this will not go on. This will be resolved. Believe me. And the wedding plans will now begin to be made, Mrs Mitchell has spoken to Mother. She has advised her that to wait would lead to gossip, to a loss of stature. Mrs Mitchell likes you. She's a good woman.'

His eyes were deep, not distant. They were firm, his voice was strong and he kissed her, his mouth open, his lips moist, tender, his hand rested on her shoulder. 'Believe me, it will not go on like this,' he said against her mouth.

But his mother's voice cut across their kiss. 'I would request that you do not indulge in public displays of affection. It is unseemly. It is not correct. You have a position to uphold, both of you.'

Patrick said nothing to his mother, just stood apart from

Deborah, not looking at either of them, not looking at the paddock, not looking at anything that was there.

The next morning, Deborah rode fast, without stirrups, her hat falling on to her back, her hair streaming out behind like the horse's mane. Her father's hunter's mane had been plaited, tightly plaited, restrained, moulded. Penny's would never be as Deborah would never be. Oh no. You won't make me tight and quiet, I shall love your son, and he shall love me and when we are married we shall kiss where we please. We shall love you, Mrs Prover. And you will love us because we are a family. And Patrick will take the role he wants, the role that will take the distance from his eyes.

She pulled Penny up, heaving on the reins, gripping with her knees, leaning back. 'We will all share this,' she shouted aloud. 'We can all be happy here. I will be loved as I would have been with Father and Mother, if there had been time.' And she was startled at the anger which she heard in her voice, because it was only love she felt for her parents, wasn't it?

At lunch, she listened to Mrs Prover discuss the guest list for the wedding. Patrick was out in the western paddocks bringing in the sheep.

'Men do not understand these things,' Mrs Prover said, writing on fine vellum with italic script.

Deborah smiled. 'Yes, Father left it all to Mother when Geoff and I were to be married.' She would make it all as easy as she could for this woman who so loved her son. 'It's so kind of you. So very kind of you to do all this. It should be me. It should be the bride's family. I'm sorry. Father would, if he were alive.'

Deborah looked at the fruit on the table, glistening with the water it had been washed in. She looked at the silver on the dust-free sideboard.

'I gather there are no guests you wish to invite.'

It was a statement, not a question.

Deborah paused, remembering Penny's flowing mane, her father's horse's plaited one, the restraint which no one would impose upon her now. 'Yes, there is one. I have a friend in Melbourne. I will bring down his address from my room.'

Mrs Prover just looked, then said, 'Very well, I shall attend to my duties,'

Deborah did not sit in the darkened sitting room alone. She walked instead down to the school and listened to the children chanting their tables, the rhythmic repetition of long-legged Italy kicking poor Sicily far out into the Mediterranean Sea.

She stood in the doorway and watched the teacher turn from one side of the room to the other, she watched him move from one child to another. She asked him if she could come each day to help and his smile warmed her. Was Edward's smile warming the children that he taught, was it warming his friends? Was the children's warmth easing into him, as it was to her today? Did he ever think of his own child, as she thought now, of hers? Did Patrick?

She helped the teacher each afternoon from then on, smelling the hot sun on the wood as she passed through the door, listening to children's voices singing 'Knick Knack Paddywack' listening to their laughter and it was far better than watching the maids working at Lenora.

It was far better than standing on the verandah watching the heat build up. Far better than watching Mrs Prover leave for Hurstland once a week in the landau to play bridge, and talk, and socialise. Far better than the dark sitting room and the ticking clock. But Mrs Mitchell did bring back the material Deborah had needed to make breeches and three open-necked shirts on the old sewing machine which only the staff had used until Deborah arrived. 'Are you sure you're a doctor's daughter?' Mrs Prover had enquired. 'You seem to have a number of very basic skills.'

Deborah brought down the photograph then of the house in Yeovil, the grounds, her parents, but said nothing of the cottage.

On Tuesday Johnny brought the mail back from town and there was a letter and parcel from Nell telling of the good cider apple harvest and how the apples had been heaped up under the trees higher than they had ever known, how the snails had been shovelled into the carts along with them. They missed her, she said. But Susie was well, and the baby was due in December. It wasn't the same without her. Was it really as hot as she had said in her letter? Was she happy? Was Mrs Prover better than they had thought? Oh, Deborah, we miss you. She also sent white cotton, Honiton lace, white ribbon, for Deborah's wedding dress.

She didn't go into school that day. She sat in her room, hearing the noise of the house all around, hearing the shearers shouting to one another as they arrived. It was 4 November. She watched from her room as they left their bikes propped up against the huts around the shearing sheds. Some had new tyres, some had improvised with rope, one had even bound his tyres with kangaroo hide. All had swag, tied over the handles and front fork and over the carrier and back fork as well, rolled and strapped. All of it was strange.

All of it was so different from Somerset and she wished she was married to Patrick now, she wished she could lie in his arms at night in their own room, and today, with Nell's letter in her hand, she wished that house was in Somerset. She held the lace to her face. It smelt of Nell.

She didn't eat dinner that night, but drank barley water in her room, the flies buzzing. She heard the shearers voting in the rep. She heard the clatter of the metal ring as their cook called them in for supper. She heard the bleating of the first of the sheep which had been brought in.

Like armies, Patrick had said to her as he stood listening to Mr Taylor giving the orders at the start of the week, telling the musterers to shift them in from the western paddocks, mass after mass of them. Like bloody armies, he had said again and walked away, though she wished he had stayed, and taken his place beside Mr Taylor. Mr Taylor had waited for him to do so. But she knew that Patrick was not seeing her, not hearing her again and wondered if it would ever end.

She rode out early the next morning, to the creek where fires had dotted the landscape during the night.

'Aboriginals,' Patrick had said over breakfast. 'They light fires to keep away the spirits. They are lost really. Their sacred places and their social life has gone. We took it all from them. They drift. That happens when there's no purpose, no challenge.'

'They're dirty,' his mother had said.

'They're different,' Patrick had replied.

Deborah walked Penny, each hoof spurting up dust as they neared the creek. There were humpies, and opossum rugs and then there were the black men, women, children. Some so very black, others less, but all with arms and legs so long and thin they seemed like spears. Deborah rode on, then turned and watched as the children paddled in the creek. The water looked cool.

It had been more than cool when her father died. There had been snow on the ground. Deb dug her heels into Penny's sides, trotting, cantering, galloping across the paddock, not knowing if there were rabbit holes in her path, not caring, not looking at the magpies, the hawks, the parrots, the kangaroos. All this was so different. All this was so strange and she was so far away from England and she wanted to be married, to be safe, to be held. She wanted to start building a family life.

Edward's letter came the next day, together with his acceptance of the wedding invitation. It was Friday, the day the shearing started. He told her of the cardinal, gold and blue colours of the school he hoped he would teach in. He told her of the street he lived in, the cut grass, the cicadas buzzing from the bushes on hot nights, the sparrows on the windowsills. The seagulls soaring up from Port Phillip Bay.

Do you remember the ship? He asked. Do you remember Orion? Mrs Warbuck? She smiled then because she did and because he was in Melbourne. He was her friend and he was only in Melbourne.

She walked out now listening to the dogs barking, nudging, yapping at the sheep which milled in the pens. She leant on the paddock watching as they scuffled up a wide gangway into the back of the building which she knew was dark and huge.

Mr Taylor was there, his hat pulled over his eyes, watching, checking, talking quietly to the overseer.

'Is Patrick still bringing them in?' she asked, her own hat low down over her face, her blouse pulled over her wrists, gloves on. She didn't want tanned arms and hands for the wedding.

Mr Taylor nodded. 'It seemed best somehow, Miss Morgan. It's a difficult situation. Both of us being here.'

His face was deeply lined, the sun had scored deep creases around his eyes and mouth. Deborah had taught his daughter how to sing 'Knick Knack Paddywack.' She was pleasant, Mr and Mrs Taylor were pleasant and he had waited for Patrick to give his instructions also.

Deborah looked out to the horizon. 'So much land. So much to do, to organise, to run. Yes, it is a difficult situation. But it will be better when we're married and we've all settled down. I'm sure it will be better then.' By then the distance would have left Patrick's eyes, she hoped.

'Tell me about the sheep, Mr Taylor,' she asked because she wanted to be able to reach out, to help the man she would marry.

He told her how some owners left wool for too long on the sheep's backs to make it look straighter than it was at the agricultural shows.

He told her how the Boss, Patrick's grandfather, had improved the stock by careful selection and breeding. She knew that but she nodded.

'Go on,' she said.

He told her about the large strong-wooled sheep that Mr Prover had bred which were capable of walking long distances to water and who could endure extreme heat without discomfort. He told her how Patrick's father and grandfather had culled sheep in the 1902 drought and this had made the stock even better. He prefered the fine long-stapled merino, he said, which had the least mutton but these were a good cross breed.

He told her how Patrick's father had died of strain really, though it was a fall from a horse which had actually killed him. He told her that this was why Mrs Prover was so protective, so careful with Patrick. It was love, he said and Deborah nodded. Her father had been protective of her mother during his lifetime – but she mustn't think of that, she must concentrate on Mr Taylor's words.

He told her that he intended to share the managership of the sheep station subtly, quietly, until it had just become a fact. It was only right and proper that the owner's grandson should play his part.

'I never knew Patrick's grandfather, but I know that is what he would have wanted.'

Deborah nodded and smiled. Yes, it had been time that she and Mr Taylor had talked.

She saddled up Penny, rode her out into the sun, out into the heat. She trotted her quietly, seeing more sheep coming in, hearing the dogs. Yes, Patrick had been right. If they were patient, it would be resolved, then she too would have a definite role, as the working owner's wife and partner.

She lay that night in the darkness, feeling the crisp linen sheet beneath her, the soft pillow. Soon she would not be alone in the bed. Soon there would be lips on hers, and the hands of the man who had hoisted her into the saddle would hold her, grow to know her.

She looked around the room well lit by the moonlight, by the stars which seemed to hang so much closer to earth than in England. In December they would be together. She would make this room theirs. She would drag in the bed from the spare room. She would paint the walls. They would have their lives. It was only then that she slept, hugging the thought of the future to her.

The next Monday the smell of sheep dung was sweet–sour, the buzz of flies was loud again as Patrick walked towards the shearing shed. On Saturday he had read the letter he had received. He passed it to Deborah, silently. There were no words he could use. No words that would pass the sickness in his throat. Charles, his Anzac friend, had died last week, Charles who had helped him carry Dave's body.

Charles had walked out into the bush behind his father's store, wedged a rifle into a ledge, cocked it and tied an empty can by a short length of string to the trigger. He had taken a second can, punctured it, filled it with water, allowed it to drip down into the lower can until the weight tripped the trigger and fired the rifle. He had waited, standing upright, the barrel against his head, looking out at the memories that he shared with Patrick.

How did he learn to do this, Charles's mother had written. How did he learn to kill himself in this way, destroying our lives? Patrick knew, all the Anzacs knew, because that was how they left Gallipoli, by stealth, following one another silently to the boats, while their guns, rigged just as Charles had rigged his, fired blindly at the Turks. Oh yes, he knew. Stealth so often won the game. Are you listening, Mother?

Why did he do it, she wrote, when he had survived such horror?

Patrick had watched Deborah read the letter. He saw tears streaking down her face. He didn't cry. Charles had written to him in October. Life was empty, he had said, he was restless. He had changed in four years of war. There was no purpose any more in weighing out sugar in his father's shop. There was no purpose in ringing up money when he had crouched in trenches, scrabbled up slopes, killed, wounded and lived life at the edge. He couldn't go on here, in Sydney, like this.

Oh yes, he knew why Charles had done it. He knew that the expectations of his family were not those of the son any longer but that the son could never tell them. Oh yes, he knew exactly why Charles did it. But he didn't cry; the pain was too deep for that. The understanding too.

Instead he walked out to the sheep that had come like armies, bleating and scrabbling. He wanted the heat, the smell. He wanted to feel again the pain in his back from shearing a hundred lanolin-soaked fleeces. He wanted to see finally, irrevocably, whether he could ever be content as his grandfather had been, his father had been. He needed to try once more this life which he had been bred into, but had now grown out of.

In the darkness of the shed the sun sliced through every crack and every doorway. He took the stall left by Dave's dad, who could not shear this week because his rheumatism, caused by handling damp fleeces, had flared again and stiffened his hands and he had said, 'You must make up your mind. You've got to do that, for Dave's sake, for everyone's sake. The indecision, the secrecy isn't fair on Deborah.'

Patrick stood quietly now and waited for the whistle. He was sweating, they were all sweating, there were flies on him, on everyone, and on the sheep in the catching pens in front of each stand. Light shone on the mellow oily floor, and on every plank and post. The shed smelt of wool grease.

The whistle blew, the machines hummed, the belts slapped, the shaft rotated. Mechanical shearing was new to their sheds. Would it be better? The shearer who worked beside Patrick stepped into their pen, took one quick look, dived a sheep, caught him under the arms, bundled him out, flicked him on to his rump, held him between his knees and started. Patrick was just behind him, gripping the wool, smelling it, feeling the grease. Christ, it was still the same.

He lugged the sheep out of the pen, on to its back, steering the cutters over the belly, throwing the wool on the floor, then the locks along the legs, throwing those also to the floor, but separately. Steering over wrinkle after wrinkle round the neck, his hand buried to the wrist in the wool. He steered it over the eyes, under the kneepads. No red stain yet. The shuffle of sheep from the pens mingled with the humming of the cutters, the yelping of the dogs. One flank cleared, now the other. He rammed the sheep down the shute. The fleece lay soft on the floor. The boy gathered it up by the hips and ran to a wool table.

Patrick lugged out another sheep. And another, and another, not counting, just feeling the pain in his back, not thinking. He mustn't think, God damn it. Then there was the rattling of tin cans on iron hoops, the shouting of the rouseabouts who were drafting sheep from the passage to be packed into the pens, refilling each pen as it became empty.

Deborah was there, watching. Why didn't she go and teach? Why didn't she go and ride? Why didn't she go away? Women were unlucky in sheds, didn't she know that? No, how could she? She didn't know anything about sheep and that's the way it should be. That's not what he had brought her out for. Or was it? Could he bear it? He had said it would all be resolved and it would. Today he would decide, one way or another.

He lugged another and another, peeling, shearing. Red stains came.

'Tar,' he called.

Sweat dripped from his face, his arms, his back, his hair. More sheep, more and more, and it would be the same next year, the year after, for ever and ever. Just like this. For Christ's sake, Grandfather, can't you see this isn't enough? Charles knew. Dave knew, even then he knew. This isn't enough any more. None of it is enough. None of it is new. None of it is a challenge.

He looked up. A boy was nibbling at a sheep, leaving the wool too long, shearing in fits and starts, mincing the long staples into short lengths. A first-time shearer. Patrick watched the set of the boy's chin, the stiffening of his lips, the straining of his back. Taylor was watching too, then he turned and walked away.

The picker-upper was racing to the wool-tables with a fleece, the sweepers were busy. All so familiar. Always the same. He lugged out another sheep, peeling, shearing. Deborah had gone, she had caught his eye, nodded and gone. Patrick heard the whistle, finished the second flank, put down the cutters, straightened and felt the pain in his back like a knife, seeing each man finishing his sheep. He knocked off.

From outside came the click of cups. The hum of machines had ceased, the engine slowed, stopped, hissed with escaping steam. Patrick walked to the doorway, his legs trembling, narrowing his eyes against the blinding light, looking at the land. You cleared too many trees, Grandfather, you and everyone else. I won't make the same mistake where I'm going.

He took a cup from a shearer. The tea was strong. His back hurt, his mouth was dry. He sat with the others on the woolshed steps watching the wool-classers strolling to their quarters. He watched the boy who had minced the fleece standing with Taylor. He nodded and went back into the shed, his shoulders firm, trying again. Patrick nodded. It was what he would have done. No good shouting at learners. It wasn't the way. Taylor was good, quite good enough, Mother, you need not fear.

And the boy would make it. It was new to him. It was a challenge.

Patrick went inside and watched the boy. He didn't mince the fleece this time, he took it slowly, steadily, then shoved the sheep back down the chute, carried the fleece to the table himself, nodding at Patrick.

'G'day Sir.'

'Where are you from?'

'Melbourne.'

'Long way from home.' Patrick walked back out into the sun with the boy.

'Didn't like it. Wanted the country. Me dad said yes.' The boy nodded and took a mug of tea, grinning at the men, at Patrick.

Taylor walked towards the steps and Patrick stepped down and stood with the manager.

'He's a real trier,' Taylor said.

'You handled it well.' Patrick nodded. 'You're a good man, Taylor, Mother's lucky.' He wanted to add that the boy was lucky to have a father such as his.

'It would be better with both of us. She forgets how old you are. It's fear, you know. She loves you. Be patient. Let her have you home and safe for a while. Indulge her, then she'll let go.'

Patrick shook his head. 'I'm twenty-seven, she's fifty-eight. I've been patient for seventeen years, Mr Taylor.'

He turned back to the shed. The men were moving back in, their patched pants rolled up or tucked into their socks, their shirts wet with sweat. Did their backs hurt as much as his, did they seem to tear as they bent down again? Did the slap of the belts, the hum of machines, the buzz of the flies go in and out of their heads like a saw that tore and hurt? They stopped for lunch and for tea and then the whistle went, and Patrick thought at first that he would not be able to straighten his back at all.

He leant against the oil-rich post. The wool-classer was still there bent over more than a dozen fleeces rolled up and laid on the table. The piece-pickers were on either side of him, and the wool rollers were working head down at their tables in front. The sweeper was pushing a clothes basket bulging with ragged wool down the board, in front of him.

Patrick watched the sheep being released from the counting pens beneath the shed, the frightened skinny sheep with their bleeding noses and bulging eyes. He watched them being counted and branded. He watched them jump, then straggle out into the endless land. For a day they had been close to one another, for a day they had been directed, handled, used. Now they were straggling away, as Charles and he had done, as they had all done. Straggling, changed, alone.

That evening Deborah said he must not shear again tomorrow, the whole thing was absurd. The shearers would just have to do extra work to make up for him. Dave's father would have to come back. He shook his head.

'No, I said I'd do it. I do what I say.'

Deborah watched every day for three weeks. Each evening she kneaded his shoulders with her fingers to ease his back as his mother watched. 'I used to do that for him,' she said one evening.

Deborah felt Patrick stiffen, but she smiled at Mrs Prover. 'My hands are tired. Could you take over?' Because there was room for everyone in this family, there had to be.

She felt Patrick relax beneath her hands as Mrs Prover laid aside her embroidery and walked towards them.

'Wise Deborah,' he murmured and leant back against her body before she moved to allow his mother in her place.

Deborah watched the mother and the son. She had rubbed her own mother's shoulders when the cold of the cottage made them ache. She picked up the Honiton lace, sewing it on to the bodice, then embroidering white silk roses. Tonight they were together, all of them, in the family they could be if she was careful, patient. There was no tension, there was no distance in Patrick's eyes. It was as though he was at peace.

Each day he worked, each day his mother and Deborah massaged his shoulders until the shearing was finished, and the peace continued, the contentment in his eyes remained.

'Why?' she asked him as they sat in the stifling heat at the end of November, just a week before their wedding.

'Because for a moment when Charles died I had doubts about my life. Those are past now. As I said before, Deborah, everything will be resolved.' And he kissed her fingertips, her wrist, her arm.

That night Deborah slept soundly, peacefully. There were no doubts left, he had said. Soon therefore he would join Mr Taylor, soon perhaps, he would tell her he loved her, as she was beginning to love him.

The next day she asked him to move the double bed into her room which she had painted herself each afternoon while his mother was out. She had made curtains with material that she had bought in town when she had been fitted for her dress.

'But ask your mother first,' she said. 'She agreed to me preparing the room. She's been in and said it was nice. It's just a formality.'

His mother said no.

She stood in front of the empty fireplace, put her hand

on the mantelpiece and said they would have her room, her
bed, the bed where Patrick had been born, where he had lain
when he was ill, where he had come to her in the morning.
She would sleep in Deborah's room.

Deborah sat on the hard settee, feeling the horsehair prick
her skin. Where Patrick had also been conceived. His mother's
room. A room which would always belong to this old woman,
which would not have the curtains she had chosen, the paint
she had brushed on to walls in the stifling hot· days. A
room in which a mother would still be present. It was too
much.

She rose and left the room, for Patrick had said nothing.
He had just looked at his mother and then at Deborah and
remained silent. Deborah walked down the passageway, up
the stairs. She withdrew Geoff's letter from her drawer. She
read it, again and again, and then Nell's, and Edward's. She
looked at the white wedding dress that hung in the wardrobe.
She felt alone, so alone again. Even now, when she was to be
married she felt alone.

Patrick knocked on her door gently before opening it. She
said nothing, just sat with the letters in her hands, sweat
staining them, staining her clothes, dampening her hair. He
closed the door behind him and looked at the walls she had
been painting, the curtains she had made. Her dress was
there, white, pure.

'You shouldn't see that, it's unlucky,' Deborah said.

He walked across to the bed, took the letters from her,
laid them on the cotton coverlet. They were finger-smeared
against the gleaming white.

'It's not important where we sleep for now, Deborah. It
will change, I promise you it will change.' He took her hands,
pulled her to her feet. There were paint stains on her fingers.
His hands were soft from the lanolin of the sheep as he ran
his finger from her eyebrow to her mouth, to her neck, to
her shoulder, her breast. Over it, round it. Her nipples
hardened beneath her cotton blouse and the breath caught
in her throat.

'I was right to want to marry you, Deborah Morgan.' His fingers were moving down, over her belly, to her thigh. She could feel the heat of them through her clothes. His mouth was on her cheek, her eyes, her neck. 'You are strong and clever and I swear to you it will change. Just be patient and then we can really begin to live.'

He left her then and she heard him later, out by the home paddock talking to Penny, his voice low, indistinct. She could still feel the touch of his finger and her nipples were still hard. He promised me, she whispered. He is beginning to love me and I am beginning to love him.

Patrick stroked the soft nose of the mare. Deborah had learned to ride quickly and well. She had painted the room, embroidered her dress. She had worked on the farm, made cheese and butter in Somerset. She was strong, useful. Grandfather had said you needed someone. He had been right. Deborah was suitable for the future he had decided upon.

CHAPTER 8

They were to be married at the Hurstland Protestant Church of St Luke which Prover money had built. Deborah stayed the night before the wedding at Dr Mitchell's house. Mrs Prover had been pleased when they had written and invited her, and had tucked her arm in Patrick's and begun to plan the last dinner they would have alone. It was fitting, Mrs Prover had said, that the daughter of a doctor should stay with one on such an occasion. She had said the same when Dr Mitchell had asked if he might give Deborah away.

The house was built of wood. It was hung with chintz curtains and was light and easy to be in. The surgery was on the ground floor and as she hung her dress on the wardrobe, she heard the door knocker. She looked through the window and soon saw Dr Mitchell hurrying down the street with a child, holding his hand, hurrying him, pointing, pulling at his bag, then running on ahead.

She ate braised steak with him and Mrs Mitchell on his return. He had just been to Mrs Miller who had three children, one of whom had cut his leg. He had stitched it, bound it. The child would be playing again by now.

There were laughter lines embedded in his face and in his wife's face that she had not noticed at the dinner party. Her father had been pale and thin. He would not allow his patients to touch him. He had never held her hand.

They sat with Deborah after dinner, and listened to her talk of Somerset, of the frost which would be on the ground, on the leafless trees, of the fires that would be burning in the grates. She told them of the myrtle but said nothing when they said it was sad they had none to give her. The thought that only she and Patrick knew why she wouldn't carry it warmed her.

She thanked Dr Mitchell for standing in for her father, and talked of a doctor's life in England. Of the villagers he treated, of the horses he rode, of Susie's baby which he would have delivered next week, or the week after, had he lived.

'Sounds much like here,' Dr Mitchell said, knocking his pipe on the empty fireplace.

'Something like here, perhaps,' Deborah said, but it wasn't. Here the gum trees lost their bark, not their leaves. Here the kookaburra laughed, not sang like the nightingale. Here the parrots flew in flocks, not perched in solitary splendour in cages in suburban sitting rooms.

She talked of her friend Edward who was staying with a neighbour. But she would not meet him tonight – it was not seemly, Mrs Prover had said. It didn't matter. He was here. He would stand on her side of the church, the only one of her friends to do so.

I wish you were here, father, mother, Nell, she whispered in the bedroom but then she sat at the dressing table, brushing her hair and smiling, because after tonight she need never talk to herself again. What did it matter that they would sleep in that dark room? Nothing was for ever, Patrick had promised her that.

Next morning she travelled to church in Dr Mitchell's car. The organ was playing, and she walked in time to the wedding march. She knew that her dress was creased from the heat, that her something borrowed garter from Mrs Mitchell was slipping down her thigh. She smiled to the guests on either side, feeling the sweat already seeping into her dress. There were no faces that she knew. Where was Edward?

She didn't falter though, she just kept on walking because there was nothing else she could do. There was no stained glass at the windows, just the clear bright light of Australia shafting on to the hats, the flowers, the altar. Onto Patrick who stood, dark-suited, turning to her, smiling, holding out his hand.

She was at his side now, and in the front pew sat Edward, his golden hair longer, his smile still broad. He was here. Someone was here for her.

'Hello, Debbie,' he mouthed, but now the rector was speaking, his voice solemn, his starched collar limp. She listened to his voice, to the drone of it, the drone of the flies. She looked at Patrick, his lashes so long, his hair so dark. She listened to the voice which said 'I will'. She felt the softness of his hands, the cool hardness of the ring on her finger, heard Edward cough behind her. Yes, she had a friend here, she had a bit of England. Deborah lifted her face to Patrick now, feeling the cool touch of his lips.

'Hello, Mrs Prover,' he murmured against them.

They signed the register and the organ played 'Abide With Me' while the congregation sang loud and lusty. These Australians are singing for you, Mother, I asked them to. I hope you can hear it. I wish you were here.

Mrs Prover was crying. Nell had cried as Will kissed Susie so it didn't matter did it? The organ wheezed and grunted as they walked down the aisle, out into the sunlight, and her hand was tucked in Patrick's arm. She too was Mrs Prover now. Can you see me, Father?

Edward was there now, smiling, kissing her cheek, shaking Patrick's hand.

'Good luck to you both, but you've got it already with her, Patrick.'

Dr and Mrs Mitchell kissed her too and after the photographs had been taken Dr Mitchell kissed her again, his moustache rough on her cheek.

'You have a very beautiful daughter-in-law, Eileen, she can only enhance your family,' Dr Mitchell said to Mrs Prover, his voice loud, his eyes looking beyond Mrs Mitchell to Deborah.

At the reception in the showground pavilion Mrs Mitchell

took her bouquet of pink roses from her and said, 'If you are compliant it will be all right. She is frightened that you will take him away from her. Once she knows that she has nothing to fear from you, that you are part of the family, everything will be fine.'

'But how long will it take?' Deborah asked.

'You have a lifetime, my dear, what are a few months now?'

Mrs Mitchell kissed her cheek. 'I shall go and rescue your husband. Have a wonderful life, my dear.' She moved towards Patrick who was being talked at by a woman in a cerise dress that clashed with the roses standing in vases all around the room. Their scent drenched the air. Edward had sent her roses on the ship.

'Reminds you of Mrs Warbuck a bit doesn't it, Debbie?' It was Edward, his hair so blond, his face and voice unchanged, but why should it be otherwise? It was only three months. His arms were round her, rocking her, creasing her dress, her veil which hung down her back, but it didn't matter. A friend of hers was here.

'You look so wonderful, Debbie. So very beautiful.' He held her away now and they moved towards the shade of the verandah and talked of his school – not yet the establishment that he wanted. Of his landlady who smoked and dropped ash in his porridge, of the cicadas at midday, and it was only now that her voice was level enough to speak.

'We have cicadas too.'

'So a grazier's wife and her old friend still have something in common?' His eyes were sharp as he squeezed her hand.

'We're friends, we have everything in common.' They knew the same things, the scent of autumn, the freshness of spring, London. England. Deborah looked round the room at her wedding guests, only a few of whom she knew, at the pavilion she had not been in before today, at Patrick's mother who had not smiled at her yet.

She told Edward all of this.

'I'm always here, not far from you. Remember that.'

She did remember this as she arrived in the Blue Mountains with Patrick. They had travelled by train, without stopping, without sleeping. They had sat up, leaning back on the seats, sometimes on one another. They had talked and talked of the cerise dress, Edward, Dr Mitchell, Dave's father who had been Patrick's best man. Her head was full of the cheers of the guests who had waved them off, Edward's warm kiss, the cold kiss of Mrs Prover. There had been no more kisses from Patrick.

They took a landau up to their hotel through deeply wooded hills and Deborah thought how low these mountains were. They were not the mountains of Switzerland, the mountains of Italy and France. This was the scarp of a plateau, a scarp with scree slopes like the Lake District, but bigger and stranger. The colours were browns, and ochres, not blue.

'They're not blue,' she said to Patrick, and she was angry, so angry and she didn't know why. 'These mountains are not blue.'

Patrick smiled. 'They look blue from a distance though, from the particles of eucalyptus oil given off by the leaves.'

The landau was open. She could smell the gums, see them covering the valleys and slopes, coming up to the edge of the road, so tall. She lifted her head to the sky. In those trees you would never feel the sun, you would curl up and die from the darkness.

There were insects and flies in her face, her eyes, her hair. At Susie's wedding there had been the freshness of early spring, the taste of cowslip wine, the noise of the bedding, friends all around.

'I wish it was not quite so strange. I wish I had my friends here.'

'You have me.' He took her hand, held it between both of his. 'I'm your friend. Your husband.'

Then kiss me, damn it, she wanted to say, but did not.

125

It was seven in the evening. The rosellas were gathering, chattering. The foyer was large, there were chandeliers, bric-à-brac on the shelves, pictures of San Gimignano and its towers, of Florence and Rome, and Deborah looked at these, not at Patrick as he walked towards the desk. Yes, you are my husband, she thought, but I wish I knew if you loved me.

They changed into evening dress, she in her dressing room, he in his. She wore blue taffeta, a necklace of opals which had been Edward's wedding present to her. For you, he had said, because we are friends. Mrs Prover had said they were unlucky. Patrick wore tails, white bow tie and a tight collar. They walked down the stairs together, arm in arm.

They dined on seafood, cracking the lobster claws. Moisture beaded on the shells, rich cool moisture.

They danced as many others did. They whirled, the taffeta rustled, the tails flew out, the musicians sweated. It was so hot. She smiled at Patrick, her husband. I'm so tired, so hot, she thought and wanted to be in the cool of England, in a cottage in a country lane with the bedding buckets beneath the window, with a man kissing her, clinging to her, wanting her. With her parents close by, and Nell too. With a man who was not the stranger that Patrick was tonight.

They bathed before bed in the bathroom attached to their room, she first, then he. There were no lights on in the bedroom as she moved to the bed in her cotton nightdress, passing him as he went to the bathroom. She didn't look but wanted to cover her bare arms with her hands, to find a room of her own. A friend, a husband, he had said. What did that mean? Edward was a friend.

She lay beneath the sheet, her nightdress cool on her damp body. There was no sound from the world beyond their open windows, there was no sound from the bathroom.

He came quietly into the room, and she saw his body in the light from the stars, from the moon. She saw his flat lean stomach, his broad shoulders which she had massaged, but always through his shirt. She saw his legs, strong-thighed, his buttocks. He was naked, he was beautiful, and her body was rigid, she was tired. Didn't he know that she was tired?

He pulled the sheet from the bed and stood there, saying nothing, just looking. He knelt, kissed her lips, her ears, her neck, her eyes and they were wet with tears and he said against her mouth, 'Don't be frightened, I won't hurt you.'

She knew then that all the anger and tiredness had been nothing but fear and that this man, her husband, had known, had cared. He was not a stranger, he was the man who should kiss her, stroke her, come into her for the very first time. Being together took away fear, as he had said before.

She kissed him then and felt his hands on her arms and neck, on her cheeks, gentle, slow. She put her arms around his neck, stroked his hair, then his shoulders. His skin was smooth, his muscles moved beneath her hands. He was still damp from the bath. He smelt of soap.

He stood and she could see the hardness and size of him. She could hear the harshness of his breath and fear came again because until now this had only been words.

He moved on to the bed, knelt over her and took the straps of her nightdress from her shoulders, easing them down her arms, right down, over her hands, and his mouth kissed her arms, her breasts, his tongue stroked her skin, her nipples and then her mouth again and the fear was leaving her as her mouth grew slack, her nipples hard. His mouth was on hers again, his chest touched hers. Oh God.

She lifted her arms, they were so heavy, she wanted him closer, closer than would ever be possible. She pulled his head down harder on her mouth, his tongue was deep in her now and she moaned but didn't know why.

He pulled away, slowly, taking his warm moistness from her lips, her mouth, and knelt astride her legs, pulling the nightdress down over her belly, and she could see him in the half light, see his face, his lips so full now, seeing all of him.

She lifted her arms to him, wanted him closer, but he shook his head.

'No, Deborah Prover, not yet.'

But why not?' Dear God. And then she felt the cotton eased from her hips, her thighs, her legs, and away from her feet and his lips were on her belly, her hips, her thighs and she moaned again, and again, and now his hands pushed apart her legs, his tongue and lips were warm on her thighs, and there were tears on her cheeks, and sounds in her throat. She gripped his hair, pulling him up to her, dragging him to her mouth, kissing him, speaking words, feeling him, hearing him as he told her that she was beautiful.

She felt his fingers gently probing, easing, and his mouth was on her breast, sucking, biting. She groaned and felt awash with pain, with pleasure, and now her arms were not around him, but reaching out to either side and her body was writhing, and she felt his skin that smelt of soap and sweat and love.

Then his fingers were gone from her, they were stroking her legs, then her breasts. She reached for him, pulled him close. She needed him now. Now.

'Now,' she shouted. 'Now or I shall die. Come back. You're too far away. Come close.' But his mouth was muffling her words, his weight was on her, his knees were nudging her legs further apart, and then at last he eased into her and there was a sharp pain, but only for a moment and then there was everything.

There was a closeness which she had not known was possible as she moved with him, clung to him, and he to her. And they cried out, again and again, and her legs were around him, her arms, and he pulled away from her mouth, looked down at her with full lips and eyes that could hardly see, then moved more quickly, more urgently, faster, faster, crying out again and again. 'Deborah!' And she felt his hot wet warmth inside her as the world disappeared under the weight of her pleasure.

They lay together, leg on leg, body next to body, arms across each other, sleeping, not sleeping, touching, kissing, until they loved again, with the dawn, when they woke.

Each day for the next week they walked amongst the pale-barked trees, some branchless for sixty feet, then bursting into a crown of leaves.

'The mottling won't happen until winter comes,' he said.

The forest floor was tufted with macrozamia palms. There were hundreds of insects, humming, buzzing, irritating. The shade wasn't deep beneath the long thin leaves of the gums. Deborah could see the sky after all.

They danced each evening, their bodies close, though it was too hot. They clung to each other at night. They stood beneath the same shower, soaped one another's bodies, kissed as the water ran over their heads, their hair, and made love, wet, dripping, laughing.

They stood often by the window, naked, watching the sun break over the mountains, bracing themselves for the heat which was never as harsh as that at Lenora and Deborah had never been so happy, so complete because his body told her of love, even if his mouth did not. She was sure it did.

They returned to Lenora and as they approached the house they drew apart. They must be patient, Patrick had said. She must be compliant, Mrs Mitchell had said, and Deborah knew that they were right, but that it would not be for ever.

They ate steak in the heat of the December evening with his mother and Patrick talked of the dancing, the music, the pictures of Florence, the towers of San Gimignano while Deborah thought of their bodies which had grown to know one another and understood why this woman feared her.

'They're status symbols,' Deborah said as Mrs Prover cut the fat from her meat. It was yellow, greasy. The lobster had been cool, white. 'But no one may have one higher than the mayor, so someone built two just inches shorter to show that he was the wealthier of the two.'

Mrs Prover said, 'Wealth of course cannot outweigh breeding. We have breeding on my side of the family. Clean blood, no convicts.' She put her knife and fork down. 'Tomorrow the rabbits are to be hunted. Next week I shall be going to the Melbourne house to shop for Christmas. You will both accompany me, of course.'

Deborah looked at Patrick who spoke quietly. 'I spoke to Mr Taylor this morning, Mother. He's going to Sydney to talk to the ram buyers again, it was arranged with me in October. We can't possibly leave Lenora unattended.'

His mother stiffened.

Deborah said quickly, 'Perhaps we, or at least Patrick, could come for a few days at the end, if Mr Taylor returns early. You see, we did our shopping in the mountains.' Deborah saw the older woman stiffen. 'I mean my shopping. I'm sure Patrick has his list to give to you, he said so while we were away.'

'Wise Deborah,' Patrick said to her in the room that had been his mother's that night.

Deborah looked at the photographs on the wall, all of Mrs Prover and Patrick. She had given her own to Edna to put on the dressing table but when they arrived the photographs were in the drawer. Deborah had brought them out, stood them up. She kissed her husband and felt his eagerness.

Their loving was different that night though; stiffer, silent. But in a week they would be alone again and so Deborah slept at last.

They rode out in the morning to the Longledge Paddock. Deborah had boned her boots, polished her saddle and bridle. Are you watching me ride out with my husband, Father, she thought as she rode along next to Patrick. Are you watching me hunt at last?

'Don't frown, Deborah, nothing's that bad,' Patrick called, smiling, his hand resting on his knee as they trotted.

Was she frowning? She hadn't realised. She was just thinking of her father and how pleased he would be.

The paddock was riddled with burrows, there were large

holes where the ground had caved in, erosion on the slopes. This would one day be her land too, she felt it already and anger stirred in her at the sight of such destruction.

'Sure you don't want ferrets? Still time to go back for them,' Bob Taylor called across to Patrick, putting his hand up to stop Edmund and Jacko.

'No ferrets,' said Patrick but his eyes did not become distant, his voice was merely firm and Deborah hugged to her the fact of his contentment.

They rode on again and Jacko and she stayed behind the guns as Bob and Patrick and Edmund, fifty feet apart, flushed the rabbits from the tussocks where they were crouching, watching them career along, watching the men raise their guns to their shoulders and fire, watching the rabbits hurtle over and over, becoming lifeless fur. Bob and Patrick broke their guns, ejected the smoking cartridges, blew through the barrels.

'Get the rabbits then, Deborah,' Patrick called. She rode across, dismounted, looked at the blood and at Jacko holding his aloft. She couldn't. She pictured her father, her mother, their flushed faces, the whisky with sugar in it. 'Another fox dead then, Deborah.'

She remounted, trotted away, hearing Patrick call, hearing him grow faint. No she couldn't, not all that blood, not that death. How could her mother? How could her father? How could they raise their glasses in celebration?

She cantered now to the gate, bent down, opened it, rode through, closed it. Turned towards the rabbit hunt. They had gone on, away from her. They were no longer calling, they were no longer watching.

At the stables she rubbed down Penny, cleaned the tack, heaved up the saddle on to its stand. In the house Edna was sweeping up the damp bits of newspaper. Of course she was. She climbed the stairs. Her boned boots were dusty. Of course they were. She entered the bedroom. Her photographs were in the drawer. She knew they would be.

She stripped off her clothes, threw them on the bed and

bathed in cold water. She dressed in a cotton skirt and blouse and walked down into the sitting room. The sweeping was finished.

She poured herself whisky from the decanter, warm, amber whisky. She drank it, sip by sip. It burned her throat. How could you have come in with your faces shining, your eyes so full of pleasure? Mother and father, I never knew you at all, did I? But I love you both so much, none of it was your fault. There was just no time.

She walked down to the empty school. It smelt of chalk, of ink, of polish. There was no laughter, no rhythmic chanting, just silence.

Patrick held her in his arms that night and promised that she would never have to hunt again, that was one of the jobs she would not be asked to do in the future that was to be theirs.

In the morning and every morning she put her photographs in the drawer, and then took them out again in the evening. She must be compliant, she knew she must, though that woman had been in the room which now belonged to them. She had laid her hands on Deborah's family and friends, on her clothes, her underclothes. Patrick said nothing when she told him.

Mrs Prover left no staff at Lenora, but Deborah didn't mind. She wanted to cook for her husband for this week. She brought the jug from the scullery, rolled out pastry on a marble slab, telling Patrick as they ate the steak pie that when the house was hers she would rearrange the kitchen, make it easier for the staff. He said nothing, just looked.

Later, as they climbed the stairs to their room he held her and asked her if she would follow him to the ends of the earth if he wanted her to.

She kissed him, caressed him, laughed and said, 'Why stop at the ends of the earth, let's make it the moon.'

That night, in the privacy of the silent house they bathed together, dried one another, kissed one another and she saw their bodies clinging together in the bathroom mirror, she saw his eyes close as his tongue traced from her ear to her neck. She saw his hand, so tanned on her white breasts, and then she saw him lift her up, kiss her belly and carry her out of the reflection to the bedroom.

They made love until there was no sound left for them to make, no more sweat to mingle and they slept as dawn streaked the sky. 'To the moon, then, Deborah,' he murmured as they woke.

At mid-day they rode out with a picnic she had made, slowly, lazily along the creek, through a copse of stringy bark and sheoak. They rode further across a line of eucalyptus trees growing on a submerged watercourse. There were others in the distance floating in the heat. There were kangaroos, so silent, an emu, so silent. They stopped at Edlers Creek.

They sat in the shade of the gums where not even the rustle of leaves disturbed the silence. They spoke in whispers and dozed in the heat of the afternoon. His lips woke her, his hands too and there, in the shade, in the rippling shade, he drew up her skirt and entered her. 'You're beautiful, Deborah. You are all that I thought you would be, and more. I love you.' He was driving deeply, slowly into her and his words merged with the passion which built in them both and there were tears on her cheeks when he withdrew and held her gently.

He bathed in the creek. She didn't. She stood and felt the cool water on her feet. She scooped it with her hands, rubbed her face, laughed when he splashed her. He dressed, told her of the scent of the spring wattle blossom, told her of the kerosene moat he and Dave had built to repel the ants when they were camping one summer.

She told him of the picnics with Nanny; of Nanny's black hat and belt, of her white uniform; of the hamper filled with sandwiches and a flask of milk; of the changes of shoes, bathing suits, butterfly nets, the books, the balls; of the river she had paddled in; of the rope which Nanny tied around her waist and hung on to for the whole time she was in the water; of the tea spread on a white cloth on flat ground; of the rich green grass it had flattened; of the peacocks and red admirals they had chased; of the tennis parties when she was older.

Patrick brought out the billy can, scraped aside all the dead grass, built a small fire out of wood and bark. He hung it by its handle from a pole supported over the fire on two forked sticks.

He took flour and water and salt from his saddle bag, mixed damper, dug a hole, put it on stones he had heated, buried it, then went back to the billy.

'Now I'll show you how we do it over this side of the world, Deb.'

The horses were cropping what grass there was. Deborah bent a blade between her fingers, then gazed around the blank horizon. No smoke.

Patrick was watching her. 'You are becoming an Australian, my Deborah.'

'I'm getting better.'

The billy was boiling, rattling the lid. He threw a handful of tea in, waited a moment, then quickly unthreaded the billy, grabbed the handle firmly and swirled it round and round, and although it went upside down above his head each time, nothing came out.

'Your turn,' Patrick said. 'So that you become even better.'

He was laughing as she took it from him, laughing as she swirled it, laughing as the tea stayed in the billy for her too.

'Ever seen a better way to settle tea, Deborah Morgan?'

She handed him back the billy.

'Deborah Prover,' she reminded him.

They ate the scones she had made and she told him of Nell's letter which had arrived with a Christmas present of a corn doll for Deborah and a carefully packed jar of blackberry jam she had sent for his mother.

'We made the jam before I left.' Her fingers had been stained purple, her arms scratched, her legs too. Soot had fallen from the chimney and on to the jam. They had scraped

134

it off and laughed because nobody would know. She laughed again now. Compliant she might have to be, but it would be good indeed to see Mrs Prover eat the soot-scraped jam that her Somerset relatives were also eating.

'Edward's term is over. He thinks he might have his new job next term. He's not sure, he's waiting. Still with his landlady, still with ash in his porridge. She talks as much as Mrs Warbuck did.'

The tea was not too strong, or stewed. The scones were moist and Patrick dropped half of his, catching it before it hit the earth. 'Where does this Mrs Warbuck live? Is she ever likely to call on him, or even worse, on us?' He spoke with his mouth full and Deborah slapped his leg.

'In Perth. Too far. Much too far.'

Patrick was quiet, then reached for another scone. 'You bake well, Deborah. Yes, Perth is quite a way from here, thank God.' He poured some more tea into her enamel mug. The steam was too warm in her face as she lifted it to her mouth. She put it on the ground.

'She's not that bad. She has a good heart. She likes the sort of dry heat that Perth has though she still talks of England as home, even though she's never lived there.' Deborah looked at Patrick now. 'Mrs Mitchell still thinks of England as home too. I wonder if I shall.'

Patrick shook his head. 'It's different if you carve out your own home, your own world.'

'But, Patrick, we can't until your mother softens. How long is it going to take?'

He looked away from her now, bending grass, scanning the horizon. No, there's no fire out there, Patrick, she wanted to say, but your mother's coming home. And then she picked up her tea and sipped it, watching as he dug up the damper, eating a bit from the edge because the centre was still not properly cooked.

She was wrong though, to question him. She must stay calm. It had been no time at all. She could wait. She knew she could wait. She'd known for so long what it was to wait.

She touched Patrick with her bare foot. 'I'm sorry, my love. It's all right, really it is.' And now he was kissing her foot, making her laugh, making her put the tea on the ground, making her drop the damper, making her beg him to stop.

'Will you come to the moon with me then? Promise me.'

But she couldn't answer, the laughter was hurting her too much, happiness was filling her too full. There was blackberry jam for Christmas for Mrs Prover, for God's sake, it was all right again.

Then he stopped, and pulled her to him, and it was then that she said, 'I promise.'

There was so much time in their lives to enjoy Lenora she must just learn to wait, and she did so gladly, because now what they had between them was love.

Mr Taylor arrived home two days later and Deborah and Patrick left, not for Melbourne and Mrs Prover, but for Shellrick for the Bensons' Christmas tennis weekend.

They travelled in the landau with Patrick at the reins and she close beside him, stopping in Hurstland to telegraph his mother who would approve, Patrick assured Deborah, because she admired the Bensons very much. Then on through the town, out towards the west. They travelled along dust-laden tracks and Deborah jumped down and opened more gates than she could count, and their laughter filled the air.

They arrived with the darkness to hugs and smiles from a family that had known Patrick for as long as he had lived, a family that had danced at their wedding and now welcomed Deborah to their home.

They hurried upstairs to bathe and change. The other guests were already holding pre-dinner drinks in the sitting room. Patrick kissed her in the luxurious bedroom as the lamps glinted on the pale blue satin bedspread. Her skin was still damp. He opened the casement windows, beckoning her across, saying. 'Remember the mountains.'

She did.

They ate a buffet supper with the other guests, some of whom had travelled for two days. They danced until four in the morning and still no one was tired. The staff cooked bacon and eggs and it was only then that they straggled up the stairs, laughing, joking, singing.

Deborah slept, but only after Patrick had carried her from the shower, their wet bodies clinging to one another, sliding against one another as their passion rose.

They got up at ten and played tennis, splitting up into pairs, the girls playing one another, the men playing other men. There was barley water on white-clothed small tables, there was the thud of ball on racket, there was fun.

'We'll all meet again at the O'Malleys' in the New Year,' Isobel said to Deborah, touching her knee, handing her a fan. 'You'll beat me then. It's wonderful to have Patrick back, and you now too. It'll all be such fun won't it, Mother?'

Mrs Benson called the maid over. 'More lemon barley, please, Jane. Yes, it will be fun to have you amongst us, Deborah. We've missed Patrick.'

Deborah smiled. 'Oh yes, it will be wonderful. It is all so wonderful.' It was as though she was back amongst her Yeovil friends, but much better, very much better.

They drank from their lemon barley and looked across to the left-hand court where John, Isobel's fiancé, was losing to Patrick. His ball went out and they laughed as he threw up his hands in surrender.

So Nell, I shall write to you of this thought Deborah as she threw a towel to Patrick, who was running towards her, sweat coursing down from his face.

They picnicked alongside a shaded creek, eating a late lunch, sitting or leaning back on rugs and palliases. Bark crackled beneath her, she watched Patrick take the silver flask from Mr Benson and drink the gin, and that evening, as they began to dress for dinner, she pictured Lenora redecorated, refurbished and the arms of this man around her each night, his lips on hers.

They drank punch that evening, ladling it from silver bowls beneath the chandelier in the huge sitting room, and they danced as they had done the night before. Other men held her, laughed into her face, kept time with her, but it was only in Patrick's arms that she felt complete.

They sang with the others, they did the conga around the stone house, their feet thudding on the verandah, and this time when they went to bed they were too tired to do anything but sleep.

Breakfast was served in good time for those who wished to attend the church service in the second sitting room. John and Isobel sat with Patrick and Deborah eating kedgeree and they talked of the band which would play at the O'Malleys' and the dresses they would wear for the Lenora Race Day Ball.

'Then we will all meet at Menridge up north. They always have a weekend in April.'

The church service was muted, they were all tired, and Patrick brought the landau round soon after, for they must be back at Lenora before nightfall.

'Come again. You must come again. It's been so lovely to see you.' Isobel kissed Deborah. 'It will be so good to have you joining us from now on.'

Yes, thought Deborah as they drove away, her lids heavy, but with the sound of laughter echoing in her head.

CHAPTER 9

Christmas was hot, and so very distant from the holly wreaths, the frost-glinting hills, the stiff grass, the ice crusted windows of England. But they had a garlanded pine tree, they ate roast beef, and pulled crackers with Dr and Mrs Mitchell who had no children and spent Christmas each year with the Provers.

As they drank the wine at dinner, breathing in the smell of the pine, there was no talk of ferrets, no talk of the war. The distance had gone from Patrick's eyes, perhaps for ever, Deborah hoped.

New Year was hotter still and they stayed up and raised their glasses as midnight came and went but there were no first footers though there was the usual New Year present from the Bensons to unwrap. It was a painting of a child cracking walnuts in front of a raging fire. Deborah remembered the walnuts she used to pick up from the ground in Somerset and which her parents had always saved for New Year's Eve. She remembered the mulled wine which Nell and she used to make as she drank the Lenora punch and made her resolution.

It was to be even more patient but she would not reveal this, and neither would Patrick disclose his. Mrs Mitchell cried, as she always did, Patrick whispered, and said that this year she must go home. Deborah nodded. Yes, one day she too would go home. One day she would feel again the crispness of the air, the scent of autumn, the freshness of spring.

'In Somerset, at New Year, they send a child up into the fork of an apple tree to fix a piece of cake dipped in cider. Then they empty a bucketful of cider around the roots.'

'It's a libation, isn't it?' Patrick said, sitting by the empty fireplace, drinking the wine.

'You know then?' She was pleased that he knew this much about her home, pleased that it was just the two of them that did. Her glass was warm with the wine, sticky too.

'Yes, I do know. It is a libation to the tree spirit so that he may grant a good crop of fruit next autumn. That old man whose cart we travelled on dropped some on the floor of the pub before he drank.' Patrick's eyes were gentle on her.

'Uneducated rubbish. Sounds like the behaviour of the blacks here.' It was Mrs Prover.

Deborah swallowed. She must not break her resolution so soon. She must not.

'But how long?' she said to Patrick in their bed that night, a bed which no longer knew their relaxed bodies, their abandoned love, because his mother was here again and there was no warmth from her yet.

But there was warmth when they took the sulky out to the O'Malleys' on the other side of town, leaving Mrs Prover at Lenora with Mrs Mitchell since she didn't want the sound of the band to bring on one of her headaches. There was warmth in Isobel's hug, in the cheers as Deborah almost won a tennis match this time. There was warmth in Patrick's kisses in their room though his mother's presence seemed to reach out to them, even here, and there were no longer such heights of passion.

There was excitement though amongst the guests about the Lenora Ball.

'When is it to be held, Deborah?' Isobel asked, clutching her hand. 'I've the most beautiful dress, it's quite the best. I can't wait. I love it when so many people come up from Melbourne.'

'We haven't quite worked it out yet,' Deborah replied, feeling the tension spread across her shoulders. How could she say that at Lenora it was Mrs Prover alone who made the decisions?

On the day after their return Mrs Prover told them that the race and ball would be held later than usual. 'I have decided on March the first,' Mrs Prover told them over breakfast. 'It was the wedding of course, everything has slipped behind because of that. We need to extend the membership though, I have sent out all the local invitations but there are quite a few young men on the list that – she paused, 'are no longer able to attend. We hadn't realised that there would be this problem. We haven't held it since the start of the war. One forgets.'

'So very inconvenient isn't it, Mother. Death, I mean.'

'Patrick my dear,' Mrs Mitchell put her hand on his while Mrs Prover ate toast with blackberry jam. 'Will you ride?'

'Oh yes, I shall ride. Dave and I planned that one of us would.'

Patrick didn't look at his mother or at any of them as he rose and left the room, his footsteps loud as he walked down the passage into the kitchen. He would leave by the back door, Deborah knew, and so did his mother.

'He is so easily influenced,' Mrs Prover said to Mrs Mitchell.

'Dave was a good boy,' Dr Mitchell said gently. 'A bit rough, but good.'

Mrs Prover nodded, but Deborah knew that it was not of Dave that her mother-in-law had been thinking.

Towards the end of January Mrs Prover left Lenora for Lorne where the Provers had their beach house. Patrick would not leave Lenora because of the race. He was busy with his horse, training it, working it. Working and training Dave's too, because he had said he would ride each of them. Mr Taylor stood and watched, leaning on the paddock fence morning after morning and Deborah stood with him.

'When this is over, he will take on the station with you,' she promised. 'But this is something he has to do.'

Mr Taylor nodded. 'I wasn't in the war, Deborah. Can't bend my leg properly. But those that were have things to sort out. We can wait.'

So they waited and watched and even though Mrs Prover was not on the station for two whole weeks, they had lost the passion they had had so often recently. There was affection, there was gentleness, but more often there was distance, because Patrick was focused again on the past, and the promises he had made.

But I will wait, Deborah said to herself as she wiped her photographs.

Mrs Prover returned relaxed, pleased. Her membership list had increased satisfactorily through contacts made at the fashionable seaside resort. 'New blood' had moved into some of the houses, but it was suitable blood.

'I was able to pick and choose those I wish to attend the Lenora event,' she said to Deborah and Patrick, but looking only at Deborah.

Deborah gave Mrs Prover another jar of blackberry jam which she had asked Nell to send out.

'As a welcome home present, Mother.'

She left the room, walking through the kitchen, out through the back door, knowing that Mrs Prover would have heard her riding boots in the passageway. She rode Penny out into the morning heat, hard, too hard. She had wanted to hear Patrick's voice coming between them, she had wanted to hear him tell his mother that he must accept Deborah as his wife, that she must share him. But he never did. For God's sake, he never did.

Penny was sweating and she reined in, trotted, and was glad that the school term had begun and that this afternoon she would breathe in the smell of chalk and polish, the sound of children's laughter, the sound of their chanting, the sound of their songs. Yes, she wanted to hear Patrick's voice cutting across his mother's but she must wait until after the race. She knew she must. He had said so.

All this will stop after the race, he had said. There will

be no need to be patient any more. He would speak to his mother. But he needed to concentrate on the race until then. He needed to complete that task first.

The ball was to be held at the pavilion in the town, and the race would take place around the perimeter of the showground. There was no need for Deborah to make a dress, she had many she had made for the voyage out. But she needed to write to Edward, to invite him to come, to have her own friend there again, and she did so, and then told Mrs Prover, leaving the room before she could reply.

Each night she and Patrick lay in bed, he asleep, drawn with tiredness from training two horses, from working with Mr Taylor in the afternoon, from taking him through the stock books from the start of the sheep station, she awake, missing him, longing for him.

'Must you work so hard?' she said one morning as he pulled on his trousers, his hands trembling.

He turned to his drawer, taking out his shirt as Deborah moved to the dressing table, putting her photographs in with her petticoats.

'Yes, Deborah.' His voice was tense, tired. 'I need to show Taylor how Grandfather built this up. I need to explain how he built up the stock. He needs to know where the stock records are, what Grandfather's ideals were.'

'But later will do.' She took his hands.

'For God's sake, Deborah, leave it.'

It was as though he had slapped her. He slammed the door shut and she called out, 'At least your grandfather did all this for the woman he loved.' But she knew that she was talking to herself again.

They spoke little for two days and Mrs Prover smiled a great deal. Deborah thought of the picnic, and the Blue Mountains, and knew that this time would come again. Soon, very soon.

The heat is growing even harsher, she wrote to Nell and Susie, and begged them to tell her as soon as the baby was born. The grass is dry, she wrote to Edward, knowing that

Melbourne, so variable, so English, was steaming in heat too. All week the grass drew drier, all week they looked to the horizon as they had been doing all summer, but now with more reason. On Friday they saw what they had feared.

The grey smoke was eight miles to the north.

'From Sinclair's Paddock,' Edmund shouted. Deborah stood with her hand on Penny's forelock. The smoke was so far away, so small, there was plenty of time surely? The stockmen, the blacksmith, the storesman were saddling horses, harnessing teams to two fire carts. Patrick gripped Taylor's arm, issuing orders, crisply, quietly, and Mr Taylor took them, calling for the spring cart to come up with waterbags. Patrick shouted to her, 'Stay here, don't you dare take that bloody horse out. Just stay here, d'you hear me?'

He ran to the stables, took out a horse, saddled her, galloped down the paddock, across country, with a blanket across his saddle, following those already on their way.

'Fire's making head,' the blacksmith called to Taylor as he careered past with the spring cart.

Deborah looked at the smoke again. It was so much darker, so much more of it. It had only been minutes.

She thought of how the post office thatch had been set on fire by a spark from the brewery wagon two years ago. The fire brigade had worn huge metal helmets, black and red uniforms, and stood on a lorry amongst their hose pipes, towing the pump behind. The village had watched as two men pumped and the flames died.

This was differentt, she knew that now. 'Will others come to help?' she asked Edna who was standing on the step, shading her eyes, watching.

'Yes, they'll come. It threatens everyone,' the girl said. 'It's a killer you know. This bloody country's a bloody killer.'

Deborah waited, as they all waited, and watched. The smoke darkened as the day wore on but came no nearer to them. It drove with the wind towards the west.

Taylor came back with one fire truck. 'We're hanging on the flank and turning it, checking it a bit, heading it towards a break.' He ran on then, as the women filled the water tank from the pump by the artesian well. Then he drove that back, the spring cart came in, and they refilled the waterbags. Edmund was blacker than the soot in the blackberry jam. He couldn't speak, his tongue was swollen, his throat too.

They fought it through the night, other stations with them now. The glow of it lit up the sky. Jacko and Archie came back for fresh horses and the spare fire cart. Deborah helped saddle up.

'Is Patrick all right?' They nodded, they could not speak either.

She rubbed down the horses, watered them, fed them, cared for them, crooning to them, not wanting to see the glow in the sky, not wanting to see its march through the night, not wanting to hear the echo of the burning village thatch, because the fire out there was so much worse.

Mrs Prover came to the door of the stables, standing upright, rigid as always.

Deborah said, 'They say he's all right, so far.'

The woman nodded and her shoulders relaxed, then tensed again. 'It's not over yet. I shall be in the sitting room. I do not care to be disturbed.'

So throughout the night Deborah stayed on the porch where the Japanese lanterns had hung at Christmas, where she and Patrick had danced the Gay Gordons with Dr and Mrs Mitchell, where the flicker from the lanterns had been reflected in the polished jarrah of the floor.

The fire burned most of the next day. Deborah worked in the kitchen with Edna and Sarah, preparing food, pies, scones, cooling water in the fridge. Patrick came back to replenish the water cart, to pick up food and water for the men. He could not speak, he brushed past her, his eyes red, his face black, picking up the baskets. She carried two, Edna two. That was all, that was enough, it was water the men needed. Patrick gulped water straight from the jug in the kitchen, it slopped down his shirt. He smelt of fire.

They came home at eight that evening. There was no glow

any more in the sky. Taylor and two others stayed out to patrol while Patrick slept and though he had bathed there was still the smell of fire on his skin, in his hair, soot deep in his pores. His eyelids and lips were swollen, his face reddened from the heat, his hands too.

Deborah sat on the chair by the bed. He needed sleep, he needed space to thrash around, but then he woke and put his arms out to her. She lay beside him, knowing now just how much she loved him and she wept to see him as he was, wept to see this land as it was, so harsh, so merciless, so beyond the control of man. Silently he made love to her, and she to him and then they slept again.

The next day, with swollen faces and silent voices, the men worked as though nothing had happened, bringing in the lambs for shearing, bringing in the sheep for face and wither trimming.

'So the flies won't infest the soiled fleeces,' Archie said, his voice still rasping in his throat.

It was a hard country, with tough people in it, Deborah thought, Edward was right, but they needed to be, if they were to survive. As the days went by Taylor worked, Patrick trained, Deborah rode and taught. Mrs Prover planned the food for the party.

But Bob Taylor and Deborah found time to smile at one another when they met at the stables because they both remembered how Patrick had taken control, how he had taken his place as owner.

'After the race it will all begin,' Deborah murmured and Bob Taylor agreed.

The day of the race was hot. Of course it was, Deborah groaned. It was always hot, but then this was better than the chilblains and the cold of which Susie had written. Her daughter, she said, was beautiful. They had named her Deborah. 'You will be her godmother, Deborah, though you can't be here.'

Deborah's back was aching as she walked into the members'

enclosure. She wasn't pregnant, she had found out yesterday, though she so wished that she was. She walked past the gunyahs of brushwood erected by the local properties. They had erected signs with the names of their stations. Patrick was at Lenora's gunyah, calling her over. She edged between the ladies with wide-brimmed hats and pastel-coloured chiffon dresses. She had chosen cotton. It was cooler but she wished now that she had sewn a new dress.

He took her round the enclosure, shaking hands, introducing his wife to those he had not seen since the start of the war, skating around those who were absent. There were new names. He introduced himself, and Deborah, chatted, said goodbye. 'Meet again, next year,' everyone said.

They stopped at the Bensons. 'Divine,' Isobel said and Deborah laughed. They talked of the weather, the riders, of Patrick's chances, of another weekend being arranged. Isobel kissed her. 'It's wonderful. You look lovely.'

Patrick moved her on. There were others outside the enclosure, inspecting the horses, chatting, laughing, and Patrick took her to see them too, Archie, Edmund and Jacko, Dave's parents, for these were employees or townsfolk.

'We'll meet at the dance tonight,' everyone said.

She and Patrick stood watching his chestnut, Dave's grey. 'Just right,' Patrick murmured. 'Just bloody right.'

'They're lovely,' Deborah said, admiring their rippling muscles, their long legs, their broad chests.

'Bred for this. Grandfather started the race. They're good sound horses. Dave's was his nineteenth birthday present, just a foal. Mine was too. We brought them along together, then nothing happened for too many years. That's why I had to start all over again.'

'There are no jockeys then. Everyone rides their own, the same as you?'

'Yes, we're used to the rough ground, the horses are used to us.'

Deborah could hear her name being called above the hub of the crowds, above the snuffling of the horses, the pawing of their hoofs on the ground. She turned. It was Edward, so tanned, his smile as broad as it always was and she knew that her smile was as wide, her warmth as great.

'You came.'

'Would I miss the chance of seeing you? And Patrick of course.' He bowed to Patrick, put out his hand and the two men laughed together. 'She's looking well, Patrick. Obviously feeding her the right food.'

Deborah laughed along with them, kissing her friend's cheek, feeling his hand on her arm, loving his English voice. She walked with him while Patrick and Taylor sized up the other horses, detailing their merits, their demerits.

'It'll go on for hours.' Deborah pulled a face. It was her turn now to introduce, to chat, to explain. She touched Dave's mother on the arm and introduced her friend from England. She entered the members' enclosure with Edward, laying her hand on his arm, showing her badge, and the one she had in her handbag for him.

He laughed at her as she pinned it to his lapel. 'Lovely Debbie, how well you look. How well you seem. How happy, and settled.'

His face was close to hers and his smell was the same as it had been on the ship, as it had been at the wedding. It was so good to have him here.

'I am settled, I am happy.' She was, because Patrick had zest, and energy, and a light in his eyes. She was because today she felt she belonged, at last she belonged and she was loved.

'This is almost Ascot,' he said to Mrs Mitchell as she came up.

'Does Ascot have sheep grazing on the course? Is that how they keep their grass short?'

'Do the ladies have to sidestep these, Edward?' Deborah said, pointing to the dark pellets scattered on the ground.

They all laughed, then made their way through to their gunyah where Mrs Prover was entertaining the Wentworths, the Mitchells and Mr and Mrs Benson. They ate fruit, salad and cold meats off white bone china plates on tables covered with starched white cloths. They drank wine, beer, ginger beer, barley water and the heat grew fiercer as each race was run. Patrick joined them, hot, sweating, checking his watch, not eating, just drinking water, but he toasted Edward with his glass when he told them that at last his new teaching post had been confirmed. Deborah heard the excitement, the achievement in his voice, and his pleasure was also hers.

'Well done, Edward,' she said. 'I'm proud of you.'

Those outside the enclosure were eating their picnics off the ground, sitting cross-legged, leaning against one another, and Edward smiled at her.

'We've come a long way, Debbie,' Edward whispered, looking at their table, at their guests, then at those outside on the ground.

Deborah smiled at him, looking across at Patrick. Oh yes, they'd come a long way. She reached across and touched her husband's hand.

There was no prize money, just gifts donated by the members. Lenora had donated a gold bracelet of opals. Shellrick a necklace. The Mitchells an antique clock.

Patrick's race was at two. He didn't win, though he was galloping neck and neck with a roan as they rounded the bend. She could hear him shouting at the chestnut, 'Get on, get on,' and she was shouting too, her hands gripped tight, then clutching Edward's arm. He was shouting. They were all shouting. But the bay faded, and though it came again it was not hard enough and was edged into second place.

'That's not the one that mattered,' Patrick said to her as she hurried through the crowd to him but his mother was disappointed for he had run his horse on Mrs Prover's behalf because Deborah had told him he must. The prize had been the necklace.

He won the three o'clock on Dave's horse though, urging him from the start, knowing that this grey liked to make the running. He was urging him ever on, his arms moving along the chestnut's neck, his knees working, his voice shouting, his body in tune with the horse until he won by a clear length.

'That was the one that mattered. That was Dave's,' he said to her as he dismounted, his breath heaving in his chest, the dust damp on his face.

The prize was the clock, and he gave it to Deborah. His mother said there was no room at Lenora for another clock, so Deborah just smiled and handed it to Edward, saying that this was his prize, for coming all this way to see her. Every time it struck it would remind him of this moment. She smiled because after tonight Patrick would be standing between her and his mother. He had promised.

Edward laughed and clutched it to him. It was dark mahogany and Mrs Mitchell had brought it from England with her but Dr Mitchell had confessed last year that if he had to live with its loud tick for much longer, it would be going back to England or on to the fire.

'Well done, Patrick,' Dr Mitchell turned to say, but Patrick was walking from them, edging between two women, then past a crowd of young men who came to stroke the grey, feeling the strength of his hindquarters. He strode on towards Dave's parents. Deborah watched as they stood, silent, then Dave's mother kissed Patrick's cheek before turning, taking her husband's arm, leaving the showground. They looked so broken, so old.

Deborah and Patrick changed for the dance at the Mitchells'. Mrs Prover was with Mrs Wentworth. They ate lightly before leaving at nine. This evening she wore her blue taffeta and Patrick kissed her neck where she had drawn her hair up.

'Beautiful Deborah.'

They travelled in the landau. Patrick carried a flask with brandy, and so did Dr Mitchell because alcohol would not be served. Deborah carried her programme. There were seventeen dances, and a space for a name against each dance. Dr Mitchell, Patrick, Edward and Mr Taylor were already written down. The musicians were playing as they arrived, the lights were on, lanterns lit the walkway to the pavilion. She entered, holding Patrick's arm, and this time she entered not as a stranger at her own wedding, but as the wife of Patrick Prover.

She danced every dance but the first was with Patrick. There was excitement in his eyes, but a tension too. He kissed her cheek hard as they whirled, towards other couples and then away. His hand was firm on her back, in her hand.

'This is wonderful, Patrick. I'm so happy.'

'To the moon, Deb, remember that.'

'To the moon, my darling.'

She danced with Edward, so light, so fast, so blond. 'You're lovely, Debbie. So very lovely. How you suit all this.' He was dancing absolutely in time to the music. The musicians were sweating. He wasn't. Patrick was dancing with Mrs Mitchell, his body bending toward her and away. Deborah felt the breath tighten in her throat. How I love you, she thought, and then looked beyond him to John and Isobel.

'They don't have dead hearts,' she murmured to Edward.

'Did I say that? I'm sorry. I was jealous. I wanted you, Deborah. I'm still alone, you know. You're not.'

His voice was low.

She danced with Dr Mitchell whose starched collar was already sodden. They didn't whirl, but danced slowly, sedately, around the outside, at half the pace of the others and talked of the race, of the future, of Patrick.

'It takes time, Deborah. These things take time.'

'It's fine now, Dr Mitchell. He's better, restful, calm.'

'He's not the boy he was.'

'He's a man, that's why.'

She looked across at Patrick as he walked through the door with Edward, feeling in his pocket. She grinned. She was beginning to know him so well. They would be sharing the flask, smoking a cigarette, talking. They were friends. The two men in her life out here in this strange land were friends. Edward would be the godfather of their child when they had one. Then he would no longer be alone.

Patrick took her in to supper. They ate cold meats and desserts laid out on tables. They sat with Edward, with John and Isobel and with Dr Mitchell's cousin. They laughed, talked, flirted, then danced again but this time more boisterously. They formed crocodiles and Deborah led one, with Edward behind, clutching her, then Isobel, then Patrick. In and out they threaded, between one long writhing line and another, then out into the showground, breaking apart, laughing, then cheering as men piggy-backed on each other's shoulders for a joust, falling to the floor, as everyone groaned and cheered.

Edward won the joust and collected his favour from Deborah. He kissed her hand laughing as the cheers grew louder. Patrick saw his mother with Dr and Mrs Mitchell and fury was in her eyes as she saw Deborah and Edward. Now he knew just how he could do what he had promised himself he would do once the race was over. It would set him free, and Deborah could never blame him, just his mother. The tension that had been in him all day went.

'So Charles, it's here, the future. Your letter finally decided me,' he murmured to himself, pushing aside the image of Deborah's happiness this evening. He looked around. This was not why he had married her, after all.

They returned to Lenora as dawn was breaking, searing the sky with red. Deborah was humming, smiling, singing as the sulky swept into the yard. They stabled Densie, still in their evening dress, and Deborah laughed as they ran in through the kitchen door, banging through into the sitting room, falling on to the settee. She laughed as he kissed her and then they heard his mother's voice, colder than it had ever been, and it brought to a halt the kiss, the breath in Deborah's chest, the whole world for a moment.

'I will not tolerate wanton behaviour in a member of the Prover family.' Deborah saw Mrs Prover standing by the fireplace then in her dark green chiffon dress. She must have been there when they ran in. Her cuffs fell in folds over her hands which were clenched, white-knuckled, in front of her.

'I will not tolerate you, Deborah, cavorting with a single man. I will not have the Prover name held up to ridicule. How dare you behave as you behaved tonight? How dare you accept favours from a single man? How dare you invite your friends to my dance?'

There was silence. Deborah sat up, her mouth dry. She heard the rustle of her taffeta, Patrick moving by her side. She could say nothing. Do nothing. Her limbs were tired, the laughter quite gone. She looked at her mother-in-law, at her husband, then pushed herself up from the settee.

'I'm tired. I'm going to bed.'

'You will go nowhere until I receive an apology.' Mrs Prover moved to block her path, her hands outstretched. There were white indentations on each hand where they had been clenched. White against the tan. Patrick hadn't spoken and Deborah knew now that he never would.

She looked at the woman who blocked her path. 'I don't know what it is that I need to apologise for but I do so. Now may I go to our room?'

'You are an impertinent girl. As I said, you do not accept favours from single men. You do not dance closely. You do not insult my son unless you are determined to prove that you are not suitable to be his wife.'

Mrs Prover was still in front of her. Her dark green dress was shimmering in the low light. It would be grey outside. Soon it would be daylight. The night would be over, but when would all this be over? For God's sake, when would life be joyous and free of all this?

You promised, Patrick, she thought, and didn't look at him, but then heard his voice.

'I will not have you speaking to my wife like this, mother, now stand aside.' It was controlled, firm. There was still no anger, just a calmness.

'I shall speak to her as I wish, Patrick. She is living in my house and sleeping in my bedroom.' Mrs Prover was looking at Deborah, not at Patrick, and her eyes said 'He's mine' as her mother's had.

'He's ours,' Deborah screamed, then, pushing past the woman, she heard Patrick say, 'Then we shall leave your bedroom, and your house.' His voice was loud, final, and Deborah was through the door, leaning back against the stair post, shaking, too tired to climb that first stair, and then the next, but she did, and leant on the bannister, her legs weak as his mother's voice came to her, raised, quick.

'It's all that girl's fault. She's come between us. She behaves as no suitable wife should.'

'For God's sake, no wife would be suitable for you, Mother. You make it impossible for us to go on. We can't stay. You are forcing us away, miles away.' There was such bitterness in his voice that Deborah felt her hands go cold. He was speaking up for her, but this was wrong. This was too harsh, too strong. 'We'll leave,' Patrick said again.

'Nonsense. Mr Taylor's house is the only alternative accommodation. He is not leaving. You have to stay here, do as I say and so does she.'

'Please stop,' Deborah whispered. 'Please stop.'

There was cold sweat on her forehead as she shouted from the staircase, 'Don't say any more, either of you. This is going too far.' But neither of them was listening and she leant her head against the bannister.

'There is a world outside Lenora, Mother. You're driving us to it. We'll go away, far away where you can't upset Deborah.'

Deborah turned then, rushing downstairs, back into the room. 'No, Patrick, there's no need for this. This is your home. Just be patient. I don't mind how your mother speaks to me. You can't leave your home. It will break your heart. What about Dave, your grandfather?'

'Get out of this room. Get out. It's all your fault. You have poisoned his mind, you have come between us.' Mrs Prover was lurching towards her, her hand raised, and Patrick came from beside the chair to grip Deborah's arm, pulling her out into the hall. 'Go to the bedroom. This is my fight. I won't let this go on any longer. It will be all right.'

She went, climbing each stair, listening to the sounds of their voices.

'Where will you go?'

'Anywhere. God knows. As far as possible. We'll start again.'

'Nonsense, Patrick. You are just making noises. I shall disinherit. You have no access to Lenora money.'

'I have my gratuity and Grandfather's bequest.'

Deborah was at the top of the stairs now. 'I hate you,' she moaned to Mrs Prover. 'I hate you. How can you do this to your son? How can you do this to him after the war he has had, and the friends he has lost? How can you do this when we could all have been so happy?'

'But you can't do anything else but live on Lenora. You're not equipped.'

Deborah was in their room now, walking to her dressing table, opening the drawer, looking for her photographs, looking for Susie's letter, Geoff's letter. They weren't here, but she needed something to look at, to hold to her as these words were shouted backwards and forwards.

It would be all right, he had said, and she loved him more than ever, because he was doing this for her, he was turning his back on so much for her, but it was all wrong. It was all going too quickly, too far. She looked in her other drawer. Where were they? She must have them and then she remembered putting them in his drawer when they left for the dance.

She took them out, the letters too. There were papers beneath, papers, tickets with her name, and Patrick's. She took them out, read them. They were tickets to Fremantle dated 4 March 1923. The papers were for the sale of three hundred virgin acres in South West Australia to Mr Patrick Prover, dated 1 February 1923.

She heard Patrick's voice in the passageway.

'Of course I'm equipped. What has the war done if not to equip me? I can wash, I can dig, I can live on nothing. I have a wife who is equipped, who can farm, knows animals, knows how to live on nothing too. Am I a fool,

155

Mother? She's experienced and strong, that's why I married her. Grandfather said you need a partner. Am I really not equipped for a life other than Lenora? Where have you been all these years? Oh yes, you've been here, waiting to smother me.'

His mother was crying. It was a high-pitched, ugly, dreadful sound. She heard him go back into the sitting room, heard his voice, soothing, explaining.

'But there is nothing to explain,' Deborah said and her voice was hoarse. The papers were cold in her hands. The words were stark, his words stark in her mind.

There's nothing to explain, Patrick, and there was just a great coldness throughout her body and she knew she must put those papers down on the bed, the papers that explained everything, together with her husband's loveless words.

But there was no time for thinking now. She must just take the bag from the wardrobe, put her photos and her letters in, her clothes. But no, that was too many. Take them out. Quick, before he comes. Before the coldness turns into pain. Because she knew it would. She had felt like this before.

Money? Take it from his drawer, you're his wife. His well-equipped, strong, wife. But don't let the pain come. Not yet. And take this dress from your body. It rustled, caught round her legs. She put on her riding skirt, her shirt, her hat, her boots.

No one heard her on the stairs, their voices were still raised, but the sobbing had ceased. She heard only anger, only rage. But Deborah was still cold. She was still cold. She must reach the stables, find her horse, which was not really hers.

Edna was in the kitchen. Deborah brushed past, out through the door, into the stables. She saddled Penny, eased the bit into her mouth, the bridle. She was pulling her out into the yard when Patrick came, standing in the doorway.

'Deb, I've done it. I told you I would. She's forcing us to leave. There's nothing more I can do. I don't know where we'll go, but I'll think of something.' He put his hand on

Penny's nose, looking at Deb, his face changing. 'Where are you going?'

'Away.' Her lips were tight.

'What are you talking about? I've done what you wanted.' Penny butted his hand, he came round towards Deborah.

'You've done what you wanted, Patrick Prover. I've seen the papers. I've seen the tickets. I heard you.' She was pulling Penny forward, into the yard. The sun was up. It was daylight. She put her foot in the stirrup, hauled herself up, holding her bag on the saddle in front of her.

Patrick was gripping the reins, looking up at her. 'Where are you going? Let me explain.'

'You lied to me. I loved you. I adored you. You didn't love me, though you said you did. You used me for this, that's all.' She waved towards the house. 'You were going to use me for the rest of my life. You have a dead heart after all.' The words were hurting her throat. 'You don't love me. Even at the the picnic you didn't love me, even at Shellrick.' The pain was coming now. It was in her chest as well as her throat and she saw her father and mother walking before her at the market. 'Only you, my love,' he had said. Oh yes, she had felt this pain before.

Patrick still held Penny. Deborah could barely see him through the tears which were rolling, silently, down her cheeks, into her mouth. She kicked the horse, who skittered against Patrick's grip.

'You're my wife. You have to stay.'

'I have to do nothing, Patrick. You've taken my life, my love. I'm going. Pick Penny up from the station.'

She kicked again, and again the horse skittered, jerking her head. She bucked. Patrick hauled on the bridle.

'All right. I did plan it. I didn't want you to know. You were making plans for a life here. I can't bear it any more. There was no challenge after the war and she smothers me. For God's sake, listen, Deb. Together we can build our life. Don't be so stupid.'

'I'm sick of the war. I'm sick of lies. Why did you use

me? Why didn't you tell me, trust me? Why pretend?' She lifted her bag and struck him. Took her foot from the stirrup and kicked him away, and now there was anger, a searing white-hot anger which overrode the pain.

'Don't go. I need you, Deb. Don't go,' he was shouting now.

'I know you need me. I'm strong and experienced. I'm equipped. I was equipped for my mother too. I was equipped for everyone and none of you ever loved me, did you? Did you?' she shouted, hitting at him again. He dodged back and dropped the bridle. She kicked at Penny again. 'Did you? Any of you.'

But then she was away, galloping round the house, down the drive, her stirrup flying, but he had taught her to ride without them, hadn't he? She thought that had been out of affection, out of kindness, but she would have needed to ride, where he wanted them to go, and the scream that she heard was hers because the pain swept over and above the anger and tore into every part of her as she finally let herself hear the words her mother had really spoken as she died. 'I love you, Denis.'

Patrick watched her go, watched the stirrup flying, heard her scream.

'Why didn't you tell her you bloody loved her?' he ground out aloud, watching the dust lifting into the air behind her, hiding her. Because he didn't. That was why and he kicked the stable door because of the anger that raged inside him, and the despair because his dream was fading.

CHAPTER 10

Deborah slowed Penny to a canter, then to a trot, finally a walk. She would go somewhere, anywhere, it didn't matter, because the pain would be there, inside her as it was now. It would gnaw, pull, tear. It would not go away. She knew it too well.

She left Penny at the station, her reins around the rail. She leant into her, breathing in her warmth, feeling the coarseness of her mane. 'You were never plaited, never controlled were you, my love.'

She ran towards the train which was about to leave.

'Where d'you want to go?' called the station master. 'Wait, it's moving.'

'I don't mind where I go,' she whispered to herself, grasping the handle, hauling herself onboard.

'That's the Melbourne train,' she heard as the train pulled away but it meant nothing to her.

She sat not seeing the land through which they passed, not thinking of her journey a few months ago. Not thinking of anything, pushing it away as it came, looking instead at her hands, so brown after all these months. She wouldn't think of the children she was leaving at the school. She wouldn't think of the Mitchells, or the Bensons. She wouldn't think of Patrick. How could she think of him ever again?

But she did. She thought of all these things, all these people. And she thought of her father, her mother and the years she had waited for love which had never been there and so could never come. She thought of the work to provide for her mother,

159

the nursing during that last year, the love that she had given and had thought was returned at last. She remembered those words. 'I love you, Denis.'

She had to stand in the empty carriage. The pain was intense, and she hummed 'Knick knack Paddywack' again and again, but nothing helped. She cried, without tears, but it didn't help. Geoff's letter didn't help. He was dead. He couldn't come back. He would if he could, but he couldn't. Patrick was as dead, Lenora was dead. Her parents were dead. Love was dead. It didn't exist.

Yes, that's right, it didn't exist. This pain would go. It had to go. No one could live with this inside them. But she had before, for so many years, and now she faced those years. She sat for hour after hour, upright, strands of hair hanging across her face, flies crawling on her mouth, her eyes. Let them.

Other passengers joined the train at stations as bare and bleak as Hurstland's had been. And then there were orchards, farms, houses. The grass was greener, but not much. It would be green in Somerset. There would be frosts, there would be crocuses. There would be Nell, there would be Susie. But there was no home for her there. There was no home anywhere.

She breathed deeply, forcing down the pain, forcing away the terror. She clenched her hands as Mrs Prover had clenched hers. But no, she mustn't think of that. She felt cold, as cold as her mother had been. But mustn't think of that. Her sweat was cold on her forehead, beaded, icy. Her breath was quick, shallow. Had her father known terror as he gulped down the ice-speared water? Did you, Father? God, I hope you did. I hope you all did. I do hope, Patrick, that when you die, you too know what it is to be alone. I hope you do, Mrs Prover, when you die.

'Where am I going to go?'

She had spoken aloud. The woman opposite looked across, then down again at her book.. Later she moved further along the train. Deborah sat silently and counted her breaths until she slept.

*

160

The cab was hot, it was safe. Melbourne was safe. There were streets, there were buildings. There were people who walked into shops, women who wore pretty hats, dresses, shoes, not boots for the harsh terrain, not hats made of rabbit skin, not saddle shined divided skirts.

The sun cast raking shadows across wide streets, not sheep-eroded soil. No, Patrick Prover, not your soil where you hunted as Father and Mother did. She booked into The Oriental on Collins Street.

The room was hot. It didn't matter. It was dark, the blinds were drawn. She lay on the bed, and rolled on her side, hugging her arms around her, feeling the sweat through her clothes. It didn't matter. She cried again, and slept.

When she awoke it was four in the afternoon. She removed her clothes, washed this body that Patrick had held, had used. She stood on the towel and sluiced water on her face, her neck, her body, her legs.

She put on a cotton dress. It was creased. She held up her photographs, lifted the blind, looked at them. At her father so tall and strong, her mother so small and pretty. At Patrick in his wedding clothes. She put them in the wastepaper bin. All long gone, all experts in the art of using.

She looked out at the tar bubbling in the streets. A shimmering haze lay over the city, over Port Phillips Bay. It was over the blue eucalypt hills, the Great Dividing Range, which kept him away from her. But although Patrick was far from her now, her love for him was here, digging deep, twisting, turning, cutting, searing. She left the room. She must walk, keep walking until it became true that there was no love. It did not exist.

The street was like an opened woodstove. So hot, so very hot, but it didn't matter, she must keep moving. In and out, through the people. It didn't matter where because there was nowhere to go. She must cross the wide streets, beware of the trams, the wagons, the cabs, the few cars. Ninety-nine feet, Edward had said. She stopped. A man bumped into her, apologised, doffed his hat, hurried on, his short busy strides so different to those of Pat and the stockmen.

Edward had said that.

Edward was here, back from the dance.

He must have been on the same train.

Edward was here. Her friend was here. She had forgotten. How could she? She hailed a cab.

'Fifteen Canberra Crescent.'

She leant forward. Edward. Edward.

'You from England then?' the taxi driver asked.

'Yes.' And Edward was too. Edward was like her, not like these people. He thought she was beautiful, he had sent her flowers on the boat, he had stood with her by the rail of the ship. He had felt the same breeze in his hair, seen the same natives diving into the sea after coins. Edward was here. She was not alone.

'Brickfielder's coming in,' the cabman said, nodding at the wind which was tossing the leaves of the deciduous leaves in the Botanical Gardens. 'Good and hot, that devil.'

'It's always hot here,' Deborah said, not wanting to listen to that Australian voice, not wanting to listen to words about heat.

Out past the Toorack mansions standing in their spacious grounds and then into the narrowing streets with their red-brick and terracotta-roofed houses. It was safer, smaller, more manageable. It was not like Lenora.

Now the houses were weatherboard with tin roofs. It didn't matter, they were small, they were close to one another. They were in streets like Yeovil, like Stoke, like England.

There were paling fences, wire fences, neat hedges. There were roses, parched but living. There were mirages on the road; large still lakes. The cab stopped. She paid the man. This was 15 Canberra Crescent. She pushed open the gate. The wood was hot to the touch. The tar of the drive was bubbling. There was some on her left shoe, black on grey, and the smell of it all around.

The blinds were drawn, the paint was blistered on the wooden fence.

'Edward, be in,' she said, passing the parched lawn to the left of the path and the limp red standard rose in the circular bed edged with pebbles. The sky was white-blue. There were cicadas in the faded hedge.

She opened the fly screen and knocked. It was dark in the shade of the porch. 'Be in, Edward.' her voice was loud.

The door opened and he was there, so cool, so blond, his voice so pleased.

'Debbie, come in.' That was all but his hand was out, taking hers, pulling her into the tiled hall, kissing her cheek, taking her through into the kitchen, sitting her down at the table, taking a billy of milk out of a zinc-lined cupboard. The drink he handed her was cool. It was the taste of the drink that Nanny had given her in the nursery, it was the taste of a time before, before the pony, before Geoff, before Patrick.

She cried then, with Edward's arms around her, hearing the voice which had shown her Orion, which had deflected Mrs Warbuck's anger, which had said she was beautiful.

'Well, I don't see you for months and then it's two days running, my dear.' His arms were loose, gentle. He tucked the strands of hair back into the pins, he stroked, he soothed.

'A row?' he asked.

She nodded. There was still too much pain to think of it, to speak of it.

'We're friends, you and I,' she said, looking up at him. 'I needed someone. A friend.'

'You have me. And quite alone. The landlady is in Queensland. Absolutely no cigarette ash in the porridge. No endless chatter.' He was not smiling now, he was searching her eyes, reaching inside her head but no one must go there, not yet. It hurt too much.

They went to St Kilda's. They took a tram, sitting in the dummy, not the trailer. They didn't speak of why she was here. They spoke of the gripman in the centre of the hollow square of outward facing seats, turning to look and laughing at the notice above his head: 'Do not talk to the Gripman.'

'Mrs Warbuck would soon deal with that,' Edward said and Deborah nodded. Yes, she would indeed. Patrick knew scarcely anything of Mrs Warbuck. It was only she and Edward. Are you listening, Mrs Prover? It is only my friend and I who know of her. Neither of you belongs to that part of my life.

'I'm so glad you're here.' she said to Edward as the conductor took their money, swinging right round the outside of the dummy, with the roadway rushing beneath him.

'I'm glad too.' His eyes were dark blue in the shade of the cable car and he touched her arm. 'Last time we travelled together there was a lot of ocean around. Seems a long time, Debbie. We had so many hopes. They've come true for both of us.'

He told her then the details of his appointment to the Prep School of the Presbyterian Public School. He told her of the acres of grounds where they were housed, and where the Senior School would join them. He told her of the plans they had for a swimming pool, tennis courts, a science block, cricket pavilion. He felt he was on the verge of life, he said, as he wanted it to be.

He told her that while he remembered the ethos of the school – God above, Satan below – he would be all right. While he dealt in absolutes he would progress. They laughed and felt the heat from the brickfielder coming in off the hinterland, full of the heat of that arid land. So you follow me here after all, Deborah thought, and would not think of the hopes she had had, which had now been dashed.

Edward had prepared sardine sandwiches and she could smell them through the bag on his lap. There were ginger biscuits too.

'There'll be rain tomorrow or the next day,' he murmured as they stepped off the dummy on to the Esplanade of St Kilda's.

Even here by the sea it was hot. There were yellow sandy beaches stretching over thirty miles from Port Melbourne to Sorrento and Portsea.

'Continuous arc,' Edward said, sitting on the beach, pulling her down beside him. 'Take your shoes off, Debbie. We're on holiday. You are escaping, I am celebrating. Let's make the most of today. We're fellow travellers, remember?'

Oh yes, she remembered. She removed her shoes, fumbled beneath her skirts, removed her stockings. She felt the hot sand beneath her toes, dug them in, covered them from the heat of the sun. It was too dry to build sandcastles but together they watched children trying.

'There are sharks.' He pointed over to the men's and women's baths along the sea front. There were several. 'There's shark-proof wire on poles around those, if you want to swim.'

She shook her head. No she didn't want to swim, but she mustn't think of father any more, any of them, or of the pain which was still there muted inside her, but which would rise and make her groan again. Edward rose and pulled at his trousers.

'Don't go.' Because if he went, the pain would return.

'Ice cream?' he asked, bending and stroking her face.

'I'll come.' She mustn't be alone. She couldn't bear to be alone. They had to put their shoes on again because the sand was too hot to walk on.

There were bushfires on the distant blue hills, the wind was clattering the propped up wooden front of the ice-cream shack.

They could smell hot wood as they queued.

'A drink as well?' Edward looked at Debbie who nodded. He turned to the woman at the hatch. 'Two ginger beers, two ice-creams please.'

'Feeding up the missus, eh? Right you are then.' There was a spurt of vapour as she unscrewed the ginger beer top, then poured the drink into two thick glasses.

One for the missus, Deborah thought, as the woman took a wooden scoop out of a bucket and stooped beneath the counter, twisting her hand, pressing ice-cream into the cones. One for the missus, and the pain was there again.

The woman placed a straw in each of the glasses. Deborah

and Edward stood in the shade of the hut. It was hardly any cooler.

'Starts in the north of the State. Probably just a willy-willy to begin with that rises, taking up dust and sand. Winds come in to fill the space, push it towards us, or so the landlady said. Should rain later.'

Lenora bloomed when the rains came, or so Patrick had said. But Deborah pushed her thoughts away. Breathe, just breathe, she told herself. Her ice-cream was dripping. She licked it but it was too sweet in this heat. She said, 'I'm sorry, I can't,' and tipped it into the bin.

'We'll go to Luna Park tonight, Debbie. We'll have some fun. You invited me to the dance. I'll invite you to the swings, to the slides.' He dropped his ice-cream into the bin too and handed her his handkerchief to wipe her hands.

Patrick had promised he would take her to Luna Park, but she would never see him again, would she? She wiped her hands, drank some more of the ginger beer, but only a little, handing the glass back to the woman.

She walked up and down, up and down while Edward watched.

Later, as afternoon changed to evening and the moon grew to the size of a melon and hung helpless above the sea, they walked past the male baths and she heard the lazy suck of the sea at the netting, saw the pier-like entrance to the baths, the turnstile. They passed the Palais de Danse with its circular tin roof. There were towers at either end.

'Would you like to dance, Debbie?'

She shook her head. She had danced enough last night. Last night would last a lifetime. She could still feel his hands, his lips as he had kissed her.

'No.'

'What happened, Debbie?'

'Nothing, everything. It hurts, Edward, too much to talk about.'

He nodded, took her hand, tucked it in his arm. 'Debbie, Debbie. You should have married an English teacher.'

166

They passed the Palais Pictures and then there was Luna Park with an entrance in the shape of an enormous grinning mouth. Two huge eyes winked. She laughed, too much, and Edward looked at her, and swept her forward into the hall of the distorting mirrors. Yes, Edward, I should have married an English teacher.

They went into the House of Ghosts, the Funny House where hot air blasted her skirt up over her head and Edward laughed. Then she laughed as he lurched and skidded on the rollers. They went down the Water Chute. It was still so hot. The moon still hung motionless in the sky. There were the sounds of voices, of women laughing, screaming, men too and children. There was no silence here. No grey endless bush silence.

All around them were the bends and dips of the rollercoaster Scenic Railway but she had travelled on trains enough today, and Edward said that he had too, leaning towards her, kissing her cheek, pushing her pain further down.

They went on the Big Dipper and Deborah screamed and screamed as others around them were doing, and then there was just the roaring rattle of the downward plunging car and she was full of fear, blacker, stronger, and she clutched at Edward. Patrick, her mind screamed, but her mouth said nothing. Patrick, how could you do this to me? The pain, the terror of her gaping world were too much and she felt Edward's arms around her, holding her.

There were screams around her, laughter, the slowing rattle of the car on the tracks, Edward's voice. Edward's English voice in the midst of all this chaos.

They took the last tram home. There would be none in the morning. The underground cable would make it sound as though the streets were humming, Edward told her, walking her down the path, hearing the crickets, then into the kitchen. Making her tea in a brown teapot with a stained rubber spout. Her hands still smelt of sardines.

She drank the tea. It was strong. She must go back to the Hotel soon. She would be alone.

167

'Come with me to see a house tomorrow. I'm buying one. Two English people together, my Debbie, bearding Australians in their den. Come with me. I don't want to be alone.'

At the hotel she had nothing but the photographs in the bin, a bag with a few clothes in. That was all. Here, in this house there were two people, both of whom did not wish to be alone. She felt her shoulders ease.

She stayed, taking the hurricane lamp out to the lavatory, then up to the bathroom, showering in cool water. The wind was still high, still hot and she stood at the window of the spare bedroom looking out across Melbourne, seeing the bushfires up on the hills. The moon still hung heavy in the sky. She turned out the lamp.

She had no nightdress. She wore nothing. She ran her hands down her breasts, her belly, her legs. 'Patrick, how could you lie to me? It was too cruel.' She spoke the words aloud.

She didn't turn as she heard Edward's voice from the doorway, didn't turn as he came almost silently across the room.

'No one should be cruel to you, Debbie.'

She didn't turn because there was such despair.

He was standing behind her, his arms were round her, his lips were on her neck, her shoulder. He too was naked. She could feel his skin against hers, warm. She looked up at the moon, Orion was there too, but this time there was no sea, no lifeboat, no sound of dancing in the background. There was Edward though, and the sound of his English voice, his lips on her breasts as he turned her round, his hands as they pulled her to him, pressing her against his body.

Now there was anger, pain coursing through her and she pressed his head to hers, kissing his mouth, opening hers, feeling his tongue. It wasn't enough. She arched away as his hands caressed her back, her buttocks, her thighs. It wasn't enough. She could still feel the pain.

She groaned as she felt his penis hard against her belly. He kissed her breasts. His hair was white in the moonlight, his back was sweat-streaked, as were her breasts, her arms, her face.

He knelt, his face between her legs. It wasn't enough and she gripped his hair, her legs trembling, and then he was pulling her down on to the cool wooden floor and he was in her, deep, slow, pushing the feel of Patrick away. Damn you, Patrick. Damn you all, and she groaned as her anger and pain merged into waves of a passion so fierce that she was crying aloud, but now Edward slowed, he soothed, he pushed up on his hands, looked down at her.

'Not yet, Debbie. Not yet,' he murmured, 'I've wanted you since I first saw you. There is all night.'

He withdrew, leaving her empty, pulling her to her feet, taking her to the bed, and Patrick was there again. She pushed him away. There was no such thing as love. She wanted the fierceness back, not this despair.

Edward held her again, kissed her, stroked her as she stroked him. He entered her again, slow and deep, then eased his body beneath her and she moved on him, slow and deep, and looked into his face, his eyes half-closed, his lips half-open. She heard his breath, quick, so quick. He pulled her down, kissed her mouth, her face.

'Debbie, Debbie,' he moaned. 'Dear God, Debbie.'

Then he pushed her from him. 'Not yet. Not yet.'

But she wanted him now, this blond man who brought the skies and seas back to her and so they struggled, her mouth searching his, her hands pulling him to her, hearing his breath, his voice, her voice, deep and incoherent. Both urgent, so urgent, and now his weight was on her, he was filling her, driving into her, faster, faster and she was moving with him, not thinking, not feeling with her mind, just fiercely with her body.

Afterwards they slept, though the night was hotter and the wind was banging the letter-boxes in the streets.

The streets were humming as they walked to 24 Urville Avenue. Their shoes were sticky with tar. Their hands, clasped together, were damp with sweat. Their laughter mingled, their glances, their hair, as he stooped and kissed her.

She liked the streets, the closeness, the familiarity – unlike Lenora. But no, she wouldn't think of Patrick, just push him away as she had pushed the photographs down into the bin. Love didn't exist, not with him. But Edward was taking her through these streets to choose his new house. Edward, her friend, who was alone like her. Who was far from England, like her.

The brickfielder was still with them, scorching, tossing the cotton palms in a garden that they passed. The heat beat up at them from the pavement. Her throat was dry. Was Edward's?

He looked at her. 'Could do with a ginger beer. We'll go afterwards, shall we, my Debbie.'

My Debbie, and yes, he was thirsty too. Are you, Patrick, out beyond those hills that are still alight with fires? She looked into the sky. The air was thick with dust.

'It'll end. It'll rain. Tomorrow,' Edward said, turning into a street with a thin strip of buffalo grass and the occasional white gum separating the pavement from the road.

'Urville Avenue,' she read.

They walked slowly along, looking at the numbers.

'Twenty, twenty-two, twenty-four.' Edward stopped, looked at her, smiled. They stood in front of a red brick single-storeyed house with a terracotta roof. 'Let's get in, out of this heat. It looks good doesn't it?' There was excitement in his voice. Deborah felt a tightening in her chest. Soon he would have a home, but what of her?

Mrs Jones answered the door, showing them in, nodding at Edward, at Deborah. Her hair was drawn back into a bun so tight that the skin on her face was stretched.

'Didn't realise you were married. What a pretty ring. You're a lucky girl, Mrs Lucas,' Mrs Jones said, wiping her fingers on her apron, shaking hands. 'We're moving to Geelong.'

'We're just looking for something of our own, aren't we, darling Debbie?' Edward was smiling at Debbie, then back at Mrs Jones. 'May we see around?'

The kitchen had one casement window on to the side alley. There was a square deal table and dresser. A gas stove with its brass nozzles jutting out. There was an old-fashioned wood burner, a refrigerator, and Mrs Jones talked all the time but Deborah could only hear the words, 'We're looking for something of our own.' *Our own*.

They looked into the larder, the scullery which looked out over the yard to the woodshed. There was a sink with a wooden plate rack above a wooden draining board that was wet and larded with dirt-drenched soap.

Our own.

They walked out into the blazing heat again. There were two kerosene tins on the dividing fence for bread and milk. Tradesmen called. People were living either side. It wasn't frightening here. It was like England, almost.

They walked down through the yard into the garden with its orange, lemon and mandarin trees. There·was a vegetable bed, some rhubarb, neglected raspberry canes. There were docks growing. She leant down, looked under the leaves, picked off the snails.

'You should put these into a can with lots of salt and water,' she said, dropping them back on to the earth. 'It disposes of them nicely.'

'You know about these things then? That's useful.'

The heat was beating up from the ground, and whirling around in the wind. There was so much dust in the air. That is what was making her eyes smart.

'Oh yes, some people think I'm very useful.'

There was a garbage incinerator right at the bottom of the garden, artichokes grew nearby. There were iris, arum lilies, marjoram, lemon balm, thyme. Not too much land, just enough.

'What do you think so far, Debbie?' Edward was smiling. He took her hand, laughed gently.

171

Mrs Jones was still talking as she led them inside and he whispered to Debbie, 'Another Mrs Warbuck.'

She kissed him quickly. Yes, she and Edward knew about Mrs Warbuck. They had shared memories that Patrick knew nothing about.

They re-entered the house, looking at the sleep-out, at the dining room. It was dark, dreary. It could be improved. It would be improved. The bathroom had a corrugated shower screen, a chip heater and corner basin. There was an outside dunny. She felt Edward's hand tightening as they walked into the bedroom. It too was dark, but still it could be improved, would be improved.

'You could do a lot with this, my love,' Edward said, 'especially when the children come.'

They drank a cup of tea while Mrs Jones swatted flies with a floppy long-handled fly swat. Edward said they would call back when they had decided. Deborah walked with him down the asphalt path and the tar was still sticky, the wind was still so hot, but nothing mattered. He had said, *they* would call back.

Edward swung her hand as they walked, laughing, putting his arm around her shoulders. 'It helped that you came, Debbie. She opened up. She thought we were married. A friend said that he found the same thing. It makes the seller feel you're more serious about buying. But, it was a strange feeling, peculiar really, almost farcical. You didn't mind, did you?'

Deborah felt his lips on hers.

'Why was it farcical?' She knew her voice was dead.

She looked up at the sky, at the sun blood red behind the screen of dust. It had been blood red behind the screen of mist so long ago with Patrick.

'Why was it farcical?' she repeated, walking on, slowly, feeling the dull pain which had never really gone. 'Why was it farcical?' She was shouting now. Standing in the street shouting.

Edward pulled her round, his lips tight, looking up and

down the street. 'What the hell's the matter with you, Debbie? Of course it's farcical. You're a married woman.'

She pulled away. 'But you said *our own*. You said it. You said *we'd* call back.'

'Oh my God, you thought I was serious.' He reached for her hands. 'Debbie, come on. You're married to Patrick.'

She gripped his hands. 'I hate him. I've left him. I want to live here with you, with neighbours in a street. You're alone. I'm alone.' She looked at him, at the blond hair that fell on his face, at his eyes, dark beneath furrowed brows.

'Debbie, I'm so sorry. I was just acting. Being stupid, pretending.'

She dragged her hands away and he tried to catch them. 'Listen to me, Debbie. Women don't leave their husbands. I can't take you in. I've got this new position. You know that. I can't afford a scandal. I've got what I came out for. We're friends, that's all.'

She started to walk away, across the springy buffalo grass, across the tarred road. He ran after her, pulling at her. 'Stop, Debbie. We're friends. It's too late for anything like that. You shouldn't have joined him. You should have come with me straight from the ship. It wouldn't have hurt my career then.'

She wrenched her arm away, leaving him standing. Everything is hurting me now, she thought and she knew that she had been a fool. Edward was right, she was mad. Quite mad with pain, and panic.

She heard him shout. 'Travelling companions, that's what we were. I thought you understood.'

She returned to St Kilda's. She sat on the beach and the red-hot wind whipped up the sand so that it stung like knives. The sun was still red, waves surged to the sand. Children ran in and out till their parents called and took them away. The heat increased, and Deborah sat on the beach because there was nothing else to do.

As the moon rose again, large, waxen, the wind dropped to a whisper, the sky clouded over, dark thunderheads appeared.

The sea was a still lake, like the road mirages of the day. Then the rain fell, sudden, large-dropped, red rain, dust-laden, viscous. But it was only a brief shower, and then the heat returned.

She sat on the beach. The moon was the same one which had hung motionless over the ship when she had felt Edward's breath on her face, and his hands in her hair. 'We're friends, that's all,' she had shouted then. 'I already have a lover,'

He was right. She was a fool. She clasped her knees, rested her head on them. Hour after hour she sat, and hoped that somehow the morning would never come. Perhaps she would die.

In the morning dawn streaked so red across the sky. She looked along the continuous miles of yellow sand, whipped up by the wind which was coming from the semi-arid continent where she had been. She was alive. 'People who want to die can't, can they, Geoff,' she murmured.

She rose and walked to the water's edge, looking across the sea. What now? Where now? Back home? How? And where was home anyway? She looked at her hands, so broad, so strong.

She stooped to the sea, cupping the water in her hands. 'Lots of salt and water disposes of snails nicely,' she echoed. 'Oh yes, Mrs Jones, I do know about these things.'

She listened to the waves lapping, heavily, turgidly. She watched the water drain from her hands back into the sea.

She rose and nodded to the relentless sun. Oh yes, and I also know, at last, that I am quite alone and I understand that love does not exist, never has existed, and therefore nothing matters anyway. Nothing.

She was heedless of the looks she drew as she took the tram to Collins Street. Heedless of the fact that her clothes were splashed with orange, that Patrick's dust had bludgeoned and marked her skin, her clothes, her hair. She showered in the bathroom, washed her hair, coiled it wet on her head, threw her dress into the bin. She put on a clean one. Her photographs were on the dressing table. The chambermaids perhaps had thought it was an error.

She took them and put them in the bin again. There was one of Geoff in her bag which she kept. His love had died with him. He had not taken it from her. There was one of Nell, Tom and Susie. She kept that too.

She paid her bill and, took a cab, not to Port Melbourne where the ocean liners left from, but to the docks. They passed horse-drawn drays, schoolboys on bicycles. Would Edward be at school now, teaching that God was above, Satan below? She could think of him now. She could think of them all because love was dead. It did not exist. There was no pain in her after that long night. There was nothing.

Along Flinders Street the masts and funnels stabbed at the sky, the drone of traffic was all around. A siren overrode it. The windows along the street were streaked with dust. There were steaming piles of horse manure; and roadmen sweeping up behind the wagons and drays. There were two lead-roofed towers with weather vanes. Would Patrick's grandfather have stolen from those too? It didn't hurt to think of it. Nothing hurt.

They went in through the brick arch to the docks, driving slowly past the bluestone-fronted mortgage stock-and-station houses.

'This is where wool is baled and cleaned for export,' the cabbie told her.

They drove past bales and crates, past blue dungareed wharfies with stained flannel singlets who looped the rope nooses over the hooks lowered from the derricks of blackened freighters. There were crates of peaches, apricots.

'For Britain,' the cabbie said.

There were customs men in shirt sleeves and peaked caps moving around, checking inventories, the shipper's agent slapping his stencil on the side of crates.

They were past them now and here she left the cab, paying, turning, asking an official for the interstate vessel bound for

Fremantle, because, what else could she do, and what did it matter anyway?

She climbed the companionway, then stepped on to the deck, walking towards Patrick who stood at the rail, watching her.

'I knew you'd come,' he said.

She didn't answer, just turned to the dock as the ship cast off. She stood with the other passengers throwing streamers to friends and relatives on the quayside and a woman beside her gave her one. As the ship slowly backed away the streamers tightened and tightened, snapped and fell into the bilgey water between the ship and the dock. Then the rain began, proper rain, heavy, wet, still dust-laden. Deborah stayed outside when others retreated. She stayed and watched the streamers become sodden and disintegrate. Only then did she turn and go to their cabin.

Book Two

CHAPTER 11

Yes, he had known she would come, Patrick thought as the ship came in between the Fremantle breakwaters. She had to come. There was nowhere else for her to go. When Edward had told them of his new teaching post he had known there was no way he would take Deborah on. She had no future outside the marriage. It was only she who had not realised that.

Patrick looked at his wife, standing silently beside him, then out across the wharf where they were now docking. The customs shed was busy. The anger and despair which had grown inside him when she left had eased. His dream was saved and he put his hand on hers because he knew that it would be all right. She would realise that he had done the right thing.

'I'm sorry, Deb, at the way I used you. I can't handle Mother on my own. It's like those frogs you told me you used to set free. You set me free. You helped me. I was wrong. I'm sorry but I offer you a future. It's what I promised you. I didn't mislead you. There isn't room in my life for love.'

She looked at him, that was all. She just looked, but he knew that it would be all right in time. She would recover, she would like the farm. It would be like Somerset again. He needed her. She needed him.

'It'll be all right, Deb.'

She followed him along Fremantle wharf, out along the narrow streets to a grocer's shop where he ordered a double stretcher bed.

'Two singles,' she said. That was all. There would be no

more misleading kisses. No more bodies which spoke of love, and lied.

Patrick paused, then nodded. 'Two singles then, please.'

He ordered a table and two chairs. The grocer said he would pack all the groceries into packing cases. They were deal and so were the kerosene cases. They could use them when empty as chairs or cupboards. Patrick ordered a Coolgardie safe and a butter cooler.

He asked Deborah what she would like.

'Sardines, ginger biscuits.' What did it matter.

Patrick read from a list, ordering flour, sugar, salt, and Deborah just stood beside him looking at his hands. She didn't listen any more. Those hands had touched her body without love. She had been a fool in Melbourne. Now, she felt nothing.

'I'll get them to the station,' the grocer said. 'And you should have some citronella oil, good for keeping mosquitoes away, castor oil around your eyes will keep the flies off, and eye ointment, for when they get through.'

She hadn't needed those in Somerset. Why should they need them here?

They walked along the waterfront. There were stacks of sandalwood for Asian temples, timber and sleepers, apples, wool, and wheat. Trains were shunting. They walked again and passed parks.

'We'll be seven miles from a town at the farm. It won't be as big as this but there'll be trees, Deb. It'll be green. There's water in the South West, not like Lenora. It's like Somerset. There are caves where the aboriginals lived. There will be dairy cattle all over the area.'

They walked again, passing bougainvillea-splashed cottages with wrought-iron balconies.

'Mrs Warbuck lives in Perth,' is all she said. Patrick didn't know Mrs Warbuck. The image was hers alone. He did not know that Mrs Warbuck had grey hair, a mole on her left cheek.

'We'll go and see her one day.'

'Perhaps I shall,' was all she said, because he was not part of her real life any more.

They passed a Woolworths and she bought slippers and socks for herself. He bought linen, cutlery, pans. A primus stove.

'Just in case,' he explained.

There was a cool breeze from the Indian Ocean. Was the hot wind gone from Melbourne? Were the schoolchildren chanting in Edward's classroom? She didn't care. Edward was not part of her life either.

At the station was a row of dirty carriages. They sat in these for hours waiting for the train to leave at midnight.

The cabin trunks, cases and provisions were in the goods van. 'I brought your Wedgwood tea service and Geoff's clock.'

'You were so sure, Patrick.' Her voice was dead, she could hear it as the train rattled, wheezed, groaned. She had groaned in her bedroom at Melbourne. She had groaned in the Blue Mountains. 'So very sure.'

He looked at her, nodded. 'I knew I could rely on you.'

She looked down at the newspaper they had bought, though she read nothing. She felt nothing either. Nothing at all.

She slept, waking at Pinjarra, watching as Patrick leapt off the train, raced into a building and came back with sandwiches and cups of tea, others followed. Had the tea been made in a billy which had been swirled around or poured from a stained rubber spout? She ate and drank but said nothing, tasted nothing. She must eat to live. She would not ask herself why she had to live. There was, she knew, no answer.

They stopped again at Brunswick Junction, then Picton Junction. They passed through land with small timbers. There were banksias sprouting yellow and orange candles, sheoaks, blackboys, zamia palms, shrubs, so many shrubs.

There were bush fires all along the tracks from the sparks of the steam engine. There were blackened burnt-out areas. There was drinking water in canvas bags slung outside the windows between the carriages. Patrick reached out of the window, half-filled an aluminium mug, handed it to her.

'Thank you,' she said, holding it between her hands, feeling the rim bang against her teeth as the train lurched. The water was warm, it slopped as the train lurched again, down her chin, her dress. She sat with it on her knees, leaving the water to dry where it had spilt.

'Premier Mitchell decided to try and make Western Australia self-sufficient in dairy produce to stop having to buy from the east. I thought it would be better for you here, doing things you are familiar with. It will be like Nell's all over again.' Patrick took the mug from her limp hand. It was empty.

She looked at him. 'So, you did all this for me then, did you, Patrick?'

He read his newspaper, a flush on his cheeks, cheeks that she had kissed and stroked, and loved. She saw him look up at her, then away. He crumpled up the newspaper and threw it to the floor. Those hands had guided hers on the reins, had helped her feet to find her stirrups. She felt nothing.

Patrick left the train again at Busselton to buy pastries and sandwiches, nectarines and apricots, and they ate them as the train rattled through land which became more heavily timbered.

'There are other settlers coming out from England, you know. They are being paid three pounds a week to work on a Group Settlement Scheme, making roads, clearing one another's blocks. They're being supplied with land and materials and have to repay the cost of preparation when they're producing. Postwar thing. The British Government are helping with the assisted passages. Some might even be near us. British people, Deborah.' His voice was eager.

Deborah looked up. 'Are we part of this scheme?'

'No, we're independent. I've bought three hundred acres. They have a hundred and sixty. It's the challenge, Deborah. Building something that is mine, can't you see that?'

She nodded and thought, Oh yes, Patrick. I can see that,

but she felt no anger, no curiosity. There was just today to get through, and then tomorrow.

There were bright red flowers on the bushes dotted all over the sand plain they were passing.

'Crimson bottlebrush,' Patrick told her, although she had not asked.

They passed Margaret River. The timbers were becoming very large, very dense, karri, jarrah and red gum, shrub and undergrowth that looked too thick to walk through. There were no trees like this in Somerset, there was no such density of undergrowth. For a moment she was angry, but then it was gone.

Patrick had arranged for a cart to meet them at the station when they arrived at five o'clock. The township was smaller, much smaller than Hurstland. It had two stores, a stables. A doctor's house. A few others. They were all wooden, all with verandahs, all with fly screens. There were huge trees all around, looming over them, around them. Deborah said nothing, felt nothing, only the flies that hummed around her head, settled, crawled. The castor oil was in the packing case.

The carter took them along a track with bush either side, but this was not bush like that at Lenora, this was dense forest. There were no mist-covered levels as there had been the last time they had creaked and jolted together on a cart. There was no smell of myrtle. She had no cutting to plant at the doorway of her new home, no love to fill the rooms, and it didn't matter. All that was past.

Soon darkness fell, suddenly, completely and there was no sound from the bush which crowded to the very edge of the track, there were no house lights to guide them. There was just the snort of the horse, the jangle of his harness, the creaking of their trunks, cases, provisions, the buzz of mosquitoes which stung their flesh. The citronella oil was in the packing case.

They stopped at the carter's home. His wife came to the door, and took Deborah's hand, helping her in.

'Thank you, but I can manage.' She didn't want hands on her, anyone's hands.

'You sound tired, my dear.' The woman sounded tired too. Her face was thin and brown, her hair was grey and pulled back into a roll. The room was lit by hurricane lamps.

I feel nothing, Deborah thought.

She sat and drank strong tea in the front room as Patrick talked to the carter, who was also a farmer. Mr Martins rubbed tobacco between his coarse hands, then pushed it into his pipe, lighting it, drawing. The smell filled the room.

Mrs Martins gave her an unwashed beer bottle so that she could start off her own yeast for bread making. She gave her two empty washed condensed milk tins, and two clip-on handles, which turned them into mugs.

'I have my Wedgwood,' Deborah said.

Mrs Martins laughed and then looked closely at Deborah. 'My dear, this life is hard.'

'My husband calls it a challenge,' Deborah said, looking round at the kitchen in which they sat, the unlined walls, at the Metters stove to cook and bake with. She listened as Mrs Martins told her how to light the fire and keep it burning with wood, not coal as she would have been used to in Somerset. She should choose good dry firewood, she said, and use empty kerosene tins for washing in, boiling clothes, heating water. But Patrick had said the farm was like Nell's – they would not need these things.

'Save the kerosene boxes, and the packing cases. It makes good furniture.'

'We're ordering some soon. He said he'd send it down from Fremantle.'

'But not yet,' Patrick said and Mr Martins nodded.

'Tools have been sent on. Should be there when we arrive.'

'But not tonight. Tonight you'll stay here,' Mrs Martins said.

They slept in the same bed, but not touching. She lay still, quite still, not asleep but pretending. She was sweaty, dirty.

There had been just a quarter of a kerosene can of water to wash in. Deborah used it first and then Patrick.

Something scrabbled about them on the galvanised iron roof. She tensed.

'It's only a possum,' Patrick said.

So he was awake too, but she didn't care. She said nothing, just lay still and thought of the lines which dragged down between Mrs Martins' nose and mouth, the exhaustion in her face, her body, the look of age on this woman of thirty-five. She thought of the snakes, the dingoes, the kangaroo ticks that Mr Martins had spoken of, the flies which had been on their faces, their eyes, the mosquitoes which had bitten them.

She thought of Dave's mother's house, the bleakness, the hardness which was so like this one, of the cottage, of Edward's new house, of the home she would arrive at tomorrow with this man who had no room in his life for love. Of the years which stretched ahead. But no, it was only of tomorrow that she must think.

They left at seven to travel the three miles to the start of Patrick's land and Mrs Martins waved from the verandah. 'Get your butter and milk from me until you have your own,' she called as the cart rattled and heaved along the rutted track.

'You're not alone. It might seem like it, but I'm here. There are others too, a little further from you. The store will deliver this far. Bring your order here. I'll give it to him. Hope the chops are all right. Don't despair. It will only take you ten years to build up to this,' Mrs Martins called, running after them, then stopping and waving, before turning back.

Deborah wouldn't let those words stay in her head. She was going to a world like Nell's. That's where she was going.

They had left the Martins' cleared pasture behind, the cows which grazed between the ring-barked trees, the felled trees, the stumps. The hens which ran behind the watertank, the out-houses, the poor square house. Ten years ... but no, that wasn't possible.

They left the track, and went through the bush following

185

a blazed trail, winding between giant trees whose foliage blocked the sun. There were flies all over their faces, their eyes, in their ears, bush flies that stung her, sand flies that ate her. There were insects, there was a solitary kookaburra that laughed once.

'Blazes were put in for you by that old boy, Spenders, from town. Follow them in, follow them out. There'll be nicks on the other side of the tree for that, Mrs Prover. Don't deviate. You'll get lost.'

She looked at the huge trees, then on up to their interlocking crowns. There was no sun to be seen. They lurched, ground on in the shadows and her spirit died even further. Mr Martins flicked his whip. 'Go on, boy.' They were moving across the forest floor where there was no track, only darkness, only insects. Mr Martins pulled on the reins, called, 'Whoa.'

Why? They stopped. She looked ahead. There were more trees, shrub, undergrowth, a few saplings. Why?

'Here you are, Patrick. This is it. You're home. Help me down with the things. Got work to do back on our block. It's nine o'clock.'

Deborah watched as Patrick climbed over her, his hands gripping the seat, the edge of the cart, easing himself down. She looked at the trees, at him, at the face he turned from her.

'Come on then, Patrick,' Mr Martins called, heaving at the back of the cart.

She looked ahead of her, all around. There were only trees, some three feet thick, some five feet. Some were saplings. There were zankias, there was scrub, there was undergrowth. There were insects. There was the darkness, the simmering heat. For God's sake. There was nothing else.

'There's nothing here. Nothing here.' She heard her words. They were low. She had thought she would never have to talk to herself again once she left England.

Mr Martins was waiting, moving the packing cases to the edge of the tailboard, but first Patrick looked up at her.

'There should have been a house put up. Spenders said there would be.'

'It's over there.' Mr Martins jerked his head to a pile of timber and corrugated iron between two trees. There were some boxes of tools also. 'Should get a humpy up by nightfall, between the two of you.'

Deborah looked at Patrick as he took one end of a cabin trunk and for a moment there was despair, dark, swirling, and then anger, but then there was nothing but a pile of timber which was her home. In ten years she would have hens, cows, and lines driven deep to the side of her mouth. But what did it matter? Why was there this pain in her chest, this thickening of her throat?

She climbed from the cart and took a case, then another. There were fleas now, all over the bottom of her skirt, all over Patrick's trousers, Mr Martins' trousers, over her legs. There was undergrowth to step over, there was sword grass to step around, suckers to trip her.

She said nothing as the sweat dripped from her face on to the packing cases she carried, as the splinters tore into her fingers. Nothing mattered, remember that, Deborah Morgan, and the breath was suddenly easier in her body. Of course, yes, nothing mattered. This was just today. Just today.

She said nothing as she carried the primus stove which Patrick had bought 'just in case'.

She said nothing as the cart left them here, alone together, in a silent world, dark and silent for she heard no more kookaburras, no rosellas, no magpies. There was nothing. There was no one. They had travelled for two hours on a horse and cart to arrive here, at a place beyond call of their nearest neighbour.

It was beyond friendship too because no one with any feeling for her at all could bring her to this. No one could buy a primus stove and then say they did not know there would not even be a humpy up when they had talked of a farm like Nell's. She was right. She must look no further than today.

Patrick moved towards her.

'Deborah, I didn't know.'

She put up her hand. 'Don't tell me any more lies. This is today. Today we put the humpy up. That's all.' She turned from him, towards the timber, the iron sheets and her face was covered with flies, one was in her mouth. There were red bumps from sand flies, from the mosquitoes. Her back, her skirt, were covered too, she felt them through the cotton, she felt them with her hand as she swept her skirt. She felt the fleas on her legs.

'It's part of the challenge, Deb.' he said.

They stood still, looking ahead, not at each other, and there was still no sound. They were so small against the trees, so impotent and Deborah shivered.

'We need to clear an area at least twenty feet square first, Mr Martins told me,' Patrick said at last, prizing open the boxes of tools, giving Deborah a mattock, taking an axe. Deborah watched him look around, walk in a circle, widening it, and then off towards the creek Mr Martins had pointed out, blazing a trail, then back.

'This is the most level area, and over there is where we'll start the paddocks.' He pointed to a position over to the left. 'That looks a bit less dense. We'll start there.'

He pushed his way through to a sapling, cutting it down with three chops. 'This is the start of our future, Deb. It will be all right. Trust me.'

She said nothing because she could not trust him any more nor love him, there was no such thing as a future, or a home like Nell's, and there was a sourness in her mouth, a tightness in her throat, but there must be no tears, because everything was dead inside her. It had to be, for her to survive.

They slashed at the scrub and the suckers, again and again, and Deborah felt the vibration as the mattock caught a sapling. It jarred right up to her shoulder, into her neck, her head. The sweat poured off her, soaking her dress. She hacked, heaped up, and dragged away the scrub which tore through her gloves, wrenching them open. She dragged away sword grass which was sharp like the pampas in the Yeovil garden. So sharp, so painful. She sucked but the blood still trickled from her finger half an hour later.

There were snakes, Mrs Martins had said. She looked for those too. She flapped at the flies, the ever-present flies. They were bitten by kangaroo ticks, and burnt them off with cigarette stubs or the heads would stay beneath the skin, festering, itching, becoming septic. They squeezed the cigarette out each time, making the heat quite dead. Quite, quite dead, like her world.

At one o'clock, they stopped, and Patrick went with an axe and bucket in the direction of the creek. She watched him, heard him, slashing, hooking, felt no breeze although she could hear a rustle at the height of the trees. At last she was alone. At last she could stop, at last she could weep.

She stood, her arms hanging by her sides, her hands throbbing, swollen, her blisters bleeding. She could no longer see the trees, their leaves which excluded the sun, their trunks, so thick. This was her future, he had said, but she mustn't think of that. She must think of today, and feel nothing.

She pumped the primus, hearing him come back with the bucket he had bought in Woolworths. It was half full, his trousers were wet where it had slopped over him. The water smelt.

'Mustn't drink it unless it's boiled,' Patrick said, squatting, pouring some into the billy, tipping some into his hands, washing his face and neck. 'First thing is the well. We can't do with water like this.'

Deborah poured some on to her hands, washed her eyes and face because he must not see her tears. They must not come again.

'We'll use the primus. No open fires.' Patrick felt the grass. It was dry. 'No fires. We've got to get some fire-breaks sorted out. We'll need to clear enough for pasture, Deb, and dig that

189

well. You'll need to walk to the Martins' each week, pick up the order.'

'How do we pay for provisions?' The billy was boiling. She waited for the tea to settle. Today no one would swirl it round their heads. All that was over. This was not a picnic. This was a life set amongst trees which blacked out the sun, amongst loneliness, amongst distrust.

'I've money of my own. Some of my gratuity left, some of Grandfather's money. Enough to keep us going until we're established.'

Deborah took out the biscuits but Patrick didn't want to stop to eat. They must build, he had said. They must have something they could call their own before darkness came and she understood and wanted to be able to touch him, to pull towards him, to be part of someone. But that was all over.

They drank tea out of the tin mugs. It was foul, brackish, but thirst overrode all this.

'Mother has really disinherited me,' Patrick said, pouring another mug of tea. He flushed and didn't look up at her. 'We . . .' he hesitated. 'We need to be careful, not overspend, but we'll be all right.'

Deborah said nothing. What was there to say? What was there to do but work? She knew that she must think only of each day if she were to get through the years ahead.

They felled one tree, throwing their axes in turn, again and again, heaving them out, then back up, down, wondering if their backs would break, cutting into one side, and then the other, choosing where it was to fall. It was at least four feet in diameter. They felt the moistness of sweat and blood on their hands, because Patrick's skin was as soft as hers from the shearing of the sheep. How could trees be so thick? How could her back ache like this and not break? How could there be so many flies? How could two people hack and saw together for so long and never speak?

The tree creaked, fell, crashed against others, then on until it lay on the forest bed. It was three o'clock. They had sawn the trunk down as low as they could, and now sawed it into lengths, levering it almost clear, heaving, sweating.

'Once more,' Patrick groaned, jamming in his crowbar, watching as Deborah took purchase on hers. The last section moved clear. They cut saplings down and now they dug the holes, fixing the saplings as uprights.

'Boil the billy,' Patrick said, his voice hoarse.

There was no water. She followed the blazed trail, her skirt catching, tearing on the scrub, the zamias. It was only about one hundred feet from the clearing. She stooped, filled the bucket, drenched her face, her neck, her arms. Her sleeves were torn, her skin black from the dirt of the forest. She washed, again and again trying to cleanse this forest, this world, from her body but beneath the dirt were the scratches, weals, bites she could not remove.

They drank brackish tea again and it was four o'clock.

They nailed the four by two timbers to the uprights, driving the nails in with the backs of the axes, banging their thumbs, not cursing, not saying anything. They were too tired to speak. Too tired even to draw deep breaths.

They nailed the corrugated iron round the sides, then put the rafters in place and nailed them too. Her shoulders were rigid with pain, her back too. Her hair hung in strands across her face, flies settled on her cheeks, her lips, on her back where her blouse had torn. They had settled too on Patrick, on his chest which once had lain on hers. She saw the muscles tense beneath his nipples as he lifted the other end of the corrugated iron roof panel but it meant nothing to her.

Love did not exist. This was what he wanted her for, and only this.

They had left out a panel for the doorway. They had cut a short panel for a window, leaving an opening of two feet square.

'When you want it closed just put that sheet of tin up against it,' Patrick said. 'But prop it with a sapling. You can cut it, Deb.'

She made a door by hanging a blanket from nails. She

made loops out of string which was bloodied by her hands, the blanket too.

She fetched another pair of gloves from the case, put them on over her swollen hands, feeling the pain as they rubbed against her burst blisters, the scratches, the cuts.

It was six o'clock. The light would go very soon. It would go suddenly, silently. She picked up a shovel as Patrick had done, clasping it, not showing her pain. They banked soil around the bottom of the corrugated iron.

'Let's eat,' Patrick said, his voice a tired monotone.

She was beyond words. She went to the Coolgardie safe she had set up earlier and felt the hessian sides. It was dry. She checked the tin on the top in which more hessian lay, draping itself down the sides. It was empty. She hadn't filled it with water. Oh God, there would have been no evaporation to keep the meat cool.

'It's dry,' she shouted. 'It's dry.'

She heard him come. The door was not shut properly either. She reached for the meat. Brought it out. It was black and writhing. It was as black as the descent in the plunging car on the Big Dipper had been and she threw it from her, hearing the rushing in her ears, hearing the screams of those all around her, feeling Edward's arms, but they weren't Edward's they were Patrick's and neither of them loved her.

She pushed him away, her mouth open, struggling as he held her shoulders, screaming again as she saw the maggots which clung to her gloves. She tore at them, pulling them off, seeing her own blood, hearing her screams and still he held her, led her to the cabin trunk, sat her down, gave her brackish tea.

'We'll get some more, Deb. We'll have cheese tonight and tins tomorrow. We'll get some more. It will be all right.'

They ate the cheese and the bread which had hardened. They wrapped themselves in sheets and lay on the floor but hardly slept because of the fleas which bred in the soil, and the mosquitoes, and the heat.

192

Deborah listened to the mopoke, to the echoes of her screams and tears, and then to the silence. It will be all right, he had said. We'll get some more, but it had been life itself which had made her scream, and she must never do that again. She had come through today. There was only tomorrow now. One day at a time. Just one day at a time. She had been brought here to do a job. So she would do it.

The next day, their eyes were stuck together. 'Bung eyes,' Patrick said. 'The flies.'

She stretched her eyelids, pulled them open. Her eyes were bloodshot, swollen, full of pus. She unpacked the eye ointment, searching, scrabbling until she found it. She bathed her eyes with boiled water, passed fresh swabs to Patrick. She put ointment on her eyes, passed it to Patrick.

She found the citronella oil and the castor oil, put castor oil around her eyes. It smelt. She gave it to Patrick. She put the citronella on, gave that to Patrick. Did they do this in Somerset, she wanted to ask him, but said instead, 'Every morning we put this on, every evening too.' Her voice was cold, crisp.

She took out the Lysol, diluted it in boiled water, dabbed her own and Patrick's cuts, scratches, blisters, ignoring the stinging. She brought water up from the creek for the Coolgardie. Put in the cheese, sweating and hardening as it was.

She brought more water up, feeling the pain of the handle against her wounds, boiling it on the billy. And when Patrick said that he was clearing a fire break she told him he wasn't. Not now, not yet. No more tears she had said to herself last night, and she knew she would cry no more but she wouldn't sleep on the floor like an animal either. If they had to live here, then they would make a home. They would not wait ten years just to have lines deep to their mouths. As a start they would not spend one more night on the floor.

'You build a lean-to on the side of the humpy, slab it around with bush timber. I'll fill the cracks with mud. Then set up the stove in it. I want a partition in the humpy between the kitchen and the bedroom. Make it out of saplings and blankets, whatever you like. But make it. We are not animals. We need food, we need rest.'

Patrick stood with his axe in his hand. 'Just who the hell do you think you're talking to? We need a fire break.'

'I'm talking to a man who married me for the use I would be to him. Use me then. The war might have taught you to live in a hole in Gallipoli, but that's not how you will turn this into a farm. You are less likely to have a fire if we cook on a stove. If we're comfortable we'll work better, and in any case this is not how I chose to live each day. If you don't do this, I shall not help you.'

She turned back to the provisions. He would do it. He had no option, as she in her turn had had no option. There was no anger inside her. There was nothing.

She made a meat safe from a deal kerosene box, storing the two tins of fuel outside the humpy. She nailed legs on to the case, and ripped the skirt off one of her muslin dresses, nailing it to the top and hooking it over nails either side. She stood the legs in tins of water to prevent the ants from getting in. They had already coated a bag of sugar with their busy bodies. A mouse had chewed a hole in the flour.

She collected all the spare flat timbers she could find, then knocked apart two packing cases. She mixed Lysol with water from the creek. It smelt too brackish. She collected more from the creek, boiled it, mixed it with Lysol. That was better. She soaked the earth floor in the humpy. She mixed up more, went backwards and forwards to the creek all morning, boiling it up, hearing Patrick banging, sawing. She then dragged in the planks, the pieces of packing case and soaked them too.

She helped Patrick carry the Metters stove into the lean-to through the humpy. He helped her carry the meat safe to the makeshift verandah where the breeze was strongest, and the Coolgardie too. She checked that there was still water in the tin above the Coolgardie, that the hessian was still damp.

She mixed up mud and filled the gaps between the stove

lean-to while Patrick set up a cupboard and then a curtain across the corner for their clothes. She collected dry firewood, lighting the stove as darkness came down, suddenly as it always did. She heated tinned stew by the light of the hurricane lamp, feeling the heat of the stove washing over and around her, beating down off the inside of the corrugated iron roof and walls. Her body was covered in sweat. She knew that she smelt but what he wanted was a workhorse, not a flower garden.

They ate outside, without the hurricane lamp so that the mosquitoes could not find them quite so easily, but the flies still crawled all over the food. She covered her fork with her hand, rushing it to her mouth. They didn't speak. Her hands and back hurt more than yesterday though she would not have thought that possible. Did Patrick's? She didn't ask.

'The flies were like this in Gallipolli.'

'Geoff died in his war. You have your challenge, you have your partner. What are a few flies, Patrick?'

She looked at her swollen hands, not at him. He mustn't see her anger. He might think he owned her body, but he owned none of her emotions.

She took the shovel and dug herself a latrine, as she had done last night, but this time she took the hurricane lamp because not even the moon penetrated here.

She washed behind the humpy in water she had brought up from the creek and boiled up on the stove in an empty kerosene tin that Mr Martins had given them. She had cut the top off and knocked the edges down as the day was ending. Patrick had run through a piece of No. 8 wire for a handle. It had cut into her raw palms when she took it from him and their eyes had met, but she had said nothing and neither had Patrick.

The water was warm. She soaped her body while Patrick washed in the creek. She poured cupfuls of water over her hair, her face, her body. She dried herself with a thick towel. She put on a clean nightdress, but didn't tip the remains of the water away. Nothing must be wasted, she was learning that much. Tomorrow she must wash their clothes. That was as far ahead as she would think.

She put on her shoes to walk back into the humpy. There were some fleas, but not nearly as many. She had guessed correctly then and must order more Lysol. Patrick had placed the two stretcher beds close together. She pulled hers away, over to the other wall, and anger was there again. She eased herself on to the chaff mattress. One day perhaps her back would stop aching, her shoulders, her neck, her feet. One day perhaps her hands would stop bleeding. One day perhaps she would feel something other than anger – but no, because then the pain would begin again.

As he left the creek Patrick took the hurricane lamp and followed the blaze to the humpy. She had been right. A home was necessary. The comfort of a warm body in bed was necessary. They weren't animals. He lifted the lamp and saw that Deborah had pulled the bed across to the other side of the space. She lay with her back to him, prone, still and that night, tired as he was, he couldn't sleep.

CHAPTER 12

The next day she bathed her eyes, eased her lids, put more ointment on, then waited for Patrick to do the same. She cooked porridge for breakfast but there would be no cigarette ash in it. Was there in Edward's, or was he in his own house now?

She collected chips for kindling from the bush, and Patrick sawed up fallen trees, brought them to the stump of the tree they had felled when they arrived. She chopped the logs for the stove, bringing up the axe, dropping it down until her head ached with the jarring, until her hands were bleeding again.

She watched as Patrick hauled in more firewood and told her they needed a horse to pull the felled trees into piles for burning or fence posts. It would be just too much for the two of them. They needed a house cow too.

'We have no pasture. We can't get a cow yet,' she said.
'Clear a horse yard. Hire a Clydesdale from Mr Martins one day a week. I'll bring it back when I go down for stores. Keep it overnight in the yard, but we must organise it so that the trees we are working on are felled by then. Return it at the end of the next day. That way you need only get in feed for twenty-four hours a week. They'll be glad of the money and you won't be paying out capital.'

She chopped, bringing the axe up and down, up and down.

Patrick nodded. 'Yes. You're wise, Deborah Prover.'

Deborah looked up. She thought of herself as Deborah Morgan now.

Patrick continued, 'Must get as much done as possible as soon as possible. Get pasture sown as soon as we can for the cattle. Must get into production. We must work, Deborah.'

'I am working, Patrick.' She brought up the axe again and again and didn't look at him as he walked away.

She carried the wood to the verandah, stacking it, hearing his axe on the trees, put some in the stove. She cut herself a switch from a sapling and swatted and flicked at the flies as she walked down to the creek, carrying two buckets in one hand. She filled them, carried them back. They cut into her raw hands. She poured the water into the kerosene tin on the stove.

She returned to the creek but this time took an axe. She felled a sapling, cut it to a length wider than her shoulders, filled the buckets again, and put them on either end of the sapling which she put across her shoulders. It dug deep into her flesh. She returned to the humpy and took her blue taffeta dress from the trunk, cut it, folded it until it was ten layers thick, sewed it, draped it across her shoulders.

She returned to the creek, refilled the buckets, and put the sapling on her now padded shoulders. That was better. She eased her way back, winding around trees, careful not to jar the sapling on any of the trees, on any of the black boys, steadying the buckets with her hands, but it was the taffeta which was torn by the end of the morning, not her skin.

She looked at it as she boiled the water. She was glad it was in rags. She was glad it was no longer recognisable as the dress in which she had danced with Patrick. She took up the switch again as the water heated and the steam rose into her face. She ignored the fleas which were on her legs, her skirt. But not so many now. Thank God, not so many.

She flaked some of the soap from the bar into the tin, carefully with a knife. She mustn't think of the Blue Mountains, of the love she once thought she had found. She took the washing down to the creek, dipped it, rubbed it with the cake of soap. There were the dresses from the voyage, from yesterday, Patrick's shirts, trousers, their underwear. She rubbed until

198

her fingers were sore, until the Blue Mountains had gone from her mind.

The mosquitoes were in her hair, the flies too. There were ants on the ground, over her feet. They stung her legs and knees as she knelt. She moved. That was better.

The wet washing was heavy. She twisted it, watching the water drip into the creek, the bank, on to her boots, her skirt. She dropped each garment into the tin, her fingers red. The clothes were spotted with blood. It would boil and go. Are you watching this, Father, Mother? The anger flared in her again and then went. She was just cold inside. Just think of today. Anger is tiring. You cannot be tired. Not here.

She carried the kerosene tin on her hip to the humpy, the rolled edge digging into her fingers. She tipped half into the boiling water. There was no stick to prod the clothes with. She used a wooden spoon from their cutlery box. She stirred, poked. The flies and the heat were thick about her.

She heaved the clothes out into the galvanised bath tub that they had brought with them.

'I bathed you in one like this, Mother, do you remember?' she said. 'I said I would never talk to myself again, Mother. Am I going mad?'

She rubbed the clothes on the washboard. The flea marks wouldn't come out. She rubbed them again. They were still there. She pushed them back into the water, put more wood in the stove, boiled and boiled and at last they were out. She left their work clothes until last.

'We never had fleas though, did we, Mother. We never had flies that crawled in our mouths, up our nostrils.' No, she wasn't mad. Just alone in the silence.

Patrick had strung up a line between two trees. She hung the clothes out. The flies covered them. White became black. Deborah took her switch, flicking at them, at the dresses, making them dirty again and the fleas were on her bloody legs again. Oh God. In Somerset there had been no fleas. She put her hand to her mouth and bit hard. No. No tears. She had said no tears.

She boiled the billy and made tea for them both. It tasted foul. She cooked tinned meat, called Patrick. They ate, brushing the flies from their food, brushing them from their nostrils. You see what I mean, Mother? Father?

'I shall make sandwiches tomorrow. We will only eat meat in the evening,' she said, rising, not looking at the washing which was dirt-smeared, fly-covered. The aluminium plate she carried was humming and crawling with flies. She used freshly boiling water to sluice the plates to guard against enteritis.

On her return she passed the remains of the washday rinsing water which was still in the galvanised bath in the shade of the humpy, waiting for the flea-marked sheets that would be soaked tomorrow night. 'I shall use the water as best I can because my shoulders ache from carrying it,' she said to herself.

'I shall grow pumpkins and pie melons as Mrs Martins does. I shall save the water for them and make jam which has no soot in it.' But no, she mustn't think that far ahead. She mustn't let herself think that there was more than today, more than just tomorrow here in this land with its trees, its flies, its hardship.

She helped Patrick begin the well that afternoon. Digging deep, wedging the split bush timber that he had prepared down the sides.

'It will take days,' Patrick said as she pulled up another bucket of soil.

'We have years,' she replied and looked up at the sky but there was only a canopy of silence above her, only the branches and leaves of the trees that crowded around them.

She ironed the next day. She placed the two black flat irons on the stove she had relit, stoked up, cut more logs for. She wouldn't think of the irons she had left behind in Somerset thinking she would never need such things again. She mustn't think of it ever.

She waited for the irons to heat. The smell of Lysol was thick. She had swabbed the floor again and again until there were fewer fleas, though she could still feel them on her legs, see them on her skirt. But they were fewer. She was sure they were fewer. She flicked at the flies. Were they fewer too? Please God, make them fewer.

The irons were hot. She picked one up, using the sleeve from her taffeta dress as a pad. She wiped it clean, ironed her dresses. Sweat dripped down her arm, down her face and smeared a muslin skirt. She changed irons, wiped the new one, ironed again. Again there were smears, marks. The air was hot. It was too damn hot. She had washed, boiled, scrubbed, made them dirty again and now they were marked even more. And she wept because there was no one who would notice here. But she had said she would never cry again.

She threw in more logs. She drank boiled water which was warm. She ironed all morning, while Patrick cleared, hacked, chopped and sawed more huge trees. She must make bread because theirs was too hard to eat so she boiled up potatoes and added their water to the sugar and flour while it was still warm then poured it in the beer bottle. God, it was so hot.

She heaved out the flour. The mice had chewed another hole. Of course they had. That's what mice did. She put down three more traps, threw out the corpses of the four that had been caught, far, far out into the bush, but she could still feel their tails in her hands and she washed them again and again. She heaped in the flour, the yeast, mixed, kneaded, left it to rise.

For the next two hours she hauled up buckets of earth for Patrick. He had dug ten feet and still no water. His face was black from the earth, his beard stubbly. His eyes were as red as hers were, tiredness was in every line of his face, every movement of his body. It was in hers too.

She boiled tea, gave him ginger biscuits. Was Edward teaching in a nice clean classroom? Was Mrs Prover playing bridge? Was Nell missing her? Was tiredness like this something you grew used to, or did you just die?

She couldn't eat. She wanted only to drink, but not this tea, not this brackish, foul tea. She tipped it away, watching it soak into the undergrowth, smelling the smoke from Patrick's cigarette. At least that kept the flies away for a moment.

He returned to the well, and she kneaded the bread again. Covered it, left it. She hauled up more buckets but then he hit a layer of clay and she watched as he stood with his head in his hands.

'Bloody bastard thing,' he groaned.

Perhaps they would leave, she thought, if he thinks we will have to drink foul creek tea for ever. Perhaps it would end now, and for a moment it seemed as though the sun had come through the crowns of the trees that surrounded them, curled in on them, towered over them, blotted out the sun, blotted out all sound.

But it didn't. He hauled himself out, walked down to the creek, washed his face, his hands and returned.

'I'll try a few yards further back,' he said and Deborah stumbled back, kneaded the bread again, put it into tins, waited in the heat of the humpy while they cooked because in here the sweat rolled down her face. In here she could pretend there were no tears, because she had promised herself she would not cry again.

That evening, in the barely fading heat, Patrick sat on his bed and began to make a chair out of a packing case. Deborah wrote to Nell and told her that they were in a place like Somerset, that they were farming, that they had nice neighbours, that she was happy. She would write again, she said, and knew that Nell must never know the truth.

She told Patrick she would call this place Stoke Farm and he nodded, banging in a nail with the axe head.

'Take the letter to the Martins the day after tomorrow, Deb. The mail man will call then. We'll get on with clearing the horse yard in the morning. You'll have to walk but that's easier work than clearing while I go. When you get back, ring-bark the trees I'll point out in the morning, all right? We can't clear them all right away. We'll just fell the most urgent, leave the rest to die.'

She washed, cleaned her teeth, wiped kerosene on her legs

to repel the fleas. It might work. It did. They were not clinging to her legs as much as usual as she walked across to her bed. He was watching her. She knew he was but all she could do was brush the fleas off and slide quickly between the sheets, her face to the wall. He would have use of her body for the farm, not for himself. She wanted no more lies, no more false love. It was better to be alone.

The next morning she walked to Mrs Martins' house, through the bush, around the great trees, carrying a basket, a billy, watching for the blazes, watching for unusual trees in case she should get lost, hacking at the undergrowth which had already sprung back after the cart that had taken them here. She left the small axe at the edge of the proper track and walked along the ruts, dust in her mouth and her eyes. The heat was great again but at least there was the light of the sun above her.

It took nearly two hours to reach Mrs Martins and she swished the flies off her back as she stood at the door and knocked. In the kitchen she walked on a proper floor, there were wooden walls around her. She sat on chaff cushions. She talked and smiled with Mrs Martins who nodded about the fleas and told her to put in an order for a kerosene spray and she would give it to the carrier who called tomorrow. She sprayed her now with the kerosene because there were still fleas in the ground.

The tea they drank was sweet, made of water from the tank at the side of the house. 'It's running low though, now it's the end of the summer,' Mrs Martins said.

Deborah arranged with Mr Martins to hire the horse. 'Next week,' she said.

He nodded. 'I'll come up before and fence in the yard with Patrick,' he offered.

Deborah and Mrs Martins walked to the hens, and she saw the fleas, but felt few bites. She looked at the water tank. They must have one. This rain water was pure.

'But put a tablespoon of kerosene on the top, it stops the mosquito larva,' Mrs Martins said.

203

She bought half a dozen eggs and put her hand on Mrs Martins' arm when this tired older woman sold her chops and stewing steak, because she had thought to order extra from the carrier for Deborah.

'It's here, for you to take back with you. There's milk and butter too. And these scones. Take those. They are a gift.'

Deborah left her order with Mrs Martins. She left Nell's letter and one that she had written to Mrs Prover, telling her that she was so sorry all this had happened, that her son was well. She should not withdraw her love, he loved her really, and love was too precious to dismiss.

She looked again at the water tank as she left, not wanting to go back to the darkness of her forest, not wanting to leave this woman with whom she could talk. 'Does it rain enough to fill it?' she asked, looking up at the white-blue sky.

Mrs Martins nodded. 'It rains enough, Deborah. There's been a long dry spell this year. It will rain soon, the cockatoos are flying inland. It won't really stop raining for months. It's the sound on the roof. It never made that sound back home in Scotland. It goes on too long. Too long, I tell Jack.'

The woman's voice was strained, her lips were tight, her shoulders hunched. 'Yes, it will rain soon and each year I think I can no longer stand it.'

Deborah felt the weight of the milk in the billy, the meat, the eggs, the old Bairds catalogue Mrs Martins had given her for use in the lavatory. 'Then why can't you go home to Scotland?'

'You stay when you love someone. You want what's best for them, my dear. That's why we're both here, isn't it?' Mrs Martins smiled. 'But one day I shall go home. That's what my egg money is for.'

Deborah looked up at the sky again, at the cows grazing amongst the stumps of felled and ring-barked trees.

'I'll see you next week,' was all she said.

The weight of the basket dragged at her arms, the track turned her ankles, the flies were in her face, her eyes. This afternoon she would be clearing, hacking, slashing. That is all she would think of. Not love, not the absence of love, not home, not Yeovil and the servants, not Lenora. She would think of nothing.

It took more than two hours to walk back. She was so tired. She picked up the axe at the edge of the track, it hung from her hand, dragged along the ground, caught on the suckers.

At the humpy she put the meat in the Coolgardie, it would last for two days. The evaporation kept the interior ten to fifteen degrees cooler than the outside temperature. She put the eggs in too. She would preserve three of them tonight. She ate a scone, then picked up the axe and moved past the horse-run, cutting a circle on the trees which Patrick had told her she must ring-bark, moving the axe upwards and downwards round the trunk, removing the bark and outer layer of wood, denying it nutrients from the soil, leaving the trees standing, but dying. No, she would think of nothing that was past, nothing that was in the future, she would feel nothing either, because all emotion had drowned beneath her tiredness.

She boiled the billy for tea, called Patrick, gave him Mrs Martins' scones, watched him eat and saw the white crumbs became black with moving flies once they had fallen from his mouth to the ground.

His hands were harder now, but still bleeding. Hers were too. She moved with him to the horse yard, taking the other end of the cross-cut saw, felling a tree he had scarfed that morning. She heard their breath heaving in their chests, the regular in and out of the saw. Would her back ever stop aching?

They worked until the sun went down. By tomorrow the horse yard would be clear. There would just be stumps like broken teeth. Deborah collected the sawdust from the base of the trees.

'For the hens I shall one day buy,' she said.

'Looking ahead. Good girl.'

She looked at the sawdust in the sugarbag. Yes, she must live from day to day and only allow herself to look ahead in this way, because, like Mrs Martins, this was her home money. But where was home? Anywhere but here, she thought.

That night Patrick watched as she heated beeswax and oil, immersing the eggs, storing them small end downwards. She knew so much. She was so strong. He was so glad she was here, so glad he was not alone and he wanted to reach out and touch her, to thank her. But he was so tired. She was so tired.

One day they would laugh again. One day they would be friends again. But this partnership was enough for now. It would build up Stoke Farm. But they must work. God, how they must work.

They did work. Deborah's hands grew hard, her blisters became calluses and Patrick's did too. Each day they grubbed out the scrub and blackboys with mattocks until their backs could take no more. They felled green jarrahs for fencing posts, but they ring-barked most of the trees for felling and burning when the leaves fell off. Dead, quite dead. They felled saplings which thrived beneath the larger trees. They used axes, they sawed. They left stumps. They cut the green trunks into lengths on the ground.

They dug the well, deeper, deeper in the one hour of daylight after tea each day. She washed, she baked, she made cushions out of the blackboy fibre. She no longer wept. She was too tired. There was no longer any anger. There was no energy.

After a week she walked to the Martins'. It was cooler.

'It will rain soon. They're bringing out your tank from town in two days,' Mr Martins said. 'Best get it up quick.'

She drove the Clydesdale back with the provisions in the cart. She guided it from the rutted track on to the blazed trail, touching the reins, steering around trees, urging Bet on, clicking with her tongue, touching her with the whip, not believing that for almost two hours she had just sat on a cart and done nothing.

That afternoon she and Patrick used the chains to snig the trees. She urged Bet to pull them together, over to a heap. The horse heaved and sweated, Deborah encouraging her with the long reins, standing to one side, seeing the chains digging into the wood, scoring the bark, the green timber which would be dry enough to burn this time next year. But no, better not think of next year.

That evening she sprinkled borax around the humpy to keep the cockroaches at bay as Mrs Martins had suggested. She put a tablespoon of kerosene in the jam tins Mrs Martins had given her for standing the legs of the stretcher beds in. There were fewer fleas. It would all get better. At last it seemed it might get better if she only thought of one day at a time.

The next morning, Bet pulled and heaved at the trees and Deborah took over the reins as Patrick levered one trunk away from a stump with his crowbar. It rolled back, jamming his leg. A branch tore it open and there was blood from the two-inch cut. He insisted that they kept heaving and pulling and only when the trees were stacked for sawing, or burning next year, did they ease the horse back into the horse yard, remove her chains, coil them, leave them and examine Patrick's leg.

In the humpy she poured Lysol on, brushing off the flies, but it needed stitches.

'Just do it, Deb,' he said, holding his knee. 'There's cat gut in the medicine box.'

'I'll take you to the doctor.' Her hands were trembling.

'You worked in a hospital. Do it.'

But that was years ago, a lifetime ago. She had only watched.

'I only watched.'

'Do it.' Her hands were still trembling. She knelt, touched the leg, the blood was running down over her fingers and the flies were hungry for it. His leg was pale, her hands were

207

tanned, hard. His hairs were black, curling. She remembered them now, the feel of them on her own legs.

She took the scissors from the drawer, poured Lysol over them, cut the hairs back. They were matted with blood. She bathed the wound again. Just remember what they had done in the hospital she told herself, but she couldn't. Did they cut and knot, or did they just sew?

They just sewed. No they didn't. They knotted. They knotted because they pull each one out separately don't they? Oh God. I don't know. There were flies all around the wound again.

'I'll take you to the doctor,' she said again, getting up, reaching for Lysol, swabbing it, covering it with gauze against the flies. God, they hummed. Why did they hum? The streets of Melbourne hummed on a Sunday. No, concentrate. 'I'll take you to the doctor.'

He grabbed her hand. 'No Deb. There's no time. We need to get on. Be of some use, for Christ's sake. We haven't got time to mess around.'

She stood quite still, looking at his bowed head, at the hands which clenched his knee. Yes, she had forgotten how essential it was to him for her to be useful. How stupid of her to have forgotten that.

She made him drink brandy, lots of it, but still his lips grew white as she dug the needle in. Her hands were quite still, quite steady. In and out, drag the catgut through, knot it. And again. And again. Then it was done. He had groaned for the last four. She had not looked up, she had not even swatted at the flies.

Now she rose, placed gauze soaked with diluted Lysol over the wound and bound it. She turned as he pulled down his trouser leg, then walked to the door.

'Deb, where are you going?'

'To take the Clydesdale back. We have to get on.' She stepped out and then across to the yard. 'The water tank is coming tomorrow.'

She heaved the cart around, hitched up Bet and bit by bit

hauled up the chains, coiling them, not knowing where she found the strength. As she left she called through the door, 'I should lie down for a bit. If you haven't time, then keep it clean. Don't go in the well.' Her voice was dead.

Patrick wanted to call, 'Don't leave me alone. Don't leave me, Deb.' But she was going and there was an ache inside him as he watched her leave and he didn't understand himself.

He was asleep when she returned five hours later, as darkness fell. Her feet were blistered, her head ached, but Mr Martins had slaughtered a beast that had broken a leg and she had been given four cuts of meat to pickle and a barrel which Mrs Martins gave her in return for her Wedgwood teapot which she would deliver next week.

She wasn't hungry. She was too tired. She touched Patrick, he moaned. She felt his leg, it was hot, but not too hot. She let him sleep while she boiled the salt, sugar and saltpetre together. She rubbed salt into the meat. Would it taste of Lysol? What did it matter. She put it in the pot and boiled it, then left it to cool in the barrel which was outside, pouring the brine over it, covering it. Yes, it must be completely covered. Nell had always told her that. She weighted down the lid.

When would Nell receive her letter? When would she write back?

'Have I been useful enough today then, Patrick?' she said as she stumbled into bed.

They erected the water tank the next day and it grew cooler still. Mr Martins came over the next few weeks to help clear when he had some spare days. Patrick worked too. She worked. God how they worked. They hired two horses and a single furrow shave plough from Jack Martins because now they had one acre to sow – only one but it was a start. It was enough for a house cow, perhaps.

'We mustn't plough too deep. We mustn't dredge up the subsoil. It'll be sour. It's not been tilled like Somerset.' But no, she mustn't think of Somerset.

She showed Patrick how to plough, not in Tom's straight

lines, but in between the stumps of trees. The left horse, Black, was nervous. He let his side of the swingle tree slap back against the foot board of the plough as he approached each stump. Once her toes were caught and the pain made her catch her breath. She said nothing. It would only be a black nail, and what was that, out here?

The next week she showed Patrick how to harrow. She walked behind and couldn't eat that night. She was too tired. The next day she showed him how to sow, filling the kerosene tin with oats, not mixed grass and clover yet because she just felt the soil was too sour.

'We need oats to sweeten the soil first,' she said.

The rope dug into her shoulder. She tucked hessian beneath, casting the oats as she walked up and down the strips which she judged to be four paces apart.

'I think we should have burned through before ploughing. It might need potash,' she said when she had finished.

'Don't you know? You should know, you worked on a farm.' He stood with his hands in his pockets and his eyes were narrowed, his lips thin.

She turned and walked away. No, she didn't know. She had worked in the dairy, she had helped Nell. She was a doctor's daughter not a farm hand but she was too tired to be angry. She would find out. That's all she could do. She would burn a patch and find out but a week later the rains came and it was too late. It would have to wait for the spring.

It was not English rain, but the rain of a large, frightening country. It was rain that dropped in torrential downpours. It was rain that hammered on the corrugated iron roof all night. It was rain that deluged their oilskins all day. It was rain that turned the ground into a sodden morass.

'Like the Somme,' Patrick said as she removed the stitches from his leg but she didn't want to hear about the war. It was April. There should be cuckoos, there should be daffodils.

They built an outhouse for the lavatory using saplings as a frame, and her old dresses, sown together as roof and panels.

She scattered ash in the dry hole each day because nausea was with her each day, as well as fatigue, and she knew that her illness must be fly-carried, though the flies were so much fewer with the ending of summer.

Water ran off the roof, through the pipe, into the tank. It was clear, pure and the tea tasted of tea, but still there was this sickness and as she dragged water up from the creek for the weekly wash she wondered if it was the water which had made her ill, not the flies.

'The well can't be dug in this, but the land can still be worked and we need all the acres cleared,' Patrick shouted as he shrugged on his oilskins.

'But there are too many, for God's sake. There are much too many,' she whispered, knowing that her words would be swallowed up by the sound of the rain.

'We need to work, work, work,' Patrick shouted as he went ahead with the mattock, beckoning her on.

'But I am working, Patrick,' she shouted back and vomited as she cleared more suckers.

She stabbed the zamia palms because Jack Martins said that they would give the cattle rickets. She held the crowbar high in the air and stabbed them through the centre. She poured kerosene in the hole in the centre, and it ran down to the root system and killed the plant.

She wanted something to travel to the centre of her body and kill the bacteria which made her so ill.

She barely ate, she dragged herself from bed each morning too early, pulling the sugar bag which hung by the door over her head, running across to the outhouse, through mud, through pools. She caught a chill and had to drag herself out several times at night, out into the darkness, stumbling, running to the outhouse, the water beating through the sugar bag, through the oilskin she had failed to do up. And still she worked.

Still she walked to the Martins' each week and brought the horse back, grinding through the mud, urging Bet on, stumbling, walking on her return.

They talked little now – they were too tired – and the wind and rain were too great, the cold too.

'There are no flies though,' Patrick said quietly, as he took her arm, looked into her face. 'There are no flies, Deb.'

'Yes. No mosquitoes. Is this like the Somme? It isn't like Somerset.' She turned from him, hauling the washing to the lines. Though there was no rain today it would not dry in the damp which pervaded the air, their bodies, the humpy.

'You're too tired, Deborah. Wrap up, get rid of this bug.'

'It won't stop me working,' she said. 'Don't worry, Patrick. Your paddocks will be cleared.'

She walked to the Martins' the following week, one foot in front of the other, hearing the mud squelch, feeling it pull at her boot, tasting the vomit in her mouth before it came, bending over at the side of the road, waiting for it all to finish.

She took the cart into the doctor's because Mrs Martins insisted.

'But Patrick needs Bet,' Deborah protested, as Anne Martins pulled her up on to the cart.

'He will have her, but later, tomorrow. Jack will ride over and tell him you'll be back tomorrow. It won't hurt if he clears a few fewer trees this week, will it?'

It was four miles into town. The rain slowed, stopped. There was still mud but now there was silence too and Deborah slept, her head on her neighbour's shoulder, and felt the warmth of another person's kindness.

The doctor sat at the side of the examination couch, his hand on hers, his old face kind, his stethoscope around his neck.

'You are pregnant. You realise that, don't you? You aren't ill, you are just far too tired.'

The words just lay there, on her mind. She said nothing.

'I said, you are pregnant. How will you manage? Have you a house yet? A humpy even?'

She nodded. Her head was almost too heavy. 'Yes, I have

212

a humpy,' she whispered. I have a humpy with an earth floor and fleas and a creek to wash in.

'You have a husband who will be happy?'

She nodded. Her head was still so heavy. 'I have a husband. I don't know if he will be happy.'

The doctor left her then, patting her hand. She lay there, looking round the whitewashed room, looking out at the darkening sky, the street. There was a house opposite and one next door. This doctor had a neighbour. He had several neighbours. She had forgotten there were such things as neighbours, streets. She had forgotten that March became April and April became May, as it now was. She had forgotten about periods. No. She had not realised that she was pregnant.

She travelled back with Anne. She slept in the room that she and Patrick had stayed in. She didn't sleep. She lay looking at the unlined walls, the luxury of wood. She lay listening to the rain on the iron roof. She remembered Edward's body, his hands, and rolled over on to her side and wept, because this was Edward's child. She had had her last period before the dance.

She left early the next morning, slapping the reins, pushing the horse on through the mud, hanging on to the side with her hand as the cart lurched. Late November the doctor had said. See me before then. Come to hospital in good time. Don't work too hard. Your husband will understand.

The rain was pouring down the front and back of her hat and she had trees to ring-bark today. No, her husband would not understand. She had the bread to bake. But no, she had bought some in town.

She had the washing to do. She had to haul water from the creek, she had to boil their clothes, scrub them, wring them. No, he would not understand.

She had all this mud to remove. She looked at her skirt, at the mud which clung to the wheels, spattered the horse. Tomorrow she had to walk back through this.

She touched her belly. She looked at the dripping trees, so dark, so threatening. No baby could come here. This was like the Somme. This was not a place to live in, this was a place to endure.

She drove down the trail to the humpy but wanted to turn, drive the horse hard, away from here. Away from Patrick who would soon hear her tell him that this baby was not his. No, doctor, he will not understand.

Now she thought of the plans she must make, because she would have to leave here, but where could she go? There was nowhere. Edward would not want the child, she was alone. She let the reins hang slack as Bet plodded on to the horse-yard.

She unharnessed the horse, changed into work clothes, looked at the burnt porridge pan on the stove, lifted it, put it in to soak. She brought the washing in from the verandah, hung it near the stove. It was so heavy. She was so tired. She must tell him. She had to tell him. But she was so tired.

She picked up the mattock, shouted to Patrick, led the horse out, hearing the chains dragging behind, feeling the rain on her oilskins, on her hands, seeing it drip down the axe handle, on to the head, on to the ground.

He was scarfing, water running off his hat. He stood.

'Doc fixed you up did he, stopped the sickness?'

Bet was jerking her head. Patrick took the halter, held it.

'I'm pregnant,' she said, looking into his eyes. 'But Patrick, it's not –'

'Jesus,' he cut in. 'Oh my God.' His eyes were dark, his lips thinned.

'It's not y –'

'Not now, for God's sake. Not now. We don't want a baby now.' There was fury in his face. He threw his axe hard into the ground. She felt the tremor of the earth beneath her feet. Bet jerked her ears back. He looked away, then back at her. 'It was that bushfire. It was after that.' He put his hand to his eyes.

'Patrick, listen. It's not –'

'What are we going to do? There's so much work to be done. There's so much to do, for God's sake. I can't carry a

214

passenger. I need a partner. I need someone I can rely on, for God's sake. I need you to work, not breed. Oh for God's sake, you stupid woman.' His voice was high pitched.

She looked at him, at his eyes which were darting from her to the humpy, to the trees which still surrounded them, the dense, dark trees, then back at her husband whom she had once loved. She dropped the mattock. It fell against her legs. Her hands hung loose.

'There are so many trees to cut down, Patrick. We should not be standing here, we should be working. You will notice no difference. You will still have your challenge.'

She gripped the mattock again, heaved it up.

'Snig the trees, then call me,' she said walking towards the undergrowth, grubbing, slashing, dragging, not thinking of the truth that had been left unsaid, because so many lies had already been told by Patrick, what was another from her? And what did it matter who the father was? Had it been Patrick's he would still not have wanted it.

She would just think of today, and then tomorrow, because nothing else was real, only the egg money, only the vomiting, only the tiredness, the work. Nothing else.

CHAPTER 13

May was followed by June, then July. They cleared in the rain and cold, they ring-barked, they felled in sodden ground. She told Patrick to grub around the roots of the saplings, expose, then cut them, levering them out from the ground as she had seen Tom do in Somerset, and as Jack Martins had also suggested. It left fewer stumps to weave the plough around, or drag out of the ground at a later date. They would burn the large stumps by heaping felled trees around them and setting fire to them all. Either that, or leave them to rot where they stood because they had no tree puller.

'You see, I'm learning how to farm this land. I'm earning my keep. Our keep,' she told herself as she dragged her mattock behind her. She placed her hand on her belly. The baby was moving now. It was there inside her, but she was too tired to feel anything.

She dragged kerosene cans of water from the creek which was swollen with winter rain and which gushed and roared and pulled hard at the can. She dug her feet in, gripping the bank with her hand, feeling the mud ooze, hauling the water out, dragging it up, stumbling back to the humpy, boiling, washing, ironing.

In a dry spell she ploughed, jerking at the right-hand horse with her whip, but the ground was so sodden. For God's sake, it was too wet. How could you plough mud? But Patrick had said to do so and so she did. She slapped the reins on Bet and Black's hindquarters.

'You're lazy, so damn lazy,' she screamed at Black as he

fell behind and the board slapped into her toe again. The nail was already black, it already hurt, what was a little more? And at last as night fell, the paddock was ploughed.

'I told you you would manage it all right,' Patrick said before he slept that night and she wanted to beat her hands on his face and show him her throbbing foot.

On Tuesday she walked behind the harrow as Patrick scarfed and felled further out. She would sow for late summer oats. The first paddock was showing green, slowly growing, and she spread super to feed the new growth and still she couldn't believe that one day this land which looked like the Somme would bloom.

Would plovers come when meadows covered this earth? Would meadows ever cover anything? Would cows ever graze here? Don't think of the months, the years. Just the days. Just this harrow which is making my legs ache, my back ache. Which turns and twists my body. My body which isn't my own. My body which belongs to Patrick, and to this baby. But they never talked about the baby.

There were boils on her neck, under her arms. Patrick had them too.

'But you have no boils, do you, baby? At least you are not out here, working. Always working.' She could see her breath. It was cold and damp, so damp, and she stopped and touched her belly with surprise. She was not talking to herself any more, was she?

On 28 July there was a letter from Nell, waiting for her as she returned the horse to Mrs Martins. It had been written in the spring, the English spring, and reminded Deborah of violets, of daffodils. It talked of Susie's baby, now sitting, laughing, smiling. It talked of the market, the cheeses.

> You'll be making cheeses soon, my dear. Will you take them to market? Will you make cider? Will you send jam to Mrs Prover? Has she written yet?
>
> The village always ask after you. Mrs Briggs misses you so much. The road mender is here again.

Your cockerel is still alive, though Tom threatens him daily. I'm so glad you are well and happy.

All my love
Nell

She read it as Mrs Martins made tea. She traced her fingers over the script, so round, so large, so generous, and she wept. Would the village ask after her if they knew that this baby was not her husband's, that she was living a lie as Patrick had done, that she had not told him? That he never spoke of it and neither did she? No, they wouldn't speak kindly of her, would they.

She looked out of the window at the sodden ground, the pines planted around the outsheds. There were no honey-stoned cottages here, no roses, no honeysuckle. No orchards out there.

She felt Anne's arms around her now, heard the soothing of her voice.

'Now, now, my dear. You are too tired. You do too much. Why is he in such a hurry? But then they all are. They know they must hurry if they are to survive. They don't notice we get tired. They don't notice that we are dying quietly.'

Deborah said nothing, just laid her head against this tired woman's shoulder and heard the clock ticking the minutes away.

'Just think, it's not raining, my dear. At least it's not raining. Not drumming on the roof. You must rest. We all get tired. So very tired.'

Deborah walked home. It was not raining but she could hear the water dripping from the trees. Anne had told her she should rest. How could she rest? Anne had told her that her own babies had all miscarried. Perhaps it would be better if this one did? She looked into the darkness of the forest. How could a child live here? How could a child bear the loneliness, the isolation, the silence? How could she not tell Patrick?

She thought of Anne's face as she had heard the rain begin

again just before Deborah left. Her voice which became thin and high.

'Your wife is too tired. She is too strained. The noise of the rain means too much to her,' she had told Jack when she had sought him out, feeling her oilskins flapping against her legs, shouting against the rain and the wind.

He hadn't listened. He had just shrugged. 'It rains. I can't stop it,' he had said. 'One day she'll get used to it. She gets like this. Don't take any notice. The summer comes.'

The boils were rubbing now on her neck as she followed the trail through the trees. She could hear the sound of the axe out across the second home paddock. She boiled up tea, sat down, read Nell's letter again, placed it to her lips, kissed it.

'I miss her so much. Will you ever see her?' She patted her belly. 'Will you ever see the real Somerset?'

No, Nell, we haven't heard from Mrs Prover, though Patrick wrote in an effort to repair the estrangement and also to tell her about the baby. But there was no energy to think of that woman, dressed in black.

She thought instead of the farm, of the cottage. She thought of Anne. It was the end of a long winter, Jack had said. It would be all right. He must know. The boil under her arm was hurting. She took the billy out to Patrick, left it with him, took her mattock and began work. It was still raining. But soon it would be summer. She had told Anne that, but she was too tired to think of the thin, strained woman any more as she dug around the roots of the saplings, too tired to think of the words she should find to tell Patrick that he was not the father of her child.

That evening she dug a patch at the side of the humpy in the light of a hurricane lamp. At dawn she carted horse manure from the horse run, piling it up. Each evening she worked long after Patrick had finished splitting fence posts or planning the next area for clearing.

'I'm digging this for vegetables,' she said when Patrick told her to come in, to sleep, for God's sake. 'We need vegetables. To stop the boils. I shall plant an orchard too. This is like

219

Somerset, you said. Then we shall have fruit. Fresh fruit. Plums, apples, nectarines and no more boils.'

She didn't add that she would make it into jam too, and sell it, because she knew now that she couldn't tell him the truth about the child, but she had decided that he must not support it.

He stood in the doorway. 'Deborah, it's late. You'll be tired tomorrow.'

She looked up: was there kindness in his voice? Was there caring? Why did her tears come so easily now? She looked down at her boots where mud clung. They were heavy. She lifted her foot to the shovel, pushing down, turning, then digging in the manure.

'I said you'll be tired. We're fencing tomorrow. I need you fresh.'

She lifted her boot to the shovel again. No, there had been no kindness. 'I shall be ready for the fencing, Patrick. I shall be fresh.' But neither of them was fresh or had been fresh for months.

She heard him turn away. The vegetable garden was almost dug. Tomorrow she would put ash from the stove on half, leave half free. She wanted to see if the ground needed potash. She thought it did. If so, they should burn off the oats when they had been harvested, and only then sow the pasture. She dug again, the baby moved. Her shoulders ached. 'I'll plant an orchard, Nell. I'll plant vegetables. I'll make Somerset here. I'll make jam too. I'll sell it. I'll pay for my baby. I must.'

She finished that night at eleven. Patrick was asleep. She washed her hands in the kerosene tin outside the door, wiped them on the towel she had made out of a flour bag edged with strips of an evening dress she would never need again. Her boil poultices needed changing. She was too tired. She turned, looking at the ground she had dug. One day it would bloom. She stared out at what Patrick called bush and which she called forest.

'Yes, I'll make it bloom. You just see.' She thought she

saw a movement, out there between the trees, a shape. She looked. It was gone. It was nothing.

She wrote to Nell, telling her that she had a friend, a neighbour. She did not tell her that the neighbour was more than two miles away. She told her that she was imagining shapes in the woods but that she had heard pregnant women were fanciful. She told her that Stoke Farm would soon grow fruit and vegetables. That she would make pie melon and ginger jam. She would order a lemon from the store, and mix that in too.

She told her that she loved her. That one day perhaps Susie's baby would meet hers, and then she doused the lamp and fell asleep within seconds.

The next day she fenced with Patrick. They had already cleared the line of fallen logs, stumps and boulders. They had already left the fence posts in piles along the line.

'It's too wet. It would be better to wait until spring, until September. The holes will be waterlogged. It will be difficult to find the depth.'

Jack had told her this when she had explained that she had to learn. 'I have to know. It is expected of me.' He had nodded. 'Farm girl, aren't you? Patrick told me.'

'But I'm not and there's so much I don't know. So much I have to learn,' she had replied and Anne had said that Patrick should be kinder, come here himself.

'No, this is my job. It's only fair.' She had felt the baby kicking. Yes, it was only fair.

Patrick was digging now, slicing his spade into the ground, hitting roots. She stood as he attacked them with an axe and mattock. He dug again. Her feet were cold, her hands numb. A boil had burst under her arm. Patrick's had burst on his back.

'We're both too tired,' she said now, watching the lines deeply etched on his face. 'We're both so tired, Patrick.'

He lifted the axe, brought it down. 'We haven't time to be tired now. Not with that on the way.' He nodded at her belly. 'It will hold us up, can't you see that?' His voice was curt, he was breathing hard. 'We've got to get this cleared, get the cattle grazing, get the buttermilk to the factory. My money won't last indefinitely. Can't you see that?'

Deborah nodded. Yes, she could see that, and suddenly guilt cut through the tiredness. But no tears, she had said what seemed a lifetime ago. No more tears, but there seemed as many tears as there was rain. Anne Martins said it was part of pregnancy. Was deceit part of pregnancy too?

Patrick cut through the roots, then dug with the spade. The hole was filling with water. She found a stick, measured it against her hand, marked it at eighteen inches. Pushed it to the bottom.

'Another three inches, Patrick.' Her voice was steady. There were no tears. There would be no tears. Not in front of him.

He dug, she measured. They placed the post into the hole, tamped it down, hearing the slurp of the mud at first, then it firmed up.

'Tread on it, Deborah. You're heavier now, at least that's one good thing. I'll line up the next one.'

All day he dug, while she grubbed nearby, coming to hold the post, tamp down when he called. Then moving on. That evening, she dug her garden. She would plant two rows of pumpkins. Mrs Martins had said you could ea* them as vegetables, eat them in pies, make marmalade out of them. She would grow pie melons, tomatoes, lettuce. That night she poulticed their boils.

At dawn they rose again. Patrick dug, lined up while she grubbed, pulling the undergrowth into piles for burning. Would the pasture need potash? She would have to wait and see. She measured. She tamped.

The next day they drilled holes through the posts with brace and bit. She took over when his arms were trembling but she wasn't strong enough. 'For God's sake,' he shouted, taking the brace and bit from her. 'For God's sake.'

The next day they wired, releasing the No.8 from its coil. It sprang and lashed out them, cutting through Patrick's trousers, whipping across Deborah's hand. The cuts weren't deep, and they didn't stop to bind them because the wire had become entangled with itself. They found the end, unwound it, saying nothing, but their breath was quick in their chests.

It was attached to the strainer post, which had a strut placed against it for greater strength. Patrick played the wire out, while Deborah threaded the end through the post holes. She was too quick, tugging the coiled wire tight as Patrick unwound it.

'For God's sake,' she heard him shout.

She slowed, feeling the tension on the wire slacken. She began to walk again slowly. Her arms ached. Her back ached. She pushed it through, caught the end, took it on again. Her boots were muddy, heavy. She reached the other strainer post. Pushed it through that hole. Returned. Threaded through the lower ones, slowly, not too fast. He would shout again. She must not make him angry. She must work. She must earn her keep. They pulled the wires taut with wire strainers.

She didn't work that night on the garden. She had seen the cockies fly inland again. She cooked, she ate.

'I'll be leaving early. It's time to see the doctor again,' she told Patrick, not looking at him as she undressed, her back to him, her swollen belly hidden.

'Be back in good time. We start snigging the next paddock first thing tomorrow. Bring back the new axe and the saw. I'll be surveying the boundaries today.'

The next day, before dawn, she walked to Anne Martins and asked her to keep her company at the doctor's. It wasn't time for Deborah to see him but she knew this thin kind woman must talk to someone before the rains came again.

The doctor lanced Deborah's boils. He told her she must rest. She must eat. She had two lives to protect. Her own and her baby's. But she told him of Anne, of the rain which drummed on her roof and in her head. Of the trembling of her hands, the flickering of her eyes and he walked out into his front room where Mrs Martins waited. He sat and talked to them both about tiredness, about depression, about fear, about the need to talk, about the rain which drummed on the corrugated iron roofs and sounded louder than it really was.

Mrs Martins just nodded, touched his hand. 'It will be summer soon, then you will feel better, not hear the rain, doctor. Or so my husband says.'

Deborah would speak to Mr Martins, she told the doctor quietly as they left.

'Tell him to bring her back to see me, or to come himself. Tell him not to leave it too long,' the doctor said. 'And make sure you rest, eat.'

She bought fruit and vegetables. She bought seed too because it was no longer enough to think of today. There was this child's future to consider.

It was raining. It poured off their hats, on to the provisions. It drummed on their oilskins. It drummed on the roof of Anne's house when they returned. Deborah made her tea and they ate scones. Anne's shoulders were hunched, her face more drawn because there had been a note propped against the billy, saying that Jack had gone to Busselton to see about some weaner pigs. He would be back, but late.

'I hate the rain. It's the noise.' Her hand was shaking, trembling. 'It's the noise, Deborah. It sounds so loud when I'm alone. There was rain in Scotland, but no noise on the roof of the house, and Mother was there, and Father and the lights of the town were all around.'

Deborah stood, came round, held the woman against her, but the baby was moving and this woman had lost her own. Deborah knelt instead, and held her, head to head, stroking the hair that was so thin, so grey and coarse.

'I'm thirty-five, Deborah. I look fifty,' Mrs Martins said, sitting up, straightening her blouse. 'Will I ever go home? Will any of us ever go home?' She waved her hand around the unlined house. 'I would have travelled to the ends of the earth for him, I said. I meant it. But it's the noise, my dear.'

Deborah stayed until eight in the evening, listening to the rain, looking at the clock, waiting for Jack. They talked.

'Go home, back to your husband. Go home. Jack will be here at nine, Deborah.'

Deborah thought of the paddock to be cleared, of Patrick, so tired, so tense. Of his anger, of his need, of his money that would not last for ever, and which she had no right to. She listened to the rain on the roof. It was lighter now. It was stopping. She stayed until half past eight. Then lit the hurricane lamp and hung it on the front of the cart, turning to Anne, hugging her, putting the eggs she had been given carefully on the front seat.

'It's stopped. You'll be all right? He'll be home soon. I have to go. It's Patrick. He said we must start the paddock first thing, you see.'

Anne was smiling, looking up at the sky. 'Go now. Take care. Bless you for your kindness.'

Deborah slapped the reins on Bet's back, feeling the lurch of the cart, the sound of hoofs in the mud, the rumble of the wheels on the track. She drew away from the house, looked back. 'It will be summer soon,' she called.

Bet had gone half a mile when the rain began again but Jack would be home now. It was all right. Deborah hunched into her oilskins, pulled the hat down. The track was under water, the surface had broken at the start of the winter. The light from the lamp was sucked away. She urged Bet on. The wind was strong, getting stronger.

'Get on, Bet.'

She could see the bush at the side, the scrub protruding through the water. The trees, the darkness. The utter darkness.

'Get on, Bet,' she called above the wind, slapping the reins, pulling up the collar of her coat, feeling the trundling of the cart. Her hands were numb on the sodden reins. 'We've got the axe for him. Get on.'

The cart lurched onwards. To the ends of the earth she had said to Patrick too. To the moon, my love. She had loved him then. His arms had held her, his lips had touched hers. There had been happiness. It seemed so very long ago, all of it.

The wind was higher, it tugged at her hat, pulling the cord against her chin. The rain was harder, beating down.

'Get on, Bet.' She was cold, but the cart was stopping, the wheels were sinking down to the axles. She climbed down, got to the back, put her weight behind the wheels, hauling on the spokes, hands slipping on the mud. Shouting at Bet, 'Get on, for God's sake.'

There was a lurch and they moved again. She hurried through the water, her boots being sucked by the mud, her feet slipping. She fell, got up, gripped the bridle, pulled Bet along, seeing only as far as the beam of the lamp. This had happened before, many times before. It just took longer to get back. But today was worse. The rain was heavier, there was so much on the ground, so many months of rain on the ground.

Was it drumming on Anne's roof? Should she go back? But she couldn't turn, not now, not on this track. It would be all right. Jack would be home. She wished she was too.

She stumbled, Bet jerked her head. They were on higher ground, the track was firmer. She climbed on the cart again. The rain was so dense it was almost impossible to see the horse between the shafts. She touched her with the whip, tapping her, shouting. She was frightened.

She sang, 'Knick knack Paddywack, give a dog a bone.' The water went in her mouth.

It had gone in Patrick's mouth when he stood by the Levels. It had gone in Dave's mouth in Gallipoli. Had it gone in Geoff's when he lay in the mud and died? Was it loud on Mrs Martins' roof? Was it loud on the corrugated iron of the humpy? Did he wonder where she was? Did he worry? Was Jack really back? Should she have left? Should she try and turn? But no, she must just try and get back.

The rain was so hard, the wind so strong. So much stronger than ever before. There was lightning. It cracked across the sky, she saw the light, not the fork, the trees were too close, shutting out the sky as they always did. Bet jerked, she felt her on the reins, but she couldn't see. There was thunder, peeling, rolling. Would these trees come down? Dear God, would they come down on the track, on her?

Don't think of that, just sing. 'Knick knack Paddywack, give a dog a bone. This old man came rolling home.'

'Are you going to get me home, Bet? Are you? Are you?' She was singing, shouting, but it was lost in the wind, the rain, the flash and peel.

The horse was straining again, but the cart was slowing. Oh God, it was slowing again. She brought down the whip. Bet jerked her head, leaned into the rain. Deborah whipped again. The cart was tilting, a wheel was going down into a mud-filled rut. She knew it was, God damn it, but then they moved again, lurched up and out.

She could hear the trees now, lashing into furies. Had this world ever been silent? There was nothing here that was silent now except for her, for there were no words, no songs. The cart lurched again, down into a hole then up, and Deborah lashed Bet again.

'Keep going. For God's sake, keep going.' But the wheel caught, stopped. She lashed again. Bet strained, trying for purchase, but there was none.

Deborah lowered herself over the side, stumbling alongside the shafts. There was just the wind and the breath in her body as she took the bridle again, pulling, straining, but it was no good. The cart was stuck.

She took the hurricane lamp. It swayed in the wind. She edged her way through the water, feeling the mud beneath its surface, seeing the wheels bogged down up to their axles.

She put her weight behind, screamed at Bet, felt her try but the cart wouldn't move. She took the crowbar from beneath the seat, levered it beneath the wheel, shouted, reached forward for the whip, lashed at the horse, putting her knee on the bar, bearing down. Nothing.

She walked ahead until she reached higher ground, until she felt firm earth beneath her feet twenty yards ahead of the cart. She searched the edge of the track until she found a blackboy, tore at the dry underside of its grass crown and heaped it on the ground beneath the trees close to the track. She tried to light it but her matches went out in the wind. She tried again, and again and at last it took. She threw twigs and small branches on, as Jack had said she should if ever this happened. By the light of the blaze at the side of the track with the lamp on the cart she unloaded the stores, taking the axe, the nails, the provisions.

She carried the wire, dragging it heavy through the water. The wind was higher now, it whipped the blaze up into the air, then down again. There was no danger of a forest fire, it was too wet, all too wet. All too damn wet.

She took the vegetables, they slipped. Fell from her hands, into the water, into the mud. She pushed her hands in, searching, feeling in the slime. Her lanced boils were on fire, her back was aching, her belly, her baby. Her hands sought the fresh fruit, the fresh vegetables, found some potatoes, a pumpkin, the greens, a swede, but only one. There should be another. In this mud there was another swede. She groped. It was lost. Oh God, it was lost. She heard a noise, a wailing crying noise, and she realised it was her. She stumbled back to the cart.

The kerosene case was all that was left to move. It was just too heavy. She picked up the crowbar, levered off its top, feeling the nails give way but not hearing them in the tumult. There were branches crashing down, lightning, thunder. She took each can separately but left the box in the cart. It was empty but just too heavy to push. She must try with it on.

Again she was down in the water, near the wheel. She lashed the whip through the air, bringing it down on Bet's hindquarters, seeing her straining in the light from the lamp. She got her back to the wheel, forcing the spokes with her hands behind her back, pulling, heaving. Shouting at the horse, who struggled for purchase, found it, pressed forward, and again, and then suddenly the wheels lurched, moved forward and she ran to the front, shouting, pulling, keeping Bet going until the high ground was reached, until they were in the light thrown from the blaze of the blackboy.

She reloaded, then leant against the cart. There was so much noise, wind, rain, and darkness, such dense darkness.

She doused the blackboy blaze, slapped Bet with the reins, rode on the cart for another mile and then it bogged again. Again she tried to move it, but failed and had to stumble ahead, through the water, the mud. Again she had to unload by the light of a blackboy, and this time she didn't try to find the potatoes which fell, or the seeds which became sodden and spoilt in the mud. But this time the cart wouldn't move.

She pushed, she heaved and Bet did too but nothing moved and so she screamed at the horse, so close she could see the fear in its eyes, so close she could feel the heat from its nose but it couldn't find the purchase, it couldn't find the strength. Still the lightning was flashing across the sky, lighting up the waterlogged track, lighting up the trees which wrenched and waved in the dark air.

Deborah felt her way along the shaft in the wind-lashed rain and heaved herself up into the cart. She took the deal box and shoved it to the edge of the cart, pushing until it fell down into the whirling water, down into the water of this land which she hated, which she feared.

She eased herself down round the side, behind the wheel again.

'Get on, Bet,' she cried. 'Get on.' But the horse couldn't move the cart and now Deborah fell into the mud, into the water, which filled her mouth. She spat it out. She staggered to her feet, back down towards the horse. She laid her head against Bet's face. It was wet, her mane was wet, everything was wet.

'Never mind, Bet. Never mind.' She felt for the harness. 'Never mind, you brave old girl. I'll take you out, ride you back, get you home.' But her fingers were numb. She couldn't undo the buckles. She blew on her hands. She moved slowly, so slowly towards the blackboy's fire. She held out her hands but the rain was so heavy no warmth came to them. She undid her coat, tucking her hands against her skin, beneath her blouse, her cardigan. The wind tore her oilskins open, drenching her clothes, whipping her coat against her body, and then away again.

She left the blaze, walked back to the cart, to the small pool of light from the lamp. She tried the buckles again but her hands would do nothing she asked of them. Her legs were heavy, her head was light. She was tired, so tired, and the noise of the wind and the rain was filling her head. Is this how it was with Anne? Were these the ends of the earth? Is this where they had both promised their husband they would follow?

'I'm sorry, Bet. I'm just too tired. My boots are muddy. Father wouldn't like that.' She felt the water on her knees, on her thighs. She felt the mud on her hands as she sank down, sitting, her head against the wheel. She was just too tired. 'I'm sorry, Father, I'm just too tired.'

Patrick left the humpy, carrying a hurricane lamp. It was midnight, for God's sake. It was midnight and they had the paddock to clear in the morning.

'Where the hell are you Deborah?' His voice didn't rise above the storm. He followed the blazes in the light of the lamp. The wind would bring down trees, less for them to do.

He eased his way to the end of the trail on to the track. It was waterlogged. He fell again and again into ruts, some of them two feet deep. He had not been this way for two months. He had not known what she had to travel across.

Why hadn't she said anything? Why hadn't she complained?

'Why didn't you complain, Deb?' he shouted into the darkness, stumbling, hurrying. There was a panic in him that was growing larger, deeper. He held the lamp up, his arm was aching. What did it matter? The wind was higher, much higher, the rain was heavier, the thunder, the lightning. He was calling her now.

'Deborah. Deb. For God's sake, Deb.'

He stumbled on, the blackness absorbing his light. She was afraid of the bush, of the darkness, and she had travelled through this each week. She had never complained. She had just done it. He had let her do it. For God's sake, he had let his Deborah do it.

He saw the light of the blackboy then. He ran, lifting his legs, feeling the water dragging at him. He saw the provisions. He ran on, down the track. He saw the horse, ran to the back, saw the deal box. She wasn't here. There was just the rain in his face, his mouth. The noise of the thunder, the crack as lightning hit a tree, the vibration as it fell.

'For God's sake Deb,' he screamed. 'Where are you?'

He went towards the front of the cart and saw her by the wheel, sitting in the mud, the water tugging her oilskins and the panic he felt as he lifted her, held her to him was worse than anything he had known before.

'Oh God, Deb. Why didn't you complain?' He held her to him as he forced each leg through the water, back to the blaze of the blackboy. 'Why didn't you complain?'

He put her on the ground near the fire, rubbed her hands, blew on them. Held her to him. 'You need warmth.' He took off his coat, pulled off his jacket, tore off her oilskins, forced her arms into the armholes.

It was warm with his warmth, she thought. So warm. He held her and for a moment she lay against his shoulder and forgot that there was no love in her world. Then the baby stirred and she stiffened. There is too big a lie between us, she thought to herself. Love does not exist. Remember that. Love cannot exist. There is no room in his world for love. There can be no room in mine.

He forced the cart from the mud, and drove it up to the higher ground and as she looked in his eyes she knew she was right because there was no love in them as he helped her to the seat. There was no love in his voice when they reached the humpy and he told her to sleep. There was no feeling in his face as he eased the clothes from her body, and washed her down with hot cloths, then wrapped her in blankets, not sheets, and put bottles of hot water in her bed, close against her.

'Get better, Deborah. Just get better,' he said and left her, dropping the hessian back down, leaving her to weep out her loneliness in private.

Patrick stood under the verandah, smoking a cigarette, his hands trembling and he didn't understand himself. He could still feel her in his arms, could still feel the weight of her head on his shoulders, the swollen belly, the baby which had kicked against his hand. He could still see the body which he had washed and which he had forgotten until then. He remembered the Blue Mountains, the smell of the eucalypts and he couldn't understand the tears that were on his cheeks, and the pain which threaded into every part of his body.

The next day Jack came. He brought Anne's fowls in the back of his spring cart as Deborah and Patrick dragged the mattocks and the crowbars from the paddock. Both felt too tired to work, but both did, because they had to, and there was nothing else for them to do.

Deborah stopped and Jack dropped the fowl down on to the ground, releasing them from the kero case. They squawked, flew up, scratched, pecked. He was heaving chicken food over to the verandah.

Deborah felt a coldness begin. There was a heaviness in his movements, a rigidity in his shoulders, in the set of his head. She ran to him, shrugging off Patrick's hand on her arm.

'What is it, Jack? What's happened?' But she knew before he told them.

'She's dead. Drowned herself, last night. I only got back at midday today. She said you'd waited in her note. You're a good girl Deborah.' He paused, looked at Patrick. 'It was the rain. I didn't listen. I didn't pay enough attention.'

Deborah walked past him into the humpy, lay on her bed. Her friend had gone. Her friend had drowned. Her father had drowned. Her mother was dead. Geoff was dead. She turned on her side.

Patrick came in, put blankets over her, sat on the bed, put his hand on her arm. 'You couldn't have done any more and you were the only one who did anything. Don't cry, please don't cry.'

She couldn't stop. Where did all the tears come from? 'They've gone, all gone. All the ones I care about go.'

She wanted arms around her, she wanted love. She turned to him. Just now, just this once, Patrick, hold me, she wanted to say. I will never ask you again.

He took his hand from her arm, turned his face from her, walked to the doorway, stood looking out, lighting a cigarette, breathing in the smoke. She mustn't see his face. She mustn't see the tears. Why these tears?

She turned on her side and hugged her belly. You are all I have, she told the baby silently.

CHAPTER 14

Deborah stayed in bed and day became night, again and again. She was too tired to move, to tired to help, too tired to do anything more than breathe, anything more that listen to the rain, drink the tea which Patrick brought her, eat the fruit that he brought back from town, the cheese, the meat.

'You must get strong again,' he told her.

'I will. I promise I will,' she said, because the work was falling behind. She knew it was. His face told her it was and that was why she was here, wasn't it?

She slept and dreamt of Anne in the bush, out there in the bush wondering, calling, crying. She dreamed of shapes amongst the trees. Seeing them, not seeing them. She dreamed of arms which did not hold her, but which once had, out there in the Blue Mountains, in the hot dry plains. She dreamed of the fire by the creek, of the billy which he had swirled around his head.

She dreamed of wire which coiled, leapt, trapped her. She struggled to rise but Patrick said, 'No, I have hired some help from town. Stay here, rest.'

'Stay here too,' she whispered but he had gone. She heard him wedge the window open, but not too much. It was cold, so cold and Patrick was too. His eyes were guarded, his voice strained. She must work, but she could not. She was tired with a child that was not his and her friend was dead. Anne was out there still crying because she had wanted to go home to Scotland and now never would. It seemed as though the rain had always pounded on the roof and always would.

On the seventh day in the evening the rain stopped. There was silence. No sound of distant trees falling, no men sawing, scarfing, chopping. She put her feet to the planks. There was no smell of Lysol. She must swab again. Fleas jumped on to her legs. She dressed. There was little strength in her body, in her hands which buttoned up her blouse, which tied her skirt at the back with ribbons she had sewn on to accommodate her belly.

She moved to the doorway, pushing past the hessian. There was water on the ground, Bet was in the horse-yard, the oats were growing. There were hens pecking the ground. She had forgotten about them. She moved out into the cool damp air, looking, searching the woods for dark shapes. There were none. There were just stumps in the paddocks, and tracks on the ground where the trunks had torn up the earth when they had been snigged and heaped up. It was all still the same. It had only been a week, after all.

She bent, picked up a branch, tore off a leaf, bent it between her fingers, looked up and longed for light to blaze through, for the trees to go, but there was still this canopy above them. She felt the sweat breaking out on her body, the shadows becoming deeper.

She heard voices now, breaking into the silence, down towards the creek. She walked towards them, feeling the ground spongy beneath her feet. She saw two fires; small, glowing. She saw two men, Patrick and another. He was dark, long-limbed, squatting. He was the shape she had seen on that dark night, and Anne was out there too when the darkness came. Anne was out there and this man had taken her.

She screamed then, so loud, so long and ran from them as they came towards her. She ran through the woods, through the undergrowth and it was tugging at her clothes, trapping her, coiling around her, but her legs were weak and she could hear Patrick's voice, and the crashing as they followed. Then long dark arms caught her, held her and a face with black hair, black eyes, dark skin was close. She screamed and fought because he had taken Anne out into the bush too. Anne had drowned but she cried all night out there. Deborah had heard her above the rain.

Patrick came then. She knew his arms, his face. He took her from this dark shape, and she clung and pressed her face into the smell of his chest. 'Don't let him take me, not into those woods. Not lost like she is.'

'Come on, Deb. You're not better yet. Come on.' Patrick's voice was firm, his hands were gentle as he stroked her hair. She had stroked Anne's but she was dead now. Her only friend was dead.

'My friend is dead. I'm so alone.' She looked up at Patrick. 'I'm so alone and he has taken her.' She turned, the dark shape had gone.

Patrick's eyes were dark, blank as he heard her words. He had this pain again. It was the work, it was all falling behind. His dream was fading, becoming confused. He didn't understand anything any more. He looked out into the bush, away from this woman who felt as she had done in the Blue Mountains. He looked out at the trees he must fell, the land he must clear.

'No, we're a partnership, remember. You're not alone. Come back to the fire. There's someone else now to make it easier. I worked you too hard. It won't be the same again, Deborah. But we've got to get you fit. Get you back on your feet.' Yes, that was it. He had to get her better or they would never win. That's all he must think of, all he could understand.

She walked back behind him, still able to smell his body, still able to see the fires, the dark man who squatted beside them, but who stood when she came, silently watching. Her breath was heaving in her chest from running. His was imperceptible. He was an aboriginal.

'This is Jimmie whose tribal land is all around here. He's come back from Broome. He's the help I've hired.'

Patrick squinted across the smoke at Jimmie. 'He knows this land, grew up here. He wants to stay. He loves it.'

'You were in the woods,' she said. 'One night you were

in the woods.' The heat from the fire was on her face, her hands.

Jimmie nodded. 'Yes.' He was very still. He wore trousers, a checked shirt. His sleeves were rolled up. His arms were so long, so brown.

'Why?' She stood as still as he did, watching, waiting.

'Because all this land here is where I tracked as a boy, where I lived, where my people lived. Where my dreamtime is. They are gone away, or dead. I have returned.'

Deborah nodded. Yes, she would want to see each cottage, each field, each brook. Yes, she could understand that. But Anne had never returned to her home. Anne was still out there, in those woods where this man, Jimmie, had been.

She looked back at the humpy. 'I'm going in now.'

She picked up her skirt, torn by the undergrowth. She moved between the two fires.

'Why two fires?' She was so tired. God, she was tired.

'To keep me warm, back and front. To keep the spirits away.' He nodded. 'And to propitiate them.'

Deborah walked now, back to the humpy. She cooked potatoes, greens, bacon. She called them to eat but only Patrick came.

'Where does Jimmie eat? Where does he sleep?' she asked as she picked up the knife. It was almost too heavy.

'He catches his own food and sleeps in his humpy. He's half-aboriginal but he's chosen their ways, not ours. Strange really. Talks like us but then he's a Mission boy. Should have gone into the Church. Brought on by the priest. Something happened, don't know what. Don't know why.' He paused. 'Finish the meat, Deborah. You need it. You must get strong.' His voice was terse.

'I'll be strong. I'll work, don't worry.'

She slept that night and dreamed again and wanted to light fires all around the house to keep her friend's cries away.

She rose at dawn, as the men did. 'Are you all right?' Patrick said as she stirred the porridge.

'Yes, I'm fine.' But the wooden spoon was heavy.

She searched for eggs, hunting in the undergrowth, in the places where Jimmie had found them before. She spread corn on the ground, watched the hens peck, heard the cockerel crow. Why hadn't she heard it before? The rain had been too loud.

She dragged her mattock out to where the men were clearing. They did the scarfing, the chopping, the sawing, and she grubbed until her back ached. It was the same as it had always been, back-breaking, monotonous, but it didn't matter because perhaps at night she wouldn't dream, she wouldn't hear the tears of the woman she had left alone in the rain: she would be too tired.

She worked all morning. They brewed tea in the billy over a fire made by Jimmie. He had drilled one piece of wood on to a piece of blackboy stem. She had used that when the darkness was split by lightning, when Patrick had come and she thought she had seen love. It seemed so far away, so long ago, and now they were without love, as they had always been.

They ate the cheese sandwiches she had made. She had brought hard-boiled eggs. They were fresh and wouldn't peel well.

'I had a cockerel in Somerset,' she said. 'Tom wanted it killed. Too noisy, too angry. He's got it now. Won't kill it, Nell says.'

It was dark here, in the woods. There was no light. It crushed her, sucked the breath from her body. She rose, paced around the fire, pushed at the ash around the edge. Would her vegetables need ash? Would the spring ever come, the clouds ever go? But even if they did the sun would not penetrate here. It was only the flies and the heat that did.

'Why did you go to Broome? Why did you leave your home if you didn't have to?' she asked Jimmie, because words kept the thought of the night away, and there were none that she and Patrick could use between them.

The aboriginal was squatting, burning the end of a stick in the fire then tracing symbols in the ash.

'I did have to. My father was white. He went to Broome to trade with the pearl divers after he transgressed the laws of our tribe, the Bibbulmun. He took us with him. You go where the man goes, don't you?' He stood up when Patrick did. He shouldered his axe when Patrick did and Deborah took up the mattock and said nothing, because he was right. She looked at Patrick. You go where the man goes. There was no anger in her, just resignation.

They worked until four, and then brewed a billy for tea and she was trembling with tiredness and longed for sleep, but feared that tonight, again, it wouldn't come because Anne would be crying.

'Then why did you come back?' she asked as Jimmie refused the scones she had baked and squatted by the fire, drinking tea from the condensed milk mug, holding it with both hands, sipping it slowly. His nose was broad, his brow heavy. Patrick dipped his scone into his tea, his eyes squinting as he listened.

'My mother was near death. She wanted her spirit to return to its proper resting place, where it existed before birth. She did not want it to wander about the world, bereft, lost. I could not dance for her because I was her son. But it was enough to bring her back. Her spirit is at peace.'

Deborah looked into the fire, then out to the woods. 'My friend is lost out there in this land she hates. I left her beneath the sound of rain. She drowned in it. She cries every night.' She watched the men's faces as they looked at her, and then at one another.

Patrick said, 'It's not your fault, for God's sake, I keep telling you.' His voice was hard, as it usually was. It was easier that way, he thought. It was less confusing. It made the ache subside. Yes. It was easier to think of the land, of the job ahead of them, and not listen to echoes of a time now past because love had been his mother's stranglehold and he wanted no part of that, ever.

'Then why does she come to me?' Deborah said, shouting at him, bringing him back to the fire, to the tea in his hand. She rose and walked away, back to the humpy, the mug dropping from her hand as she did so. Anne would never leave her. She would never leave her now because Scotland was across the other side of the world, across oceans, continents, and how could a spirit travel so far?

That night the fires outside Jimmie's humpy burned green wood and there was the smell of smoke, the sound of chanting, and as Deborah lay there it drowned out the sound of Anne's cries. She rose and walked out into the darkness, towards the song that Jimmie sang, towards the dance which he played out in the light from the fire, the white dotted marks on his face vivid against his colour, his fibre armband and hair belts like shadows on his body. He beat his feet, sang his song, threw his spear and there was no fear in her as she watched. No fear in her as he finished and came to her out of the circle of light, and spoke to her in the silence.

'I have danced for her,' Jimmie said and here, even in the dark, she could see the white on his face.

There was peace in Deborah's head, peace in the bush around them and she nodded. 'Even though we are here, on your land.'

Jimmie looked up at the trees, the stars.

'I am here now too, where my spirit existed and will exist again beyond death. I am here where I can travel the paths of the great heroes of our life. I am here to live the law which I have been taught. I'm home, Deborah.'

Anne never came again and the next evening Jack found carved and decorated grave posts on his wife's grave.

'I carved for her,' Jimmie said.

August became September and spring arrived. The rain was past. She slept at night. More land had been cleared, fenced. She hauled washing from a creek which no longer roared and tore at the kerosene can. She ironed and ignored the black marks. She baked, top dressed the oats, felt the baby move more strongly each day, felt its weight bearing down.

She watched Patrick shave once a week and his face was not so drawn. She combed her hair each night and in the mirror her lines were not so deep. They worked as before, alongside one another though not together, but the anger was quite gone in her, there was only acceptance. At last there was that.

She planted pie melons, pumpkins, tomatoes. Half in the ash, half not. She bought strawberry runners, cucumbers, rhubarb, to make sure their boils did not return. She sawed a deal kerosene box for the baby's crib. She rubbed it down and guilt would not allow her to accept Patrick's help.

As the sun warmed the earth and dried the sodden ground to firm greenness she walked through the bush, blazing a trail wherever she went, listening to the robins, the thrushes, seeing the brilliant flash of the parrots, the rosellas. She heard the screech of the squeakers, the caw of the crow and she held her belly and said, 'Listen to that, my child. You listen. It's not silent after all.'

There was golden wattle in the bush and its scent was in the air. Wisteria grew on shrubs and logs. There was coral creeper, clematis. She picked them, placed them in Nestlé's milk tins and the scent of them drowned the Lysol. There were shrubs that flowered, there were blue wrens, cockatoos which flew to the coast, a sign of fine weather.

She wrote of this to Nell, telling her that there was beauty after all in this place where she thought she would find none. The winter was gone, she was calm. Work was easier because Jimmie was here. The baby was due in eight weeks, she said and she had written to Mrs Prover to tell her of the child but had heard nothing.

In October Jimmie found a swampy valley with boronia growing and took her through the bush, away off to the right of the trail when he next went to Jack's to collect the horse. His feet made no sound, no mark. He had no need of blazes but she looked for landmarks, for strange trees because she was learning the way of this land and knew she might lose him, then herself, for ever.

They found the valley. The scent was rich, heavy. She knelt on the moist ground, her face in the flowers, but picked none. 'They should stay here,' she said, 'where they belong.'

'That is as we think too.' His voice was quiet. 'My mother spoke of these often.'

'Did you remember them in Broome?' It was quiet in the valley, warm. There were flies, but not too many.

Jimmie squatted beside her. His fingers were gentle as he touched a petal. 'I remember the scent. I remember her words as she told me. I can't remember the sight of it. Do you understand?'

Yes, she understood because the distant days with her parents were the same. They walked back to the trail and it didn't matter that her knees were wet. He told her of the stories he had learned at his mother and grandmother's side about the land and its animals, the rocks and trees, and the waterholes. He told her of the tales he had learned from the dreaming.

He told her that his totem was the kangaroo. That he might never eat its young, for it would be like eating his own child. But she didn't want to hear about that with her own child moving inside her and so he told her instead that the Milky Way had once been a native road to the sky country until one day some women on the road had lit a fire and burned the road which was really a sacred wooden emblem. So, Edward, she thought, you showed me Orion and now I know the Milky Way. I shall tell your child these myths.

As they walked he spoke to her in his own language but it had double vowels and when she tried to repeat his words they made her larynx hurt and she stopped. She was sorry, she said, and he smiled.

'I left here twenty-five years ago when I was four. Two years later my father was dead. I was brought up from the age of eight in your language by the priest. I know Gregorian chants better than most whites. Aboriginal parents were not

242

considered suitable to bring up children with white blood. We were taken from our kindred, from our culture. It broke our black hearts but pleased the whites. The priest called it an act of love, but it was an act of possession. I chose to leave when I discovered the truth about what they had done to my mother. I brought her back to her home.' They were at the trail now and she could see the cart tracks, the blazed trees.

She watched him walk through the bush towards Jack's, not needing to use the track as they did, and she touched her belly, feeling her child, then lifted her hands to her face, smelling the boronia. Jimmie had loved his mother enough to look after her, bring her home. She was heavy with a child who would love her too and at last she knew that she would never be alone again.

At the end of October she showed Patrick and Jimmie her lettuce which were thriving. 'This end had ash. We need it, Patrick.'

She pulled a plant out, knocking the soil back on to the earth, breaking the roots off, throwing them on to the compost which she had layered with Bet's manure. She pointed to the weaker plants at the other end of the plot. 'See, there's a difference. We need to burn off the oats, then plough.'

He stood, drawing on his cigarette, his eyes squinting against the flies. 'You're right. That all right by you, Jimmie? If the wind's low, we'll burn off when the oats are in.'

She watched as Patrick looked across at the aboriginal who stood as still as always. 'Yes. It's the right thing to do. My people burned off. The regrowth was lush.'

'Fine. I'll leave the scything to you then, Deb. You can manage?' He ground out his cigarette beneath his heel. 'I want to get that far paddock fenced this week.'

She watched him walk with easy strides towards the green wood he would be splitting for fence posts. There was a quiet courtesy between them as there had been between Mr Taylor and the ram buyers.

She scythed the paddock the next day, digging the blade

into the earth again and again until she had regained the knack and then the spindly oats keeled over, neatly, quickly, and she breathed in the scent of harvest time. She skirted the stumps and looked out towards the bush which they had ring-barked in the autumn. The leaves were dropping. Soon those could be felled and burned.

Her back ached, but then it always did. Her shoulders ached too but her hands no longer blistered, the calluses were too deep for that. She worked all day, brewed tea, but not for the men because they would boil a billy and eat the bread and cheese she had packed for them, the lettuce she had washed and dried. For there were to be no more boils at Stoke Farm, no more tiredness which made the rain seem as though it was inside their heads.

After two days she turned the hay, seeing the motes in the still air, squinting against flies that she barely noticed now. She walked in the bush, down to the creek, passed the wattle, the wisteria, the coral creeper. She dug up the roots of a clematis and planted it at the corner of the humpy. Next spring it would bloom.

She turned the hay again two days later and Patrick sent Jimmie with the cart into the paddock. Together they threw the hay up on to the cart. Dust fell into their eyes, dirt into their hair. They ducked the stones, the twigs, and laughed. It was the first time she had heard Jimmie laugh.

'I love the harvest. At home, in Somerset, we used to drink cider, eat sandwiches,' Deborah said.

'You will be able to tell your child your history. Keep it alive for him, and for you,' Jimmie said, climbing on to the cart, the oats hanging out across the seat, so that he had to duck. They laughed again and she placed her hands on her belly.

'Did you hear that, my love? Soon you'll be here. Soon I can talk to you. Soon you will laugh with me.'

They heaved the oats into a stack to the rear of the humpy and would burn off the field the next day if there was very little wind, but first Jimmie ploughed around the edge, making a break. Black pulled as Jimmie directed and didn't let the swingle tree bang back against his foot. Deborah shook her fist and again they laughed. Patrick too.

This break soil was shot through with chaff. It crumbled well. She looked at Patrick and he at her and they nodded. Yes, after the burn this soil would grow pasture, she knew that now, and there would be plovers to show her child next year.

Patrick tied No. 8 wire to a piece of red gum and Jimmie drilled wood against blackboy fibre placed on the log, and the gum smouldered and caught alight. Deborah watched as Patrick ran parallel with the break, but ten feet inside it, in and around the stumps which Deborah had drenched with water from the creek. They didn't want them burning yet, only under controlled conditions.

The breeze was a barely perceptible westerly and the fire caught, crackled and burned back on to the break and there were no sparks to rear up and light the still green bush. Again and again he ran along, burning, while Deborah stood at the edge and heard noise that she could not grasp and felt heat that she could not believe on her face.

She remembered the bushfire at Lenora, Patrick's swollen tongue, lips, eyes, his body which had needed her comfort and the loving which he thought had produced her child, and she looked away from him, because the guilt, the regret was too strong and there was something else, which she would have called love, if she thought it existed.

By the third week of November the spring-sown oats were coming on well and had been dressed with super. That night she made a white frill for the baby's crib out of boiled flour bags and a net as protection against flies and mosquitoes. She pulled it hard against her bed but there was so little room in the humpy and it was so dark. But then she caught the scent of the stocks which cast the Lysol into shade. She had overcome that, she would overcome the darkness and make more windows.

She looked up at Patrick who was working on his five-year plan and then out of the door, seeing Jimmie's fires towards the creek. It was almost as though they had neighbours; as though the silence and the isolation were lifting.

'I'll make scarecrows tomorrow,' she said, lifting the lid of her trunk, dragging out a velvet dress. 'The rosellas will get at the oats.'

He nodded, not looking up. 'I'll clear and drain near the creek. Could grow maize for the cattle. We must get a cow now the baby's due.'

He put his pencil behind his ear, pulled out his cigarettes. The smell of sulphur flared. He drew on his cigarette, looked at the dress she was holding up. 'I heard in town that the English groupies are coming down from Perth. You should keep that. There'll maybe be a party this Christmas.'

That night she didn't sleep. Her back ached, her mind played with his words. The groupies were coming. There would be people near her, working in this bush, making it bloom, making it into Somerset. There would be parties. There would be help. They could corrugate the roads, clear the trail. There would be friends for her child to play with, to attend school with. There would be laughter, there would English voices. There would be women visiting her humpy. Yes, at last the isolation was lifting.

It was then that the pain gripped her, across the back, then into her belly, tightening, then releasing, ebbing, leaving. She lay until dawn as the pain came and went.

She hauled water up from the creek that morning, running it into channels alongside her vegetables, watching it seep into the soil which was not yet cracked and dry. She watered the clematis. If it died she would plant another root in the autumn.

The pain came again, clenching at her, tearing, and she leant against the corrugated iron of the humpy and was afraid. She clutched her belly, the breath high in her chest, sweat on her forehead, between her breasts. She called when the pain was ebbing but no one was near.

She walked out around the ploughed and sown paddock, out beyond the winter-sown oats which were growing straggly and which rosellas had fed on this morning. She must get the men. She couldn't be alone. They must get the cart. The baby couldn't come yet, she had the scarecrows to make, the windows to arrange. The pain was coming again. It tightened, clenched, and she stood still, gripping the post that she had tamped into the earth and which Jimmie said cut across his songline. Patrick had said he must just climb over.

Think of that, not the pain. It would go. The others had. The doctor said she would know when labour began. He had said she would have lots of time. He had said to breathe but it hurt too much to breathe. He said she would have hours of time. Hours of this?

Think of the crib she had made, the boronia, the history that Jimmie would one day pass on, that she would pass on. Think of Somerset, forget the pain. Oh God. Oh God. But it was going, easing. She could walk again.

Keep by the fence, out through the gate. Out across the stumped land, around the heaped trunks. She could hear the sound of axes chopping. She called. They didn't stop, couldn't hear her, and the pain was building again, tightening, grasping her. How long had the pause been? How long did this one last? It was longer, surely it was longer.

There were no fences here. She leant against a felled gum. She could smell the eucalyptus of its leaves, the scent of the gum. Here was another pain starting. She pulled at the bark. It peeled. Her nails were deep into the palms of her hand. She could hear moaning and it was from her. Wait. Just wait. It was going. Easing. Almost gone. Not quite.

She called again and this time the chopping stopped. She couldn't move from the trunk. She leant against it, her legs weak, watching them running over the uneven ground and now she straightened because she must be strong. It was not Patrick's baby. He reached her first.

'I need to go now,' she said. Her lips felt stiff. 'I must go now.'

Jimmie ran through the bush to collect the cart. Would he smell the boronia as he passed? Had his mother leant against the trunk as she was doing? Had his father put his arm around her, easing her along, supporting her as the pain came again as Patrick was doing? But Jimmie had told her once that childbirth was the preserve of the women and she longed for Anne, for Nell, because the pain was coming again and she mustn't let it show to this man, who was not the father of her child. She had no right to his care.

The cart took less than two hours to reach them. Jimmie had trotted Bet. There was sweat on her withers, on her haunches. There was a chaff mattress in the back on which Deborah lay, moaning as the cart lurched and jogged down into the potholes. Surely the holes in the road would go now that more people were coming. Think of that, not the pain. Look up at the trees which met above the track.

Patrick changed horses at Mr Martins'. He striped the reins over Black's back, trotting when he could. There would be sweat on the horse's haunches. There had been sweat on her father's hunters. There was sweat on her. Jimmie sat in the back turning his face from her when she groaned because this was not where he should be.

'I'm so sorry, Jimmie. There should be women here. I'm so sorry.'

'Don't be sorry. It is a time for celebration.' He poured out water on to a towel, wiped her forehead, slapped at the flies which crawled on her cheeks and near her mouth. She felt them on her eyelids as she closed them but the pain was here again. And again, and again.

Patrick urged Black on, threw the citronella oil into the back and the castor oil. 'Put it on her face, for God's sake. She can't have those bloody things all over her, not now. Not now, for Christ's sake.'

The hospital was light, airy. There was a bed, a proper bed. There were blankets and sheets that were starched; crisp and starched. Patrick stood at the door, and Jimmie too, so black against the white. She turned, looked at them, heard Patrick say, 'Get on to the station. Pick the iron up and the wood. We haven't got much time.'

Jimmie nodded, looked at Deborah. 'Soon you will have your child. Soon.'

He left silently, swiftly, and the nurse was undoing the buttons down the front of Deborah's blouse and she wanted the door shut, because Patrick was a business partner and he shouldn't see her swollen breasts when he wanted iron collected. He hadn't got much time. This was taking him from his schedule. There was the super to put on the oats. There was the cow. She was taking him away from his work and she was not there to help because of this baby that was not his.

The pain swept over her and her waters broke, gushing to the floor and there were women's hands holding her, calming her, soothing her and she called for her mother, for Nell, for Anne as they sent Patrick from the room.

They hung her clothes on hangers in a wardrobe. She had forgotten there were such things. She lay on the bed watching, looking at the light which streamed through the glass window, through the fly screen. She looked at the floor, the wooden floor, at the dado panelling on the walls. There was no rust-specked corrugated iron here, no fleas, no propped-up window.

'The windows. I haven't done the windows,' she whispered.

Then the pain came again and the nurse brought Patrick in. He sat by the bed, his hat in his hands, turning it, turning it. She looked away from him, from those lips that had once kissed her, from that body that had once lain on hers, and wished that this child was his. But the pain was here again.

Luke was born at ten p.m. She was so tired, so torn, that she did not stir until the nurse put her son into her arms. She felt his warmth, his weight. He stirred and she looked at his face, at his lips, his closed eyes, and couldn't believe that anything so perfect could exist. That anything so small could call from her such all-consuming love.

At ten-thirty Patrick was allowed in to see his child and his wife and as he looked down on them, at the baby swaddled in white linen and Deborah, pale and tired, the pain reared up in him again. He touched her face with his finger, then the child's face and his skin was so fine that he barely felt it.

He sat by the bed, took Deborah's hand. It was scarred, rough, her nails were torn, her palms callused. He bent his head and kissed it. 'We have a beautiful baby,' he said. 'Do you feel all right?'

He watched her nod and look away, down at the child. 'I shall be fine. I shall be back as soon as I can. The nurse knows of a pram that is no longer needed. I shall be able to bring him out to the paddocks in that.' Her voice was distant.

'Shall I stay?' he asked, not ever wanting to leave, and he couldn't understand himself.

'No, go. You have work to do. I'll send a message via Jack about collecting me. But go.' Her face was turned from him, towards the window. Her voice was cold and he felt the pain deepen and set as he rose, walked to the door, opened it, wanting her to call to him to stay, but she did not.

Deborah heard him leave, heard his footsteps down the passage. She had wanted him to hold her, take the baby in his arms, say that he would never leave them, but why should he say that when they were just business partners?

The baby stirred and she touched his fine hair with her finger. 'But I have you, my little Luke. I have you and you are all mine.'

CHAPTER 15

Patrick didn't visit except briefly, on Sunday. He was tired, rushed, quiet as he stood above the cot and then sat with Deborah.

'The Groupies have come, Deborah.'

But she knew. Sarah, who had come on the Group Settlement Scheme, was in the next bed. She had left England three months ago and had been weeping all day and all night because of the fleas in the Fremantle Immigration Hostel and the size of the trees, and the heat, though it was not yet really hot.

'You look tired, Patrick.'

'Been busy.'

She nodded. There were no words that could travel easily between them, there were only minutes that dragged in this light wooden building until at last he rose, nodding at her, touching her hand.

'Remember that if you are getting the cow, we must have a mature one, not a heifer. We won't need a bail. I can milk her without.'

Sarah's husband was kissing his wife, leaning over, murmuring, stroking her hair. Deborah looked away, watching Patrick walk from the ward, hearing his boots on the floor, and then she picked up her child, hugging him to her, telling him that she loved him, only him. Because she knew, as Patrick's footsteps faded, there was nowhere else for her love to go.

Sarah's tears were quieter that night and her voice was soft as she told Deborah of her voyage, via Tenerife as an assisted passenger. But Deborah didn't want to listen because Edward had been with her in Tenerife, he had been with her for days, nights.

Sarah told her of the Immigration Home, of the fleas, of the rows of beds and horse-hair mattresses, of the mosquitoes, of the hours they had spent walking in the Fremantle streets, or down by the water waiting to be given their instructions. She told Deborah of the people who had told them about the size of the trees and how it would take years for them to begin producing with their limited financial means.

'I don't believe it,' Sarah said. 'Nothing could be as bad as they said.'

Deborah looked away now. How could she tell this girl that she *must* believe it?

'I'm glad my baby came early. My husband is in a twenty-foot humpy with another family. I don't know what a humpy is. I thought I would have brick walls around me, a floor, light,' Sarah said. 'I want to go home, Deborah.'

Deborah nodded, eased herself from her bed. The floor was cool on her feet. There were few flies. The hospital had fly screens. She held the girl in her arms while Sarah told her that her Ernie, her husband, had survived the Somme to take up the offer of a new life.

'We're being paid three pounds a week. We've been given tools. In Fremantle they said the tools were laughable for the size of the trees and the scope of the bush. But it'll be all right, he says. They're going to be taught to farm by a foreman, but how can you farm forests, Deborah?'

You clear them first, Deborah thought. You scarf, you saw, you grub until you have hands that are as hard as the trees you work on and lines that are as deep as mine and Anne Martins' were. But she just said, 'It will be all right.'

But would it? Because she and Patrick had money behind them. Not a lot, but enough. They had knowledge, not a great deal but it was sufficient. They had Jimmie. They had good land. She knew that this was much more than the Groupies had and what would happen when they had to repay their loans? At first they would only repay the interest, but then it would be the capital. How could they do that and live as well?

'It sounded so good. How we'd all mix in and set up the farms, clear each other's land. How we'd be self-sufficient in two years. They didn't tell us about the shacks or the flies, the mosquitoes, the size of the trees.'

'It will be all right. It really will be all right,' Deborah said but she gripped Sarah tightly. 'It will be all right.' But self-sufficient in so few years? It was an impossibility.

After two weeks, Patrick collected her, brought her away from the light, from the lined wooden building, from the other women in the ward, from Sarah.

'I'll come and see you. You are only three miles to the west . . . I will come and see you,' Deborah called and recognised the look in the girl's eye. It was the same as had been in Anne Martins'.

They jolted along the track, leaving the town behind and she wanted to stay where there were houses, where there were people. She wanted to jump from the cart with her baby and stay. She pressed her lips to his forehead.

'Such a silent baby, for a silent land,' she whispered.

Patrick talked of the cow he had ordered, but which hadn't yet arrived. 'When does the flush season end?'

'About now, but don't worry. It will be all right,' she said. It seemed to be all she ever said to people. 'Have you started draining for the maize? The cow will need the fodder. We should order bran and pollard to supplement the pasture.'

They talked of the need for a fowl house. 'Otherwise the dingoes or the foxes might get them, Patrick. If they're together I can use their manure too.'

'Soon then, when I have more time. The pumpkins are doing well and the pie melons. The strawberries are ripe,' he said.

'I shall make jam. Now that the Groupies are here I can sell it to them. I can sell it in town. The hospital will take some, I asked.'

They fell silent now and she listened to the rattle of the cart, the rasping of Bet's breath. They had nothing to say to one another if they were not talking of cows, of maize, of fowl, and Deborah looked down at her son and the sight of his face soothed her pain, swept it away.

They left the track for the trail and she hadn't realised what a path they had worn.

'We'll clear this over the next month,' Patrick said, 'turn it into a track. 'Now the Groupies are here, there's talk of a road gang that'll lay logs, corrugate the track. Make it passable all year round. It will be good having others here.'

She nodded. The town was so far behind them, the trees so close. People so distant.

'I'll make more windows,' she said, not wanting to think of all the bush that was around them.

He nodded.

They were coming to the clearing now and she wouldn't look at the humpy yet. She wouldn't look to see if the clematis had bloomed. She looked first at the ploughed and sown paddock.

'Soon there will be plovers,' she said to her son and then looked further to the oats, and to the land which they had cleared, then to the sky which at last she could see with ease. Then she looked at the shack which would be so dark after the lightness of the hospital – but it was not there.

Instead there was a house like Anne Martins'.

It was there, where the humpy had been. It was made of timber with a verandah. There were three steps up to it. There was a front door with six panes of glass in the top and large proper windows either side. There were two tin chimneys fitted on to stone bases.

She turned. Patrick looked at her but said nothing. She handed him the baby, eased down from the cart, walked towards the house, climbed the steps carefully. She was still torn, still sore, but she felt no pain as she pulled open the fly screen, pushed open the door to her own house.

The living room had an open brick fireplace, a mantelpiece

with Geoff's ornate clock on it. The walls were lined. The kitchen had a No. 2 Metters stove. There was a shelf over it. There was a cupboard made of a kero box. She opened it. There were her pans, her mugs, the milk tin mugs. There was another cupboard next to it. She opened it. Her Wedgwood was stacked inside.

The provisions were still on a table with the legs in tins holding water and kerosene. Did Sarah know to do this? She must tell her. She opened the solid back door. There was a rear verandah with the Coolgardie. There were stacks of gum logs for the open fire, and chips for the stove. There were the bags of super to keep dry when the rains came again. There was an outhouse with a roof on and a dry lavatory inside.

She returned, walked through to the living room. There were wooden floors, the faint smell of Lysol. There were flowers. Patrick stood in the doorway, holding her child, looking first at Luke and then at her.

'Oh Patrick. It's so wonderful. Oh Patrick.'

She wanted to come into his arms, to come home, to thank him for all this, to love him for his kindness.

He moved then, away from her towards a door.

'We need some sleep to get the best out of ourselves,' he said. 'We need a home. Come and see the bedrooms, Deborah.'

He opened the door and stood silently as she passed him, brushing against him, smelling him, and then she looked and she felt her throat thicken as she saw, not two beds and a cot but just hers, hers alone and the baby's crib. That was all and she knew then that she had wanted much more, for one foolish moment she had wanted so much more than this.

There was a curtain hung across the corner for a wardrobe. There was a mirror on the wall. He pointed to the large window. 'I knew you needed light. Jimmie and I built that for you.' He pointed to the bed. 'Now the baby won't keep me awake too.'

She nodded, looking out across the bush, down to the creek. At night she would see Jimmie's fires burning. At night, when she was alone in her bed she could see some warmth somewhere. At night, when she was so alone and her business partner slept next door.

'It's lovely. You were right. We will sleep and work so much better.' She didn't turn as he laid her child in the crib. She didn't turn as he left the room but she did call out, 'Thank you Patrick. I am so happy.' She gripped the windowsill. Her bed was so bleak, so alone. There was no love, not even when he thought this child was his. How foolish to think there would be. How bloody foolish. She pressed Luke to her.

'But I have you,' she said, carefully, loudly. 'I have you.'

Patrick walked to the cart, lifted out her bags, lifted down the pram. He was tired. He and Jimmie were both so tired but he had said it must be finished and it had been, though it was not scheduled until next year. He had put her bed in her room because they must sleep. The baby would keep him awake. She had said she was happy but he had hoped for something else, though he didn't know what. For God's sake, he didn't know what.

But that night he tossed and turned because he couldn't sleep. She wasn't there when he looked across in the darkness as she had been in the humpy. She wasn't there when he woke in the morning and he left without breakfast because he couldn't understand himself.

All the next day Deborah boiled sugar bags, dried them on the line, edged them with the skirt of a cotton dress which was holed from last summer, turning them into towels. She wanted to be busy, she wanted to make a home. She didn't want to think any more of the adults living separate lives within this house.

She fed her baby, crooned to him, carried him gently out into the bush, showed him the robins and the crows, showed him the parrots, the rosellas, showed him the paddocks that she had sown. In the evening she held him up to the kookaburra who sat on the fence post, his head on one side, his expression ruffled, and listened to his full-throated laughter.

Jimmie came as the day ended. 'My people's babies are born pink,' he said. 'But not this pink.'

He led her then with Luke to see the brush-tailed possum who lived in a tree near his humpy. He held the child and told Luke that one day he would grow and hear his mother's history, as he, Ngilgi, had heard his people's. They listened to the mopoke and then Patrick came and stood by the fire with them and they talked of the maize they would grow and the boody rats and birds that would try and eat it.

'Should we call you Ngilgi?' Deborah asked.

'No, you should call me Jimmie. It is my tribe who should call me Ngilgi and there are none, are there?'

They ate supper on the table in the living room that Patrick had made for the humpy and she told him that she wanted to make jam tomorrow to sell, because she was not able to clear the trees with him yet.

They soaked string in kerosene outside on the ground in the light of the hurricane lamp. They tied it on the wide part of the old bottles she had been saving and burned it. The tops came off easily. She rasped the edges until they were no longer sharp while he returned to his plans and his accounts, and she was glad that for a moment they had worked together, that she had been able to smell the scent of his skin.

She boiled up the pie melon the next day, adding ginger to some, lemon to others, held up the wooden spoon, nothing dripped. The jam was ready. There was no soot in it, she wrote to Nell that night. She picked strawberries, ate some, gave some to Patrick and to Jimmie and made jam with the rest. She sent some in with Jimmie to town and gave Patrick the money that night.

'There's no need for this, Deborah.'

'There is every need, Patrick,' she replied, and returned to the letter she was writing to Nell.

Jack came at the end of the week, to say that Deborah must now take over the mail stop. He couldn't cope any longer. She would have to be the base for the Groupies too, because their foreman was even further down the track.

He stooped over Luke's pram, lifting up the fly net, smelling the castor oil around the baby's eyes.

'He's beautiful. Anne would have loved him,' he said and kissed Deborah's cheek. 'It's time you had some company. Make sure you ask them in for tea, make sure you talk to them, tell of how things are. We don't want any more tragedies. But he seems a little hot, Deborah. It might be the cord. Anne would have known.'

The baby was hotter still that night and it wasn't the heat of the summer which was baking down again. She looked at his cord and it was redder than it had been earlier. She stood by the window, looking out on to the fires behind the trees, walking him up and down, up and down. She heard Patrick moving, then heard his knock on her door. He came in.

'I heard you moving.'

'He's hot, Patrick. I don't know what to do.' She wanted to clutch him. Her baby was ill. Anne would have known what to do, she didn't. But Patrick had heard her, he had come.

Patrick felt the baby. 'I'll see if Jimmie will go for the cart and we'll take him to the doctor.'

She nodded. He left. She saw him hurry behind the water tank, across into the trees, his stride still long. She moved out to the rear verandah, hearing the frogs, the mopoke. 'You are ill, and you still don't scream. You are so good, my Luke, my love.'

She spoke to keep the fear at bay. She knew so little. She wanted Nell, Anne. Jimmie came, pulled off the child's clothes, felt his stomach. 'Wait,' he said and left. They stood, neither speaking, just looking at the child. Jimmie returned and rubbed ash and herbs on to his cord.

'He will sleep now.' He turned and left, silently.

Luke did sleep and so too did Deborah, after she had watched the aboriginal return to his fires, knowing that she would never know this land as Jack and this man did. She also knew that here at Stoke Farm were three adults who might indeed be separate but who were also linked and it gave her a measure of peace.

She spoke to Patrick in the morning of the need to leave the sacred places alone, the boulders, the trees where the Bibbulmum ancestors had trodden.

'Remember,' she said, 'telling me your grandfather cleared the land too well. We mustn't do that. We mustn't destroy.'

Patrick nodded. She had said 'we' and he talked that day to Jimmie so that he could note on his five-year plan the areas to leave because that was what Deborah wanted. It would make her work more efficiently, he told himself, if he made concessions. That was all it was.

Sarah and the other six women came in a spring cart to collect the mail, to pick up the milk and bread which Jimmie had brought up from Jack. Sarah brought her baby, Mollie, and she cried and the other women laughed and said that Mollie should have some of Luke's silence.

They drank tea from mugs, because there was no place here for Wedgwood as these women told her of the work their husbands were doing. Of the humpies two families had to share, of the kerosene tins they had to use, of the tiredness as they helped their husbands clear their own blocks, but only after the the men had finished the group work for the day. They told her of the fleas, the flies, the snakes, and now they didn't laugh.

She sprayed their legs with kerosene because of the fleas which they brought, and which were still anyway on her floor. She told them of castor oil and citronella oil and golden eye ointment because they had bung eyes. She gave them jam to take away because she could not make money out of these people, who had so little, and who she knew had so much more to go through.

The next week she brought in the oats. They were seeding and would fall. She scythed and the heat beat up from the ground and down from the sky. She was slower, weaker, but it must be done. It was her job. She fed her son, loving him, holding him, drowning in the sight of him, crooning Knick

259

Knack Paddywack to him. She laid him in his pram in the shade of the trees. She worked again, all through the day. Working, feeding, while the men cleared elsewhere.

They burned off the paddock, carefully, so carefully and she told Sarah and the other women the next week how she had learned that burning off should be done with care, out here, in Australia, where the land was king. She had learned that they needed to burn to get potash, that they top dressed with super. She gave them two beer bottles from which to culture yeast and handles for their condensed milk tins.

She held a plate supper on Christmas Eve and each family brought food. There were sausage rolls, cakes, pies, there was ginger beer which Deborah made from a root she had kept going, there was Jack's home-brewed beer. They danced to the sound of an accordion that Ernie played. There was a sapling on the verandah which Patrick had cut for her and which she had draped with coloured paper. All around them in the bush were small trees with masses of orange and yellow flowers.

'We call them Christmas trees, because of their time of flowering,' said Jack.

Sarah and Deborah arranged games for the children and as night came they slept on chaff mattresses on the floor of the lounge while their parents danced, but not Deborah or Sarah, because they were both still too sore. Instead they watched the dust-kicking dances of the others and Deborah remembered the Blue Mountains and Patrick's hand against her back, the heat of their bodies as they swirled to the music.

As darkness fell they danced by the light of the hurricane lamp and Patrick talked to Jack, and then they both talked to those men who were drinking beer and talking of burning the bush, not clearing it first. They told them that the bush would only grow back more lush. They must clear first.

They left at midnight and it wasn't until then that Deborah realised that there were no fires from Jimmie's humpy. He had gone.

Patrick handed her a present of working gloves and she

handed him a hammer and put the hat they had bought for Jimmie to one side. 'An aboriginal will always leave his work if he feels the white man's magic seeping into him,' he said, nodding towards Jimmie's humpy.

'Will he return?'

'Yes. This is his homeland, isn't it?'

She missed the fires that had flickered through her window each night. She missed the third adult in their corner of this looming bush, and she missed the help which Jimmie had given Patrick because now it was she who took the end of the saw again. It was she who wielded an axe, stopping to feed Luke from her still swollen breasts every few hours.

It was she who woke to find that the dingoes had got three hens which they had strewn around, so that the ground was splashed with blood and feathers littered the air, but now she didn't cry at such things, she cursed as Tom would have done.

'So maybe I'm becoming a farmer then, Nell,' she wrote that night after she and Patrick had felled a tree, cut it to length, taken off the bark and split it into posts for a fowl house and pen, driven picks into the ground, dug a fence hole eighteen inches deep. They had no need to measure them now; they had dug so many, tamped down so many.

Jimmie arrived the next morning and split some five by five sections eight feet long, then trimmed them to shape with an axe. They all cut more trees and made the billets three feet long then cut them into slabs one and a half inches thick and Deborah knew now, more than ever, how much luckier they were than the Groupies to have this extra help.

Patrick set a dingo trap when the house and pen were complete 'The bastards will only try and get beneath.'

She used the manure on her garden. She grew sweet-scented stocks in the shade of the verandah where Luke lay beneath his net, feeling the benefit of any breeze. Patrick and Jimmie completed the well. She took the water for her vegetables from there, for her flowers, for the fruit trees she had planted. She hung and cooled her jellies within it, her butter too. It was

261

1924. Her vegetables were growing, her fowls were penned and laying, her flowers were filling the air with fragrance and she relaxed into her love for her child, the peace she was finding.

They bought a mature cow. It ran in the home paddock which was high in mixed grass and clover as the first light rain of early autumn came and Jimmie looked at Luke and said that he had become a coba-jeera, a baby – as he had come to smile, move his lips, touch the balls that Deborah had hung on his pram, the child spirit had left to return to its home.

'But still so quiet,' he said and looked at Deborah, at Patrick, who nodded. Deborah looked out to the trees which barely rustled in the cooler air.

'It's this land,' she replied and returned to making fly paper which she had devised by mixing gum from the red gum and castor oil. 'It's this land, that's all.'

She gave the fly paper to Sarah and the others when they came as they did each Tuesday. She gave them lettuces, tomatoes, because they too had boils as she had done.

'It's diet, but the flies too,' she said. 'The vegetables will help.'

She passed around the mail, watching them take their letters, not opening them here, but putting them in their pockets, touching them again and again as they talked, smiled, but seldom laughed.

Nell had written to say how well Susie was, how another baby was expected. How was Luke? How was the farm? Was the cow a good milker?

Deborah milked Dora, the Guernsey house cow, each morning, each evening, tempting her in from the field, tying her to the post, giving her bran to eat, squinting her eyes against the flies, dodging the swinging tail, the kicking hind leg. She listened to the hiss of the milk in the pail, stripping properly while she talked to Luke who lay in his pram, telling him of the separator she would buy next year when they had another cow, telling him of the letter she would write to Nell about the virtues of Guernseys over Jerseys. She told him that Sarah and her baby, Mollie, would be in their own humpy next week and at last away from the shared shack which was driving both families to the point of breakdown. She told him that she was glad she was not about to go through her first winter here, in South West Australia, as these Groupies were. She told him how worried she was because the roads had not yet been corrugated and sometimes Sarah and the others would not be able to come for their mail and she remembered her own hours on that sodden track. And she told him how much she loved him, how at peace she felt.

'It will be bad for them though, if we don't see them, and bad for us,' she said.

Before the rains began to fall heavily she asked the Groupies to Stoke Farm in March to eat potatoes that were to be cooked in the heat of the stacked felled trees as Patrick and Jimmie burned the first of them.

'It's a celebration,' she told them. 'It's a milestone, one that you will reach too next year and it's a chance to talk, all of us again.' She knew that they must not go into winter without some cheer.

They came on two spring carts, which they tied near the house, giving nose bags to the horses. They walked with Deborah around the fenced paddocks where the pasture was showing green, towards the heaps that were burning, sending up showers of sparks. Deborah had tried potatoes in the high ground towards the creek. They had been successful.

She edged the potatoes now into the ash of trunks which had been snigged into heaps and which Jimmie and Patrick had set alight at lunchtime. She handed split saplings to Ernie, to young Mark, Mr and Mrs Taylor's son, to others and they laughed, for once they laughed.

She felt the heat of the fire on her face, smelt the gum, heard the crackle, took Luke from a woman who had held him for her and moved away so that he did not become too hot.

She looked as the flames devoured first one part of the heap, and then the other. She listened to the hiss and spit as a new part caught alight, shooting up flames. Patrick pushed at the logs, shoving them together. She saw him pass cigarettes to Ernie and knew that he would be telling him to sow oats first, and then to burn off. But would he? The Groupies had been told to plant mixed grasses and then barley in ground not yet sweet.

She touched Sarah on the arm. 'The winter will be hard. Just remember that it will pass and that next year we will be burning off like this on your block. Just remember, Sarah.'

'But at least the winter won't be hot. At least the flies will be gone. We're used to rain in England, aren't we, Deb?'

Deborah nodded. Yes, she too had thought all of that, so had Anne.

The rains came, the roads were barely passable and sometimes quite impassable. The women failed to come some weeks and when they got through, it was only some of them, and their faces were thinner, their eyes were duller. Sarah did not come at all. Her friends collected her mail and Deborah sent milk in a small billy. She sent notes. At the end of April she sent a chicken whose neck she had rung because Sarah's friends said that she could not stand the sound of rain on the roof and wouldn't eat or speak.

In May Deborah left Luke with Jimmie because Sarah must not give up like Anne had done. She followed the trail he had blazed for her through the bush. It made the journey to Sarah only a mile and a half. Her oilskins dragged at her legs, caught on shrubs. Her boots collected mud, the billy with the milk and the basket with the eggs caught again and again on sapling branches, and water showered all over her.

She dragged on, hearing nothing beneath her hat except her own breathing. Her hands were cold, numb, her feet too. It was so dark here, in the depth of the bush. Were Jimmie's spirits here, all around? Was his mother?

Sarah was sitting on a chaff mattress on her stretcher bed. Just sitting, holding her child, looking at nothing. There was no wood on the floor. There was no light in the humpy.

Deborah stood at the curtained door and shook her oilskins outside, hanging them on the peg beneath the verandah.

She threw chips in the stove, lit it. Cooked eggs for her friend, boiled the kettle for tea. Put in fresh milk, sat with her on the bed, told her of her first winter. Was it only a year ago? She told her that her husband needed her, that the farm would not produce without them both, that the sun would come again. Her child needed to hear her voice, she needed fresh air, wet though it was.

They talked for three hours and it was after five, almost too dark Deborah knew to see the trail, but she could not leave this woman yet as she had left Anne Martins. They talked for another hour and Deborah told Sarah that she too could follow the blazes that Jimmie had made. She could come through the bush with Mollie if she wished. But only in daylight. It was only when Sarah smiled and talked of the clearing that she would do with Ernie that Deborah felt her shoulders ease and relief seep through her.

She left when Ernie returned, carrying one of his hurricane lamps, edging over the ground towards the bush, saying that she was perfectly capable of finding her way. She was an old hand at this, wasn't she? Ernie must stay with his wife.

But it was dark, too dark. She should stay at the humpy but she wanted Luke. She had work to do, for she had realised as she spoke to Sarah that she had not worked either, as she should, once Jimmie had returned. All she had been doing for the past months was breathing in the smell of her child, growing flowers, vegetables, milking cows. She put her hand to her face and the palm was too soft, the fingers too.

She was into denser bush now, and she lifted the lamp higher, spotting the blazes, walking on slowly from one mark to the other. But wait, she'd lost them now. She stood still, moving the lamp around, her head up, her hat back. Yes, it was there. For God's sake, it was there.

She edged slowly forwards. Would Luke be hungry? Would Patrick feed him? Her arm ached. She had only travelled a hundred yards or so and already her arm ached, for God's sake. She must work harder, she was too soft. She changed hands, and the lantern slipped and almost fell, the light lurched, her heart stood quite still, as she did. But though it flickered it did not go out.

She could hear the drips of water from the trees. She listened to then as she put one foot in front of the other. She was frightened. This land frightened her. The darkness, the size. She looked up. There's no Milky Way here, Jimmie. She walked on. Her arm was shaking. She changed hands again and wished that someone would come.

Patrick did. He came out through the trees, into her beam of light and took the lantern from her.

'Jimmie is with Luke. I've fed him.'

She nodded, feeling the comfort of his presence, wanting to tell him, but she said instead, 'I needed one of Jimmie's fire sticks. I can believe there are spirits here, you know.'

Patrick walked on, slightly ahead, but so that she was still in the circle of light and she told him of Sarah, of the Groupies, of the toughness of their lives, of the heartache, of the difficulties, of the hope which many still held. She spoke of Nell and Susie's baby because in their house they did not discuss these things and out here, in the dark, she wanted to hear the sound of voices.

She said that she would dig the drains near the creek tomorrow so that they could get the maize in. That perhaps she could leave Luke under the shelter of Jimmie's humpy.

Patrick didn't turn but said, 'There is no need for you to work like that, Deborah.'

'There is every need, Patrick,' she replied, and there was, because he had fed a child tonight that was not his. He had built fowl pens, he had cleared land, burned logs, built a house. He had fed and housed her child. He had come to find her. 'There is every need, Patrick. We came here to start a dairy farm.'

Throughout the winter, and as spring came, she worked. They built a temporary cow bail, erecting tall posts with a bar at the top and bottom and a swinging bar attached which could lie open or be pegged shut, and bought another Guernsey cow. She separated the milk in flat pans, leaving some that was fresh, making sure there was enough for Sarah's family too. She churned the remainder, turning the handle of the wooden box until she heard the swish of buttermilk, felt the stiffening of the handle as the wooden paddles strained.

She washed and salted the small amount of butter. She mixed the skimmed milk in with the bran and pollard and fed it back to the cows, one of whom was in calf. It brought Somerset back to her, but those days were gone. Too far away. A lifetime away.

'We'll need a pig next year,' she told Patrick as she packed up the fly papers she had made and which were selling well. 'They can have the skimmed milk, we can sell the pork.'

She was busy again, she was tired, but it was right that she should be. She watched as Patrick drove the cart down the track that they had widened during the winter. She had planted maize by the creek, and potatoes again, and more paddock was cleared. Sarah was better but she herself was so tired that as she lifted her son from his pram and showed him the plovers the effort drained her.

'Listen to their song,' she murmured to him as November waned, holding Luke now one year old in her arms, feeling him push her away, turn around, lift his hands to the birds. Sarah had said yesterday that Luke had been too quiet at the tea party Deborah had given for their children's birthdays, much too quiet, but Deborah had laughed because any child would be quiet in comparison with Mollie.

'He's too quiet,' Patrick said as he sat doing his farm diary.

'He's concentrating on trying to walk. He'll find his tongue when he's done that,' Deborah replied and planned a Christmas party for them all, including the Groupies.

On Christmas Eve everyone danced, except for Patrick and her. Everyone sang and lifted their glasses to absent friends because one group settlement family had left. They had walked from their land, unable to survive after Don had pushed gelignite into a hole he had made in a jarrah to bring it down. The gelignite had exploded too soon and he had lost his hand. He couldn't work, and therefore no longer received the three pounds a week that the family needed to survive. They couldn't eat and therefore they had left.

'Where will they go?' Patrick asked Ernie.

He shrugged. 'God knows. Perth probably, but they can't go home. They have to repay their passage out first and then find their fare back.'

Deborah didn't want to listen to this, she didn't want to see the darkening of the settlers' eyes, the despair which was lurking as their land was still so far from productivity.

Neither did she want to listen to Mollie's shrieks of laughter as she crawled alongside her son who just breathed silently.

CHAPTER 16

On the eve of 1925 Deborah raised her glass to Jimmie, who was again absent, but he would return, Deborah knew that now.

At dawn she dragged the pram out over the paddocks while Patrick carried the saw and the axe. They laid out barriers of saplings and Luke played behind them on the hot parched earth well clear of the dead ring-barked trees which could and did drop their branches at any time.

She scarfed, sawed and now her hands were as hard as they had ever been. She checked Luke every few minutes. Watching for snakes, spiders. He was nearly fourteen months old, where had the time gone? He was so strong with a smile that lit her day, his arms were tanned, his legs sturdy. It was because he walked so well that he didn't bother to shout, or shriek, a fact which seemed to bother everyone but her. It *is* because he walks, isn't it? she wrote to Nell.

At lunch they boiled up a billy, drilling wood against wood as Jimmie had taught them, showing Luke, laughing as he pointed, laughing as he walked so carefully, then sat so heavily.

'He's still too quiet, Deborah,' Patrick said as he stared into his mug of tea. 'He's been walking properly for a month and he's still so quiet.'

She held her child on her lap, feeding him toasted rusks that she had made, tomatoes she had grown.

'It's this land, that's all. He mustn't be pressurised. There is no need to talk yet.'

'But he makes no sound, Deborah. We're not talking about words.'

She rose then, walking her son back to the saplings, feeling his hand around her finger, slowing her pace to his. 'See how well you walk my darling, and they expect noise from you too.' She was walking too fast now because this was her son and there was nothing wrong. Absolutely nothing wrong and she didn't know why everyone was talking to her as though there was. It was just because Mollie was talking, shouting, shrieking. Growing up wasn't a race, for heaven's sake. It was absurd. Why couldn't they all see that? Then Luke fell and his face crumpled as he rubbed his cheek with his hand. She lifted him, held him, longing to hear his cry.

'You see, he should have cried out, Deborah,' Patrick called out to her. 'But come on anyway. We're still behind.'

That evening she clipped the wings of the fowl then rubbed kerosene on their swollen legs, holding each bird beneath her arm, feeling its bones as it struggled, remembering her cockerel back in Somerset. Nell had written to say that it had died. They hadn't been able to eat it. Tom had said it would be too tough anyway. Great softie, Nell had written.

She had sent her twenty pounds, the money from all the eggs since she had left, and from the hens they had sold at the market, and the pig that she had owned with Mrs Briggs. A surprise, she had said, though perhaps you don't need it? Or perhaps you do, my dear. I know how hard farming can be.

Do you, Nell? Do you know how hot and dry this land can be? Do you know how wet, how large the trees? Would you have managed better than me? Would you have managed better than the Groupies? Because all of us are far from being self-sufficient yet.

And how is Luke? Nell had written. Has he started to say Mama? Has he called Patrick Dada?'

Their letters would have crossed, Deborah knew, and she tightened her hold on the strugging bird's neck, rubbing the kerosene firmly but gently. 'You'll get better now. There you

270

'go.' She could smell it on her hands. She caught each one in turn, holding them, rubbing them. Then she sprinkled kerosene onto the ground to keep the fowl lice and fleas down.

She scrubbed her hands in the bowl outside the front door, hard, so that it hurt, so that she would not think of the sounds which Luke would not make, so that she did not hear again Patrick's voice saying, 'He's too quiet, Deborah.' Wasn't it enough that they were behind with their schedule? Wasn't that enough to think about, worry about? Why didn't he just concentrate on that, like the other settlers were doing?

She milked the cows, hearing the hiss, stripping each udder, turning them out into the small home paddock, pouring the milk into the separator pans in the corrugated iron outhouse they had built and lined with asbestos. The cream would rise overnight, she would skim it off in the morning. She thought of how they needed pigs for the skimmed milk, not of her son.

She heard Patrick calling her. It was late, he said, and they were building the hayshed tomorrow, it should have been done last week, so come to bed, for God's sake. She leant her head against the coolness of the asbestos. That's right, she would think of the hayshed, of the sawing and banging there would be when night became day. She could only think of one thing at a time, for God's sake.

There were no fires by the creek as she walked on to the verandah, there was only the Christmas tree draped with lifeless ribbons. There were only the two adults here, marooned on the farm. That was why there was so much talk of Luke when there was no need. When Jimmie came back it would be different.

At dawn she skimmed off the cream, milked the cows, drank warm fresh milk, put some aside for Luke, for Patrick, put the rest in the flat pans. She watered the peas, the beans, the lettuce, the tomatoes, the pumpkins, the pie melons, the onions.

Down by the creek too many of her potatoes were being eaten by wallabies, and quokkers, and too much of the maize.

She told Patrick as they dug holes for the hayshed uprights. He shrugged. 'When Jimmie gets back.' His eyes were shaded, his mouth thin. She dug deep, not listening, not looking at him again, just at her son who was staggering towards the ball they had bought him. She watched him as she reached it, sat and looked and turned it and touched it with his mouth. She smiled. He was perfect. It was all nonsense. They were just tired and busy.

Jimmie returned in the middle of January. The hayshed was finished, the roof was on, and one end was boarded up.

'It's enough,' she told Sarah and the others. 'Later it will have more sides.'

It wasn't enough because the cows broke through the fence two weeks later and ate some of the hay which Deborah had scythed, turned, raked and carted, too tired for laughter as bits fell on her and on Jimmie.

They repaired the fence, put on extra sides and it held their schedule up.

'For God's sake, this is holding us up,' Patrick shouted as he split, carried, hammered. He sucked his hand and Deborah drew out the splinter which had driven deep into his palm. He pushed the Lysol she handed him, slapping it to the ground, watching it spill and soak into the earth. 'It's holding us up,' he shouted, walking from her and she was glad that he was thinking of the things that he should be concerned with, not problems that didn't exist. She smiled at Luke.

The next day she gave Patrick the cheque from Nell to pay into the bank when he went into town for the provisions. She had ordered a small separator. She worked with Jimmie all day, one or other of them watching, checking, but never listening for Luke. No, never listening she realised now.

'Tell me about the island the priest sent your mother to,' she said as they sawed, as they pushed and pulled and the sweat dragged off them both because she mustn't think the thoughts which were echoes of the words which had been spoken to her recently. 'Tell me of the mother you loved so much.'

He told her then of Dorré Island which had been set up for the sick aboriginals who were all just herded together. He told her how his mother had been sent there when his father died and how he, Jimmie, had pleaded with the priest to let him take her home. 'We know best,' the priest had said and sent her across the water to live in huts where others had died, to live on an island where the spirits of the dead were trapped.

'She sent the nurse with a bambura, a letter stick. I took a boat, I brought her here where her spirit could go to the land beyond the Western Sea, to Kur'an'nup. She died when she saw her totem coming for her.'

Deborah watched as he sawed, as he pushed, as she pulled. 'The Gregorian Chant is a long way from Kur'an'nup and totems,' she said. 'I can see that they don't mix. I can see why you leave at Christmas.' She looked across at Luke, where he played with the bricks Jimmie had cut and rubbed.

He told her then of the stories his mother and others of the tribe had told him from the Dreaming which enriched his knowledge of his world; of the stories told to children that showed that they should give, not steal, that they must share; the stories which were songs of the land and its animals, rocks and trees and of its waterfalls.

'People and children must communicate, must talk, must pass on their knowledge. There are ways other than speech, Deborah. Sometimes our people used signs. It is only fear that stands in the way of seeking these other paths.'

She took the crowbar then, jamming it beneath the trunk, hissing at Jimmie to do the same. Saying that there was no time to talk, not here, not now. He eased his crowbar beneath the trunk, they rolled it, slowly, slowly, the breath hard in their chests and said nothing more.

Patrick's hand was septic by the time he returned. She bathed it with Lysol and this time he did not strike it from her hand but when she finished he picked up Luke, held him close, kissed his head, showed him Jimmie's fires down by the creek. 'Fire,' he said. 'Fire, Luke. Fire, fire.'

273

She wanted to snatch her son away from this man whose face was too close to her child, whose voice was too loud. This is a quiet land, that's all. This boy is a product of this land you brought us too, that's all, and Jimmie was supposed to have made things better by his return but nothing was better, because echoes of their words were in her now.

They cleared as February became March and after some early rain fell they burned the heaps, pushing the potatoes in with green sticks, eating them charred. The men drank beer, the women ginger beer but it was sour in her mouth.

They took some bottles, potatoes and onions to Sarah's block one week later, laughing as the sparks burst into the sky, feeling the heat on their faces and Deborah would not listen to Mollie who shrieked with delight. She looked out across the few acres that had been cleared, the stumps, and forced herself to wonder when these settlers would be able to produce enough to be self-sufficient, when Stoke Farm would. That was the real problem, couldn't they see that, for God's sake.

Dora's heifer calf was born as heavy rain brought the pasture through green again. They had built a shelter with four bails, but needed a proper cowshed, she told Patrick, who said that there wasn't time. Not now, not yet. She felt the calf's tongue on her fingers, she held up Luke to see, to laugh, to shriek but he did not.

At the beginning of March Sarah and the other women came for the mail, for butter, for human contact as they did each week and talked of the poor potato crop, of the peas which had only filled half a kero can; the land which was being cleared at last, of the roads which would not be corrugated for years yet.

They talked of the replacement Groupie for the man who had lost his hand, of the tears his wife, a Londoner, had shed on seeing the humpy, of the barley a Group to the north had grown and allowed to seed, choking the cows.

'If only they had known to cut it earlier,' they said.

They talked of the jam they had made, the bottles they had

turned into jam jars, of the rains that would isolate them again and turn the tracks into mud.

Deborah brewed more tea in the kitchen, carried it into the front room and where there had been whispered voices there was now silence as she entered, a reddening of cheeks, and awkwardness, and then talk began again, but it was too loud. They ate her scones and asked about sales of the jam in town.

'There's very little market now,' she told them, picking up Luke, blowing into his fine hair. 'The fly paper will begin to sell again in the summer.'

The rhythm of the morning was uneasy and she was tired, too tired to talk and laugh and the women left, walking out along the trail which Patrick and Jimmie had widened and cleared, corrugated with logs, laying them side by side, filling in the cracks with earth.

Sarah stayed though, taking the mugs through to the kitchen, washing them in the kero can with water from the pan which Deborah had boiled. They washed and wiped and talked of Jimmie's mother, of Ernie's cracked rib following a fall in the bush and then again there was silence, broken only by Mollie's crying, because Luke had wanted her brick.

Sarah put her mail in her basket, and her eggs which she had bought from Deborah and which were still warm. She picked up Mollie. 'I'll follow Jimmie's trail,' she said and Deborah nodded.

'You always do.'

'I know. Deborah . . .' Sarah paused on the verandah, looking at Luke who clung to Deborah's skirt as he handed Sarah a brick. She laughed, stooped, took it. 'Thank you, Luke. Say ta,' she said to Mollie, who buried her head in her mother's neck and said nothing.

There you are you see, thought Deborah. She says nothing too, sometimes.

'I'll see you next week, Sarah,' she said now, wanting her friend off her verandah, wanting the solitude of the pastures where there were no voices to stir up fear in her.

She turned, but felt the touch of Sarah's hand on her arm, then heard her voice, loud, firm saying, 'The doctor said that you hadn't been to him for the yearly check-up. He says that you should. Better for things to be picked up sooner, rather than later, Deborah.' Sarah was gripping her arm now, her eyes intense. 'It's not fair to Luke. It's not fair to you or to Patrick. You must take him.' Sarah was pulling at her. Her round face was serious. 'There is something wrong with your son, Deborah.'

'Get off my verandah, Sarah. Go home. Take your child and go home. Don't take my peace away from me.' She was shouting, she knew, because Patrick and Jimmie were at the hayshed and had turned to look. Sarah left, taking her child, and Deborah picked up Luke, took him through the house, hurried down to the creek, and sliced the shovel into the swamp as he played beside her. She must dig more drains, that's what she must do.

She sliced, cut, dug, and then deepened it, throwing her shoes on to the ground, getting down into the trench, working with her feet in the mud.

'Don't listen to them,' she ground out to herself. 'They don't know what's important. They don't know we must get the work done. We can't waste time.'

Patrick was coming, she could hear, but there was no time to stop work. He had said so. He was standing beside her, as she sliced in the shovel, heaved at the sodden earth.

'You need to get Jimmie to put up a fence around the maize. It needs to be sunk into the earth,' she shouted.

'Stop it, Deborah.'

'The kangaroos can't get in then. We'll need the fodder for the cows now we've ordered more and there's Dora's calf.'

'Stop it, Deborah.' He was shouting now, his hands were taking the shovel from her, throwing it through the air. 'Stop it. I heard Sarah. She's right. If you don't take Luke, then I shall.'

She turned, looking at him, then at her son. When would

276

they all just leave her alone? 'You will not take him anywhere. I shall take him.' But she would not. Oh no, not really.

'When, Deborah?'

'Soon.' She was crying, she could hear it in her voice, feel the tears on her cheeks, taste the salt in her mouth and she shrugged off his hands on her arms, stepping out from the trench, forcing her wet, mud-stained feet into her shoes, picking up her child, walking with him into the bush, away from that man who was her business partner and nothing else. The man who had brought her here to solve this one problem for him. That's all, just one problem. There wouldn't be any others. How could there be any others after all this? She looked back to the cleared paddocks, and then down at her callused hands.

At the end of March the sand was carted in for the cowshed and the new dairy, and rocks were brought in, which Jimmie and Patrick broke up. Luke smiled at the noise and Deborah thought of the old man who had sat with a sack across his shoulders next to the road, next to her cottage, and she wanted to be with Nell, wanted to hear her say that Luke was all right. That all children were quiet, that Susie's two were just the same.

'When, Deborah?' Patrick said as she brought them tea.

'Soon, I said. There is is no time while you're building this.'

She milked, she collected the eggs, she cleared, she drained the land for more maize.

'When, Deborah?' Patrick said as the foundations were cleared of roots and boxed up with boards the following week. 'When, Deborah?' as he and Jimmie humped in the sand and cement over the broken rocks and evened it three days later, putting a large square block of timber into the dairy floor as a stand for a larger separator, as the cowshed floor was roughened, to make it non-slip.

'I have the washing to do. There is no time.' She boiled the clothes, coloured yellow from the sand in a kerosene can which had rusted and which stained the washing further. It didn't matter. She ironed and black marks stained her only white linen table cloth, but it didn't matter. She did not ask the women in any more for tea, she handed them the mail on the verandah and sold the eggs in town.

Patrick and Jimmie kept the cement damp for four days.

'You can go now,' Patrick said.

'There is too much to do,' she replied. 'The walls, the roof. We are too busy, we are behind schedule. Soon.'

He didn't shout, he just turned away and his face was cold.

That evening she walked down to Jimmie's fires, standing in their heat, feeling the rain on her, watching it spit into the the fire, on to the gums. She breathed in the smell and wondered how people could say such things about her son, how they could find the energy to worry about such absurdities. Why weren't they too tired, as she was?

Jimmie was squatting. He watched her, then drew emu tracks in the ash, kangaroo tracks.

'These are some of the signs we use. You whites think us stupid but it is just that we speak little. When our babies are born the tribe teaches them, signs to them, talks to them too. One day you should tell Luke of the story of the Milky Way. One day he should tell his own child. One day he should tell his child of your Somerset.'

She nodded and turned from him. He too was absurd. She didn't sleep that night, just sat on the bed and listened to Patrick as he paced, and watched the fires which glowed by the humpy, and then looked up at the sky. The next day she received a letter from Nell which said that her son should not be so silent, that there should be laughter, cries, Dada, Mama.

The next day she took Luke to the doctor in town, who said she must take the train to Perth, to a specialist. He wrote the letter while she sat with Luke so quiet on her lap. She heard the scrape of his pen, the rustle of the paper as he put it into the envelope.

Her bag was packed. She had known in her heart what

he would say and so had Patrick because he had come with her, sitting alongside her in the doctor's surgery, watching the doctor lick the envelope, then press it down with hands that had black hairs growing below the level of his starched cuff. She had never noticed that before. There was only a twice weekly train service to Perth. That train wouldn't run today, she thought. I shall go home, wash, iron, dig, grub and go later, some time later. But the train was running after all.

Patrick took her to the station in the cart. 'I'll come,' he said, as they waited.

'You need to work on the dairy. You need to get the sides up. You need to get the roof on. There is so much to do, Patrick.'

Her voice was dead. I can't tell you anything, the doctor had said. I can only suggest that there is a problem. The train came in chugging, whistling, steaming. Luke looked, pointed, and Patrick took his hand, rubbed his cheek against it. He put her bag on the train, helped her in and stood on the station as they left and didn't know how a man could live with such an ache inside him.

They travelled slowly, stopping for refreshments at small stations. They travelled through the night and she looked up at the stars that were so close, at the Milky Way, and she told her son about the women who burnt the emblem. As the miles passed he slept on her lap, his head warm on her arm, and she wanted to hold him too tightly, never let him go, take him from the train, run through the dark night to a place where no one would find them and tell her things she couldn't bear to hear. But she did not, that would be absurd.

They arrived at Perth at midday. It was so light, the streets were so wide, the buildings so solid and large. She had forgotten that anywhere like this existed. She carried her bag in one hand and Luke sat on her hip. She hailed a cab which took them through these wide streets to a hotel. She washed Luke, washed herself.

'Sleep,' she said to her son. But he wasn't tired and so she travelled with him straight to the hospital with the letter stiff in her pocket.

'Mr Wilson will see you now,' the receptionist said and smiled but Deborah could not. 'Your doctor has telegraphed.'

She took her son into the room, into the large light room. Mr Wilson sat in a leather chair behind a desk. He rose, came round, shook her hand, touched Luke's cheek, pulled out a chair for her and another for her son, but she shook her head.

'He'll stay on my knee, he's not used to large light rooms and strangers.' Her voice was still dead.

She watched Mr Wilson read the letter, leaning back in his chair, his hair shot with grey. He looked at her and smiled.

'So, you named your son after the apostle who was a doctor,' he murmured. 'Have you a doctor in the family?'

'My father. He's dead.'

'He would be pleased.'

She nodded. Yes, that is why she had given her son that name. Are you listening, Father? Make this all right. Make my son all right. At least do that for me. Make this whole thing absurd.

She talked and listened, answered questions, nodded as Mr Wilson took her son to other rooms, other places, doing tests, taking X-rays. She drank tea out of white crockery, not milk cans. She ate biscuits she had not made. She listened to the rustle of starched uniforms. Make my son all right, Father.

Mr Wilson brought Luke back at half past five, carrying him, talking to him. The child was smiling, his eyes were bright. He held a bright red ball out to his mother.

'Come back in the morning, Mrs Prover. We should have some news for you by then. The ball is for Luke, he's been a splendid boy. You must be very proud of him.'

She took Luke, put the ball in her pocket, nodded. Walked out of the hospital, took a cab to the hotel, fed Luke in the dining room but couldn't eat anything herself. Perhaps she would not go back. Perhaps she would find a ship and travel far away. But she knew that she would not.

She walked with Luke through the city. Past the art gallery, then down to the river – too shallow to use as a port, Mrs Warbuck had told her – down past White City which had merry-go-rounds, side shows, boxing booths and over by the river there was a large slide like the rollercoaster which she and Edward had ridden on and which had loomed large and dark as she had screamed. She hurried past because the scream was there now. It had been there for months and so had the darkness which swept over her like a storm but which she had refused to acknowledge.

At the hotel she took Mrs Warbuck's address out of her bag. She had given it to Deborah on the ship. Was it really only two years ago? It seemed a lifetime. It was faded, creased, and Deborah was too tired. Luke was too tired and Mrs Warbuck talked too much. Far too much when her child was so silent.

They arrived at the hospital at ten a.m as they had been instructed. Her father had always insisted that his patients were punctual so she must be now because it would help to make the news good. It must make the news good.

Mr Wilson came from behind his desk again, took Luke into his arms, smiled, talked to him, showed Deborah to her chair. A nurse was there and poured tea from a white pot into a white cup and the liquid was so brown against it. She watched as Mr Wilson sat down. She looked at the clock. It was ten past ten but that didn't matter because they had really been here on time.

'I was here on time. Really I was.'

Mr Wilson nodded. 'Yes, I know.' He sat with her child on his knee, his voice gentle. 'Your son, Mrs Prover, will never speak. He is absolutely dumb, but he can hear. That is the good news. His hearing is perfect.'

She couldn't move, she couldn't breathe, and then she saw the hands of the clock move and pushed the cup and saucer away from her, pushed it across the polished desk. She rose and took Luke from him.

281

'He's mine,' she said. 'He's mine and you're wrong.' She pushed past the nurse who stood in her way, like Mrs Prover had done. She reached for the door handle and Mr Wilson came to her, took her by the shoulders, led her back to the chair and his voice was as soft as her father's would have been, if he had lived and known that his grandson was dumb.

'You would have been, wouldn't you, Father,' she whispered.

Mr Wilson took back Luke and the nurse put sugar in her tea.

'Drink it,' the nurse said, her blonde hair tied in a bun beneath her cap.

It was sweet, too sweet. 'I don't like sugar. Edward had your colour hair,' she said. 'Luke has mine.'

Mr Wilson looked at her. 'Listen to me, Deborah. As I said, Luke's hearing is perfect. He has some congenital defect of what you would call the voice box. It is quite irreparable. You will never hear his voice.'

'Will I hear him laugh?'

He shook his head. 'Nor cry.'

She wouldn't cry. She would sit here and listen to this man. No one would hear her cry. She had said that so long ago.

So she listened and drank the tea, and then another cup, and another as he told her that speech is given to us so that we can not only tell other people what we are thinking, but know ourselves as well, because words are part of our thinking processs.

'Without speech thinking can become muddled, confused, almost non-existent, almost imbecilic, Deborah,' he said.

'But my son cannot speak, you said. Why are you telling me this? Are you mad, or just cruel? Perhaps he is just late. Perhaps you are wrong.' She was shouting. She knew she was shouting.

The nurse's hand was on her shoulder and Mr Wilson stroked Luke's hair. Her son's hair.

'I'm not wrong, Mrs Prover. Please believe me, and neither am I cruel or mad. There is sign language. It is essential that your son learns this. It is essential that he uses it to convey his ideas accurately. He must get used to constantly observing and analysing the world around him as we do. He must get used to talking to you, to your husband, to the world. Using sign.' Mr Wilson was putting Luke from his knee and they both watched the child walk over to the low table and bang the spoon which the doctor had given him on the wood. He listened to the sound, looked at Mr Wilson and Deborah, then turned away as she said, 'Spoon.'

'If he could sign, if you could also sign, if the family could sign it would open up his world. The movements are much more simple than the muscle movement needed for ordinary speech. That's why we usually only learn to speak in the second year of life.' He paused. 'The sign for milk, Mrs Prover, can be made at four months. Luke could be fluent by three years of age, then everything would be possible. He could explore the thoughts of others, discover their history, their feelings, their humour and develop his own personality. He could learn to read and write.'

He talked for longer. He gave her the address of a woman in Busselton who had a deaf and dumb son and who could teach her sign language. She would have to work hard. They would all have to work hard. They had lost time.

She left at half past twelve and walked through Perth. She took a cab to Mrs Warbuck with her son on her lap because she wouldn't believe all this. She couldn't believe it. Not her son, not her child that she loved so well. Nothing like this could happen to her child.

Mrs Warbuck was surprised to see her, but pleased. She gave them lunch. Salad with chips. Deborah hadn't eaten chips for years. They were hot and crisp. She blew on one, gave it to Luke who took it in his hand, ate it slowly, bits falling on to his knee, on to Deborah's knee on which he sat.

Mrs Warbuck talked and talked as she had always done and didn't notice that Luke was silent. She didn't notice that Deborah said little. But the noise was too much, the soft smart furnishings were too much, the light streaming in through the windows was too much, the neighbours whose houses were either side and across the road were too much.

'You have so much, Mrs Warbuck,' she said at last, getting up, walking to the door, holding her son close to her.

'You're not leaving? You haven't even finished lunch.' Mrs Warbuck's voice was sharp but it didn't matter. It didn't matter that she was rude. Nothing mattered after the doctor's words.

They had to wait until the next day to catch a train back down to the south-west. She walked with Luke through wide light streets she didn't know. There were cars, trucks, there were drays and men who cleaned the streets of manure and Deborah pushed the knowledge of Luke's silence from her. She would speak to another doctor. She would travel the world if necessary.

Luke was tired when they finally caught the train. She was tired too but couldn't sleep though it was dark with the darkness of the bush and there was rain now and it was cool.

'He's wrong. I know he's wrong,' she whispered to Luke, touching his cheek, watching the rise and fall of his chest. She looked away, out across the bush, then up to the sky where the Milky Way hung so close to the earth, as Orion had done on the ship.

She rubbed her face with her hands. She didn't want to think of the ship, or Edward, or Mrs Warbuck, who spoke so much and so long. She didn't want to think of the rollercoaster, the hot room in Melbourne, the despair, the two bodies which had clung together in what she had thought could have one day been love, but it was there in her mind and so was her guilt. But that had always been there.

Her son stirred, his lips moved. She looked at her hands, so rough, so chapped, so tanned. She looked at Luke's, so small, so soft. How could hands speak?

She turned back to the window, to the darkness which was so profound. No, the doctor could not be right. There was no defect in her family. There was no problem with speech. She

284

thought of Mrs Warbuck again, she thought of Orion, of the ship, of the light, of the hot days, of the scent of Australia as they had arrived at Fremantle, Edward's laughter as they stood at the rail and watched Mrs Warbuck leave, of his voice as he told her of his uncle who had just died.

Deborah felt the coldness begin then, in her fingertips, her hands, her arms, the panic which swept her and made her want to walk, but she could not move because her son was asleep on her lap. She heard Edward's voice as he told her of his uncle who had been dumb.

She didn't move, she just looked at her child and said, 'What have I done to you?'

She knew now that Mr Wilson had been right. She knew now that she would never hear Luke's voice. That it was Deborah Prover who had been absurd, all these months.

CHAPTER 17

Deborah left the train at Busselton. She sent a telegram to Patrick saying that she would be on the next one. She walked to the address which Mr Wilson had given her and knocked on the door. It was only eight-thirty in the morning, but what did it matter. She had lost months already.

Beth Murdoch answered in her apron, her hair straggled loose from her bun. Deborah stood. She could find no words. Suddenly there were no words in her mind.

'Help me,' she said at last. 'Please help me. My son can't speak.'

The older woman took her into her house, where there were geraniums on tables near the window, pictures on the wall and rugs on the floor. She poured tea from a pot which already stood on the table. She gave milk to Luke, and toast.

She listened as Deborah told her of Mr Wilson but not of Edward. That was her pain, her guilt. Mrs Murdoch smiled and said of course she would help, that Deborah must come each week and learn a little more, that she must take home the knowledge and teach it to Luke, to Mr Prover.

'My son is deaf and dumb but is now grown up and in America. He's at college training to be an architect. He's quite independent and one day he will come home and see me. I never thought he would be able to earn his own living, live alone even,' Mrs Murdoch said, pouring more tea, passing sugar that Deborah had no need of now.

She told her that while signing might appear to be a chaotic mixture of symbols there were actual grammatical constraints as there were in speech. Signers can set a whole scene up so that you can see where everyone or everything is very quickly, she said, visualised with a detail that would be rare for the hearing.

'Before David learned to sign he couldn't count. He made notches on a stick when he ran out of fingers. Signing has transformed his life, and ours. It allows him to deal with things at a distance without actually handling them. It has allowed his imagination to flourish, his personality to develop.' She pointed to a photograph of a blond young man. 'So like his father.'

Deborah nodded. Luke had chestnut hair. He was not like his father. He was like his father's uncle and the pain knotted in her.

Mrs Murdoch said that Luke would learn well between twenty months and thirty-six. 'But it's never too early to start, my dear, nor too late. 'You will find it difficult though, Deborah. You won't be as receptive. Children are like sponges, they soak it up.'

'I'll learn. We'll all learn.'

She left then, and walked around town, seeing which shops would take her jam, which would take her fly papers. Her local markets were insufficient. She would need to pay for the travelling each week and it must not come out of the farm money because all this was to benefit her son.

On the train journey home she thought of Beth Murdoch and her son, who wrote each week but hadn't been home for two years. Luke would not leave her though. They loved one another too much.

Patrick was waiting at the station, his face strained. The pouring rain ran off his oilskins. He had brought hers. She sat in the cart with Luke on her lap beneath her waterproofs. The cart lurched, Bet whickered and strained. The track to the station was gravelled. She heard it beneath the wheels.

She told Patrick then and he nodded. 'I thought so. We all thought so. I'm so sorry, Deborah.'

The bush was closing in on them as they left the town.

'I'm going to Busselton once a week to learn to sign. We all need to learn to sign. It will help him.'

'All of us? Me and Jimmie too?'

The horse was pulling the cart through the mud, the potholes had been filled in with sand. She thought of the wide Perth streets, the light, the neighbours. She thought of Edward's uncle, she thought of her son and knew she had no right to ask this of Patrick, but she must. For Luke.

'It is important that he is fluent, that he feels at ease amongst others, that we sign as well as speak. I'll work harder to help. I have markets for my jam and fly paper in Busselton to pay for my travelling. Please, you must make time, Patrick. I'll teach you what I learn and I'll work harder to make up your time and mine.'

'I thought you meant we'd all have to travel. That's no problem. We'll learn. Of course we'll learn, Deb, and there's money available to pay for your travelling.' Patrick's voice was low. 'We have enough for that, for God's sake, and there's no need for you to work any harder.'

But you don't understand, she thought, there was every need.

Each week she and Luke travelled to Busselton and learned how much space a signer needs. She learned the etiquette of signing, the starting of a conversation, keeping it going, taking your turn, interrupting, and ending. She learned how to show attention, how to get attention. She returned at the end of each day tired. She paid the carter to take her to Mr Martins' and then she walked, carrying Luke.

She taught Patrick and Jimmie too.

Patrick said, 'Leave Luke with us. It's just more tiring for you to take him.'

She refused. This child was her responsibility, more than ever now, and Patrick must not be inconvenienced any more than he already was. Besides, she could not bear that Luke should be out of her sight.

Each Tuesday she gave Sarah and the others tea and they

were kind. They listened to her, they watched her hands and Sarah learned as Patrick and Jimmie did. But there were deep lines on Sarah's face. Their cow had died. It had eaten the leaves of the zamia palm and developed rickets.

'You should have stabbed them,' Deborah said, 'poured kero down to the roots.' She tried to sign it and knew that she should go to Sarah's land and show her how but there wasn't time. She must work harder on their own land to make up for the time she was in Busselton.

May became June. The rains were heavy and the cart could not get through. Deborah dug drains in the wet instead of travelling to Busselton, impatience burning into her, watching Luke playing in the bark humpy she had built nearby. She kept his line of vision to her clear. She made signs to him, using her face, her eyes, her mouth, talking to him too, always talking because she had wasted so much time.

She dug drains that filled with water and covered her feet. She was cold but it didn't matter. She heard the mud slurp on to the shovel, heavier than dry soil would have been, but it didn't matter. She cleared with Jimmie and Patrick. She washed, she ironed. She milked the cows in the cowshed. Patrick bought another two. One calved. She was up all night. It was a bull calf. They would sell it for veal. She worked all the next day.

'No, I'm not tired,' she said when Patrick told her to stay in bed for longer. How could she be tired, when she was taking so much time from his schedule?

The rains became easier and the following week she began travelling again, hearing the wheels rattling on the tracks, feeling the throbbing of the headache which never seemed to leave and the heaviness of her eyelids, which must not close.

June became July. Patrick bought a horse and spring cart. She drove Bernie to the station instead of walking. She sold her Wedgwood and Geoff's clock in Busselton to pay towards the cart.

'But there is no need,' Patrick said.

'There is every need,' she replied.

She rose each morning at dawn and milked the cows, even when she was going to Busselton. She turned the small separator, washed it. They took the buttermilk to Jack's where the carter would collect it, along with what the Groupies were producing. Sarah was not among them. She took Luke with her. Always he must be with her, to learn, to develop.

July became August, storms brought trees crashing to the ground and Ernie was hit by a falling branch from a dead ring-barked tree. Jimmie worked his farm for him while he lay on his stretcher bed in the humpy and Deborah missed the fires by the creek, missed the stories he told them all of the children and the spirit kangaroo and the bush mice, or of his droving days and the Hereford herd with their whitewashed faces that he had driven down from North to Central West Australia.

Jimmie had learned to sign quickly. 'We are used to it. We use it in our rituals, we use it when we are hunting and require silence. It is not the same, but it makes me receptive,' he said.

In September the travelling was easier but she was even more tired because the days were longer and therefore she could do more work. She dug her vegetable patch, she manured it, planted it. She clipped the hens' wings and read to her son, each evening in her own room, and relished their time of solitude, preferring it now to the campfire.

In late September Jimmie came back for the fencing and though the camp fires were burning by the creek again she put her son to bed and read to him, putting curtains up because Luke was drawn to the flickering light, to the sight of Jimmie, of Patrick by the fire.

'It's too late, my darling, you must sleep,' she said each night. 'Jimmie is too busy for stories, too tired after such a long time at Sarah's. A quiet time is better for you too.'

She said the same to Patrick, to Jimmie.

'We're not tired,' they said.

In mid October she grubbed out the scarlet runner which was choking the pastures.

'So pretty, so very pretty,' she murmured, her hands working, her shoulders, her eyes as she tried to sign to Luke as well as pull out the long vines with their red pea flowers. So very pretty but so prolific. She showed them to Luke telling him they were naughty but nice, watching as he laughed so silently, watching his fingers curve, his little finger lift and his mouth turn down. 'Yes, that's right, bad.'

She eased her back, looked across at the thick mat over the grass and clover. She would have to grub out every single plant, it was the only way. She tugged. It was like wire. She looked across to the distant paddock. The men were working, Jimmie was uncoiling the wire. He would leave for Sarah's again tomorrow and there would be no fires for Luke to lift the curtains and point to.

At the end of the day the scarlet runner lay in mounds about the paddock. She gave some pieces to Luke to carry, watching as he stepped on the ends, and staggered, fell, rose again. Watching as he learned to walk clear of them. She hugged him to her, kissed his neck, knowing that with his love she was at last complete.

Jimmie came over, laughing as the boy rushed to him, signing hello. He laughed again as he tossed the child in the air.

'Careful, Jimmie. Be careful. You might drop him. Come here, Luke.' Her voice was sharp. Why was that? Why did she feel so angry at the sight of those two faces close together, why did she feel anger when Luke turned, as he did now, and waved to Patrick? It was tiredness of course. It was too much, all of this. Just too much. She called sharply to Luke, 'Come back, with Mother.'

Jimmie walked towards her, looking at the heap, bending and tugging at some runners that were still rooted. 'It will clog the hay-mower. It will destroy the crop and the machinery. Love can be like that. It can root in too deep. It can overgrow, smother.'

Deborah watched Luke bring her some of the bright red flowers. 'Mrs Prover was like that.'

'Yes,' Patrick said as he came closer, signing hello to Luke. 'It drove me away.'

Luke came to her then and she turned from these men. There was food to prepare, there was Luke's lesson, there was his bath. There was the story she would read. She walked from the men, holding Luke tightly, telling him that she loved him, so much. So very much.

Throughout October she worked on the weed because Ernie sent a message that he was feeling better, he could manage, and so Jimmie stayed and helped Patrick with the fencing in her place, then they both brought in the silage, digging a pit, excluding all light. Each night they told stories around the campfire again and Patrick took her son with him so she went too, but each night she slept badly and dreamt of her father and mother walking away from her, without the pony.

In November Ernie's leg was bad again and Jimmie returned to Sarah and Deborah slept well, at last she slept well.

The other women collected Sarah's mail, delivered her eggs because she couldn't leave Jimmie to do all the work alone but Deborah had no time to visit, because her son needed her.

'I was wrong and left it almost too long,' she wrote to Sarah. 'I must spend every minute I have with him.'

She grew and bottled rhubarb, made strawberry jam. She took it to Busselton to sell and each day she hauled at the scarlet runners until it was gone, all gone.

The late spring hay was ready. They hired a hay-mower and she walked in the paddocks collecting up the sticks, the branches from the dead trees, the stones while Luke played beside her and then cleared the mower after each circuit of grass which clogged the blades.

She travelled, learned, taught Patrick, taught Jimmie when he returned at the end of each week to stay overnight in his humpy and there was no time left for him to tell stories to her son and there was even less time for her to sleep. She had to sew new clothes for her son. She had to turn

292

pieces of material into patchwork to sell. She had to salt pork.

She was too tired to listen to Patrick at the table as he told her of their tasks for the next week, so that he had to repeat it again and again. She was too tired to ask the women for news, though some were thriving and others were not.

There was no time for a Christmas party that year. She was too tired, there was too much to do. Instead Christmas Eve was quiet and Christmas Day was a day on which they gave presents but also worked and signed. It was a day when they talked in the evening with Jimmie, who had stayed this year because Luke had lifted his arms to him, then lowered his hands and signed, 'stay.'

He talked to them around his fire of the myths and legends, the hero ancestors of his people. He told them, and signed to Luke when he could, that in the dreaming state which you arrived at in the rituals, you were not just re-enacting, you were really there.

He told them that in the north-west the men dreamt their children. That even if they had not been home for five years, but had seen their child in their dreams that child was theirs. He told them that in the south-west it was the mother who dreamt the child.

He told them of the berries the women would collect, of the game the men would hunt. He traced in the ash the tracks of a kangaroo and an emu but then Deborah said that the mosquitoes were biting her son and they must go in.

That night she watched her son's hands signing on the sheet. He was asleep. He was sleep talking and she wept because the travelling was worthwhile, her son would talk.

The heat of the summer gave way to the wet of winter. Patrick grew winter oats, barley, field peas. She scythed a bit at a time for the cattle. They had five cows, four milking, one dry. She drew her water from the well, boiled her washing, hung it to drip in the damp of the verandah, brought in gum logs for the fire, chips for the stove from the rear verandah, heaped the super further beneath the verandah to keep it dry.

She screamed when Patrick came in covered in red, but it wasn't blood, it was red gum which he had been chopping. He laughed, and Luke tried to laugh too, but her own laughter was stifled in her throat, beneath the throbbing of her head.

'You're tired,' Patrick told her as he washed his face, his arms, his hands.

'I can't be tired,' she said and turned away. She had to work, she had to travel and that was all there was to it and she had to read to her son when he came in each night from Jimmie's humpy, a pattern which had begun again after Christmas Day.

'He needs English stories too. That's part of his culture also,' she told Patrick when he demurred and said it was too late.

They brought a larger separator and she milked each morning though her head ached and her shoulders were stiff and tense. The Lister separator was set up in the dairy. She carried the milk across, turned the handle faster and faster until the bell stopped ringing. If she slackened off it rang again, so loud, too loud. It rang, too, when she stopped turning to change the kero buckets filled with skimmed milk. It rang when she filled the bowl with fresh milk. It pierced her head.

She heard it as March became April even when she left the dairy, even as she stirred the porridge.

'You're tired,' Patrick said again.

She could barely hear him above the noise of the bell. 'I'm not tired,' she shouted.

'Let me go to Busselton instead. You stay here.'

'I'm not tired,' she shouted again because how could this man who had been deceived leave his farm for a whole day to help a child that wasn't his? Couldn't he understand that? But of course not. It was her secret. He was her child. Her beautiful child, who held his arms to her and whose neck she kissed. He was her son whom she loved and whom she would protect. He was her son who loved her, and only her.

Luke was developing well now. He was two years and almost five months. He was talking too. He was using the space around him to speak to her, to speak to Mollie who came with her mother now that Ernie was slightly better. Mollie giggled at Luke, and Deborah wanted to slap her because she couldn't sign, and because she laughed at her son. Sarah signed, though not properly yet.

'I'm too busy to spend any more time, Deborah,' she said as she collected her mail. 'Ernie's leg is still stiff. I've had to stab the zamias for him because we've been issued with another cow. Did you know Mrs Burgess's son has drowned in the creek? She needs company. I've been going. Can you?'

Deborah couldn't go. She had to travel to Busselton the next day, she had to work, she had her son to teach, the separator to turn, the milk to get to the carter. How could she go, she wanted to scream. How can I do anything more than I'm doing? How can anything be more important than this?

In May she arrived home from Busselton in torrential rain. She carried her son into the house, into the kitchen, wiped his face, his hands, put him into his playpen until she had bedded the horse.

Outside, her fingers were stiff on the horse's harness. She blew on them, tried again. They were too cold, too wet. How could she sign when she went in to Luke? Her head was ringing. She could hear the bell of the separator but it couldn't be working. It needed her. Everything needed her. The bell was louder as she drew the horse from the shaft, as she led it into the horse-yard, then into the stable they had built from slabs. She had a splinter in her thumb. She hadn't felt it, her hands were too callused.

She brushed the horse down, gave him his fodder, checked his water, looked into the dairy. It was empty, the skimmed milk was in the kero cans but she could still hear the bell, it was splitting her head. She leant against the wall. Her hair was so wet that it dripped down her neck, underneath her oilskins which were so heavy. She poured the skim into billies. Tomorrow some could go into the cows' feed, some could be sold. They needed pigs, for God's sake.

She walked across to the verandah, up the steps, into the house and Patrick was there now with her son in his arms and her son was signing to him. 'Did you dream me, Daddy?'

She stood and watched as Patrick looked up at her and said, and signed, 'Yes, you are my son.'

She felt the blackness coming then as the pain in her head surged and knocked against the inside of her skull, as the noise of the bell overcame everything.

Patrick travelled to Busselton every alternate week after that.

'You will stay here with Luke. It's bad for the boy. It's tiring. Hadn't you thought of that?'

He came back and taught them all that Mrs Murdoch had taught him. He took her jam, her patchwork cushions and sold them. She didn't work out in the pastures with Jimmie because of Luke. It was too wet. Instead she washed and ironed as she had always done. She salted the pork she had bought from Jack. She practised her signing. She preserved eggs but then the rain eased and she scythed the oats and barley as the cattle needed them.

She carted some to Sarah, heaving the stooks off the cart, then carried them through into the outhouse while Luke stayed beside Sarah's fire.

She drank tea in the house they now had and still Mollie giggled at Luke. Sarah told Deborah that Mrs Burgess was drinking because she could not come to terms with her grief but Deborah did not want to hear of death from drowning. She did not want to hear of the loss of a son. She had no time to visit the Burgesses' house. Sarah must go if she wished. Deborah had no time.

In early spring they burned the heaps and did not ask the neighbours though Patrick wanted to. 'There's no time,' she said. 'We're behind, for God's sake. I'll cook some for the four of us.' She sold those that their neighbours would have eaten to help pay for the Busselton trips.

They built a cow-yard and race-way leading both to and from the cowshed. They built a big wooden gate to close the cattle in the yard. Jimmie and Patrick built it with strainer posts and rails to a height of six feet. It was large enough to hold up to thirty cows.

'We're getting there, Deborah. At last we're getting there,' Patrick said as he wrote in his notebook that night.

'Yes, he's nearly three and talks so much,' she said.

Again they didn't stop for Christmas and in February the women who came for tea told her that Mrs Burgess had died. She had walked out into the night, down to the creek where her son had drowned, and had been found beneath the water in the morning. Sarah was weeping at home.

'She couldn't come. She was too upset. Too tired.'

But Deborah didn't want to hear of a woman who had died in a creek. Too many had died beneath water. She handed them their mail, gave them Sarah's to leave on their way to their homes.

She listened as they talked of the land they had cleared, seeded and which was now supporting house cows, but nothing more. They told her of other Group Settlers who had been put on land not properly surveyed, with foremen who knew too little, of those who had already walked off, been broken by the lack of equipment, the flies, the fleas, the hardship, the poor stock.

'We're so lucky,' said Mrs Williams, and Deborah looked at her, at her face which had aged ten years in two. Of her hands which were as callused as her own.

'The Government is setting up a Group school too. The children will be ready for it soon. Even your boy Luke. He could go.'

Deborah looked at her son who was playing with the older children. They were kicking his ball but they were leaving him behind. He was signing for them to wait. But they didn't see, they didn't make space for him. He signed for them to come back as they threw it high into the air near the home paddock, but they did not.

School was too far away. She would not think about it because after school came college and Mrs Murdoch's son had left her, had gone away. No, school was too far away to think about.

She did not visit Sarah. She helped the men instead to build a pig run for the three sows and the boar they had ordered. Cutting the slabs, building the pens; one for the boar, one for each sow, enclosing the yard, digging deep for the posts, tamping them.

She felt the sweat rolling down her back. She squinted her eyes against the flies, breaking off to chop at a tiger snake which they disturbed as it basked in the dry grass. She checked again that Luke was within the enclosure which they had ensured was snake-free.

She brought out tea and while they drank it, she watched Jimmie and Luke speaking to one another of pigs, of piglets, and Jimmie making snuffling noises while Luke's eyes laughed.

She watched and listened as Jimmie said, 'My people were taken from their woodland dwellings and put into stone-walled houses on the missions, shut away from the air that was their breath of life. Some love can be like that.'

She said loudly, 'My son is only three, too young for stories like that.' She threw her tea on to the ground and lifted Luke into her arms, carried him away from the two men who had looked at her with eyes that were dark and she didn't understand them and neither did she understand the rage which had risen within her at Jimmie's words.

She and Patrick travelled alternate weeks, and in October Mrs Murdoch told them that they need only come every two weeks, that though they were late to signing they had learned so much.

It gave them more time. Deborah cleared the pastures of broken branches before the mower was used. She helped the hay up on the cart and laughed as bits fell on to Jimmie, on to herself, on to her son. She smelt it on her son's skin in the evening.

She heard from Sarah who was coming for her mail again of the school which had been erected, and was now functioning, of the teacher who insisted that he would teach each and every child to swim because of the Burgess tragedy and she knew then that her son would never go to that school.

'He's too vulnerable,' she told Patrick that evening as they sat on the verandah watching Luke, who was nearly four now, walk down to Jimmie's humpy as he had begun to do every day.

'It's the best thing for him, Deborah. He should go.'

'They teach them to swim. He couldn't cry out if he needed help. It's too big a risk.'

She watched her son squatting beside Jimmie, she watched his hands move, his eyes following the stick which was drawing symbols. He would smell of smoke. He would not want her story again tonight but she would read it none the less. She always read it, using her hands and her mouth, and her body. He was her son. He should hear her story too and she moved to ease the ache which twisted inside her at the sight of Jimmie with her son.

'Listen, Deborah. He should go to school. He needs the company of others. We don't see enough people any more. He must have the chances that Mrs Murdoch's boy has had.'

Deborah left the verandah, walking towards the boy, calling to him, and Patrick wanted to take her in his arms, to tell her that he existed too, to tell her that it wasn't enough any more just to have her working beside him, that the ache that pulled at him he knew at last was love.

It had been love all the time, but he hadn't known it until she had fallen to the floor that night when Luke had asked if he had dreamt him. He hadn't known it until he had carried her to her bed, taken her clothes from her, and felt tenderness, as well as passion. He hadn't known it until he had felt a savage loneliness tear at him as he covered her, left her and returned to his own room.

That night as he had lain alone he had remembered the cold which had seeped into them both as she had stood at the edge of the mist-shrouded Levels and listened to him talk of Dave. He remembered the myrtle which she had made and which he had thrown to the ground.

He had thrown her love away too because he had not recognised the pain within him for what it was. He had not realised that love did not have to draw the breath from another's body, it did not have to suffocate and destroy as his mother's had done. It did not have to possess and spoil, but it was too late for him now. He had hurt her too often. Her love for him did not exist, she had turned elsewhere.

Now he watched her stoop and pick up her son and it was as though he was watching his mother and he knew that he must stop this, but he didn't know how. All he knew was that he must be careful because Deborah had been hurt enough already by life, by people, including him.

CHAPTER 18

In November an Agricultural Show was held, as it had been for the last few years, on the outskirts of the town.

'We shall go to celebrate Luke's birthday,' Patrick said, though in reality he wanted them to mix and mingle, for the boy to be with others. 'Bring your sweet peas, your jam, Deborah. Enter it for the prizes. It would be good for sales.'

She came, sitting on the cart with him, holding Luke's hand, travelling along the track through the bush, showing the boy the wild orchids that she had learned to spot in the undergrowth, pointing out the magpies that flew across the track in front of them.

They veered left around the town, drawing up at the showground, leaving their cart where others had been tethered, fixing the nose bag, petting Bernie.

'I'll teach you to ride one day,' she told Luke. 'Everyone should be able to ride.'

She looked at Patrick. Did he remember Penny? She did. She remembered the feel of his hand as he eased her foot into the stirrup, his face as he laughed at her, the feel of his fingers on her ankle. She remembered too the careering gallop away from Lenora, away from his mother, from his lies, from his lack of love. She remembered her own lie and felt despair twist inside her.

She walked on, Luke's hand warm in hers. The heat was building, the grass was drier than it had been just two weeks ago. She remembered how they had stooped, touched the grass, looked at the horizon on Lenora.

'It's dry,' Patrick said now, coming to take Luke's other hand, looking around. 'There wasn't so much rain this winter and it's hotter than usual. Jimmie said he'd check the firebreaks today, said he'd rather do that than be here.'

She nodded, looking out across the show ground, like an English fairground, like the fair where she had swung on boats with Patrick. It had been cold then though, so cold. Did he remember?

'He prefers the solitude of the bush and after a life like his who can blame him? He must be so lonely,' she said. The ground was uneven, she caught her foot on a dry rut of earth, steadied, then continued. They were passing sideshows, displays and exhibits housed in long tents.

'He's going to buy a block. Should have enough in two years,' Patrick said. 'By then we'll be able to manage without his help, but he'll still be near us. He seems part of us. I'd miss him. Luke would too.' They had let go of Luke's hands and were signing as well as speaking. They no longer thought of it, they just did it and left his hands free, so that he could too.

Luke was looking away from them, at the merry-go-round. He turned, signed to them, his lips up, his eyebrows working, his mouth too and they laughed and nodded, following him across, sitting him on the small horse. They listened as the music began again, as the horses began to move, as he clung to the pole and smiled but did not shriek as the other children were doing.

There was so much music blaring, she thought, so much sound. There were pigs grunting over to the right in their pens, there were cows lowing, sheep baaing. There was bunting. It was tiring. They'd had so little noise in the bush and she thought she preferred it now.

She lifted Luke from the horse as the merry-go-round stopped, felt his arms around her neck, saw his delight, his excitement.

'More, more,' he signed.

'Later,' they laughed.

She put her strawberry jam into the preserve tent and her

302

sweet peas into the flower tent which was heavy with the scent of stocks, snap-dragons, roses. There was pink myrtle in one bowl along with carnations.

'Next year I shall grow roses. How about that, Luke?' she said because the scent of the myrtle was strong and it brought back too much. She hurried past. Patrick must not smell it, it would hurt him too much.

They walked alongside the tables which were covered in cloth. It was as though she was back in Somerset, as though she was back with Nell.

'I haven't written for too long, Luke,' she said to her son, signing to him, smiling as he pointed to the flowers and signed, 'Pretty.'

A woman stopped and looked. She stood between Luke and Deborah, in their line of vision. Luke moved to one side, touching the woman, smiling, signing at her that the flowers were pretty.

She didn't understand and shrugged at her husband. 'He's not all there,' she said and moved along.

Luke looked at Patrick, at his mother and he was no longer smiling and there was hurt in his eyes. She took his hand and walked with him from the tent, quickly, too quickly so that Luke had to run.

'It's too hot in these tents,' Deborah said. Her voice was shaking, her throat was tight. She shouldn't have come, she shouldn't have brought him here, amongst so many people who did not understand.

She stopped, turned to Patrick. 'There are too many people here. Too many people everywhere. They don't understand him. It's all just so difficult.'

'No it's not. You must show them, that's all. We learned, others can.'

He took her arm, cursing the woman inwardly, cursing the crowds who pushed past them because his throat had tightened and his shoulders had tensed as the woman had said those words. But somehow Luke must be eased from Deborah and today was the start.

He steered Deborah towards the stock, the poultry, the grasses and clovers, then towards the roped-off section where the vehicles were on display.

He lifted Luke on to his shoulders, pointed out to him the T-model Ford utility.

'It'll carry half a ton in the back. I'll have the money next year. I'll wait until then. Don't want to have to worry about interest.'

She wasn't looking at the truck, she was looking at Luke who gripped Patrick's face. She looked at Patrick's hands on her son's knees.

'He can't sign,' she said. 'Put him down while you go and look.'

Patrick looked at her face, patted Luke's knee. 'You're all right for a bit aren't you, Luke.'

He moved along the rope, away from her. She followed, looking at the vehicles, and then back at her son. She wanted to reach up, take his hand in hers, that hand that lay on Patrick's face. Luke turned, he lifted his hands, he signed, 'Nice cars,' wobbled, and she shouted, 'Put him down.'

Patrick had hold of him though. He didn't fall. 'I told you, he's fine.'

But he lowered Luke, sent him across to Deborah, stooped beneath the rope, beckoning to the salesman. He turned to Deborah. 'Why not give him another go on the merry-go-round, I'll meet you there, then we'll have the picnic.'

He watched her walk between the crowds, beneath the bunting, which hung lifeless in the still hot air. He knew he must go gently with this woman who had grown to love her son too much.

They ate their picnic in the light shade of a red gum. They peeled the shells off the hard-boiled eggs.

'Give me the shells. I'll grind them for fowl grit,' she said. She poured tea for herself but Patrick drank beer. She watched as Luke put his finger into the glass and sucked it, grimacing at its bitterness.

'Only a little,' she warned.

They ate cheese she had made and watched others who picnicked too. They were in groups. Mrs Taylor was there with three other Group families. They waved and laughed, lifting their mugs, their glasses to one another and to Patrick and Deborah.

'Sarah should have come,' Deborah murmured, cutting up tomatoes, passing them on a plate to Patrick.

'She's too tired with this pregnancy,' he said, biting the tomato, catching the pips which spurted from it in his hand.

Deborah looked up, her hands still. 'I didn't know.'

'She's showing now, has been for a while.'

'I haven't noticed.'

'You don't notice very much these days.' He was wiping his hands on his handkerchief.

Deborah thought of her friend, of the lines around her mouth, of Ernie who still limped, still struggled to develop his land and was sorry, so sorry, but then Luke stood and pointed to the children playing football, children who were kicking, running, shouting, pushing, laughing.

'Me too,' he signed.

'It's too hot,' she said. 'They're too rough.' She forgot about Sarah as she remembered the children who played on mail days, who didn't watch for her son's signs, who shouted directions, pushed, shoved. She packed away the picnic, wanting to be away from here, wanting to be back at the house where there were no others, where there was no danger to her son, no hurt for him. She felt anger tighten in her as she looked from the hamper to Patrick.

'We shouldn't have come. It was cruel. These are the children that will be at school. How can he play with them, how can he shout for the ball? They won't understand him if he starts signing. They'll block his line of vision, they won't give him space. And how could he shout for help if he was swimming as this teacher insists? Remember that woman in the tent. Remember the look in his eyes.'

He said nothing, just nodded, drained his beer. 'It'll be all right, Deborah.'

He turned to Luke. 'We'll go back now, see how your mother's flowers have done, how her jam has, shall we, Luke?' and she wanted to pull him from her son, and tell him it was not all right. That there were people in this world who were thoughtless, and unkind, but they were walking away now, and she put his empty glass in the hamper, smelling the hops in the heat of the day. There was nothing to do but follow them through the crowds, through the heat, through the tent doorway into the humid heat.

Patrick said to her quietly as she stood by the table where her jam had won second prize, 'There will always be people like that woman. But there will also be people like Jimmie and Sarah too. She is teaching Mollie to sign now.'

She said nothing and they moved to the flower tent where her sweet peas had been highly commended. She plunged her face into their petals, their fragrance. She hadn't known that Mollie was learning to sign. She hadn't known that Sarah was pregnant, and confusion pulled at her, and regret.

She walked back through the crowds, past the merry-go-round while Patrick carried Luke, calling out to Deborah to slow down, it was too hot. She didn't though, she carried on until she reached the horse and carts, until she reached Mrs Taylor's. She wrote a note, put the flowers and the jam in the back.

'I've sent them to Sarah,' she said to Patrick.

'She'd rather you took them yourself.'

She shook her head.

'I haven't time.'

She travelled to Busselton at the beginning of December and talked to Mrs Murdoch about her son, about his travels, about a mother's loneliness.

Mrs Murdoch smiled and said, 'My husband and I talk of him often. We sit here each evening, reading his letters. We show them to his sister who lives round the corner. She was always by his side when they were young. Yes, of course we miss him but he's happy. We have one another, as you have your husband.'

Deborah went to her jam markets and showed them her second place rosette and they increased their orders, and on the train home she thought of Mrs Murdoch, of her husband, her daughter and knew that it was different. There was no such companionship for her, no such sister for Luke. She must be there for him, for ever, as he would be for her.

As Christmas approached they mowed the pastures for hay, and two of the sows had litters, squealing, wriggling piglets, and Luke pointed, touched, stroked as she held the pink bodies. She wrote to Nell and told her that the skimmed milk was being put to good use, that Luke was signing very well, that he was joking, that he was growing, that she could see the boy and the man he would be.

They checked the firebreaks again as the weather grew even hotter. They felled and snigged as many of the ring-barked trees as they could into heaps, in case there should be a fire. She drew water from the creek and the well for her fruit trees.

She still read Luke a story, although Jimmie told him many around the fire in the evening. He still signed in his sleep at night and she would watch as she lay in her own bed, pulling back the curtain which Patrick had put up and which now hung between them.

In the daytime she kicked a football for him, because he signed so often of the boys he had seen playing at the show and Patrick did also at the end of his day's work.

'I'll take him out with me in the paddocks,' he said, but she shook her head.

'It's too hot, he's too young,' she said.

Luke signed to Mollie when Sarah came for her mail, but Mollie blushed and sat on her hands, burying her face in her mother's side.

'It's the baby. She's become silly,' Sarah said.

Luke signed to the other children too because they were

on holiday from school and had come with their mothers to collect the mail, drink lemonade, and talk of swimming in the dammed creek.

Deborah gave them the football to kick, to make them run and not talk of swimming and school. As their mothers drank tea on deal chairs on the verandah Deborah watched Luke standing on the parched earth, signing at them to kick the ball to him. She watched as they ran, not looking, just shouting, just passing the ball, her son's ball and she wanted to snatch it from them, throw it far away.

The mothers talked of school, of the teacher who was excellent, of the Group Christmas party that would be held there on Christmas Eve, of the dancing, the food arrangements, the school concert and Deborah just poured the tea and wouldn't think of it, wouldn't talk of it.

She talked instead of Sarah's baby, due in March, of Ernie's leg which was still so stiff, of their new cow which was thriving, of the scarlet runner which Sarah and Ernie would need to grub out by hand.

'I'll ask Jimmie if he would mind helping, instead of clearing with Patrick. I can take his place on the snig chain,' Deborah said.

'Perhaps you could come over instead of Jimmie. You could bring Luke,' Sarah said, touching Deborah's arm. 'It would be good for him to play with Mollie. It would be good for him to be in someone else's home. We could have the other Groupies over.'

'I haven't time. There's the jam, you see. No, I shall send Jimmie.'

That evening she told Patrick of the boys' thoughtlessness, of the fact that their mothers had done nothing.

'I shall teach him at home,' she said. 'It will be kinder to him.'

Patrick smoked his cigarette and said nothing.

Jimmie did go. He stayed for two weeks and there were no fires, no stories and she read to her son every night for much longer than usual and she slept well, so very well.

The week before Christmas was very hot, the piglets were growing, the cows were milking well, the fowl were laying. She was up at dawn watering her vegetables, her fruit, cutting maize for the cows, milking, separating, and carting the buttermilk to Jack who then took hers and the Groupies' in to the station.

She was making cheese too because the Busselton shop had asked if she would. She was snigging with Patrick, she was putting Luke on the horse's back, laughing as he smiled, promising him a pony one day, promising him that they would both bone their boots and ride across the land together, always together and she wouldn't think of her father, who had never ridden with her. She wouldn't think of her husband who had, but only because it might be useful.

Sarah collected her mail on the Tuesday and said that the Christmas party would be good. Deborah and Patrick would be able to see the school, Luke too. Deborah didn't sleep well that night and when she did she dreamed of Mr and Mrs Murdoch sitting together because they loved one another and though their son was gone there was no loneliness in their house.

In the morning, she hooked the snig chain to the trunk and told Patrick that they didn't have time to go to the school, it was too dry, they must clear the break between the northern paddock and the bush.

'It will be good for the boy to mix. It will be good for him to have his freedom. Remember the frogs, Deborah, how you set them on leaves, set them free. Your son needs friends.'

'I don't see what frogs have got to do with this. And anyway, he sees his friends on Tuesdays. They don't know what he is saying. They don't make space for him. They take the smile from his eyes. He has us.' She was bending over, wedging the crowbar beneath the trunk, looking across at Luke who was kicking the ball at the edge of the mowed paddock.

'He needs more than us,' Patrick said.

'He has Jimmie.' The sweat was dripping down her face.

'When he's here.' Patrick's voice was curt. 'You should have been the one to go to Sarah's.'

She turned from him then, taking the crowbar away. She slapped the long reins, urging the horse forward, not wanting to hear any more, not wanting to listen to this man, not wanting to look at his eyes which were so dark, at his body which had once known hers but never with love, never as Mr and Mrs Murdoch had known one another.

'I've told you, I don't remember the frogs. Somerset is a lifetime away, as well you know, Patrick Prover.' She was shouting now, because she did remember them but what had they to do with her?

On Christmas Eve she carried pumpkin pie, salad and cold pork to the Christmas party. Jimmie would not come. He stayed in the humpy and Luke waved until he could no longer be seen.

'We won't stay long, my darling, and tomorrow will be our day,' Deborah told him, holding him as he stood and waved to his friend.

They urged the horse along the dry rutted track. 'Won't be long before we're coming along here in the Ford,' Patrick said.

There'll be no need to come along here, not for a long time, Deborah thought because she had decided that she would teach Luke herself, but she said nothing because school age was still so far away.

'Will Jimmie put the Christmas tree on the verandah this year?' she asked, because she didn't want to think of school any more, or other people any more.

Luke signed, 'Yes.'

There were mosquitoes around her face. She could smell the citronella oil on them all. She looked at the sky, at the bush. It was so dry.

The school was two miles from them. The teacher's small house was set behind the wooden building which was lit by

310

hurricane lamps with lanterns hung on a framework in the playing space outside.

Sarah was there with Ernie and she put her arms around Deborah and hugged her. 'It hasn't been the same without you,' she said. Her hands were waxy from the candles she and the other women had put on the schoolroom floor to make it slippery for dancing and she showed Deborah the garlands they had picked from the bush and hung around.

She held Deborah's arm, walking with her, showing her the drawings on the wall, showing Luke the desks which had been stacked outside tonight but which he would never sit in, Deborah thought.

They drank ginger beer. 'From the root stock you gave us,' said Mrs Taylor. 'We've missed you the last two Christmases. You were so kind to us, so helpful.'

There was a Christmas tree set into a bucket and they tied on small presents which had been bought with the shilling the men had contributed at the parties their wives cooked for and arranged every two months.

'I didn't know,' Deborah said.

'We told you, but you were too busy. You didn't register,' Sarah said and tied on a present for Luke. 'We missed you. You've given us all so much. We could not have survived without you. I could not have survived.' Sarah kissed her friend, her arms warm on Deborah's neck.

The men were setting out rows of low benches and lighting the lanterns. Sarah sat with Deborah on the front row as the men gathered at the sides because there were too few seats. Luke and Mollie were next to Deborah, sitting quietly, watching the children with their teacher beside the school building. These neat clean children were the ones who had played football with Luke's ball, who had not seen his signing.

The accordion player started 'Oh Little Town of Bethlehem' and the children marched in single file from the school to the stage area singing, their voices lifting almost to the stars. They arranged themselves in two rows, the tallest behind.

They sang all the hymns of Deborah's youth and her heart broke because she would never hear the sound of her son's voice soaring like this.

She looked straight ahead, not at Luke, not at Patrick who was standing near. Her throat was thick. No, there was no place for her son here, no place at all. She felt Sarah's hand on her arm, her warmth, her kindness, then her friend stood and moved across to the children as the tall second row eased forward into the front, making a long straight line. There were twenty children in all. Sarah stood before them, facing the audience and spoke to Deborah, just to Deborah, saying that this evening was for her, really. It was in gratitude for her help, her steadfastness, her courage. They had missed her these past two Christmases, this last year. They had missed Luke and Patrick too.

'This next song is for you all, but particularly for Luke,' Sarah said, standing to one side and waiting as the men brought more lanterns and stood quite still, holding them up, lighting the area more clearly between the audience and the children.

As the moths flew amongst the lanterns, they heard the accordion playing, 'Knick Knack Paddywack' and the children sang, but they also signed, each one of them, with clear confident hands.

But Deborah couldn't see them because of the tears which were in her eyes and on her cheeks, falling on to her hands which were clasped on her lap. She could see her son's hands though as they signed back and his smile as he looked and listened.

There was dancing until eleven, but Deborah sat at the door with Sarah who was too tired, and Ernie who was too lame, and watched others sliding along the floor, gliding along it, dancing the Lancers, dancing the waltz. She thought of the dance in the village before Patrick had proposed. The floor had been too rough for gliding, the men had lifted their feet, and she smiled at the memory. It was all so long ago.

'They are so very kind, Deborah.' It was Patrick. There

was beer on his breath and tiredness in his eyes. It was in hers too and she longed for their lives to be different. She longed for love to warm them but there were too many lies, and the biggest was hers.

'He will be safe with friends like these. It will give him confidence, as you gave those frogs confidence.'

'Do you remember dancing in the village?' she replied because she didn't want to talk of her son. She knew that they would be kind, that he should go to school, and she couldn't bear the thought of losing him.

'So long ago,' Patrick said. 'Yes, I remember. I remember holding –'

Mollie came running up then, pulling at her mother's skirt, shouting, 'Where's Luke? I want to play with Luke.'

'He's over with the bigger boys. Over there by the bush. I saw them just half an hour ago,' Patrick said, standing up, taking the child's hand. 'Come along, we'll go and find him.'

Yes, it was no good shouting. He couldn't answer. Her son couldn't answer, Deborah thought as she stood up, looking beyond the line of the lanterns, seeing the children laughing and shouting, playing tag. But tonight a start had been made. Tonight it seemed that Patrick was right, people could be taught. She put her hand on Sarah's shoulder. 'Sit still, I'll go with them. It's time we were going. They'll be tired tomorrow, both of them.'

She followed, leaving the circle of light, walking towards Patrick who was beckoning to the boys. She saw him hold the shoulder of one, shake him, turn him round, start after him towards the bush and she was running too.

Deborah reached the boy, grabbed him. 'Where is he? Where is Luke, for God's sake?'

Patrick was calling to her. 'Leave him, he didn't mean any harm. Leave him. Come with me.'

The other boy was leading Patrick along a track. It was too dark to run, but she did, panting as she caught up.

'We use this track for nature class, you see. I know me way.

We was playing, see. Cowboys and Indians. We thought we'd got everyone. We called, see. We shouted when Mrs Taylor called us back for cakes. It's through here.'

She could hear the breaking of the dry twigs beneath their feet. She could hear Ernie now behind them, catching up, carrying a lantern and Mollie who was crying.

They eased around two trunks which had been stacked beside the track, then out into a clearing and Deborah pushed past Patrick because in the light from the stars and the moon and Ernie's lantern she could see Luke, tied to a tree and there were tears on his cheeks.

He lifted his face to her as she ran, and the boy said, 'We didn't mean it. He wanted to be an Indian. He signed to Mollie that his friend was like an Indian. We forgot him. He didn't call us.'

She was undoing the knot but it was too tight. She tore at it, until Patrick said, 'You hold him, I'll do this.'

She was on her knees then, holding her son's face to hers, kissing him, telling him it would be all right, then shouting at the boy, 'If you tie his arms down, he can't speak. He has a whistle. But he can't blow it if he hasn't got his hands free. You must never tie his hands, you stupid boy.'

The rope was slack now, she rubbed Luke's arms.

'We forgot he was different, Missis. We forgot he was dumb.'

She lifted her son, feeling Patrick's hands beneath her arms, helping them both up. 'They didn't mean any harm, Deb. Take him to the cart. We'll go home. Ernie, tell Sarah it's all right.'

They skirted the lanterns but there was sufficient light for her to see her son's face, to see the shock, the fear, to see his hands signing, 'He said I'm different.'

He wept all the way home, sitting on her knee shaking, and she said, 'He'll never go to that school. I won't have him treated like that. We shouldn't have gone. You shouldn't have made me go.' She was shouting, crying. Her child's pain was hers.

'It's all right, Deborah. They didn't mean it. You can see that. This will be a lesson to them. They will learn from this.'

'But even if they did, there is still the swimming. He can't take a whistle in the water. It's impossible. He will stay with me. I must look after him. I can't bear this.' The tears were gone now, she was holding Luke, rocking him, rocking herself while Patrick cursed the evening, which had begun so well.

Jimmie's fires were alight when the cart creaked, jerked and finally stopped. Patrick handed down the boy to Deborah but Luke wriggled from her arms and ran through the bush towards the humpy, towards the fires, towards Jimmie who rose as Luke ran to him.

He squatted and watched Luke's hands, face, eyes, telling him that the boy had said he was different, that Luke knew he would always be different. Luke told him that he couldn't call to the boys, that they had tied him, leapt around him, pretended to kill him. That he had been frightened, that he could not tell them that, because his words were in his hands, and they were tied by the rope. That they had forgotten him, that he couldn't call.

Deborah came and stood, feeling the heat from the two fires as Jimmie looked at her and then back to the child.

He said to Luke, 'You are a mute. I am a mute because I am the last to speak my language. I had no one to pass on my rituals, my law, my myths to but now I have you. You have made it possible for my tribe's history to continue because we have a special language. We have your language. Yes, you are different. Yes, you are shocked, you are frightened. But you've learned tonight and so have your friends. They will not do this again.'

He looked up at Deborah and Patrick and she watched Jimmie draw shapes in the dry soil, in the ashes. 'I shall teach you to track, I shall teach you our games. You will learn how to lie still against a log and not be seen. How to trail a kangaroo without being seen or smelt. You may show them that. You may show them how to track. When the time comes I shall tell you the secrets of my people. You may not tell them. That is for you alone, because you have something extra. You have that difference and only you may call me Ngilgi.'

There was silence now around the fire and Deborah felt that these men were taking her son from her, and she came forward, lifted him. 'It's time you were in bed.'

She took him to her room, signed and told stories, kissed him and couldn't smile when he signed that he was glad he had his friend Jimmie. He was glad he was special.

Summer became autumn and the rains were close. They didn't go to the parties because Deborah chose to go to Busselton on a Saturday now because it suited the shops better, she said, but Patrick knew it was not for that reason.

Luke played with Jimmie, made himself as still as a log and taught the other children too when they came for the mail or milk or meat in the early evening. He drew them emu tracks and kangaroo tracks as Jimmie had shown him. He stood quite still with the wind blowing his scent away from the kangaroo as Jimmie had shown him and the children learned the value of sign, because speech would destroy the hunt.

The older children allowed the young ones to play football with them now, and they made space for him to sign, they watched him, until he and Mollie were tired and moved across to paint, or play with a model of the T-Ford utility that Patrick had carved him.

In the evenings, as the rains came, Deborah told him not to go down to the humpy in the dark. She would read his stories, tell him tales, and when Luke signed that he missed Jimmie, she said that the daytimes were enough.

'Quite enough,' she shouted and was glad that it was dark and wet outside, and that she had her son with her for the long evenings.

She told Patrick too, that it was enough for Luke to have friends here, that she would school him, that he could play with them when they came, that it would be safer. She would never rest with that teacher and his fetish for swimming. That there might be new children who would not understand his difference.

Patrick just nodded and waited, because Luke no longer smiled during the long evenings.

CHAPTER 19

In March 1928, Sarah had her son and returned from the hospital before the rains had clogged the track, before the cold had begun and as the grass was becoming green again after the heat of the summer.

Still Patrick worked, and waited, looking at Jimmie, talking quietly. Ernie came in late March and asked Deborah to stay for four days with Sarah and the new baby.

'I have to see a specialist about my leg.'

Deborah was feeding the pigs, leaning over the pen, scratching their backs. She had given one to Sarah. 'Yes, I'll bring Luke too. It will be good for us all to be together.'

Ernie shook his head. 'It might be better not to. Mollie's not well. We're worried that Luke might get it. Sarah's had it, but not the baby.' He looked at Patrick who was heaving bags of super on to the verandah. 'Can you cope with Luke? We wouldn't ask but Deb's the only one Sarah wants.'

'No problem. We can cope. It's better this way, Deborah.' He looked at the boy, at the mother who rested her hand on his hair as she always did. 'Jimmie and I will be fine with him. Just fine.'

The waiting was over.

Deborah didn't want to go. She didn't want to leave her house, her son. They had never been separated. He needed her.

'I'll read him his stories,' Patrick said. 'Jimmie will too.'

She felt the anger surge again. It should be her voice that her son heard, but she nodded at Ernie, because his face was

318

so lined, his eyes so kind. 'I hope they help you, Ernie. Of course I'll come.'

She left one hour later, her clothes in a bag, vegetables with her, fruit, a piece of pork, cheese, her mattock. Ernie laughed.

'We're not asking you over to work, Deb.'

'Might as well, if you're to be away.' She smiled at him, at her son, and pulled the boy to her, kissing him, nodding at Patrick, at Jimmie, wishing that they could go, that she could stay.

She didn't see her child's eyes shade over at her kiss, at her hug, at the voice that told him she would miss him, think of him, but Patrick did and knew that she was beginning to lose her son.

They waved until the cart could be seen no more. He nodded at Jimmie then and they told the boy that they had four days in which he must learn to swim. It was to be their secret. He was a big four now, nearly four and a half. When the time was right, he would go to school and Luke smiled and it was as though the sun came out and Patrick's heart ached for Deborah.

They took provisions, they took ground sheets but no tent because they would build a humpy. They took the cart along the track towards the high reaches of the river. They travelled for four hours through bush Patrick didn't know, but which Jimmie did.

Jimmie told them of the rich flora and teeming fauna his people had found when they sat down in the forests by the rivers and waterholes, how they shared it all with the birds, animals and reptiles that they believed to be their 'elder brothers' and which became, in the passage of the centuries, their ancestor gods.

He told them that Bibbulmun signifies many breasts and Patrick laughed, and Luke's eyes did too, though he couldn't have known why. It was just happiness, just freedom and Patrick recognised the boy he had once been, travelling away from his mother with his grandfather, and again he ached for Deborah.

'We had neither chiefs nor kings.' Jimmie's voice was soft, sing-song. The sound of Bernie's hooves was gentle on the rain-softened ground. There was peace all around. 'We gave our women more liberty than many tribes. Our only god was a serpent that dominated the sky and sea and punished evil-doers.'

'Like our God,' Patrick said while Luke signed, 'What is a serpent?'

He nodded when Patrick told him.

'Perhaps like your god.' But Jimmie did not want to talk of God. He didn't want to think of the priest who had denied his mother the right to her own choice in her illness. He didn't want to think of the whites who had taken him from her when his father died, and put him in the children's mission, and his mother in another area, as though aboriginals did not know what it was to love. All she had wanted to do was to take him home with her. And that was all he came to want too.

'Perhaps,' he said again.

'Did you have boomerangs?' Luke signed.

'No, not here. Too many trees. We had kojas which are stone axes fastened with wattle gum that we used as tools, and spears or clubs for hunting. One day I shall teach you how to spear dodge. We were all taught it as soon as we could walk, and swim. It will be something to show your friends.'

Luke smiled, they all smiled.

They made camp beside a series of rock-bound pools, then Jimmie rubbed himself in grease and before the light faded he dived deeply, going down, down, counting, always counting, before turning, to paddle his feet and rise to the surface, striking out to the bank. 'It's deep, twenty feet. Remember that, Luke. The depth of the dam is six of you.'

They swam naked, all three of them. Patrick and Jimmie held Luke between them, playing, taking fear from his mind, turning it into sport, into a game as Jimmie's people had done with their children. When it grew quite dark, they dried themselves and sat between the heat of the two fires and Jimmie told them that the soap and water the mission

320

insisted upon had cracked his skin. Aboriginal people needed oil.

Patrick handed out long pronged forks with pork steaks on for them to cook. Jimmie made damper and buried it, laying it on hot stones to cook. The billy boiled and Patrick showed Luke how to swirl the tea and he laughed and Patrick promised he would teach him how to do it, one day when he was old enough, as he had once shown his mother, and again he ached for Deborah.

They sat quietly then, savouring the smell of roasting pork and Patrick thought of the pigs she had nurtured, of the cows she had milked, of the work she had done, of the life he had brought her to and he felt the sharpness of the pain it brought him.

'Remember, we must keep this a secret, Luke. Your mother must not know yet.' His voice was soft and he smiled as Luke nodded. He watched his son's hands as he signed to Jimmie.

'Did your people fish in the rivers?'

Jimmie was resting his elbows on his knees, twisting his fork. 'Oh yes, in the rivers, the sea coasts, the estuaries. The Bibbulmun would welcome others too at the time of spawning and crabbing. They welcomed them to the wild potato harvest in the forests of the karri and the jarrah.' He looked up at the sparks which spurted into the air as Patrick pushed another log on to the fire. 'In the wastes of the north west they cannot afford that generosity.'

Patrick turned his steak over, then helped Luke to do the same. The smell was good.

'It's very different from Victoria, that's for sure.' He looked at Luke, at the freedom in his eyes. 'But in some ways, so much the same.' Did his mother miss him while she ruled Lenora? Had she realised what she had done? He knew that she had not, because she was still so full of frustrated love that she had been unable to write, ever. He was quiet as the fire spluttered. He would write again this Christmas as he had done last year, because he knew now what it meant to love a child.

Jimmie touched his meat with his finger and nodded to them both. 'It is done.'

They were in the water early the next day, although the rain was falling and Luke played, smiled, but could not let go of Jimmie, or of Patrick. They dried off by the fire, boiled a billy for lunch and then walked through the bush, following a trail that only Jimmie could see, watching his signs, doing as he indicated. As they ate the rabbit he caught for their evening meal he told them of his people who could not understand the fences which the white man put up enclosing cattle, sheep, horses within their boundaries.

'They built them across our foodlines and we couldn't understand what they were for. To us, nothing was owned. Animals weren't owned, they were just part of our world. We didn't understand why it was wrong for us to kill and eat a cow or a sheep. They belonged to the earth, to nature. We were hunters. We could not understand why we were punished.

'When the towns were built, like Perth or Busselton, Luke, they were built on our homing spots. Our tracks to our food grounds were covered by your houses and your streets. Our mungaitch honey groves were cut down to make way for your flocks and herds. We could no longer hunt for the bai-yoo nuts of the zamia and the warrain, and the joobok roots. They were behind the fences of the white man. We were trespassers in our own country.'

His voice was soft, patient. He pulled at the rabbit meat that he had hunted and cooked, sucking his fingers as they sucked theirs.

'Soon there was no more wandering, no more friendship visits. Our food disappeared and my people were sent by your people to unfamiliar places, to reserves which were not on our homeland, not within the land of our spirits. That is why there is no one here now. That is why I'm alone. But if I were to meet a fullblood he would lift his stick against my half-caste smell, as my uncle did to me. But in my heart I am as black as he. I hear the songs of my ancestors, I feel the spirits but I am alone.'

322

There was silence and Patrick looked at Jimmie, at the acceptance in his eyes, at the darkness of the bush and there was nothing he could say, because he remembered shouting 'bastard blackfella' many times in his youth at Lenora.

Luke signed then, in the light of the fire, 'You are not alone. You have me.'

They were in the water again the next day, but Luke still couldn't let go. Again he played and paddled to Patrick, but only as long as he held Jimmie's hand, not releasing his grip until his small cold hand grasped Patrick's fingers and then his neck and he could press his small wet face against Patrick, who kissed him each time, and said that he was almost there.

They only had one more day before they must be back. It would not do for Deborah to return and find them gone. She must not know, not yet.

That night Jimmie told them of the wanna-wa which was an ancient dream dance.

'It lasts two weeks, there are three performances daily. I remember how day after day the same songs and motions were practised until each dancer was perfect. So you see, Luke, you have been practising these last two days. Soon it will be right as the wanna-wa dance became right. But there are sacred and secret parts of the wanna-wa and one day, I shall tell you of those. When you are of an age. But only you.'

Patrick watched as the boy reached out and touched Jimmie's hand. He nodded and listened now as Jimmie began the opening stanza of the dance, squatting by the fire, his voice low, then high, the double vowels impossible to reproduce.

> Warri wan-gan-ye,
> Koogunarri wanji-wanji
> Warri wan-gan-ye.

He seemed not to draw breath, and neither, it seemed, did they as they listened and the fire crackled and the song went on until Jimmie was tired, and Luke was asleep in Patrick's arms.

That night Patrick stirred, feeling coolness where Luke should have been sleeping against his back. He rolled over; the boy was gone. Jimmie was gone. He crept from the humpy. He passed the gum logs which were smouldering in their ash. He moved down to the creek where he knew Luke would be. There was panic in his throat, fear throughout his body. He walked silently and stood near the water.

Luke was there, naked, alone, standing up to his thighs in the dark. Patrick scanned the creek and there was Jimmie, opposite, motionless, unseen by the boy. Patrick raised his hand and Jimmie nodded.

They waited as Luke moved, easing into the water, deeper, up to his belly. He was too small, for God's sake, and it shelved steeply here, it was twenty feet deep. Patrick wanted to shout, but he said nothing and watched his son step forward, the water rippling behind him and then Luke's arms went up, and his head, his mouth opening in terror as he felt no ground beneath his feet, as he sank in soundless panic and now Patrick moved, but Jimmie waved him back.

'Be still,' he signed in the light from the low bright stars. 'Be still.'

But that was his son there, beneath the water, and now he knew the fear that Deborah lived with, and the love. But then there was a flurry of arms, a head, a spitting of water, and Luke was up, he was thrashing.

'Take it easy, remember what we said,' Patrick whispered to himself. 'Kick, use your arms. For God's sake, use your arms.'

He was ready to move to the edge again. Deborah was right. Their son could not cry out. He could not use his waterlogged whistle. He could drown. He'd been wrong.

But now Luke was swimming. In the starlight he was moving to the bank, towards Patrick who stayed motionless. He watched his son turn and swim back again, across the twenty-foot depth, towards Jimmie, who melted back into the bush as Patrick now did.

Both men watched while the boy swam and they could hear his breath, see his smile, and they waited until Luke was finished, and climbing out of the water on to the bank. They returned to the humpy then, quickly, quietly, pretending to sleep as Luke came back to lie between them.

The next day they all swam in the morning and professed surprise, delight, as Luke struck out from them and later they talked all afternoon about school, about friends, about life as it now could be.

'But this must be our secret. We must be careful because your mother loves you. She wants the best for you. You must remember this, Luke,' Patrick said.

'But when will you tell her?' Luke signed.

'When the time is right,' he replied and felt a great sadness because he had lied yet again to Deborah.

Winter passed and Deborah fed grain to the two sows who were in pig and in the spring collected cape weed with Luke which they also liked. Daisy had a bull calf which Deborah decided they should rear for meat, rather than kill immediately, because the freight bill would be less than the price this year. Blossom had a heifer and that was good news. The milk herd was growing.

Each morning she milked, separated, cooked breakfast of porridge for Luke and Patrick, and their own bacon. Its smell was as sweet as it had been in Nell's kitchen. She walked through the bush each week with Luke on a Friday to see Sarah, Mollie and Bob, the new baby. She listened to his gurgles, felt the grip of his hands on her fingers and was relieved that the lines were less deep on Sarah's face. Ernie's leg was better, they had two cows now, and soon there would be more. Next year they would clear the land of the ring-barked trees, though Patrick told Ernie that it should be done now, because there was another very hot summer coming.

She travelled to Busselton only every three months. The tracks were too muddy in the winter and by the spring she was too busy, there were too many piglets, too many calves; too much ploughing, sowing. There were too many fowl to clip and feed, too many photographs at Mrs Murdoch's of her son in America, too many stories of his success, of his travels which meant that he could still not come home.

In November the grass was dry, too dry again. Luke stooped as they all did and bent the blades of buffalo grass she had sown at the front of the house, and in front of Sarah's when she had stayed for those four days with her. They didn't go to the agricultural show.

'It's too hot,' Patrick said. 'Too bloody hot, too dry.'

She was pleased, so pleased. She would stay here with her son, not walk in humid tents with people who did not understand. She called Luke to her, giving him leaves from her vegetable patch, and peelings, watching him walk to the fowl pen, whistling his special tune for them, smiling as they clucked around him.

He brought back the bowl and signed that he wanted to go to stand in the creek. 'It's so hot, Mother.'

'No, get water from the well, pour it over you, my darling.'

'I want to stand in the water,' he signed.

'I said no.'

Patrick called Luke then, took him along to the well to draw water, spoke to him quietly. 'Soon,' he said. 'Be patient. Now is not the time. It's worrying, all this heat. Leave it for now.'

Luke nodded.

The next day was hotter still, the next week even more so and her vegetables wilted. She watered them with well water, with clothes-washing water, with dish-washing water. They lay on their beds at night, feeling the heat oozing from the wooden walls, from the iron roof, feeling sweat rolling from their bodies.

The crops were too dry. They harvested the hay, the barley

326

before it headed. They heaved the stooks on to the cart and were slower this year, in this oven heat, and all the time they looked to the sky, to the bush that was as dry as tinder.

As Christmas approached Patrick said that they must not walk through the bush but stay near the house, or keep to the track within sight of one another. There was such a danger of fire. At the Christmas party the children signed again for Luke and then played as the adults danced, but only in front of the school house, not out in the bush.

'Because of its dryness,' Ernie said, though it was also to set Deborah's mind at ease, to make it possible for Patrick to tell his wife that there were no obstacles now for school because others also took great care.

'I will in the New Year, at the right moment,' he told Luke.

'I'm five now, Dad.'

'I know, Luke. I'm just waiting for the right time.'

But Deborah was too tense here, with the school desks heaped outside the school, with these children whooping their Indian sounds around her son, who was playing and happy, but still so vulnerable without her.

They ate the suppers that they had all brought in the light of the lanterns but no billy was boiled out here where the land was so dry, and a spark could set off a fire. Then there was dancing again. She watched Sarah dance with Ernie and was glad to see that her friend was stronger, that at last they could see the future ahead of them.

'Will you dance, Deb?' Patrick asked.

She shook her head, turning, checking on her son. No, she could not dance with this man who had once held her naked body, whom she had once loved and whose body she had not held against her since she left Lenora. She could not dance with anyone else either because then she couldn't listen for her son.

In January the heat was more intense. Deborah bathed Luke's face, told him not to run about, and her son looked at Jimmie who nodded and she wanted to scream, 'Look at me. I am your mother.'

She ran water over his wrists and by midday there was a gusting northerly wind, and she remembered the bricklayer in Melbourne and the heat and dust it brought.

She told Luke how it rose, how it sucked along the dust and he asked how she knew. 'A man told me,' she said, but did not tell him it was his father.

At lunchtime she was scanning the sky, so was Jimmie, so was Patrick.

'Got the breaks done OK?' Patrick said to Jimmie. 'We got them all, didn't we?'

'We got them all.' Jimmie's voice was soft.

They were standing on the verandah and her washing was waving in the wind, the fences were shimmering in the heat.

They brought the cattle closer to the house. Would Sarah know to do this?

'I'll go through the bush,' she said at two o'clock. 'I'll tell Ernie to get his stock in close.'

'You'll bloody stay here,' Patrick said, his voice hard. He wasn't looking at her, he was looking at the sky where Jimmie pointed.

She saw the clouds then above the skyline of the trees and knew it was smoke. She had seen it before at Lenora. She had seen it here, but only far away, only small.

'Where is it?' she asked.

'Beyond the Taylors'. Six miles away only, for God's sake. There was a burn there last year. The wind's blowing it on to that. Should be OK.' Patrick was standing quite still. 'Bloody should be anyway.'

They stood and watched and the clouds became thick and black so quickly. Bernie was neighing, pawing the ground. The smoke was closer, not much, surely not much, Deborah thought, shading her eyes, checking the direction of the wind. It would bring the fire to them but the burn would check it. They watched, waited and barely breathed. It didn't check.

'Get the buckets, fill them from the well. Get anything that takes water,' Patrick shouted, running across behind the house. 'Come on, all of you. Luke too. Anything that'll hold water.'

She heaved out the wash tubs, the galvanised bath and filled the cans, slopping water as they brought the containers back to the house. They doused bags.

'It should have checked,' Deborah said. 'It should damn well have checked.' Fear clutched at her because the fire was so much nearer, because there was nowhere to run to. She had felt the heat as they had burned off fields, she had heard the noise and knew that a bushfire was a million times worse.

She stopped, looked up at the smoke which was so much closer now. It had spread, it was billowing, rolling, and now there was a surge of sulphur and orange. Someone's hayshed. Oh God. Sarah? But no, it was too far to the north. The Burgesses' then?

The clouds were moving closer, the wind was still gusting. Why couldn't it drop? Why couldn't it change, blow back on itself? She looked around. The trees were so dry but at least the bush was cleared around the house. Thank God it was cleared, but there were still crops in the field. Crops that were so dry, so tinder dry, that they would feed the fire.

'Get in the house now, Luke. Just get in the house.'

She could hear the fire now. He could hear the fire, she could tell from his face.

'Two miles away I reckon and the bloody wind hasn't shifted.' Patrick was panting. He ran back for more water.

She could see tree tops catching alight from the sparks and from the heat. Too many, too quickly. 'For God's sake change,' she shouted. She hurled water on to the walls as high as she could, then looked past the house to the east. There was another fire there. She pointed to Patrick who was running past, taking water to the cow bails.

'Over there. Look, over there,' she shouted and then looked back, seeing the main fire leaping from tree top to tree top. She knew that sparks would be showering on to the parched dry undergrowth, that the ground fire would be leaping, burning, racing towards them.

'Oh Christ, if they meet there'll be an updraught.' Patrick ran on, slopping water, throwing it on to the cowshed. She hauled water up from the well, ran to the house, to the outsheds. The dead ring-barked trees at the edge of the most distant paddocks blossomed into flame, torching the dark smoke, searing the sky.

'We didn't get them all down. How could we get them all down?' she was shouting as she threw water on the house, as Patrick and Jimmie hurled it again and again on the outhouses, on the pig pens, the fowl houses, rushing to and from the well. Then out to the cow shed again, throwing it on to as many panicking animals as were in there.

Luke came on to the verandah. 'Get back into the house,' she screamed at him. She looked at the two fires, they were creeping, then leaping, coming together, and then they met out there in the valley where the boronia grew. They heard the updraught, felt the movement of the air, saw the flames and they were shouting to one another, screaming, pointing to the stables because they were furthest out, pointing to the hayshed whose sides were smoking.

There was burning wood in the air, sucked up by the draught, thrown hundreds of yards, leaping the fire breaks, starting other fires, nearer to them. Oh God, much nearer to them and she could hear their roar and no one could shout above the noise which was approaching. She dragged at the bucket in the well, running with the water, throwing it, running back, again and again.

The hayshed burst into flames, the smoke was orange, the noise obscene. There had been no flames near it. It was just the heat. 'Oh God, my son.' Deborah threw more water, feeling the heat from the walls of the house, from behind her, from each side of her, breathing in air which was so hot it hurt.

Patrick was shouting but the noise was too fierce. The fire was out of the bush now and into the paddocks. She turned. Bernie was trying to break through the fence. She pointed. Jimmie ran, out across the yard. The cattle were running, charging the fence. Patrick ran.

She kept throwing water at the house. The sky darkened, the sun was blacked out. The fire was at the edge of the home paddocks, skirting them, not bearing down on them, going on south. Her arms ached, her back ached, but that was nothing. Sparks could still explode, leap on to her house, her son, on to her animals.

She turned. Patrick had headed off the cows but one had tried to jump the fence and was down. She threw water as the flames were reflected in the darkness of the smoke. There was such a roaring and the fire burned on, sweeping past, nearly past, thank God. Her breath was tight, the heat was too much, it sucked what air there was. The fire was eating up the paddock fences.

The wheat went up, then the barley.

But then the fire was beyond them, the ground was black and smoking, the fences were like charcoal sticks, the trees were like blackened stumps. The house was steaming, the outhouses too. The noise was almost gone, suddenly gone, and Luke came out to the verandah.

'Stay there,' she shouted. 'Just stay there.' She ran down to the home paddocks, where the few free cattle were charging again.

She stood with Patrick, waving them down, calling to them, stroking them as they stopped, as they stood and trembled, and she wouldn't look at the distant blackness that had been their farm. She wouldn't look at the fences she had dug and tamped and wired with Patrick, at the ground she had cleared, ploughed and sowed, the hayshed they had filled, the burned cow that Patrick was shooting now.

She would look instead at the pasture on the home paddocks which had survived, at the house, at the cowshed and the pens which still stood. She wouldn't grieve, because that which was burnt would grow again and her son was safe, but there were tears on her cheeks and it must only be the smoke, for God's sake. It could only be the smoke because she didn't love this place, it was just her job, wasn't it?

Patrick was running now, with a shovel, with an axe, and

Jimmie was with him because the fire had changed course, it might reach Sarah's and they had too many ring-barked trees near the house. 'Keep the buildings wet,' Patrick yelled at her. 'Douse what fires you can. Be careful.'

She nodded and watched them as they grabbed Bernie, put a halter on him and rode him, together and bareback. There was no time for tears, not when her friend was out there in the path of the fire. Not here in this country which gave no quarter.

She gave a small cloth to Luke because he wanted to help. She told him to soak it and slap it on the verandah, on any parts of the house he could reach. She carted water to the pig sties, the fowl house, the stables, the cow sheds, the dairy. Later when she could get near it, she threw water on the remains of the hayshed.

All around them trees were still smouldering, still bursting into flames. She doused those near the house. She worked until darkness fell, but there would be no real darkness tonight because the sky was still lit by the reflections of the flames in the smoke, or by the flames themselves.

Ten o'clock came, then eleven and she fed Luke, put him to bed, went out again and worked, dousing, smelling the smoke all around, feeling the swelling in her mouth, the tightness of her chest, the rawness of her eyes, tasting the smoke, and all the time she looked at the progress of the smoke in the sky and wondered if the men would come home alive, if Sarah still lived.

They did return, but not until dawn was breaking while she was still dragging water up from the well, and tussocks in the far paddocks were still smouldering. She saw them come down the track which had not been in the path of the fire. She saw Jimmie leave and go to his humpy, every movement showing his exhaustion, side-stepping the fallen logs and branches everywhere, some of which she had doused.

Patrick dropped his mattock and axe on the buffalo grass which had survived. She watched him climb the steps and his movements too betrayed his exhaustion.

She let the rope dangle and walked into the kitchen, through into the lounge. He was slumped at the table, his hands blackened, as hers were, his eyes red and swollen, so much worse than hers, his lips large, his eyelashes and hair singed and he looked as he had done at Lenora.

She went to him, stood by him and felt the heat of him, saw his cracked lips, the blood from them on his chin.

'They're burnt out. Everything's gone, even the house, everything. Just when things were turning out better for them. But they're alive. At least they're alive.' His voice was a croak as it had been that day and this time tears streaked down his face and fell black on to the deal table. 'He was going to clear the trees next year. They were too close to the house, the fire just came on. We used the bags when it broke out of the bush but it leapt us using the ring-barked bloody trees. We could do so little, so bastard little.'

He leant his head against her. She felt his weight, she felt the heaving of his body as he wept and she put her arms around him and felt love stir, though she hadn't known it still existed. She felt his arms come round her, felt him cling to her. She was bending to kiss his hair, his poor singed hair, when Luke threw open his bedroom door, ran to them, pushing Deborah aside and signing to Patrick. 'You're back. I'm glad you're back.'

He climbed on to his knee, stroking his face, making his own small hands black too, signing, 'Is Sarah all right?' and the moment had passed like the fire and she knew that she had only imagined the stirrings of love.

CHAPTER 20

At midday Deborah and Patrick harnessed up the cart. They threw in their axes, their hammers, what nails they had. Deborah packed a hamper with water, milk and food and hoisted Luke on to the seat of the cart. They looked towards Jimmie's humpy and saw him come, bringing his axe.

'Sarah's?' he said.

They nodded. He climbed up into the back and Luke clambered over the seat to sit with him. The track was bordered on either side by smoking trees, charred on their trunks, their foliage gone. The undergrowth was smouldering but there was no danger. There was little left to burn. There was just silence.

No one spoke as they travelled. Their throats were too raw, their chests too, their tongues too swollen and Deborah was glad that they knew how to sign. It took them two hours because trees had fallen across the track and had to be levered to one side with crowbars, not with hands because the wood was still too hot.

They entered the clearing which had held Sarah's home. There were just smoking ruins where the house had been, where the chaff-shed, the fowl shed and the cow bails had been.

Sarah was there, at the edge of the clearing sitting on dry grass which was unburnt, near to their creek. They had erected a tent which Ernie had thrown into the creek as the fire surged forward. In front of it Mollie sat beneath the shade of a gum tree. This was the edge of the fire's path.

Just fifty feet further away and the house would have been saved.

Deborah climbed down and carried over the food while Patrick and Jimmie walked towards Ernie, standing looking at the ruins of his block.

Sarah turned. There were no tears, just acceptance. 'It's over, Deborah. We'll walk off. There's nothing else.'

Deborah held her, telling Luke to go to Mollie, that he should look after Bob who lay in his pram, crying.

'You will not walk off. You have nowhere else to go.' It hurt to talk. Her voice was a whisper.

'But it's too much to start again. Just too much. We have no money. It's too big a job.' Sarah was crying now and Deborah held her with arms that were tender from the heat of the fire.

'We're here to help. I'm not going to let you go. Besides, I can't bear to be alone again.' She pushed Sarah from her, laughing. 'You won't go. I need you.'

Sarah smiled then, shaking her head, but then more carts arrived bringing the Taylors, bringing Mr Burgess, the Smiths, and they started cutting down the still smoking trees to make slabs and posts for rebuilding. They wore thick gloves and the wives took out drinks every half hour to ease already swollen throats.

Deborah watched as these men scarfed trees with their axes, while others sawed them, then split them into slabs. Sarah and she took Bernie and the cart from the slab area to where the new house would be built while Mrs Taylor and Mrs Smith laid out food which they had brought with them.

They ate in shifts and there was the noise of children playing on the unburnt ground near the creek and the sound of axes, saws, shovels, hammers all around them. They worked, all of them, until it was dark, turning the smoking trees into building material, then lit the frame of the house which they had erected on unburnt ground with hurricane lamps and worked on for another hour. At nightfall they all returned to their farms to milk their cows, separate their milk, feed their stock, and Patrick told Deborah that he didn't need the Ford utility this year, that he would plough the money back to make up the deficiency in fodder that there would now be, for them and for Sarah and Ernie too.

They were up before dawn, milking, feeding, separating, and they left the buttermilk on the track for Jack to pick up, because he had come yesterday and said that he would do this for everyone as his contribution.

Again they worked, stopping in shifts, and after the last lunch break the house was finished. Each cart that had come that day had brought furniture, mugs, blankets, sheets, kerosene cans and flowers.

'It will all grow much more lushly now,' Deborah said as she helped to arrange the chairs, and then to light up the stove. 'If you stay, that is.'

She looked across at her friend. The women were laying out drinks on slabs which were supported by logs, putting muslin over the lemonade, the water. There was no ginger beer. It was too raw for these parched throats. She came and stood beside Sarah on the verandah and her friend was crying, but so was she, because there were so many friends out there. There was such a community, such bravery, such compassion. It was like her village in Somerset and now she knew that this was home.

'Will you stay, Sarah?'

It took four days to rebuild the fences, the sheds. Then they moved to the Taylors' and rebuilt their hayshed, then on to Stoke Farm and rebuilt theirs, and the fences too.

'I'll plough soon. It will bring a good crop,' she said to Luke as they watched the men gathering for beer, now their throats were better. 'I'll show you how to sow. I'll show you how to scythe when you're older.'

The women were putting out food and ginger beer. There were balloons on the fences, on the verandah uprights, there were garlands from the undergrowth near the creek. They would dance tonight, they had all agreed, because Sarah and

336

Ernie were staying, because this had been a good time, a marvellous time. Deborah hugged Luke to her, holding him close. Yes, they could be happy here.

There was still the smell of smoke in the air, still the darkness of the fire's path around them as they listened to the accordion and ate pork, potatoes, salad and marron from the dam on the Taylors' property.

There was talk of next year, of the silage that they had all stacked in the ground, some of which was safe, of the fodder they would have to buy, or borrow. Of the stock they would have to replace, of the depression which was threatening the buttermilk prices, but tonight nothing mattered. They had pulled together, they were a community. The depression wasn't here yet. They would have to deal with that when it came.

They danced, here on the buffalo grass, swinging one another in the Gay Gordons, and the Lancers. As usual Deborah did not dance, but as she watched Sarah and Ernie together, so close, she felt the pain twist inside her and looked for Luke. He was by the humpy with Jimmie and the other children.

She started towards him but Patrick moved alongside her and gripped her arm.

'Please dance with me, Deborah. Just once.'

'Luke's been with Jimmie too long. He's tired.' She was looking beyond Patrick now, to her son.

'Please, Deborah, dance with me.' Patrick took her by the shoulders. His voice was loud and then he said softly, 'Dance with me as we did in the mountains, as we did at Shellrick.'

The music was slow, it was a waltz and the air was warm, not hot. He drew her close, and they moved to the rhythm of the accordion. She was too close to him, she could smell his skin as she had smelt it so long ago. She eased back but felt his arm stiffen, pull her against him, and she couldn't understand this man who had never loved her but who still remembered the mountains.

She couldn't understand the pain which was gathering inside her as she felt his body down the length of hers, the sense of loss. Love doesn't exist, she reminded herself, not in this man.

She looked away from his neck to her house, to the paddocks, to the sheds, and lifted her hands to see the calluses in the light from the hurricane lamps. Patrick's hands had once been as soft as hers had been. She felt his hand close tightly on hers and she looked for her son because she couldn't bear these echoes of a time when she thought there had been love.

She pulled away as the accordion stopped. 'I must find Luke.'

The music started again and Patrick caught her hand, holding her here, with him. Tonight he had to tell her he loved her. Tonight he had to tell her that because of that love he had deceived her again.

He pulled her to him again, and they danced together too closely. Much too closely, Deborah thought. It wasn't fair. It reminded her of the nights they had stroked, kissed, clung, all without love from him, but so much from her.

'I love you, Deborah,' Patrick said, into her hair. 'I love you more than anything else in the world. I've always loved you. I just didn't know.'

She heard the words that she had once longed to hear, but she knew that love didn't exist. She had told herself that for so long. So why were there tears on her cheeks, and in her mouth? Why couldn't she hear the sound of the music? Why could she only hear the sound of his breathing, the sound of his voice telling her of his love?

He pulled her away now from the other dancers. He pulled her outside the light of the lanterns, near to the fence they had erected when there was only darkness, only rain.

She looked into his face and there was love in his eyes. At last there really was love in his eyes and she knew that it was in her own and that it was in her lips as he kissed her, gently, so gently. Then he kissed her again and now there was passion, and then there was joy and his arms were round her, and hers were around him.

'I love you, Deborah Morgan,' he said against her mouth and she smiled.

'Deborah Prover,' she said and he held her close and Luke came to them then and she remembered the lie that lay between them. Then she saw Luke stop and turn to Jimmie and sign in the light of the lamp.

'Has Dad told Mum that he taught me to swim? Has he told her I can go to school? Has he told her the water was very deep?'

She saw Sarah come and pull Luke away, looking across at Deborah, anxiety on her face. She heard Patrick's voice speaking of love but she was cold, so cold. Her son had been in water, cold water. Cold deep water. It was water that had killed her father. It was water that had taken his love quite out of reach.

She pulled back, wrenching herself free from this man who had told her he loved her, but only so that he could take her son away. Her son.

'You taught him to swim,' she said. Her voice was cold. 'You lied to me again. You told me you loved me to take my son from me. I hate you, Patrick Prover.'

His face turned pale and he looked from her to Luke who was standing with Sarah. 'Go to Jimmie, Luke,' he called. 'Go to Jimmie.'

Deborah spun round to him. 'Don't you dare tell my son where to go. You have no rights with my son.'

Patrick caught her by the arms. She could feel his fingers digging into her tender flesh. She could see his singed eyelashes, his eyebrows, but there was no compassion in her for this man who had lied again.

'I do have rights. He must grow away from you, Deborah. You must let him go. You mustn't do to him what my mother did to me. Please, my darling. I love you, I love him. I was going to tell you.'

'How dare you talk of love? How dare you say you have

rights? You have none. He's not even your son. Do you hear? He's not your son, he's mine.' She screamed this and knew she had heard those words before, but it didn't matter where, or how. This child was hers, nobody else's. He was hers.

She pulled against his grip. She must get to her son. She must make sure that he was safe. She must keep him with her, always, but Patrick was pulling her back, close to him. He held her head between his hands, forcing her to look into his face, his eyes. She felt his breath on her face.

'Do you think I didn't know he was Edward's? I've known almost from the day he was born. He has the same mouth, the same nose, but I love him and I am his father. I dreamt him, remember that, Deb. I dreamt him and now you must let him go.'

His eyes held hers for moment, but only for a moment and then she wrenched free, running from him, running from Sarah's outstretched hands, down towards the creek, to the humpy where she could see her son sitting with Jimmie. She lifted her skirts, jumping over logs, hearing sticks break beneath her, hearing the accordion which still played.

'Luke,' she called as she drew close to the fire, and he turned and in his eyes she saw for the first time the look which had been in Patrick's when his mother smothered him.

She stood, not hearing the music, not hearing the crackling of Jimmie's fires, just looking into those shadowed eyes which only held rejection, not love. She looked at Jimmie whose eyes were kind and knowing. No one moved, no breeze rustled the trees, there was just the flicker of the fire, the orange of the flames, and those eyes.

'I just thought you might like to go for a swim with the other children tomorrow,' she said, and smiled though her heart was breaking. She nodded, turned, and left the circle of light, stepping carefully, so carefully, away from her son.

She could still hear the sound of the accordion, still feel the ground beneath her feet, but inside her there was just a vast emptiness. She looked up. The moon was huge as it had

340

been on the beach. She leaned against a tree, touching the papery bark, tearing it, rolling it between her fingers.

Patrick came then and held out the cutting of myrtle that he had taken in the spring to give to her when he told her he loved her.

'The scent no longer causes me pain,' he said, standing in front of her, pressing it into her hand. 'I know it's because of you. I don't know how to tell you how much I love you, how much your son loves you, when you allow him to breathe.'

She turned the myrtle over in her hands again and again and then moved towards him, pressing herself against him, feeling his arms around her, hearing her voice telling him of her father's death and how her mother had screamed. 'He's mine.'

He held her and listened when she told him that when her mother had died she had said, 'I love only you, Denis.'

He held her as the accordion played on, as Jimmie's fire burned, as words which had remained unsaid for far too long passed between them.

He held her till the accordion died and Jimmie's embers were smothered and said, 'We'll go back to Somerset if you want to, Deborah.' His lips were soft on her forehead. 'I shall never stop loving you, I shall never stop wanting your happiness.'

Deborah felt his arms that were holding her so close, his lips that were kissing her so softly and with such love and knew that they would stay here where they belonged and that she would give myrtle and roses to the daughter they would one day have.

EPILOGUE

After courageously enduring and surmounting enormous natural odds, many of the 1920s 'Groupies' and independent settlers were finally defeated by the 1930s Depression and had to 'walk off' their land, hungry and penniless. Some survived though, and some prospered.

All of these brave people, however, played their part in bringing to fruition Sir James Mitchell's dream of a Western Australian dairy industry. All of them helped to make South West Australia what it is today; flourishing and beautiful.